Praise for *Lost Along the Way*

"Duffy delivers a summery novel about friendships, with both hardship and hilarity." —*Philadelphia Inquirer*

"Duffy effortlessly explores complex issues, especially how much pressure women put on themselves and one another to be perfect and have everything together." —*Library Journal*

"A rollicking beach read." —*Kirkus Reviews*

Praise for *On the Rocks*

"Alternately humorous and touching, this novel is a fast, fun read. . . . [Abby] is someone you'd want to friend, freezer full of ice cream and all." —*RT Book Reviews*, four stars

"With its more realistic and modern ending, this engaging novel offers readers relaxing and light yet thoughtful summer escape." —*Library Journal*

"Duffy's second novel is tenderly introspective. . . . Abby's attempts to navigate the ever-changing rules of dating are infinitely relatable and will prove to be an ideal beach read for fans of Elin Hilderbrand and Sarah Pekkanen." —*Booklist*

Praise for *Bond Girl*

"I'm crazy about *Bond Girl*. Erin Duffy is a fresh, funny, and fabulous new voice in literature. . . . Great story. Delicious debut."

—Adriana Trigiani, author of *Lucia, Lucia* and *Brava, Valentine*

"Witty and very racy . . . Trust me, you won't be bored with this Wall Street story." —*Washington Post*

"A compelling, fun read." —*Kirkus Reviews*

"*Bond Girl* is a sparkling debut, smart and snappy but never weighed down by financial terminology. Who knew Wall Street could be this much fun?" —*Entertainment Weekly*

"Duffy's first novel is a sharp, witty look at the intricacies of the trading floor and the people who populate it. . . . Filled with too-good-to-be-true anecdotes and enough of a biting, cynical bent to offset the chick-lit romance angle, *Bond Girl* is a fun read." —*Booklist*

Regrets Only

Also by Erin Duffy

Lost Along the Way
On the Rocks
Bond Girl

Regrets Only

A Novel

Erin Duffy

_wm_

WILLIAM MORROW

An Imprint of HarperCollins_Publishers_

P.S.™ is a trademark of HarperCollins Publishers.

HarperCollins books may be purchased for educational, business, or sales promotional use. For information, please email the Special Markets Department at SPsales@harpercollins.com.

FIRST EDITION

Designed by Diahann Sturge

Library of Congress Cataloging-in-Publication Data has been applied for.

ISBN 978-0-06-269824-7
ISBN 978-0-06-285463-6 (library edition)

18 19 20 21 22   LSC   10 9 8 7 6 5 4 3 2 1

For Patrick, Andrew, and Cate

Regrets Only

✾ Prologue

I CAN'T REMEMBER how I got here. I assume I drove, because I'm here and I'm holding my car keys, but I don't remember leaving my house, which is probably normal under these circumstances. I stare at the lights in the ceiling, counting no fewer than seven fluorescent bulbs, one of them continuing to buzz, and flicker, and flash because it can't make up its mind as to whether or not it wants to stay lit. I chose a chair in the corner of the waiting room even though there were other seats available, and it's underneath the air-conditioning vent. I'm cold, and I can feel goose bumps that I have an urge to scratch rising up on my forearms underneath my blue blouse. I focus on the glass coffee table in front of me, women's magazines fanned out in a semicircle as if picking up a few new recipes or exercise strategies would make sitting in this waiting room any less torturous. I don't know anything about Tara Redmond except that Tara Redmond doesn't really sound like the name of a lawyer. Tara Redmond could be a class mom, or a Girl Scout troop leader, or a nursery school teacher. You want Tara Redmond to hand out smiley face stickers, read stories, and help you sell cookies to the people in your neighborhood. You don't necessarily want her to help you get your life back after you eagerly gave it away. You don't want her to be the one responsible for fixing all of your mistakes.

I'm not the only person sitting in this waiting room, but I'm apparently the only one who's willing to actually look around and acknowledge that anyone else is here. The other three women busy themselves staring at anything except each other, as if they could make themselves invisible simply by avoiding eye contact. One of them is pulling relentlessly at a loose thread on the cuff of her blazer that apparently needs to be ripped off right this very minute. She's tugging at the string so fiercely I'm beginning to think she might unravel her sleeve before Tara Redmond comes and saves her from a completely self-provoked wardrobe malfunction. Another is reading a book, but she hasn't flipped the page in twenty minutes. Unless she's reading *Fifty Shades of Grey,* it's pretty clear she's checked out entirely and has no idea what's going on around her. The third woman is playing some kind of game, I think Candy Crush, on her iPad. I know this because she didn't turn the volume off and the stupid music is playing way too loudly in an otherwise silent waiting room. If I had the energy I'd go over there, rip the iPad out of her hands, and smash it into a billion little pieces on the glass coffee table, right next to the most recent copy of *Cosmo* and a small box of Kleenex.

I notice that we're all in different stages of this process by the way each of us has chosen to deal with her wedding ring. The woman trying to rip off her own sleeve has her rings dangling around her neck, as if continuing to wear them on some part of her body will make her divorce a little less real. She's still in the bargaining phase of the process, hoping that she can work things out with her husband. Meanwhile, her soon-to-be ex has probably thrown his ring down the garbage disposal with last night's takeout, and she's sitting here nervously ruining her clothing and affectionately stroking her pavé diamond ring as it hangs on a fragile gold chain. I feel badly for her. Holding on to the dream of how things should've been isn't going to help. I'm still new to this, but even I know that. She should ditch the necklace, and the glazed-over stare, and start focusing on her new reality. That's just my opinion. It's too bad she's not going to ask me for it.

The fake reader is still wearing her rings, a tasteful diamond solitaire and a platinum band, which are strange things to be wearing when you're sitting in a divorce attorney's waiting room. She's in denial. She's probably going to leave this office and text her soon-to-be ex-husband to ask if she should pick up his dry cleaning on the way home, even though they no longer live together. The younger woman playing Candy Crush twirls her ring around, and around, and around again on her finger nervously, debating whether or not she should just admit defeat and take it off. She's probably the talk of all the other women in her morning barre or spin class (*Did you see that she's still wearing her ring? Poor thing, her husband left her and she can't even bring herself to take it off! How sad is that!*). I look down at my naked ring finger. My ring came off almost immediately, although I don't remember doing it or have the faintest idea where I put it. I've been walking around totally numb now for two weeks, and I fear that this might be how I walk around for the rest of my life, which is a terrifying thought. I hope things work out for these other ladies, even though I don't know them at all. We're all just strangers in a room. All of us united by a piece of now useless jewelry, and by needing the services of Tara Redmond.

A short woman wearing black pants and Chanel loafers pushes open a door next to the table with the magazines and announces that Tara is ready to see me. I stand and brush my sweaty hands against the sides of my pants. I gathered my hair into a low tight bun before I left the house this morning because I tend to play with my hair when I'm nervous, and I don't want Tara Redmond to think I'm a mindless nitwit who didn't even notice that her husband of less than two years was cheating on her. My clavicle is too pronounced from the weight I've dropped since this whole mess started, so I opted not to wear a necklace or earrings. *Allure* magazine recently informed me that a delicate pendant or statement necklace could draw attention to that area, which is fine if you're trying to get a guy to fall in love with your clavicle. It's not fine if you're trying to pretend that you're over the fact that your husband fell out of love with your clavicle and with every other part of you as well. The raging depression that immediately followed the surprise end of my marriage completely killed my appetite. It was as if an alien invaded my body and began to switch off every biological process that wasn't absolutely necessary for survival, and my taste buds were the first things to go. I don't understand people who eat when they're depressed. Who finds out her marriage is over and says, "Sure, I'll help you pack up your sock drawer, right after I make myself a grilled cheese with bacon"? I'm not suggesting that there's a right or a wrong way to deal with this, I'm just saying that eating isn't high on my list of things to do right now. I've decided to focus my waning energy on breathing and blinking instead.

I don't even know how to introduce myself. "Hi, I'm Claire Stevens"? Or "Hi, I'm Claire Mackenzie"? How can Tara Redmond possibly begin to help me when I can't even tell her my own name? I've tried to find solace in the fact that she's certainly dealt with bigger messes than mine, but maybe that's not actually true. I have no idea how big of a mess I am, relatively speaking. Maybe this situation is more messed-up than 99 percent of the cases she has. Maybe that's part of her job description—for five hundred dollars an hour she'll tell you how screwed-up you are on a scale of one to ten and then give you a bright green lollipop to make you feel better on your way out the door. Maybe she'll give me a magazine off the glass coffee table as a parting gift when our meeting is over. "I'm sorry your marriage is over, Claire whatever-your-name-is, but please take my copy of *Good Housekeeping* on your way out. There are some great tips in there on how to deal with the really big problems in life: like how to disinfect your dishwasher, and clean the crumb tray in your toaster oven." I really have no idea what to expect.

Tara is older than I thought she'd be, with silvery white hair and dark tortoiseshell glasses and sensible heels that she probably kicks off next to her chair when she's not seeing clients.

"I'm Claire Mackenzie, but please just call me Claire." It seems like an honest statement. I'm still married. I still have to use my married name.

"It's nice to meet you, Claire. I'm Tara. What brings you to my office?"

"I need some help. I'm here to file for divorce." Once again, it's probably better to start with the basics.

"What's the reason for the divorce?"

"My husband has been cheating on me for months with his high school girlfriend." It hurt so much to say that sentence I could barely even stand it. I hadn't really said it out loud to anyone, because I still couldn't believe this was happening. My parents know—they're the ones who directed me to Tara Redmond and who are paying her fee—but that's it. I haven't even told my friend Antonia back home in Chicago yet, because the truth is too painful to admit out loud. I don't have any friends in Connecticut, and I doubt there are support groups for women like me, and if there are, I have no interest in join-ing one. It won't make me feel better to share my story with other women suffering from similar betrayals. It will only make me feel worse.

Tara stares at me for a few seconds and I wonder if she's wait-ing for me to give her all the sordid details. I don't know what kind of woman she is. Maybe she became a divorce lawyer be-cause she likes hearing all the grit behind a sacred union that went from "'til death do us part" to "I want the silverware." I stay quiet. I'm not going to fill her in on everything yet. I don't want her to know that I came home when I wasn't supposed to and my entire world shattered in an instant. How can I possibly explain the details to anyone when I'm still having a hard time understanding them myself?

I don't feel like I'm old enough to be a divorcée or that it's a label I particularly like. Divorcées are older women who go to Jazzercise and call everyone "darling." They have overplucked eyebrows that don't match their hair color, and nails that are long, and square, and synthetic, and painted bright red. They hang out in piano bars wearing low-cut animal print tops while slugging martinis with extra blue-cheese-stuffed olives. They say things like "Don't get mad, get everything!" and "Divorce means half as much husband and twice as much money!" I am not one of those women. I haven't been married for that long, not even two years, so there isn't anything for me to get. My nails are short and unpolished because I have a baby and my hands are constantly covered in ointments or shoved into scalding hot dishwater. I don't like martinis or olives. I'm too young to have my marriage fall apart, but my marriage fell apart, and I didn't even notice it was happening.

Men are supposed to cheat on their wives after years and years together because they're bored, or they grow apart, or they develop irreconcilable differences. What kind of irreconcilable differences do we have that I'm not aware of? I had a baby. That occupied nine months of my body and then eight months of my entire life. That's seventeen months that I've been busy creating a person and keeping him alive. We only had three months to grow apart! It can take longer than that to get a mortgage! It took longer than that to have my name changed on my passport!

We haven't even been together long enough for him to feel the seven-year itch.

"I'm sorry," Tara says. She doesn't ooze sympathy, but I still believe her. It must be hard to do this for a living—to spend years listening to other people tell you about their heartbreaks, their betrayals, and their disappointments.

"Thanks. So, obviously, I need a divorce." I sound equally unemotional. I don't want Tara Redmond to know anything more than she absolutely has to. I want her to go home tonight and tell her husband about this incredibly strong woman she met in her office. She doesn't need to know that I sat on the floor in my shower this morning and cried for twenty minutes before pulling myself up, and that if I had a bigger hot water tank I'd probably still be in there.

"Do you have any children?"

"We have a son, Bo. He's eight months old." I resist the urge to flip out my wallet-sized picture of him nestled on Santa's lap at the mall three months ago.

Tara scoffs, as if to say, *It takes a special kind of guy to cheat on a woman with a baby at home,* and she'd be right. Owen is special. Maybe I shouldn't be surprised to learn that I'm not the only one who knows it. "Are you seeking sole custody?" she asks, writing in her notebook with a shiny silver pen.

"It's more complicated than that." *Here we go. Here's where you earn your paycheck, Tara.* "I'm from Chicago."

"Okay. Where is your husband from?" She's still writing in neat cursive handwriting across a large white legal pad. I examine Tara across her desk, and I decide that I like her. It takes a real woman to let her hair go gray like that without trying to dye it. She's confident, and knows who she is. She's probably never had to think twice before introducing herself.

"He's from here. I moved east to be with him."

"So, what are you saying, exactly?" Tara's large brown eyes flicker with sympathy behind her glasses. It's pretty clear that she knows where this is going, and that the information she's about to give me is not what I want to hear. "You want to take the child away from his father?"

It's a question I've been trying to answer myself since this whole mess started. Owen might be a lot of things, but he's not a bad father, and a boy needs his father. I don't want Bo to grow up without that relationship in his life, but I can't stay in Connecticut when my entire life is back in Chicago. I'm going to be a single mom. I need my own parents, and my own friends, and to be comfortable in my home. People say it takes a village to raise a child, and my village is in Illinois, not Connecticut. What other choice do I have? "I want to go home. I know that taking Bo away from Owen isn't ideal, but I'm his primary guardian, and I don't know anyone here. I don't have any friends. I don't have a support system, and I have an infant. I want to take Bo to Chicago and start our life over there. Owen can come see him whenever he wants. He has a ton of frequent-flier miles. He travels a lot for work."

"I understand, Claire. I wish I could tell you that this is going to be an easy battle, but it's not. Does your husband—"

"Owen. Please just call him Owen." I feel rude correcting her, but I can't stand to hear him referred to as *my* anything.

"If I keep calling him my husband, then I have to keep calling myself Claire Mackenzie, and I'd like to rid myself of the moniker as soon as possible." So far, I'm pretty happy with my performance of "strong woman in lawyer's office."

"Does Owen know that you want to go to Chicago?"

"Yes," I admit. "He told me that I can't go. Do I have to listen to him?" I know that it's a stupid question, and one that won't help my cause of trying not to appear stupid. I suddenly feel like I've swallowed nails. I researched this particular dilemma on the internet, and I know I need his permission to move. I'm just hoping that someone who didn't get her legal degree from Google would have some better information for me, or some interesting ideas as to how I could get around this particularly annoying law. I glance at the large framed diploma from Yale Law School mounted on the wall above her desk. Yale means she should be able to get creative, and get me the hell out of here without my needing to break multiple federal statutes in the process. Yale means she should be able to fix me.

"Claire, it's not that simple."

"Things stopped being simple for me when I discovered this affair, so I don't find that surprising." I mean to sound sincere, but I'm afraid it comes off as dismissive. I'm not capable of feeling anything at the moment, but if I could, I'd probably feel badly about that.

"Unless Owen gives you permission to take your son out of state you're going to have a hard time getting a court to give you permission to leave. It's considered kidnapping."

"That's ridiculous. I can't kidnap my own kid. I'm his mother."

"I feel for you, Claire. I really do. I see this all the time. It's more common than you'd like to believe. I know it's a horrible situation for you, but legally your options are limited without permission."

"Oh, okay." My eyes are dry and itchy and I wonder for a moment if maybe I've forgotten to blink since I sat down in this chair. "So he can actually keep me from going home?"

"He can. The law was designed to protect children from becoming pawns in divorce hearings. It's meant to provide safety and continuity in the child's life, and to have both parents present. Sometimes, unfortunately, those same laws create uncomfortable situations like the one you're in right now. I know it's not what you want to hear, but I want you to understand that realistically there's not much you can do."

"He was my only reason for being here. What am I going to do? I haven't been here long enough to make any kind of life for myself. We moved here a month after I had my son. I don't know anyone. I barely leave my house."

"Custody battles are never simple, and there's not much you can do unless you file suit for sole custody. But, that's not easy to get either. You would have to prove that Owen is an unfit parent. Do you have leverage you can use against him? Is he involved in Bo's life?"

"He travels all the time for work. He's never around. Is that reason enough?"

"Again, I'm sorry, but no. Plenty of parents travel for work and if that could be used as a reason to have sole custody then there'd be a lot of women with a major problem, too. When I ask if he's unfit, I'm referring to drugs, alcohol, abuse, or neglect. Has he ever endangered Bo?"

"No," I admit. "I have a better shot at being able to prove him to be an unfit human than an unfit parent. Owen loves him. He travels a lot, but when he does he always calls home and talks to him on FaceTime and he always goes directly into his room when he gets home late to kiss him good night. He even wakes up with him in the morning most weekends so he can have some one-on-one time with him and so that I can sleep in. The only leverage I have is that he cheated on me in my own house. Is that enough to get sole custody?"

"No. It's not. It sounds to me like you're going to have to work out a joint custody schedule where you both are involved in Bo's life. If Owen wants to be a part of his parenting, then a court will rule that it's best for Bo to let him. You just described a loving father."

"I'm having a hard time understanding that any of this is happening, and now you're basically telling me that there's nothing I can do?"

"Imagine what the courts hear every day, Claire. There's child abuse, drug abuse, alcohol abuse, violence, neglect—they've seen it all. An ex-girlfriend breaking up your marriage . . . well, I know it seems like the end of the world to you, but it's not."

"So what are you saying?" I ask, even though I fully understand what she's saying. There's no way out for me. I'm stuck.

"The deciding factor in cases like these is what's in the best interest of the child—not what's in the best interest of the wife. I know it's hard to hear, but relocation is very hard to win unless the man involved has some really serious demons. Is he offering to pay you child support?"

"Yes. He said he'd pay me alimony, too, and that I could keep the house." Somehow, as this conversation progresses, Owen's managing to look more and more like a good guy. He has no problem paying child support! He's offering me alimony! He moved out of the house no problem! He won't contest the divorce! What a gem.

Tara removes her glasses and folds them gently on top of the desk blotter. I hold my breath, because I know she's about to seal my fate, and brace for the impact. "I'm sorry," she says. "I wish I had some better news for you, but I have to be honest. No judge is going to hear this and think that your moving home and removing Bo's father from his life is the right course of action. If you try to fight this in court, you'll lose. I don't want to waste your time, money, or energy pursuing that option."

"I see."

"The rights of the parent are paramount to everything else. Without his permission you don't have much of a case, and I don't want to give you false hope. If he decides to let you go, then we can have a very different conversation. What you need to focus on is setting up a joint custody agreement you'll both be happy with. That's your goal as your divorce moves forward."

This is my new résumé: Claire Stevens–then Mackenzie–then Stevens again, Connecticut divorcée, mother of one, wife of no one, lonely, isolated, thirty-six-year-old mess.

"What about the girlfriend? My son is only eight months old. He can't tell me what's going on in Owen's house. I don't want her around my Bo. Please tell me that there's something I can do to prevent her from being in his life."

"There is. You can absolutely work that out in the custody agreement, and considering Bo's age, and the fact that your husband and the other woman haven't been together for a long time, you can definitely restrict her access to him. We can take care of that, no problem."

"Okay, good. That's something."

"We'll work out a custody situation you're comfortable with. If Owen violates the agreement in any way, then you may have a few more options, but let's talk about that if it happens."

"Okay. Thank you for your time. I guess it's helpful to know where I stand." It's the first time since this started that I feel like I really understand anything, even if it's something that I don't want in the slightest. Nothing else in my life makes any sense at all, but at least I have some clarity as to where I'll be living. That's good. That's a good thing. I need to try and find the smallest sliver of a bright side in all of this because if there's not one I'll probably go to bed and stay there forever.

"We'll still file for divorce. If he's agreed to give you child support and alimony it should be pretty straightforward, and easy. I want to help you, Claire. If anything changes and you can bring me something we can use to show a judge that Owen is unfit, we can go over your options again."

"I understand. Send me whatever papers you need to send me in order to get the divorce started. Thank you." I exit her office and walk through the waiting room, the sleeve unraveler, the fake reader, and the game player all still in their seats. Maybe they'll have better luck.

 # Chapter 1

Two weeks earlier

"WE HAVE A surprise for you," Owen said. I opened one eye, my right cheek still pressed into the pillow and slightly wet from drool. My son, Bo, had been sleeping through the night for a while now, but I still collapsed into bed by 9:00 each night completely exhausted. I used to work long hours at my job. I was up early and often stayed until almost 7:00 P.M., and I never, ever was tired the way I was tired now. I worried that my epic fatigue wasn't entirely physical—that some of the drain I was experiencing was due to the fact that my brain was turning into a marshmallow thanks to lack of stimulation and adult conversation, but the worry quickly flitted away because I was too tired to focus on it. I barely made out the burning red numbers on the alarm clock on the bedside table next to Owen's side of the bed. 8:00 A.M. For a mother with an eight-month-old, 8:00 A.M. might as well be noon.

"You let me sleep in. Thank you!" I yawned, and rolled onto my back, my cotton Gap nightgown twisting around my waist, and I immediately pulled it down around my knees, lest Owen see the paunchy belly I was still battling. Owen sat up in bed next to me, already dressed in khaki shorts and a gray T-shirt, holding Bo on his lap. I reached for them both, the men in my life, and pushed myself up so that I could kiss both of them good morning. Bo immediately reached over and grabbed a fistful of my hair, which was his new favorite thing to do. "Good morning, handsome," I said, as I eased his hands free and pulled him over onto my lap. "How are you this morning? Did you sleep well?"

Bo's big brown eyes sparkled while I held him. I liked to think that it was because there was no place he'd rather be than in my arms. The feeling was mutual.

"Pretty good, actually. Thanks for asking," Owen teased.

"Oh, I'm so glad." Bo cooed and I wiped a string of drool from the corner of his mouth, before running my finger over his lower gums to see if any other teeth had broken through overnight. Nothing. Still just one lone little jagged tooth jutting up through swollen pink flesh, and I had to admit that it made me happy. Teeth placed him squarely on track to becoming a toddler, and I wasn't ready to let go of my baby yet. The longer he stayed that way, the better. "Thank you for letting me sleep in."

"You're tired," Owen reminded me. "I've been gone for a few days, and I hate leaving you guys alone when I'm traveling. I know it's hard that all of the work falls on you."

"I know. I love being home, and I love Bo more than anything, but while you were gone I was wondering if maybe it was time for me to go back to work. Is that crazy? I'm starting to feel like maybe I'm ready for more." Part of me felt like I was a poor excuse for a mother admitting that maybe I wanted to leave my child to reenter the workforce before he was even a year old. But if I didn't want to go back to work, part of me would feel guilty for just giving up a career I'd worked hard to build and liked quite a bit. Guilt and I were going to become good friends, because we'd be spending an awful lot of time together going forward no matter what decision I made. Being a woman was annoying like that.

Owen paused for a second as if he was considering it. "No. It's not crazy. You always said you might want to go back. What made you start thinking that it's time?"

"I don't know. I feel like I want to at least see what's out there. Maybe I'll know what I want to do for sure when I have a better idea of what's available to me."

"Okay. The little man wears you out. I can't imagine how hard it would be to work and also be a mom, but if anyone can do it, you can."

"Millions of women do it. It's one of the reasons why we are the superior sex."

"I see."

"Anyway, you're right. I'm totally exhausted. It's more than tired. I feel like I need to be plugged in in order to function properly. It's nothing I could ever explain."

"We should take a vacation," he said. "Let's go to Alaska or something."

"I think Bo is a little young to take a vacation like that. We can't just leave an infant and take off for Alaska!"

"People go on vacations all the time. Becoming parents doesn't mean we have to spend the rest of our life within spitting distance of Connecticut."

"I know that. But I think we should wait until he's a little older. Let's talk about it again next year. Though a vacation sounds dreamy. I'm running on fumes."

"I know that, too. And I think—actually, *we* think—that we needed to do something to say thank you for taking such good care of us all the time." Owen tilted his coffee mug toward me so that I could take a sip without having to put the baby down. I rubbed my face against Bo's and inhaled the scents swirling around my bed: Owen's sweat because he didn't shower before he got into bed after returning home from his most recent business trip, the dark roast coffee, Bo's baby detergent, and the formula that had dribbled onto his pajamas. If I could bottle this and save it and revisit it for the rest of my life just so I could remind myself how perfect things were at this moment, I would.

"Oh yeah? What would you guys like to do for me?"

"We want you to leave. See you tomorrow."

"Huh?" I asked. "What are you talking about? Where would you like me to go?"

"I was thinking the Greenwich Hotel might be a nice place. Oh, and also SoulCycle, and Bliss, and Drybar. We think you should go there. You have time to eat something and shower, but then you need to get out of here because you can check in at noon and your spin class is at one."

"Wait, what? You're serious? You're sending me to a hotel? In the city?"

"I wanted to give you something special to say thank you. You need to spend some time taking care of you. I know it's been hard and you sometimes feel overwhelmed with everything here and I wanted to make sure you knew how much we love you and how important you are to us. Go pamper yourself. You used to spin with Antonia all the time back in Chicago, but you never go here. I know it won't be the same without her, but you could still get a nice workout in, and then go get a facial and your hair blown out, treat yourself to dinner somewhere downtown . . ."

"That's where we stayed when we got engaged! That hotel was amazing!"

"I know. I know how much you liked it. I also remember how much you liked the cookies, and the room service menu."

"Room service! Oh God, I could order room service! And go to sleep in a giant bed all by myself and wake up whenever I want!" I hadn't done that since before Bo was born. It felt like a lifetime ago. In some ways, it was.

"Anything you want. They have my card on file. Charge anything you want to the room, but you have reservations that will take up part of the afternoon, and if you're serious about wanting to start looking for jobs, you should go shopping and get yourself some new clothes for interviews."

"You want me to go shopping, too?" I couldn't believe what he was saying. This was every woman's dream come true. I immediately imagined myself ransacking Bloomingdale's and didn't feel guilty about that at all.

"Why not? You haven't been since Bo was born, and if you're

going to be hunting for a job you'll need some new clothes. It's funny that I had this booked and you just mentioned the work thing. Perfect timing, huh?"

"Yeah, but I haven't totally decided on that, yet!"

"It's just a matter of time. Go ahead and buy a few new things. Enjoy yourself. I don't want you to think about us even once."

"Impossible," I said honestly.

"True, but you can try."

"This is the most wonderful, amazing, thoughtful gift in the entire world and I can't believe that you did this for me. Do you understand that a day alone to do nothing but pamper myself and sleep is better than a two-week trip to Bali? I mean that! I'm not even exaggerating!"

"I know you're not. And that makes me really happy. You deserve it. Now go get in the shower and pack a few things and come downstairs. I'll pour you some coffee."

"You are the greatest husband in the entire world."

"Nah. I'm just smart enough to know that I need to show my wife I love her."

"You'll be okay with Bo all by yourself?" I asked. I wanted to know that I was needed, but the never-ending neediness was what was making me want to throw on my Nikes and run like my hair was on fire. The constant emotional war I was waging against myself was really starting to get old.

"Of course. It'll be a guys' day. I'm happy to have some quality time with the little man. Right, buddy?" Owen clapped his hands together gently in front of Bo and he mimicked him by clapping his own hands, a skill he'd discovered he could do earlier in the week. I'd sent Owen videos of him clapping and laughing and it was the most adorable thing in the entire world, but I knew that watching his son actually start to interact in person was infinitely better than anything I could capture on my iPhone. They should definitely sit in front of each other and clap for the next twenty-four hours until I returned. "Don't forget your spin shoes," he ordered.

"I can rent them there!" I said. I had spin shoes somewhere, but I had no idea where. They got tucked away during the end of my pregnancy in Chicago when spinning became totally unenjoyable. I wasn't even entirely sure they made the trip to Connecticut.

"Good! One less thing to pack. Now, go get that gorgeous ass in the shower and go be a crazy single girl in Manhattan for the day."

"This is unreal," I said. "I love you so much it hurts, you know that? Part of me hates to leave you because you're just getting home. I haven't seen you since Tuesday and now we won't get to spend any time together today."

"Do you want me to cancel it?"

"No."

"Didn't think so. We'll have dinner this week. I'm not traveling again until next Thursday. You're stuck with me until then."

"That's not called being stuck. It's called being lucky."

I POURED THE rest of the coffee from the coffeepot into my favorite mug, and looked outside at the beautiful spring morning.

Two squirrels ran across the backyard playing, or maybe they were fighting, I wasn't sure. I glanced at the plot of dirt where I was planning on planting tomato plants in May, which would be my first attempt at gardening in suburbia, and I realized that those squirrels were going to be the bane of my existence this summer. In Chicago, I worried about how I was going to find a parking space on the street outside my townhouse. In Connecticut, I worried about how to keep squirrels from snacking on my tomatoes. I couldn't believe how much my life changed while I wasn't paying attention.

"Stop stalling," Owen ordered. "We'll be fine without you for a night. Have fun," he said. "I really want you to relax and enjoy the quiet."

I leaned over the back of the chair where he was sitting, wrapped my arms around his neck, and buried my face in the crook of his neck, a place that seemed like it was molded to fit me perfectly. "You are the best husband on earth," I gushed.

"Don't I know it," he answered. He ran his hand over my ponytail as I released him and scampered off. I grabbed my purse off the hook near the door.

"Are you sure you'll be okay without me for a night?"

"We will be fine! I'll see if my mother wants to stop by."

"Okay," I said, the concept of a night in the city now even more appealing. Owen's mother, Marcy, was not my biggest fan, though I had no idea why. The only reason I could come up with was that I was pretty sure she was one of those women who never thought anyone was good enough for her little boy despite the fact that her little boy was almost forty. She wore pantsuits, and fake pearls the size of golf balls, and she always had lipstick smeared on her front teeth. Her ash blond hair was way too light for her sallow complexion, and she basically bathed in an orchid-scented perfume that you could smell a block away. If she was coming, then I was definitely going, and fast.

The rickety door clanged behind me. I descended the stairs of the porch down to the driveway, and climbed into my waiting chariot, which came in the form of a Volvo. I noticed the crocuses starting to peek up through the mud. It was only March, but you couldn't miss the signs that winter was effectively over: heavy jackets swapped for cotton coats, the sounds of birdsong in the trees and car radios through open windows. Winters in Chicago were brutal, but my first winter on the East Coast hadn't been bad at all. Of course, I had an infant, and therefore only left the house for appointments with the pediatrician, so my experience was limited.

I drove south on I-95 toward the Cross Bronx Expressway that would eventually lead me down the West Side of Manhattan. I had only driven into the city three or four times in the last year, once because Owen made me so that I wouldn't be afraid of driving in New York, and once because we went to see a play on Broadway and I missed the train I needed to take in order to get to the theater on time. We'd only been in Darien for seven months, and between the baby, and Owen traveling, it was hard to get out and find my bearings. Thank God for GPS, or I'd probably spend the next six months within three blocks of my house. I couldn't help but be proud of myself; the

Midwesterner cruising down I-95, crossing state lines into New York and heading downtown like it was absolutely no big deal. What had I been so afraid of?

Sometimes when I woke up at night, when my pillow was too warm and needed to be flipped over, or when Bo cried because his poor gums were being shredded by teeth that didn't seem to want to make an appearance, I stared at Owen while he slept. More often that not, his sandy hair had fallen over his face, and his skin looked so soft, and he lay so still that sometimes I had the urge to put my hand on his chest and make sure he was still breathing. He almost always lay on his side, his head propped up on his elbows, and his legs bent at the knee, and I'd have to pinch myself because I couldn't believe he came into my life and turned it upside down and moved me to a different time zone and I couldn't have been happier.

I wouldn't have imagined that I'd meet Owen in a bar the way we had a little more than two years ago, or that he'd want me and not my friend, Antonia, since the guys always wanted Antonia, and rarely ever wanted me. That was what happened when your best friend was a curvy Italian girl with thick, dark waves that flowed over her shoulders and lips that could be used as a flotation device, and you were just a normal all-American girl with mousy brown hair and lips that were barely visible to the naked eye unless they were lined with a pencil and coated in gloss. It didn't offend me. It just meant that if I were sitting next to Antonia, and someone was staring in our direction, he was most certainly not focused on me. Except Owen was.

"That guy is checking you out," Antonia said as she glanced

over at the bar on that random Wednesday night in Chicago when my entire life changed.

"No, he's not," I said. I didn't even bother to turn around and see who "he" was. "No one is looking at me, and honestly, I don't care. I've decided that I'm totally fine with my single life. I'm really happy where I am, you know? I feel like I went through the stage where I was terrified that I was going to either die alone, or be forced to join Tinder and spend all of my free time mindlessly swiping left, and I'm through it now. Besides, whoever *he* is, I'm sure he's looking at you anyway. People always say that once you hit your mid-thirties you become happy with yourself and it's really true. At thirty-four, I finally feel like I've got a grip on my life. Things are pretty good for me the way they are. I'm lucky. I don't need anything else."

"I'm happy to hear that, but you should probably turn around and say hello," she said. She grabbed her drink and sauntered away, and I spun around in my chair and came face-to-face with the handsome, clean-shaven, smiling man who was going to change my entire life. I was happy with my job, and my apartment, and my friends, and then Owen appeared, and everything I didn't think I wanted all of a sudden seemed like the perfectly logical things to have.

"I'm Owen Mackenzie," he said, and I had to remind myself to blink. Owen was ruggedly handsome with sandy brown hair that fell over his right eye and a mildly crooked front tooth. His voice was commanding and soothing at the same time, and he smelled like Irish Spring, and beer, and Tic Tacs.

"I'm Claire," I managed to choke out, my voice sounding

squeaky and foreign. I took a sip of my beer, hoping it would shrink the burning knot in the back of my throat that threatened to crush my voice box. I couldn't believe I was having this kind of reaction. Who got tied up talking to a cute guy at this stage of the game? "Are you from Chicago?" I asked.

"Yes, and no."

"That was meant to be an easy question to answer," I teased.

"I'm originally from Connecticut, but I work for an internet travel company, so I'm from here as of about six months ago. Before that, I'd never been here in my life, which is absurd. This town is fantastic. I love it," he said, and immediately I conjured up images of gray clapboard houses in bucolic Connecticut; all manicured lawns and shiny SUVs, freshly baked apple pies and vibrant orange leaves in fall. I imagined an Ivy League diploma hanging on his bedroom wall next to faded Pearl Jam posters, and an old, battered lacrosse stick tucked in the closet. Even his name sounded perfectly New Englandy: Owen Mackenzie. I liked it. I liked it a lot.

And that was that. We had endless phone calls, romantic weekends on Cape Cod and Nantucket and Manhattan that used up all my frequent-flier miles, and after six months we decided to move in together because that's what you do when you're in your thirties and find someone who makes everything better just by entering the room. It was hard for me to be bothered by his relentless travel schedule since it was his job that had ultimately brought him to Chicago and into my life, but it was hard knowing that he spent a fair amount of his time in lonely hotel rooms with minibars and room service menus. I liked to write him notes when he traveled. I tucked them inside the pockets of his sports coat, or hid them in the zipper compartment of his travel bag, or placed them inside his dress shoe, just so he'd know that he was missed. I liked letting him know that I was thinking of him, because I was thinking of him, constantly. Not thinking about him was an impossibility, which seemed silly since I'd managed to live thirty-four years without ever knowing him at all. My old age was apparently morphing me into quite the sap.

Until I met Owen my love affair was with my career. I constantly worked because I thought that was what you were supposed to do when you graduate from Notre Dame with a degree in communications. I enjoyed being a social media consultant, and I was good at it. I was so good at it that at one point I was approached to head up branding and marketing at a start-up and I almost said yes. I was thirty-four years old. For all of my twenties and almost half of my thirties I'd dedicated myself to the pursuit of more: more money, more security, more recognition, more satisfaction, more of everything because that was what ambitious women did when they were unattached and motivated and hitting their professional stride. Then love suddenly dropped itself right into the middle of all of that, and I decided that it was time I pursue something else. That was how it often happened in real life, if you were honest. If I was honest.

I got married and then quickly became pregnant, so quickly that when I told my mother I was expecting she smiled but fell quiet for almost a full minute while she tried to figure out if a September ceremony and a July due date meant that I was pregnant at the wedding. (She was good at a lot of things—math was not one of them.) I left my job and devoted my time and energy to being Owen's wife and Bo's mother and cooking and cleaning and singing and snuggling and I was happy with that decision. Until recently, I was very happy with that decision. What bugged me now was that I was starting to realize that my potential return to the workforce might not even be possible. I lost my rhythm. I lost my contacts. I lost my stability and my confidence in a lot of ways. It's not easy to step out of anything for almost a year and then just step back in. Things change quickly, and there's not much of a job market for a woman who takes a year off to get married and have a baby and then changes her mind. I risked being seen as unreliable, and uncommitted, and unwilling to give my entire life to the job, and that was exactly what most jobs want you to do. I'd be seen as someone who had her shot and gave it away and there was nothing I could do about that now. I should've thought about it before we moved, but I didn't, because I was too busy nurturing my family to worry about the atrophy of my career—too in love to see that trading one for the other would likely be the last business decision I'd ever make. I didn't like to admit it to myself, and certainly not out loud to anyone else, but I was having a hard time making peace with the fact that my transition to becoming a housewife was probably permanent whether I wanted it to be or not.

My phone rang. I glanced at the dashboard and saw that it was Antonia, so I pressed the green button. "You'll never guess where I'm headed," I said.

"Chicago?" she teased.

"A spa in Manhattan. Owen got me a day of pampering and a hotel room. How amazing is that?"

"I'm sure that's well deserved, bella," she said. "Glad to hear that husband of yours is still treating you right. You got one of the good ones."

"You will, too," I said.

"*Si.* I'll find my *amore* when God wants me to. There's a plan for everyone."

"Sure seems that way."

"How's my little Bo doing? When are you coming home for a visit?"

"Soon. As soon as the thought of flying with an infant doesn't terrify me."

"You better make it soon. I need to get my hands on him. Who's going to teach the baby to speak Italian?" Antonia asked, only half-joking. "I hate you for leaving me, you know," she reminded me.

"You are my Italian love Yoda. Aren't you supposed to be telling me that if you love someone, moving is a small sacrifice to make?"

"You're right. I just miss you. How are you?"

"I'm okay. Except, I'm starting to get the itch to go back to work. Is that weird? Does that mean I'm not satisfied with my life or something?"

"Not at all! It's been almost a year. Go back if you feel that way. You're a modern woman. You can do anything you want."

"Yeah." I sighed. "Anything you want is a great concept as

long as you only want one thing. I want a lot of things. That's the problem."

I didn't know if I really wanted to go back to work, or not. It was certainly a thought that had been crossing my mind more and more lately, probably because I was starting to come out of the new mom fog and realized that maybe there was more that I could be doing for myself in this particular phase of my life. It wasn't easy staying home. It wasn't easy transitioning from someone who had a life and a career and a paycheck and a role to play in the real world into someone whose life revolved around an infant, and there was no career and there was no paycheck and there was nothing that was mine anymore. If I wanted to buy a new pair of jeans, I needed to use a credit card that Owen paid for, or even worse, ask his permission to use it. I hadn't thought about the fact that not working gave away all of my autonomy and a lot of my identity. If I went back to work, what would it even look like? My mind meandered through all of the scenarios: Full-time or part-time? Nanny or day care? Then, out of nowhere, a thought that made my heart stop. My wallet wasn't in my bag.

I didn't know what made me think of it, or why I hadn't thought of it until I reached Westchester County, but I passed by the exit for Larchmont and immediately remembered that I'd taken Bo for a walk yesterday afternoon, and stopped for a latte in town, and my wallet was still sitting in the bottom of my UPPABaby stroller next to an empty water bottle and a wad of napkins from Starbucks.

"Shit! You've got to be kidding me," I said as I exited the highway and turned my car around to head back north on I-95.

"What's wrong?" Antonia asked.

"I forgot my wallet. Do you believe that? I'm going to miss my appointment if I don't hurry."

"At least you realized it before you actually got all the way to the hotel and couldn't park your car."

"Good point. I'll call you later from the hotel, okay? We can have a proper catch up while I enjoy room service in my pajamas."

"Sounds good, bella. Enjoy."

I hung up and moaned in frustration. This was an annoyance, but it wasn't the end of the world. Owen would no doubt lord this over me forever, and make fun of me for a million years about how I couldn't even manage to get my life in order to leave the house for an entire night. I turned my face toward the sun as I drove back onto my quiet little street, with its cracked sidewalks and its huge trees, and thought about how lucky I was. I loved my little house and I loved my little family and I'd love them both even more after I spent a night away from them sprawled out alone in a king-sized hotel bed with the "Do Not Disturb" sign hanging on the door.

I left my purse on the front seat of the car and my keys in the ignition while I sprinted inside to get my wallet out of the stroller in the basement. Bo would be sleeping, thankfully, so I could pop in, get my wallet, pop out, and it would be like none of this ever happened. I ran my hand over the arm of the swing on the front porch, and thought about how we really needed to use it once the weather warmed up. It was one of the things I loved about this house, and I'd decided that I was going to put a good amount of miles on it this summer. I pushed the front door open and breezed into the foyer, my skin still warm from the thirty-minute drive home with the windows down, and the fresh air blasting my face. I was opening my mouth to call Owen, but I stopped.

I stopped because I was halfway into the kitchen, heading for the basement stairs, when I came face-to-face with our Realtor, which was odd. She was drinking champagne out of the bottle and toasting a frozen waffle in the toaster oven Owen's mother gave me at my bridal shower, which was very odd. She was also clad in nothing but bright purple lingerie, which was nothing short of completely fucking horrifying.

I heard a crash: the champagne bottle. I heard a beep: the toaster. I heard a scream: mine, but that might have only been in my head. I reached out to steady myself against the wall, because I was fairly certain I was about to pass out and crack my head open on the hardwood floor.

"Claire!" someone cried, and not in the "Oh, it's so good to see you!" kind of way, but in the "Oh shit, what are you doing here?" kind of way, which was not what you wanted to hear when you were standing in your own kitchen.

"I forgot my wallet," I muttered, because shock made you say really ridiculous things that weren't appropriate for the situation in the slightest.

"Oh my God, Claire," Dee Dee—our Realtor—said.

"I think it's in the stroller," I added. I had no idea why.

Dee Dee was on her hands and knees, picking up glass from the shattered bottle, which was nice of her.

"Oh my God," Owen said. Then, he reached over and touched my shoulder, and the feel of his hand on my body was enough to snap me out of the protective daze I'd fallen into.

"What the fuck is going on?" I asked, even though what was going on was obvious to anyone with one ounce of common sense and two functioning eyeballs.

"Claire, I'm so sorry. I'm so sorry. I never meant for any of this to happen," Owen said as he struggled to pull on his khakis, like that was going to make a difference at this point.

"You never meant for this to happen?" I asked. "What happened then, Owen? She stopped by to borrow a waffle, reached into the freezer to grab one, and her clothes fell off?"

"Claire, it's not like that. Please . . ." Dee Dee started, which was mind-boggling because I had no idea why she was in my house to begin with, and no one had asked for her opinion. How did I not see this coming? My mind flashed to our first meeting, when Owen casually informed me that our Realtor was his high school sweetheart, and how my mind stuttered on that fact for a split second, and then moved past it because I stupidly believed that my husband wasn't looking to cheat on me. Not my husband. Not Owen.

"DEE DEE IS great," Owen said casually. "You'll like her." I stood outside the cozy-looking colonial on the quiet little street and couldn't find anything obviously wrong with it from the outside, which was more than I could say for other houses I'd looked at online, most of which seemed haunted, or at the very least had hosted a murder in the basement.

"You know her?" I asked. The lot was square and neat. It was fenced. It was clean. It had an herb garden, and a tree for a tire swing. I pulled the emergency Twix bar from my purse, ripped open the wrapper, and ate half a stick in one bite. I was enormously pregnant, starving, and cranky. Admittedly, not the best state to be in if you were going to spend a day house hunting, which was why I decided to stash candy bars in my bag.

"We dated," he answered. He didn't provide any details other than that. They dated. That could mean so many things.

"Dated like you went to the fifth-grade dance together?" I mumbled through bites of chocolate and caramel.

"We were together for three years of high school."

The candy stuck in my throat when I tried to swallow it, and the caramel that was mashed in my molars made it difficult to speak. "You never mentioned this before," I managed to choke out. This seemed like a very serious act of omission. There are some things that you can't just forget to tell your wife. Like, "I'm an assassin for the mob," or "I have a highly contagious venereal disease." When you were a pregnant Midwesterner looking for a new house on the Eastern seaboard, "I used to date our real estate agent" is right up there with some of the worst omissions out there.

"What's the difference? I haven't seen her in a long time, but she sells real estate here, so it would've been silly not to use her.

Don't tell me you're jealous?" he joked, grinning and reaching over to rub my stomach.

"I'm not jealous! I just think you should've mentioned that you've seen our Realtor naked."

"Okay. Going forward I'll make sure I give you a heads-up every time I run into someone I've seen naked. I wasn't aware that was the rule," he teased.

"Thank you. I appreciate that," I said with a smile. I nudged his ribs with my elbow, and he leaned down and kissed the top of my head.

A gleaming black Mercedes pulled up in front of the house, all sleek and streamlined and shiny. Dee Dee removed her sunglasses as she stepped out of the car, tousled her long beach waves, bumped the door with her hip to help it close—which was unnecessary as neither of her hands was occupied—and extended both arms toward Owen, ready to wrap him in an embrace. She wore a tight black pencil skirt and a deep blue sweater set, a huge pearly smile, and lipstick that was way too bright for day. Long, knobby giraffe legs jutted out from under her skirt, and her razor-thin heels only made them look longer. I sucked chocolate off my fingers, and looked down at my own fat feet, which were jammed inside New Balance sneakers. The ponderous stumps I now called legs (thanks to seven months of baby and Twix bars) were encased in black maternity leggings below a long white tunic clinging to curves in all the wrong places. I looked like I'd rolled out of bed, picked my clothes up off the floor, and strolled out of the house without stopping long enough to brush my hair, never mind curl it. I didn't know what I'd have done differently if Owen had bothered to tell me that he used to date our Realtor, but let's just say that had I known she was Owen's ex-girlfriend, I would've at least left the candy bar at home.

"Oh my God!" she squealed. "It's so good to see you! You haven't changed a bit!"

"It's great to see you, too," Owen said.

"It's so nice to meet you, Claire," she sang. I hated that she knew my name, and I'd only found out that she existed two minutes ago.

"You too," I replied as I shook her hand, praying that they didn't stick together from candy bar residue.

"Congratulations!" she said. She glanced at my enormous belly. "When are you due?"

"Thanks! I'm due in July."

"Only three more months!" she said.

"Yes. Ten weeks, actually," I replied. I was counting down the days until the end of my pregnancy and the subsequent return of my ankles, and the difference between three months and ten weeks was enormous.

"Then we better find you a house fast. I can't imagine you'll be able to fly out here much longer."

"We're hoping we can nail something down while we're here," Owen said. He placed his hand on my lower back and pulled me a little closer to him. "We need to be here in August so we can get settled before my job starts."

"I totally get it. I really think you're going to like this place. Let's go inside!"

We followed Dee Dee up the driveway and entered the house through the basement door, because you had to climb an entire flight of steep stairs up a hill in order to reach the front porch—not something a very pregnant woman needed to be doing.

"I don't love the fact that I can't push a stroller into the back-yard," I'd said. "What will I do with the baby if we go for a walk and he falls asleep in his stroller? I can't just leave him in the driveway."

"This town is very safe. You could actually leave him in the driveway. It wouldn't be a problem," she offered. "Or else, you could push the stroller into the basement." I appreciated her effort, but I was pretty sure that even if this was the safest town in America, I wouldn't leave a sleeping baby in the driveway. Not the first kid anyway. "This house is really special," Dee Dee said as we climbed the basement stairs to the hallway outside the kitchen. "It just came on the market and it won't last long. It has really good bones," she added, which was what real estate agents said when they wanted to sell a house that probably needed an awful lot of work. The place smelled of cinnamon, and dried lavender, and lemon—like a sachet tucked away in the back of an underwear drawer, and like really clean wood. "Let's start upstairs," she suggested.

The wooden stairs creaked, and groaned, and moaned as we climbed to the second floor, as if they were mad at us for being there. The staircase was missing a spindle, and faint outlines of stains were visible on the creamy wool carpeting in the hall-way upstairs, but the moldings were beautiful and the ceilings were coffered and the floors peeking out from the sides of the runner were sanded and glossed. The room at the top of the landing was small and square, with two large windows and one small closet, and not much else. Next to that was the master bedroom. There was a wall of built-in shelves that would be a wonderful place to display family pictures, homemade Mother's Day cards, and eventually, macaroni necklaces way too special to tuck inside my jewelry box. The windows weren't particularly big, but they got good sunlight, at least in the early afternoon when we visited the old, charming house that had really good bones. The master bathroom had two vanities, a large steam shower, and a heated floor, which I'd never even heard of before. Who needed a day at a spa when you had this place thirty feet from your bed?

"Is that a Jacuzzi tub?" I asked, all of a sudden falling in love with this house, which was totally surprising.

"The owners just renovated both bathrooms on the second floor, and replaced the central air unit. I think you guys would be very, very happy here," Dee Dee said, which was hard to argue with.

There was a second bathroom at the end of the hall, a perfect guest bathroom for when my parents came to visit. The bedrooms weren't big, but neither was our family. They weren't luxurious, but who needed that? They were clean, and they were functional, and I could see us living here. I glanced at Owen and knew that he, too, felt like this was our home.

"There are a ton of new restaurants in town, Owen," she said. "Claire, you'll love them. There's a new farm-to-table restaurant called Farmhouse Kitchen that is absolutely amazing.

They specialize in using the whole animal. It's impossible to get into, but I know the manager, so I can get you a table whenever you want. You have to try it, you'll love it. Trust me."

"What do you mean, they use the whole animal?" I asked.

"It's nose to tail," she said.

"Why would I want to eat pig nose? Or pig tail for that matter? Neither sounds like a draw to me. Then again, I'm pregnant. So unless they serve no fewer than twenty different ice cream flavors, I'm not all that interested in a lot of things," I joked.

"Let's go downstairs. I want you to see the kitchen," she said, as she escorted us into a perfectly updated, stainless steel, granite topped, Sub-Zero masterpiece. "There's nothing not to like here, right?" she asked. All I could think about was Antonia and how she would die for this kitchen. "The hardwoods are original," said Dee Dee. "Aren't they beautiful?"

I FORCED MYSELF to stop thinking about our introduction, and how I'd been a witness to the beginning of the end of my marriage. "You told me this was our dream house," I reminded her, just in case that would make her feel bad about her sleeping with my husband on a beautiful Saturday afternoon.

"I think maybe I should go," she said. She picked up a pump from the floor, then glanced around nervously for the other one.

I took a step toward her. "You told me we would be happy here, and that you would help us get settled, and that it was nice to meet me." I was having such a hard time understanding how one person could be so underhanded, so evil, so manipulative, and how I could be so stupid to not even recognize it. I was too busy admiring the hardwood floors to notice who was standing on them next to me.

"I'm sorry, I can't do this," Dee Dee said, though she didn't seem nervous, or guilty, or even uncomfortable. She seemed more aggravated than anything, which really didn't fit the situation at all. At least pretend.

"You're nearly naked in my kitchen eating my waffles. You're already doing this!"

"Claire, leave her alone," Owen pleaded.

I turned and faced him. No wonder he had gotten up early and showered and dressed before I was even awake. It was all calculated. Every last move he made to get me up and out of the house today. "Don't say another word, Owen. Don't you dare speak one more word to me, or to her. The only reason I haven't gone wild is because Bo is sleeping upstairs, and one of the three adults in this house should give a shit about that!" I hissed.

"Call me later," Dee Dee said to Owen. She scooped her dress up off the floor and dropped it over her head.

"Call me later?" I whispered, as the front door closed quietly behind her. Did Dee Dee not get that they weren't two teenagers who'd just got busted making out in the basement after school? Did she not realize that she'd taken the best thing that had ever happened to me, and broken it as easily as she'd broken the champagne bottle? I turned to face Owen, and it was as if I'd never seen him before in my life. His head had grown horns, his nostrils breathed fire, and his eyeballs spun in circles in their sockets. "You sent me into the city for a day of pampering, telling me that it was because you loved me, when really it was so you could sleep with our real estate agent." *This isn't happening,* I thought. *Not my Owen. Not my marriage.*

"She was my girlfriend. Not just a real estate agent," Owen said.

"Is that supposed to make some kind of difference?"

"No. I don't know why I said that," he answered. His face was flushed, and he was fidgeting relentlessly, and I didn't know if it was because of shame, or regret, or neither, or both, but whatever it was looked remarkably like the onset of a seizure.

"I'm your wife. That's supposed to make a difference. I thought we were happy."

"We were. We are."

"No. No. Happy people don't have affairs. They certainly don't have calculated getaways in their own house that they facilitate by shipping their wife away for an evening. Did you have big plans? Were you going to cook her dinner?"

"Don't do this to yourself."

"You had her in this house while our son slept upstairs! Have you lost your mind? Who are you? Who does that? What just happened here? I woke up this morning and believed that I had the most perfect little family in the world and now I'm standing here and I have no idea what's happening. You sent me away so you could have the house to yourself. Do you have any idea how fucked-up that is? And I would never have known. I wouldn't have known anything if I was better organized. Oh my God," I whispered. Owen had manipulated my entire life.

None of it was real. I basically just discovered that I was living in *The Truman Show*.

Bo cried. He woke up from his nap like he always did, and he cried like he always did, and I ran up the stairs to get him just like I always did, except this was nothing like any of the other times those things had happened. I hurried to his room, pushed open the door, and rushed at the crib by the big bay window. I scooped him up and buried my face in his sailboat-covered romper as I sank down to the floor in the corner of his room next to the rocking chair. I cried silent, hot tears that ran down my face and dripped onto his collar, and rocked him softly for as long as he would let me. I rocked, and quaked, and held him tighter than I needed to, because he'd suddenly become the only thing in my entire world that I knew for certain was real.

Chapter 2

HE MADE ME a cup of tea. Because nothing says "I'm sorry I cheated on you with the class of 1998 homecoming queen" like a nice hot cup of Darjeeling. My head was spinning. The kitchen pitched back and forth while I sat at our round kitchen table, the one with white painted legs and a distressed wooden top that I loved, but worried wouldn't be big enough for the whole family in a few years, assuming that Owen and I had the additional kids we'd once dreamed of having. I stared at the cookbooks shoved on the shelf above the counter next to the stove. I'd promised myself that I was going to organize them before the end of the weekend. They really should be alphabetized, but oddly enough, the fact that books by Rachael Ray were shelved in between books by Giada De Laurentiis and Rick Bayless didn't seem like much of an issue anymore.

A filthy kitchen towel hung on the door handle of my stainless steel refrigerator. I kept meaning to wash it, but I never remembered to add it to the laundry pile until after I'd already thrown in a load, filled the machine with Tide, and pressed start on the washing machine that was conveniently hidden in a closet in the upstairs hallway. I hoped Dee Dee didn't notice how dirty it was. It was bad enough she knew that I couldn't keep my husband. I didn't need her thinking I was a slob, too. I held my mug tightly, but I didn't take a sip. My fingers and toes were numb, and a prickly heat was making its way from the nape of my neck down my arms and my chest until my entire upper body felt like it was on fire. I wanted to leave but I couldn't. Bo was asleep upstairs for the night and the last time I left him with Owen when he was sleeping upstairs, a nearly naked woman somehow ended up walking around my kitchen. It didn't seem wise to make that same mistake twice—also, I had no idea where I left my car keys.

"I don't know what to say," he said. This was not a good way to start the conversation. He should have at least started by apologizing for not locking the front door. I'd never be able to unsee his affair. It was now part of my mental Rolodex, one of those defining moments in my life that I'd never forget. It was in there, lumped together with memories of my college graduation, our wedding, and Bo's birth. It wasn't fair.

If I'd ever thought about how I'd react in this situation (and I could honestly say that until now, I'd never thought about how I'd react in this situation), I would've thought that I'd never stop screaming—that I'd scream so loud the neighbors down the street would hear me. I'd have expected to yell, bang, threaten, wail, and break anything breakable that I could get my hands on, and that would probably include Owen's nose or jaw. But that wasn't what was happening. I'd stopped screaming, and had now gone completely numb. I was waiting for the tears, but none came. I was wondering if maybe I wasn't smart enough to handle all of this information at once—if my brain tried to process anger, hurt, shock, disappointment, resentment, disgust, sorrow, betrayal, embarrassment, and horror simultaneously and became overloaded. Maybe it decided that it really wasn't up for the challenge, so it went with numb and said, "Here you go, Claire. This is really all I can do for you right now." I didn't know what was happening—just that I was eerily calm despite being devastated, and that had never happened to me before. Then again, neither had this.

"How long has this been going on?" I asked. Though I knew I didn't want the answer.

"About six months," he answered. Why do men do that? I wondered. Answer questions we don't really want the answers to?

I tried to do some basic math, but couldn't because I was having a hard time understanding why the bulletin board hanging on our wall was swinging like a cheerleader's ponytail. Six months. That was a long time to be having an affair without your wife noticing. Six months was a long, long time to be an idiot. Then, the worst thought of them all: six months was almost the entire time we'd been living in Connecticut.

"Why?" I asked. "Why did you do it?" I felt like I swallowed something sharp, and it was slicing through my esophagus as it made its way to my stomach.

"It's not your fault," he said, which obviously made me feel oh so much better.

"That's not what I asked you. I know it's not my fault. I also know that you absolutely think that it's at least partially my fault. Why don't you just tell me the truth? Because I don't think I can handle any more insults today."

"I don't know, Claire. We haven't talked in so long. We haven't done anything, or spent any time together, and it never seemed to bother you."

"This is how you're going to try and convince me that you don't think it's my fault? I had a baby. *We* had a baby. I'm sorry that you're having a hard time taking a backseat to the infant upstairs, but I don't think having an affair is the way to go about dealing with your own feelings of inadequacy. Why didn't you come to me? Why did you move me out here if you weren't even going to care enough to have a conversation with me about how you felt before things got to this point?"

"You think this was all calculated? I don't know the answers to those questions, Claire."

"How is that possible?" I wailed, those nails I swallowed making their way down into my stomach and stabbing me in a million different places. I felt my insides beginning to churn and imagined my stomach lining shredding, and decided that enduring that would actually be less painful than this conversation.

"It wasn't one specific thing. It's been a lot of things. We've grown apart. We don't have anything to talk about anymore."

"That's ridiculous! We talk all the time. We talk about Bo, and our families, and your job, and your friends, and I talk about *Sesame Street*, and the music classes at the YMCA. I'm sorry that I'm not up-to-date on global economics at the moment, but this time in our life will pass. I'm going to rejoin the human race soon. I told you I was thinking about going back to work! You try being at home with a baby all day, and let's see what you have to talk about!" I couldn't believe that he was using the fact that I was a stay-at-home mom against me. What, Dee Dee had so much more to offer conversations because she could talk about vaulted ceilings and hardwood floors? Is that the stuff on which scintillating conversation was made these days? Is that really why my husband cheated on me?

"I'm not judging you. I'm just saying that it's made things hard on me."

"So you have an affair? It never occurred to you to try talking to me about it? Hey! There's something we could've talked about!"

"I didn't mean for any of this to happen. We just started talking and one thing led to another."

"In person? On the phone?" I asked.

"What's the difference?" he answered, which was a stupid question for him to ask. How did he not understand that it mattered—all of it—every sordid, dishonest detail?

"It makes a difference. You know it makes a difference," I insisted. One wasn't better or worse than the other, but I wasn't going to be the idiot in the room for another second. I needed to know what was going on in my marriage, in my home, in my life, even if it was too late to change any of it.

"We started texting and emailing. It was nothing at first. Just funny email forwards. Things like that."

"You started flirting with your ex-girlfriend on email. That's just awesome. I didn't know about it because I'm not the kind of wife who feels the need to search your computer while you're in the shower. I trusted you. I trusted our marriage. I don't know how we could be on two completely different pages."

"I know. I don't know what happened, Claire. I don't know. I wish I could give you some explanation to help make this easier for you, but I don't have one."

"And then what? She asked you to coffee? How did you get from texting to sneaking her into the house while I'm out? That's not a short progression. It doesn't just happen. Things happen because you allow them to happen, or because you encourage them to happen. Stop pretending like this was something you had no control over." The prickly heat continued to move lower, now my knees were burning, and itching, and I half expected my skin to start melting off my legs and fall onto the floor.

"We have history, Claire!" he said. He stood up from the table and bumped into it, causing some of my tea to slosh out of the mug and drip off the edge onto the floor. I wondered how long it would take me to care that it had happened. A few months from now, someone would probably come see this house when it was up for sale and sit down at my table, and her elbows would stick to it because I never cared enough to clean up the sugary tea that Owen made me to ease the shock of his infidelity. I didn't give a shit about the spilled tea, or the unalphabetized cookbooks, or the dirty kitchen towel that needed to be washed. I cared that he didn't care enough about me to tell me that he wanted to be with someone else. I cared because if I hadn't forgotten my wallet, this might've gone on for months, or years, and I never would've known it. How long could he have kept lying to me? How long would I have failed to notice? It wasn't a fling. It was a relationship. It was a relationship that started in the halls of their high school in 1995, and continued in the breakfast nook of my kitchen in 2016.

"Everyone has history!" I screamed back. "What kind of explanation is that? Just because you dated her twenty years ago doesn't mean you get to sleep with her now! Marriage means you let go of history, and you focus on the future. Did you not pick up on that when you were talking about forsaking all others? Are you that dense that you don't even understand what a marriage means?" We were now into the insult part of the program. Next up, breaking of sentimental objects, followed shortly thereafter by hysteria.

"I don't expect you to understand, and I'm sick knowing that I've hurt you. I didn't want you to find out like this."

"How did you want me to find out, out of curiosity?" I asked. I was pretty sure there was no good way to break this kind of news. I found it interesting to discover that he did.

"I wanted to at least be able to sit you down before you had to see it for yourself."

"Oh," I said. "So you were going to tell me about this. Thank you for being so thoughtful as to wait until I could be safely seated. Do you love her?"

"I can't answer that."

"You just did." Extreme heat now enveloped my entire body and I knew what it felt like to be trapped inside of a box that was on fire. For the record, it sucked.

"No, I didn't. I enjoy being with her. She likes to do things. I travel so much, and when I'm home you don't want to do anything. You're so tired all the time."

"She doesn't have a baby! That's the best you can give me? 'I cheated on you because you sleep too much?' Are you kidding me with that?"

"You always do this," he said. I didn't like that this conversation seemed to be steering back into the "it's your fault" lane.

"Do what?" I challenged.

"You never take responsibility for anything! I can't have a conversation with you about anything! You're impossible to talk to!"

"This isn't a conversation!" We were now yelling so loudly I glanced at the window, praying it was closed. It wasn't. Awesome. "This is my finding out that you cheated on me and that our marriage is over. This isn't a conversation. It's an assault on my head and my heart. I'm allowed to react however the hell I want!"

"You're right," he said, suddenly remembering what exactly had happened to me today. "If you want to go to counseling, I'm willing to try it. I'm willing to work on our relationship if you are. As bad as this is, I don't want to lose you. I don't know what I was thinking. I wasn't thinking at all. I'm sorry, Claire. I'm so, so sorry."

"Counseling? You can't possibly think that I would ever take you back after you did this. You're not that stupid. Is there any part of you that thinks we can make this work after what you did? Do you think I'll ever trust you again, ever?"

"No," he admitted. "I don't expect you to take me back." He held his head in his hands, and then quickly ran his sleeve across his eyes. He was crying. The only other time I ever saw Owen cry was when Bo was born. That was the beginning of something. This was the end of something. Sweat began to pour down my arms.

"I'm sorry, Claire. I really am."

"You can apologize for the rest of your life, Owen, and it won't undo this. We will be eighty years old and you can still be apologizing and it still won't be enough."

"What do you want me to say?"

"There's nothing to say," I whispered. "It's over. You knew it would be over the second I found out about this, and you did it anyway. You brought her into our home. You sent me away so that you could play house with your girlfriend and our son. I don't know who I married, and I don't even know who you are anymore, but I know that we are over, and that's something I never would've expected. Not ever."

"You can have the house," he said, because that was the way to make your wife feel better after telling her you don't love her anymore. "I'll pay you alimony. I'll obviously give you all the child support you need. I won't make this any harder on you, or on Bo, than it already is." I hadn't thought about what would happen when this conversation was over—the logistics of everything—the packing of suitcases, the removal of tooth-brushes and deodorant from the medicine cabinet, the monthly checks that would now arrive in the mail. I hadn't thought about how we were actually going to untangle our lives and go forward separately. The only thing that had concerned me up until now was the emotional fallout of this mess, but there was more to it. The physical disconnection might actually hurt more. "As awful as this is, it doesn't have to be ugly," he informed me. "We can try and be friends."

"It's a fucking divorce, Owen. It's ugly. I'm not doing any of this conscious uncoupling crap where we still have dinner every Saturday and you live in the basement or something. You picked someone else over me. It doesn't get any uglier than this. Don't try and convince yourself otherwise. And I don't want the stupid house."

"What do you mean?" Owen asked, because that was the part of this conversation that was hard to believe.

"I want to go home," I said, my stomach heaving. I'd never wanted to be home more in my entire life. Fight or flight instincts were kicking in, and I was going with flight, as in, the next one to Chicago.

"You are home," he said, because he apparently was a lot more stupid than I'd ever thought possible.

"Home to Illinois. I want to just take Bo and go home. I'll worry about putting my life back together there."

"Don't be ridiculous. You can't take him to Chicago. He's my son, too," Owen said, and I immediately felt my mouth go dry. I hadn't expected him to put up a fight, which, in retrospect, was me being more stupid than I'd ever thought possible. He loved Bo. Bo might be the only person on earth he loved other than himself.

"You weren't thinking about him when you banged your

high school girlfriend. Why are you bothering to think about him now?"

"You can be mad at me all you want. I don't blame you. I'm mad at me, too. But you can't leave here with my child and think you're going back to the Midwest. It's never going to happen. Never."

"What does that mean?" I asked. It hadn't occurred to me that I couldn't go home. I'd been trying to figure out how fast I could pack and book tickets out of here.

"It means you can't leave. I'm sorry."

"Well, if you were my father, and I was seventeen, and asking for the car keys, that would be an acceptable answer. As I am most certainly not seventeen, and you are most certainly not my father, that means shit to me. I'm going."

"It's illegal, Claire. I'll fight you until the very end. You can't go anywhere with our son without my permission. I'll give you the house, and all of the money you need. But I'm not giving you Bo. No shot in hell that happens."

The reality was beginning to set in, and it felt like a sharp punch in the chest.

"I'm going to see a lawyer," I said, which was meant to sound threatening, even though I was sure that was what he expected me to do.

"I think you should. I promise you, though, no matter how much you hate me right now, you're not going to be able to move. Bo's life is here. Our life is here . . ."

"There is no *our* life. Not anymore. There never really was. There was your life, and me isolated in this stupid house in this stupid place that you moved me to. I never had a life here. I've just existed."

"There's your life, and there's my life, and they both happen here."

I had a hard time computing what had happened to my life in the span of a few short hours. How did I miss the signs? We had a nice morning together. Owen gave me a gift, and made me coffee, and encouraged me to hurry so I didn't miss my spin class. He kept telling me to go, to get up, to leave the house, to trust that he and Bo would be fine without me for the day.

He kept telling me to leave.

Without warning, I put my head between my legs, and vomited all over the hardwood kitchen floor that Dee Dee promised me was original.

Chapter 3

THE FIRST FEW days after you find out you're getting divorced are kind of weird days. You don't really follow through with the plans you thought you had because they all suddenly seem pretty stupid. For example, Owen and I were going to take Bo to the swings on the playground and then maybe stop at the grocery store on the way home to buy some organic apples, and an organic chicken, and some dinosaur kale for dinner, and now these seemed like pretty silly things to do. I didn't need apples. I didn't need chicken. I didn't really need dinosaur kale when I thought I needed dinosaur kale because I didn't actually like it, I just felt like I should. We'd talked about going to the aquarium, or maybe heading up to Boston for a weekend, or maybe driving to the beach on a sunny afternoon and having a picnic. It was safe to say that we weren't going to be doing any of those things now, so my calendar for the foreseeable future had suddenly opened up. In light of recent events, I decided to forget about all of my previous plans and make some new ones. I removed my wedding ring and placed it in my top drawer underneath a pile of socks that I never wore, but for some reason hadn't thrown out. The affair had been going on almost the entire time we'd been here, and I've been walking around town with my stroller and my diamond ring like an idiot, and that wasn't going to happen again. It was going to live in my sock drawer until I figured out where to sell it.

I knew Owen was going to come by at some point to get all of his clothes, and I knew he was going to do it soon, and that was why I decided that I had to destroy them. Women throw their husband's clothes out of the window and onto the front lawn all the time, but that seemed like a cliché, and also I didn't actually know when he was planning on coming to collect his things, and didn't want to risk having his wardrobe all over the lawn for weeks on end. People in suburbia talk. So, keeping the destruction confined within the walls of my house seemed like a better alternative for now. I grabbed scissors from the drawer and cut holes in the pockets of all his pants, so that he'd lose his change, his keys, and anything else he threw in there, but he had made me lose my marriage and my mind, and those didn't seem like fair trades, so after I was done with that I moved on to his dress shirts. I cut nipple holes in all of his button-downs, and half of his golf shirts, and that made me feel marginally better, but it was fleeting, because really all that did was ruin a round of golf or make him late for work, and that didn't seem sufficient, either, and so I looked for something new again. I gazed at his blazers hanging neatly on the racks, and thought about how not that long ago I tucked love notes in his pockets, and had to resist the urge to slam my dominant hand in the doorjamb to punish it for being so stupid. There would be no more love notes in his pockets, or his shoes, or his bags, but that didn't mean I couldn't leave something else instead. I spastically hurried down to the kitchen, grabbed a bag of dried beans from the pantry, and brought them back up to my bedroom. For the next ten minutes I proceeded to put handfuls of them in his shoes, in the pockets of his sports coats, in his winter coat pockets, in his baseball hats, in the small zipper compartments of the travel bag he carried with him on business trips, in his tuxedo, and even in the jar of pomade he used to style his stupidly perfect head of hair. I stepped back and exhaled. I needed to catch my breath because cutting holes in pockets and golf shirts, and scattering beans all over someone's belongings was more tiring than you'd think. He would move, and he would take his clothes with him, and he'd never again find another love note from me, but for years to come he'd find beans in his belongings, which would drive him crazy, and remind him that once upon a time he drove me crazy, too. Throwing clothes out of the window was fleeting, but beans could be forever. When I was done cutting the pockets and the nipple holes and hiding the beans, I laid back down in my bed and realized that those things didn't even begin to punish him enough for what he'd done to us. It was a start, but going forward I was going to have to get creative, and that was fine, because I had nothing but time and a lot of creative energy to expend, not to mention the fact that I was royally pissed off.

It was a good thing that I got to work on the clothes and the beans, because two days later Owen showed up and packed a few of his bean-filled bags and left the house to move in with his mother. I waited a while to call my parents and Antonia to tell them what happened. I would've thought that I'd have called them right after he left, but I didn't. I watched him leave with his shoulders slumped forward and his head hanging low like he was ashamed of what he'd done, but I wasn't buying it. He let it go on for too long. He let her in our home. He wasn't ashamed he cheated on me—he was ashamed he got caught. It took all of my strength not to chase him out into the front yard, and beat him with the golf club he kept in his closet in case someone broke into the house in the middle of the night and he needed to scare them away, but I didn't. I decided that I was going to try and handle this mess with some dignity. I didn't know how successful I'd be, but trying to bash in his skull with athletic equipment couldn't be a good place to start.

It took me some time to process everything, and for some reason, I just wasn't ready to tell anyone that it was over. I was embarrassed, because I felt like admitting Owen cheated on me somehow meant that I failed—that I wasn't a good enough wife. I was angry, for obvious reasons, and hurt, for obvious reasons, and numb, for obvious reasons, and I felt it was best to hunker down with Bo and keep our personal crisis to ourselves. There would be plenty of time for people to know, but only a few days to deal with it in peace, and I wanted to make those days last as long as possible. So I did. I didn't leave the house for over a week. Owen still had some clothes in the closet, and I still had my scissors and a giant bag of lentils. I was good.

I missed my job, if for no other reason than a job would have allowed me to not feel like I was failing in every aspect of my life. My mind wandered, a meandering string of thoughts that skipped and hopped through various scenarios of how different things could be for me right now if only I hadn't stopped working. I was good at what I did, and if I had joined that start-up I would've been part of an amazing company that I'd helped build from infancy. There could've been venture capital money, and then an IPO, and then I could've been present to ring the opening bell at the New York Stock Exchange while throngs of sweaty businesspeople applauded and cheered and screamed. But I'm not. Instead, I'm in bed in Connecticut, because I quite dumbly decided that I'd rather be someone's wife and someone's mother over someone who rang the opening bell. I exercised my right as an independent, modern woman in the year of our Lord 2015 to leave everything I'd worked for and move east for a man, and nobody tried to stop me. If I'd left my life in Chicago for any other reason—say, to join the circus, or try my luck in Hollywood, which, for the record, might have actually worked out better for me—I'd have had more than a few people tell me to reconsider. But I left for a husband, and so instead I got a goodbye card signed by my colleagues and congratulatory hugs on my way out the door.

That was messed up.

And so here I was, living where I didn't want to live without the person who was responsible for my living here. Even worse, I didn't have a job, and I didn't have a life, and I didn't have an IPO, and I could be angry at Owen for all of that, but the truth of it was I was angry at myself, too. I didn't hedge my bets, and instead I went all in on the wrong thing. I gambled on Owen—on us, and our family, and what we could do—and I should've gambled on me and what I could do for myself instead. If I had, well, things likely would've turned out differently. That was something that I'd have to reconcile at some point, after hours of expensive and intrusive therapy, innumerable self-help books, and probably a few bottles of vodka, too.

By the following Saturday I was ready to talk, if for no other reason than I was afraid if I dodged any more phone calls from Antonia she'd think I was dead, which in some ways, I was. My parents were understandably shocked when I told them what was happening, but it didn't take long for my father to tell me that he never really liked Owen, and that I could do better, or for my mother to remind me that any man who was unfaithful to a woman with an infant wasn't the type of man I should be married to. This was all useful information that did nothing to make me feel better.

If I could've held off telling my parents forever I would have, because once you tell other people about the worst day of your life, you can never again pretend it didn't happen. It wasn't bad enough that I had to deal with the horror of my failed marriage, but now my parents would have to deal with it, too. All of the time and the money spent on my wedding and it was over before I got most of my pictures out from under my bed and into an album. All of the people who came to toast us and to celebrate the beautiful life I was about to have with my new husband were going to wonder what was wrong with me that

I couldn't even manage to make it last two years. I wasn't sure why I felt shame, but it was overwhelming.

"What do you want me to tell people?" my mother asked.

"Why do you have to tell them anything? Why does anyone need to know?" I asked.

"People ask how you're doing, Claire. You don't live in a vacuum."

"Don't I?" I said. I was being unfair, I knew it, but I also didn't care. It didn't seem right that I had to be dragged through the gossip mill at home and not even be present to defend myself. It made me sick to think of people running into each other in the deli in town and talking about poor Claire Stevens while they were waiting for a turkey sandwich. I was humiliated in Connecticut, and I would be humiliated in absentia in Chicago, and that was more humiliation than I felt like I should have to endure. Shame and embarrassment would follow me for the rest of my life, but now it would follow my parents, too. They were just as much a part of this divorce as I was. Any hope for more grandchildren, now gone. Any hope for nice holidays with their only daughter and son-in-law, gone. Not to mention the fact that they'd certainly now feel like I was their responsibility, and they'd worry about me, and stress about me, and stay up late at night feeling sorry for me and wondering how I was going to figure out this new life all by myself, and that would break their hearts, and knowing that would break mine all over again. "I'm sorry you're dealing with this," I whispered. I also wasn't sure why I was apologizing, but I felt like I should.

"Stop. We aren't dealing with anything. We're just worried about you," she said, as expected.

"I'm fine. I don't want you to worry about me. I've got this," I said. I covered my eyes with the back of my hand and splayed out on my bed, because it somehow felt better to have this conversation while horizontal.

"You don't sound like it. Why don't I come stay with you and Bo for a few days?" she asked.

"Please don't, Mom. I appreciate it, but I'm a big girl. I can handle it," I said, which wasn't technically a lie. I was handling it. I didn't say I was handling it well. "I know you want to help, but I need to figure this out on my own."

"I can't believe this happened to you," my mom said, her voice quivering. "I could kill him, Claire. I swear I could kill him."

"Yeah. Get in line," I replied. The sobs I'd been holding back finally forced themselves free. "I don't want you to worry. I'll let you know if I need anything. Right now I need to just get my bearings. I'm going to be okay. Please, I don't want you guys to stress over this."

"I know you are. It's just so unfair. You're so young, and now you're going to be divorced with a baby," she reiterated, just in case I had forgotten.

"Yeah. I know," I said. If any part of me had been wondering if maybe I should let my mom come and stay for a while, it was gone. I couldn't possibly handle seeing the sadness on her face, or hearing the pity in her voice, or listening to sentences like the one she just uttered, which made me want to slam my head into the wall. We needed to keep space between us for a little while, so that I could lie and tell her that I was rebounding like the strong, independent woman that she raised. It wouldn't benefit either of us to have her see the truth for herself. "I have friends here. I have a life. I don't need Owen. I just need to regroup. That's all," I said, because that was what my mother wanted to hear, and I immediately realized I needed to protect my parents from this divorce almost as much as I needed to protect Bo from it, too.

"Your father plays golf with a lawyer out here who used to work in New York City. We'll get you the name of the best divorce lawyer there is. Don't worry about the cost. We'll pay for it." Tears welled again. So far, nothing she'd said had done anything to help get me out of this mess, but a lawyer could. A lawyer was the best gift someone could've given me right now, and it made me miss my parents so much I thought I might die.

"I don't know how to thank you. If you can do that for me, it would be an enormous help. I don't even know where to start to try and find a lawyer."

"You take care of you and Bo, and let us take care of the lawyer. I'm so proud of you. If you need anything from us, anything at all, any time of day, you call. I'm here for you and so is your father. You'll get through this. You're tough. If you change your mind and want us there we will be on the next flight out."

"You know it," I said. I looked down and realized that over the course of this conversation I'd managed to chew off every nail on my right hand. Awesome. "I love you. I'll talk to you soon. I'm really sorry, Mom." I said it again because I couldn't not say it no matter how hard I tried. I was sorry. I just didn't know exactly for what.

"I'm sorry, too. And neither one of us should be. The only one who should be apologizing is Owen."

When I hung up I realized that telling my parents had just made everything worse, and that that conversation was one of the worst things I'd ever endured in my entire life, and I was going to delay having to put myself through that again for as long as was humanly possible, so Antonia was just going to have to wait. I was still battling numbness, fatigue, and a tingling sensation in my extremities that may or may not indicate an impending stroke, but at least I'd soon have a lawyer who would help get me off the East Coast. Other than Bo, that was the only thing that mattered. I put my ringer on silent, and swore that I was done with the phone forever. Me and my fancy New York City lawyer would get this all straightened out, and there'd be no need for anyone else to know about it until it was all over.

SIX DAYS AFTER I told my parents, and almost a full two weeks after waffle-gate, I made my way into the city to meet with my lawyer, Tara Redmond, and it did not go as planned. Much to my horror, she basically told me that I should just slap a UCONN bumper sticker on my car and learn to love the fall foliage on the East Coast, because I wasn't going anywhere. My plan for not having to tell anyone else about the pending divorce until

I could also say that I was moving back home wasn't going to happen, and so once again I was forced to readjust. I couldn't avoid Antonia any longer. I sat on the edge of my bed and ran my big toe along the fibers in the carpet while I picked up the phone and dialed Antonia's number. I knew she would answer because it was 7:00 P.M. in Chicago and on Friday nights Antonia went spinning from 6:00 until 6:45 and by 7:00 she was in the market next door to the gym buying a salad for dinner. If I was at home, I'd be with her. I should be with her.

"Ciao, bella! What's up?" she said. "The music in class tonight was terrible. You'd have been so annoyed. What's the latest and greatest from the East Coast?" she asked. Hearing her voice made my heart ache. I missed her so much. I missed the life we used to have together. I missed the way she managed to make me smile even when I thought it was impossible. I wondered if she'd still be able to do that, or if this was something that not even she could make better. "Where have you been? I've sent you a few texts and you haven't written me back. What, you have cool friends in Connecticut with riding boots and ponies and you're too busy to talk to me now?" she teased.

"I caught Owen having an affair with our Realtor. I met with a divorce lawyer and she told me I can't ever move home to Chicago," I said. I heard the words come out of my mouth, but I still couldn't believe them to be true.

"I'll be there as soon as I can," she replied.

"Thank you," I whispered before I hung up. I was a big girl, and I didn't need my mother flying in to help take care of me—but allowing my best friend to do it was a different thing entirely.

I rolled onto my back, pulled the covers up over my head, and decided that for the time being, when Bo slept, so would I.

BO WOKE UP early the next day and we headed downstairs to have breakfast. "How are you doing today, buddy?" I asked. I was determined to hold it together for him, to make sure that he didn't notice that anything had changed. I would've worried that Bo noticed that Owen wasn't around, but since he typically traveled at least two or three nights a week, it wasn't all that unusual for him to be gone. Bo probably didn't notice that anything had changed, which was crazy since everything had changed right in front of him in a very big way. He reached up and grabbed the small diamond pendant hanging on my neck and babbled while he twisted and turned and bit it as I defrosted applesauce I'd made a month ago and stored in ice cube trays in the freezer. "Okay, little man, I have to put you down for a second, but then we'll sit and have breakfast together, all right?" I sat him on his play mat with an activity board and a toy flashlight that lit up blue, red, and green and made the most annoying noises in the entire world. I handed him a frozen bagel I kept handy for when his teething became particularly painful, and watched as he clapped and smiled and shoved as much of it in his mouth as he could with his fat little hands. Something inside me warmed at the reminder that Bo still loved me more than anything on earth, even if Owen didn't. It was just the two of us now, I thought, and my brain coiled itself tightly around a horrifying thought: *I'm going to die.* Not today, but eventually. This realization was the second worst thing that had happened to me in the last twenty-four hours.

No one knew how to make Bo's oatmeal the way he liked it—how I ground it in my mini Cuisinart and mixed it with applesauce and cinnamon. No one knew that I could sneak avocado into his Greek yogurt without him noticing, or that he liked when I read *Elmo's 12 Days of Christmas,* no matter the time of year, before he went to bed. Owen didn't even know this stuff. He never paid attention when I cooked for Bo, and thought that I was being crazy for making most of his food instead of buying it at the grocery store like his mother used to do. I could drop dead in the dry cleaner, or the driveway, or the grocery store at any moment. If it happened in the grocery store, I hoped it would at least be in the aisle that sold Bounty and Ajax. Maybe then the store manager would be able to use me to demonstrate just how absorbent the two-ply paper towel really was.

These weren't thoughts that happily married people had early on in their union, but once you became a single mother, your perspective changed. The entire world seemed unfathomably dangerous. I used to walk down the stairs in heels! Thin, spiky heels! What was I thinking? I felt irresponsible just owning them! I immediately scooped Bo up off the floor, ran upstairs, and reached under my bed to find the tattered brown tote bag that I last used on our honeymoon in Aruba. It was probably a pretty safe bet that I wouldn't be going on any beach vacations or a second honeymoon anytime soon, so I took the bag over to my closet and started to fill it with my once beloved shoes.

The sidewalk outside my house was craggy. Whenever I walked on it, fragmented pieces of stone and brick caused my knees to buckle and turned my ankles. It was just a matter of time before I pitched forward, smashed my head into the corner of a broken brick, and bled out on the pavement. For all intents and purposes, it was a death trap, and I couldn't believe that it didn't turn up on the inspection. Then there was the blinking light at the intersection of Avenue What's It Called and Boulevard of Broken Marriages. That thing was just begging for some millennial with a selfie stick to come plowing through it at a high rate of speed and ram into the driver's side door of my sensible four-door sedan. Don't even get me started on the hurricanes in the Northeast. People must have a death wish just living here. It was going to happen. The only responsible thing to do was prepare.

I wished I had my laptop, but it was downstairs on the kitchen counter and that might as well have been seven miles away. My mind continued to race with the staggering amount of information I needed to get down on a piece of paper somewhere, so that Antonia would know what to do once I was gone. I couldn't rely on Owen to handle this information. I apparently couldn't rely on Owen to do much of anything, and this was not the time to be taking any big chances. First off,

I needed to start a spreadsheet with all the important information: the name of Bo's pediatrician, the phone number of the pharmacy, the location of Bo's birth certificate, and the temperature I set the thermostat when he went to bed at night. Antonia didn't know what foods Bo liked, or where to find the recipe for his favorite sweet potato purée. Neither did Owen. I was the lone keeper of all of this information, and that was a major responsibility that I couldn't believe I was just noticing now. I decided that I needed to make a death chart with links to all of the recipes I used, so that while Bo was adjusting to life without his mother, he'd at least have his favorite homemade teething biscuits that I cut into giant stars with a Christmas cookie cutter.

I had a notebook where I jotted down recipes I wanted to make for him as he grew older, finally got teeth, and could eat more grown-up food. I wanted to make him homemade granola bars, and Oreos, and graham crackers, and cinnamon biscuits that had just the right amount of sweetness. I wanted to make miniature calzones, and potpies, and meatballs that were stuffed with cheese and coated in garlicky pesto. I was already thinking about these things and he had only cut a single tooth. I decided to create a separate spreadsheet that I would save in my death folder. From now on, everything was going to be documented and painstakingly cataloged so that there would be no confusion. I moved some of Bo's favorite toys—the flashlight, a stuffed elephant, an ark filled with little pairs of plastic animals and one creepy-looking man holding a stick that I could only assume was supposed to be Noah, and a board puzzle—up to my room so that he could play on the floor next to my bed. I crawled back under my duvet and let it wrap me, and warm me, and remind me how miserable life outside this bed was, and suggest that I should never step foot out of it again.

❧ Chapter 4

ON A RAINY early April afternoon about two weeks after Tara informed me I was going to die in Connecticut, Antonia showed up on my doorstep. She arrived with two bags, a laptop, and an Apple Watch that served as an alarm clock, a calculator, a datebook, and maybe an actual watch, though I wasn't entirely sure, because she was always late for everything. She flung herself on me and wrapped her arms tightly around my shoulders. "I'm so sorry. I'd have been here sooner but I had to meet with two couples who were about to leave on a three-week trip to Tuscany and the vineyard they were supposed to visit totally botched their wine tour. It was a mess and I almost had to rebook the whole trip. Anyway, it doesn't matter. I'm here now. I have no words, bella. I don't know what else to say." I leaned into her, and emptied my lungs of all the angst and pain that had been building over the last two weeks. The wail was almost inhuman, a long, moaning, wheezing shriek that just seemed to keep coming as Antonia hugged me. "Let it out. It's going to be okay," she promised. I had no idea how she planned on making that true.

She moved her things into the guest room upstairs, which

I hadn't put much thought into decorating because I wasn't expecting any overnight guests, and now I regretted it. If Antonia was going to put her life on hold for me, I should at least be able to offer her a room with an area rug, but the floors were still bare, and cold in the morning despite the fact that it was spring. Then, she hurried back downstairs and into the kitchen, scooped Bo out of his jumper, and kissed him a million times before she held him over her head and let his fat, swollen gums drool all over her forehead. Really good friends will drop what they're doing and fly to Connecticut to take care of you and your son when you discover your marriage is over. At least, the really good friends who work from home will. A lot of people would've just sent a card and promised to call every Wednesday night after the six o'clock news to see how I was doing. A lot of people would've promised to visit but would never have actually shown up. A lot of people aren't Antonia.

I hated to admit that I needed help. Until now, I'd never have thought I'd be the type to need someone to stay with me to help me pull myself together, but I did. I felt like I was living underwater, and that I could come up for air for a brief period of time, but would inevitably end up submerged again, all of my senses foggy, and my equilibrium off, and my body cold no matter how many blankets I wrapped around myself. I wished I could be one of those girls who spent the day after a breakup driving around town with the windows down singing Kelly Clarkson while the wind blew through my hair, but instead I was lying in bed watching Rachael Ray teach me how to make my own takeout, and wondering when that became a thing.

Antonia didn't wait long to get into the details. She poured herself a glass of water and sat down at the kitchen table. "How did this happen? Who is this woman?" she asked. "Do you know her?"

Of course I knew her. Every married woman knew her—the ghost from her husband's past that lingered around longer than she should, the quiet threat she'd never admit was a concern, the well-rested, non-wrinkled, annoyingly perfect tramp with a thigh gap who reminded women who became mothers of the people they used to be and never would be again. She was my worst nightmare. "She was Owen's high school girl-friend. I didn't know that at first."

"Oh, come on," Antonia said.

"Yep. It's that ridiculous. The day we moved in she came over with a bottle of wine and gave us a toast." Recalling that day now felt like reliving a traumatic event. "She said, 'Good neighbors make great friends.' I didn't realize how good, I guess." Dee Dee had clinked her glass against Owen's and I remembered noticing that she had no fewer than four bangle bracelets dangling off her wrist. Maybe five. "I should've known she was trying too hard."

"She was maneuvering her way in before you had even un-packed?"

"Yes," I said, pushing the memory from my clouded mind because I couldn't stand to have it in there for another second. "I'm so happy you're here," I said. I sank into a chair next to her. "What am I going to do?"

"You're going to take some time to process everything, and to take care of yourself. Then, you're going to start over."

"That's a lovely thought for someone who doesn't have an infant."

"I'll take care of him. You take care of you."

"Okay," I agreed, because no one else was going to take care of me, and I figured I'd better get used to that. I dragged myself into my room, which was a complete mess, but I didn't really care. It was my bedroom, and my bedroom alone now, and that meant if I wanted to empty out Owen's entire dresser looking for someone else's underwear, and leave the contents strewn all over the floor, I could. I rolled around in the bed like I was a warm donut trying to coat myself in sprinkles. Owen's side of the bed was usually off-limits; he didn't even like it if our feet touched while he was sleeping, and now I wasn't sure how to handle all of the extra space. Was I supposed to just keep my side, because I liked it there? Or sleep on Owen's side, because I could? Or sleep in the middle so that I didn't have to decide what side of the bed to sleep on? Part of me wondered if I should get a sleeping bag out of the attic and sleep on the floor, removing the bed from the equation entirely. But I liked the bed. I was positive that Owen and Dee Dee never slept together in my bed because I was incredibly particular about how I made it. My grandmother once worked as a maid in a hotel, and she taught me how to make absurdly tight hospital corners that were nearly impossible to move. I spent no less than five minutes every morning smoothing my fluffy, downy, pale green duvet across the mattress until there were no creases or indentations anywhere. A box-pleated dust ruffle skimmed the floor underneath it, hiding tote bags, photo albums, paperbacks awaiting donation at the library book drive, and what I called my "pre-baby" clothes that would be more aptly called "clothes I will never fit into again." It was admittedly frilly, and admittedly girly, and I admittedly didn't care when Owen complained about those things one bit. The bed was my happy place. If Owen so much as sat on it during the day, it was obvious. There was no way in hell he and Dee Dee rolled around in it without my noticing. None. It was now the only thing in the entire house I was comfortable touching without ski gloves.

I couldn't get the sickening thoughts to stop running through my head. *My marriage is over. My family is broken. The demolition expert's name is Dee Dee. Her hair is blond and in perpetual beach waves, even though it's not beach season. Owen is with her now. I am alone.* There was an empty plastic bag from the dry cleaner hanging on the doorknob of Owen's closet, and I wondered which shirts he took with him when he left. There was usually a pair of sneakers tossed in the corner next to the dresser, but those were gone, too, as was the red sweater he'd left thrown over the back of the armchair by the window. *He's gone. His dry cleaning, and his sweater, and his sneakers are all with him, and I am here alone in our giant bed to fend for myself and our son. I don't know how to do this. Plus, I just noticed that the paint is chipped on the wall opposite my bed, down by the floor molding, and a crack is starting to spread up the plaster. I don't know how to paint. There are lots of things I don't know how to do. That includes how to get up.*

"YOU'RE GETTING IN the shower," Antonia informed me the following morning as she deftly yanked the blankets off my bed, leaving my lower body exposed. For some reason, I was wearing one of Owen's blue cotton T-shirts, the one that was so soft and thin you could almost see through it, and a pair of my cotton underwear, the one that was so old and ratty you could almost see through it. I wasn't sure why I didn't have on pajama bottoms, or at least a pair of cotton shorts. I assumed it required too much effort to find them, but I couldn't remember, so that was just a guess. The T-shirt was both torturous and comforting—I wanted to curl up inside of it and at the same time rip it to shreds. At this moment, I couldn't clearly identify any emotion at all. They were all tangled and knotted like necklaces in the bottom of a jewelry box. I wished Antonia could release them with a safety pin—poke and prod the massive, snarled ball until she nudged one free and untangled the whole mess, but she couldn't. No one could untangle this. I was pretty sure I was going to stay knotted forever.

"Okay," I finally agreed. Antonia reached over and gently clasped one of my hands in hers. She wrapped the other one around my waist, and slowly helped me to my feet, like the problem was with my leg and not my heart. We walked together into the master bathroom, and I sat on the edge of the porcelain tub while Antonia turned on the steam shower. I never used this tub, even though it was one of the things that I'd liked most about the house when we bought it. Now, as I sat on it with my head hanging low because it required some kind of superhuman effort to hold it upright, I noticed that there seemed to be a ring around the bottom of the tub, a watermark that hadn't been buffed away. Was Dee Dee in my tub? I wondered. Were they taking baths in here while I was at the playground behind the elementary school or at the aquarium in Norwalk?

"What are you thinking about?" Antonia asked, as if she knew that my mind had wandered somewhere dangerous and unnecessarily painful.

"If Dee Dee and Owen ever had sex in this bathtub," I replied, honestly.

"You can't do that to yourself. This is your home. You'll drive yourself crazy wondering."

"How do I not wonder, Antonia?" I asked. "Everywhere I look all I see are Owen and Dee Dee naked and laughing at his stupid wife who didn't even realize what was happening in her own house. I wonder if they did it on my dining room table, or on my living room rug or on the kitchen counter. Every inch of this house is contaminated. There's no way to get rid of her—believe me, I tried. I read the labels on every cleaning solution under my kitchen sink, and they promised to rid my house of mold, mildew, grease, grime, dust, dander, ants, roaches, and rust, but not one of them promised to wash away tramps named Dee Dee who ate my waffles and slept with my husband, in no particular order."

"Okay. So what do you want to do?" she asked.

"I need to move," I said, the immediacy of the thought shooting currents through my body.

"I don't think that's a bad idea at all. There's no reason for you to stay here."

"Do you think I need permission to move?" I asked.

"You'd have to ask your lawyer. If his name is on the deed

I'd imagine you do. But as long as you stay local, I don't know why he'd care. You should talk to him. Be rational, and calm, and let him know that you don't want to be in this house. All things considered, he shouldn't give you a hard time."

"I need a new Realtor." For some reason, the emotional knot loosened just enough to allow me to locate a single emotion: grief. Tears came violently, almost as forcefully as the water that sprayed out of the showerhead and all over the beige tile on the floor.

"It's okay," Antonia said, dropping on her knees in front of me and wrapping her arms tightly around my hunched, tired body.

"This isn't fair. This isn't supposed to happen like this. I was a good wife," I whispered, because the tears were choking my words before they could make their way out of my mouth.

"I know you were," she assured me.

"I wasn't jealous, or petty, or difficult. I didn't pick arguments for the sake of picking them. I bought his favorite toothpaste at the drugstore and made him pork chops with vinegar peppers just like you showed me every time he came home from a business trip."

"And I'm sure they were delicious," Antonia said.

"Why did he leave us? Why weren't we enough for him?" I finally had the courage to ask the big question, the same one I'd bet every woman whose marriage ended in divorce asked herself countless times and could never answer.

"It doesn't have anything to do with you. He's being an idiot. He's probably about to have some kind of midlife crisis, and is trying to reclaim his youth by dating his high school girlfriend. He's a cliché. The problem is with him. It's not with you."

"I didn't think he had it in him. I didn't think he was the type to have an affair, you know? I thought he was too honest, or too righteous to ever do it. How did I miss this? I feel like he's not the man I thought I married. Who have I been with this whole time?"

"You don't need to make this into a *Dr. Phil* episode. It's simple, bella. He reunited with her, he liked going over all their old times, and she doesn't have a toddler wrapped around her leg or pulling on her beach waves all day long."

"I told you about those, huh?"

"Yeah. You did."

"I wasn't jealous, Antonia. I wasn't. I wasn't worried, or nervous at all. She was just a blip on my radar. I was happy and thought Owen was happy and that that meant there was nothing to worry about. I should've known. She helped us move in. I thought she was just being nice. How could I miss that? She came by before we'd even moved into the house!"

"HI, GUYS! WELCOME to the neighborhood!" Dee Dee sang, and I mean *sang,* as if she were auditioning for a Broadway show. The trip from Chicago had seemed endless. Riding eight hundred miles in a U-Haul one month postpartum now topped the list of things there was no shot in hell I'd ever do again.

"Dee Dee? Is that you?" Owen asked, as he wiped his hand on the back pockets of his jeans and hopped out the back of the truck. "What are you doing here?"

"I wanted to say thank you for the business, and to welcome you to the neighborhood. I knew you drove yourselves out here with the baby, so I thought maybe you could use some help unloading! Claire, the last thing you need to be doing right now is lugging heavy boxes around, right?"

I walked around to the driver's-side door and eyed the five enormous men standing in the street. "You hired us movers?" I asked. I'd heard that it wasn't uncommon for Realtors to leave a bottle of wine at the house, or a basket of flowers, or to make some kind of gesture to the new homeowner to say "thank you" and "welcome to the neighborhood." I'd never heard of someone showing up with a team of large men to help unload your furniture. "This is seriously amazing! All I want in the world right now is for Bo's room to be ready for him. I don't want him sleeping in the middle of boxes. I don't know what to say."

"You don't have to say anything! These guys will get your truck unloaded, pronto. Bo's room will be ready before you know it." She pushed a piece of her hair behind her ear and it was shiny, and bouncy, and annoyingly perfect. "Now. Let's get you guys inside. You've spent enough time with this truck, so leave this job to the pros. In the meantime, I brought a bottle of wine. How about we go inside and celebrate your arrival back home?"

"I'm down for a glass of wine," Owen said, rolling his head in circles and kneading the muscles in his upper back. "I'd love one, actually. I'm sure we can find glasses in here somewhere." He motioned toward the boxes in the truck as the starting defensive line for the New York Giants climbed inside and started lifting furniture like I lifted Twix bars.

"I brought some with me!" Dee Dee singsonged.

Of course she did.

"I'M SO STUPID," I moaned.

"She's a knee-jerk reaction to something, and he's going to wake up one day and realize that he made a huge mistake. He will. You need to show him that you aren't breakable."

"How am I supposed to do that?" I asked, even though I had a few ideas. I'd seen this play out in the tabloids a million times. I could do the revenge body thing, like Khloé Kardashian. Get in kick-ass shape, cut my hair, and wear a beautiful, uncharacteristically bright dress to a red-carpet event, or in my case, the grocery store. That was option number one. The second option was to go the Taylor Swift route, and pen a song about him letting him know without equivocation that we were never getting back together, and have it play all over the radio. The third and least likely option was the J.Lo option, where I'd hire a slew of backup dancers who were barely of legal drinking age, and start dating one of them to prove that young, hot, muscular men were interested in me, despite having breasts that looked like deflated water balloons, and a muffin top that barring surgical intervention would likely stay with me until death. All of these options were good. I had no problem with any of them. The problem was that exactly none of them were applicable to my life. I didn't have a red carpet, or a record label, or a dance troupe available to make my revenge fantasy come true. I was just Claire Stevens, suburban mother and housewife. That sucked.

"You start by showering and get dressed. I don't care if you want to wear sweatpants, but put on clothes that you could theoretically wear outside of the house."

"Uh-huh," I grunted.

"Then you go and take care of your son. It's not his fault his dad is an asshole. He doesn't deserve to lose his loving, normally attentive mother to grief. He needs you. You need him."

"Uh-huh," I said again, the tears slowing down at the thought of Bo sitting downstairs with his plastic soccer ball and wondering where both his parents had gone. I was thirty-six years old. Owen ruined a portion of *my* life, but he'd just changed Bo's entire life. The entire freakin' thing. I was the only person in the world who could keep him feeling happy, and safe. "Then what?"

"Then you stop avoiding your mother's phone calls and let her know how you're doing. If you don't she's going to show up on your doorstep next."

"I haven't been avoiding her. I just feel too guilty to talk to her. I don't want her to worry. I need her to believe that I'm okay because if I now have to deal with the fact that I destroyed her dreams for her own child, while also coming to terms with the fact that I destroyed my dreams for my Bo, I will drown in guilt."

"There's no reason on earth for you to feel guilty, Claire. You didn't do anything! Stop taking the blame for this. Call your mother. Let her know you're okay. Better yet, start working on actually being okay."

"You make it sound like I don't want to do that!" I wailed. "Of course I want that but it's not that easy, Antonia! It's not like I can snap my fingers and make everything better. Believe me, I've tried."

"You can find yourself again, Claire. I know you can."

"Right. I'm sure that's easy," I said. "No problem."

"I'm not saying it's going to be easy, but you'll never get there if you don't stop feeling sorry for yourself. One day at a time. One foot in front of the other. That's what you need to tell yourself every single morning until the day comes where you can do it without needing to be reminded."

"Thank you," I said. I wiped my eyes with the hem of the T-shirt and for a second I thought I caught the scent of Owen's cologne, or his aftershave, or his hair gel, whatever that particular scent came from I wasn't entirely sure, but it belonged to Owen and therefore made me nauseous. Antonia was right that I needed to figure out a way to move forward, and while I had no idea how I'd do that at the moment, I could figure it out eventually. Before I did anything, though, before I made one single move, I had to get out of his fucking T-shirt. I stood and drew my shoulders back as if having better posture would somehow make getting on with my life easier, and pulled it over my head. I handed it to Antonia. "Get rid of this," I said. I wondered briefly if I would come to regret that decision, if maybe there was still a part of me that wanted to keep a few things for nostalgia. Before there were bad times, there were a lot of good times—didn't they deserve to be remembered?

"I'm going to be here for you every step of the way," Antonia said, wrapping the shirt into a tiny gray ball. "I can work from the East Coast for a while. I'm here as long as you need me to be here."

"Bo lives with me, you understand that, right? You won't be able to sleep past six thirty in the morning even once the entire time you're here."

"Sleep is overrated," she said with a shrug.

"Oh my God. You are the best friend in the entire world. I don't deserve you."

"Yes, you do. And I know you'd do the same for me."

"I hope one day I can."

"What?" she asked.

"That didn't come out right."

"I know what you meant. Now go ahead and get in the shower," she ordered. "Wash your hair. You'll feel a million times better."

I closed the glass door behind me and let the water rinse the last two weeks away. I reached for the pink disposable razor I kept on the bottom shelf of the shower caddy and shaved way too much hair off my legs and my armpits. I washed, exfoliated, rinsed, moisturized, plucked, and brushed, and when I was done, I wrapped myself in a soft beige towel, and raked my wet hair into a ponytail. I'd hoped to feel like a warrior when the whole process was over. I didn't. Instead, I just felt like a really big mess who was very clean and very well groomed. For now, that would have to be enough.

Chapter 5

ANTONIA HAD MOVED in with me almost a month ago, and I felt like I'd made some serious progress since then. Bo and I went on some long walks in the warm May sunshine and spent some quality time together, strolling around the park at the end of town or sitting on benches to watch the dogs play on the grass, and getting out of the house did a lot to help clear my head. I was very proud of this fact. One Monday we went to the playground, and I pushed him on the swings while the other mothers talked to each other and pretended I wasn't there, but the playground's not really a place to make friends when you're a grown-up, because everyone's too busy trying to make sure that their child doesn't fall off a jungle gym, or run toward the gate into the parking lot, or eat twigs off the ground. Two women in tunics sat on a bench drinking out of bright-colored thermoses, and most people would assume it was coffee, but I was fairly certain it was booze, because they were laughing an awful lot and seemed to be having way too good of a time considering they were sitting on a bench in front of monkey bars. I'd like to be friends with those girls. I'd get a shiny green thermos and fill it with a weak mimosa, too, and then sitting on a hot park bench wouldn't seem so much like cruel and unusual punishment, and more like a brunch picnic. That sounded like a lovely way to spend a morning with a baby in suburbia. Another mom stayed on the periphery and barked into a headset, and she had on shoes with a heel and carried a briefcase, so she was probably working from home for the day, and probably couldn't wait until she could go back to the office and talk to other women with brains, instead of the loner hanging out at the swing set (me), and the drunks hanging out by the monkey bars (women I wished I was friends with). She didn't seem unfriendly, she just seemed uninterested, but I couldn't really blame her because the playground wasn't interesting at all, it was just more interesting than being in my house, and that was the only criteria it needed to meet for me to feel like it was the best place on earth. I promised myself that the next time I took Bo to the swings I'd brush my hair so that I looked a little less scary and a little more friendly, and bring a thermos, just in case the stars aligned and the drunk girls asked if I wanted to sit down with them. I knew this was unlikely to happen, because I'd seen every John Hughes movie ever made, and the outsider was never invited to sit with the cool kids at their lunch table, but I didn't care. I decided that I needed to set some new goals for myself, and making a mom friend at the playground was currently at the top of my list.

I'd planned on making the playground part of my regular routine, but instead the weather gods intervened and decided to make it rain for eight straight days. Not the kind of rain where on the first day you think, *This is the best sleeping weather ever!* And then the next day, you think, *This is awesome. I can organize my spice drawer, and clean out my garage, and finally get around to throwing out all the underwear I haven't worn in two years.* It rained the kind of rain that made you check the attic to see if the roof was leaking (it wasn't, thank God), and the garage to see if your Christmas decorations were floating around in three feet of water (I had no idea. The garage scared me). I felt so guilty that I hadn't done anything with Bo for over a week except read him books and plop him on his play mat in front of the TV, and I was really getting sick of feeling guilty for one reason or another all day, every day, so I was ready to look for alternatives.

Every Friday at 9:00 A.M. the children's room at the library held story time for kids who were at least nine months old and it had been on my list of things to do, but up until now I hadn't been able to get my act together fast enough to make it there on time. I hated to admit it, but part of me didn't really want to go out and be with other people, which I knew was silly, and immature, and counterproductive, but I couldn't help it. I feared having to listen to other women talk about their husbands and their kids and complain about how hard things were for them because their husbands left the toilet seat up. If this experience had done nothing else for me, it had given me some perspective. Still, I knew that Bo would probably like the library and I wanted him to socialize and start to make friends. One of us should have some kind of life here, and I didn't want my grief to prevent me from doing something that he'd enjoy. I woke up early this morning and got showered and dressed. Rain or no rain, we were going.

I wrapped Bo up in his raincoat and carried him on my hip out to his car seat. When we arrived at the library, I parked my car and carried Bo quickly through the parking lot, falling in with the chaotic net of rain shield–covered strollers and trying to remember the last time I felt this uncomfortable. All of the other mothers seemed to know each other, and the cliques were evident even to someone who didn't know anyone. Women pushed by each other trying to get through the entrance first, so that they could jockey for seats, and they whispered and gossiped and openly judged each other and I had no idea why. It was like *The Real Housewives of Connecticut* meets *The Hunger Games*, and I was afraid that I wasn't currently equipped to handle this.

Rain continued to pour down, drenching the hem of my pants and causing Bo to bury his head in my shoulder. I hurried up the ramp and into the lobby past a friendly-looking elderly woman seated at a cracked wooden desk in the corner. The placard on her desk said her name was Barbara. I smiled as I walked by her, and she smiled back, the first smile that I'd received from anyone in town in a while, which felt really, really nice. I moved past the line of strollers that had been parked against the wall, black and gray and one purple one that stuck out like a purple stroller would, and pulled Bo up higher onto my hip. His sneakers were soaked and I was happy that I put plastic bags over his feet, the way my mom used to do when it snowed in Chicago, so I knew at least his socks were dry. I dragged him here in the rain for my benefit, though I told myself the whole way that it was really for him—that he would somehow be better off if a stranger read *Goodnight Moon* while thirty other toddlers sneezed on him. But I really came here for me. I came because I needed to try and meet some other women to socialize with so that I could spend my time doing something productive and not wallowing over the fact that my husband had left me. Also, I needed to send a picture of me and Bo in the children's section to my mother as proof that I was actually up, dressed, and out of the house. We'd smile and I'd snap the perfect happy selfie and text it to her, and maybe she'd breathe a little easier at her yoga class this morning because she knew she raised an independent daughter who could handle anything. Right.

I followed the crowd down a large staircase to the basement and into a room filled with rows of folding chairs and a giant toy chest filled with puppets. I lowered myself into a seat in the corner and cautiously placed Bo on my lap. The folding chair creaked when I sat, the metal cold and unforgiving under my now bony butt. Somewhere, a bell rang, and all the moms lingering in the back discussing their playgroups and their luncheons and their tennis lessons shuffled in and took their seats. I held Bo's hand too tightly, and he grunted as he tried to pull it free of my grasp. I quickly took a selfie with my phone, and texted it to my mom with the caption "love from the library!" Convincing her that I didn't need her help was going to be easy. I was a social media consultant in my previous life. People used to pay me to carefully craft fiction and sell it as a reality. Making things look better than they actually were was kind of my specialty. If anyone was able to dupe her parents into believing that life wasn't a total mess, it was me.

The girl reading took her seat at the front of the room, the book in one hand and a caterpillar puppet worn over the other like a giant, multilegged oven mitt with a face. The puppet wasn't what caught my attention. She had a nose ring, an eyebrow ring, and no fewer than four hoops in her right ear, and those were only the ones that I could count from the back of the room with an astigmatism in my left eye. Her hair was bottle-dyed black, her lips painted a shocking red, her fingers strangled by stacks of silver rings. She appeared thin, but was drowning under drapes of black fabric and lace-up combat boots. She looked like she'd rolled out of a Marilyn Manson fan club meeting. She wasn't who I would've expected to read to a bunch of children on Friday mornings. I leaned back in my chair and watched the girl make the puppet speak. I was out of the house. I was dressed. I was making progress. None of those things were small things. Not to me.

I heard them snickering before I saw them. I heard some of them say, "Shhh," not because they were causing a minor disruption to Goth-girl's caterpillar reenactment, but because they were afraid I'd notice them looking at me. I glanced at Bo, so enthralled with the existence of the caterpillar that he had no idea women were gossiping about his mother right in front of him. I prayed I'd make my way out of this mess before that ever changed—before things became hard for him, too.

I quickly glanced over at them and, as expected, Dee Dee's friends—Becky, Stella, and Stephanie, the triumvirate from hell—were seated next to each other behind me. I'd only been introduced to them once, a few months after we'd moved here, and once was more than enough. I was hoping to maybe meet some women to be friends with at this story hour, but it had never occurred to me that I would also have to dodge women I wouldn't want to be friends with under any circumstances whatsoever. I hadn't fully thought this through. It was a good thing I already sent the happy selfie, because things had just taken a drastic turn for the worse.

I met them when Dee Dee invited us to her Christmas party. "Christmas Cocktails," the invitation read. Owen wore a tie, which was rare, and I wore my Spanx, which was not rare at all, and we bundled up and left Bo with Marcy so we could enjoy a night out, just the two of us. The party took place in a private room at a restaurant in town, and I'd thought that a holiday party would be a great place to meet people, because people were happy at the holidays, and also usually tipsy, and that makes for easy conversation. I wanted to show Owen that I was still fun and hip and so I went to Dee Dee's party, and I laughed and I smiled and I tried very hard to make everyone like me. I wanted to feel like I fit in. I wanted Owen's friends to become my friends, too. I tried not to think about that night too much because when I did, I wanted to smash my head in with whatever blunt object I could get my hands on.

"You just have to meet my friends, Claire," Dee Dee said, as she grabbed my hand and pulled me over to three women standing together by the bar. One by one, she introduced me to the women in her crew: Becky, a steely blonde with a fake tan and a faker personality (I didn't like her); Stephanie, a steelier blonde with a faker tan and an even more fake personality (I disliked her even more); and Stella, a dead ringer for Julianna Margulies, who didn't seem to have a whole lot to say unless she was agreeing with Dee Dee, Becky, or Stephanie. She tossed her curly hair over her shoulder and stared down her nose at me, and I didn't like her either, though I liked her better than the rest. They flirted with Owen like they owned him because they'd known him longer, and like I was only visiting their silly little world. They flirted with Owen right in front of me, and right in front of their own husbands, and drank too many Cosmos, and too many glasses of wine, and no one seemed to care one way or the other, because they were all just old friends, and it was all just harmless fun.

Until, of course, it wasn't.

"Look at her roots," one of them said now. I think it was Becky. She seemed to be the ringleader, and I was pretty sure without her the other two wouldn't have said anything at all.

"She's not even that pretty," Stephanie added. "I can't wait to tell Dee Dee we saw her. She will just die." It took all of my strength not to stand up and scream, "I didn't do anything! Your friend broke up my marriage! Not the other way around!" But there was no point. I knew that women like these would never change, but that didn't make their insults hurt any less. I looked at their toddlers, all of them wearing miniature North Face anoraks and jeans, and felt my insides ache. It was only a matter of time before they became the class bullies who would no doubt stuff Bo in a locker or jam his head in a toilet bowl. It was only a matter of time until they learned from their mothers that it was okay to judge, to ridicule, and to exclude, for sport. I felt tears well in my eyes at the thought of one of these kids hurting my Bo, still staring at the caterpillar puppet with such amazement I could barely stand it, his pudgy little hands clapping along and his lips still stained from the cherries I swirled in his yogurt for breakfast.

I sat still and watched the wildly animated performance quietly, pretending like I didn't hear their chatter, when we all knew that I had. When the session was over, I pulled Bo up off my lap and headed toward the door. I wasn't going to say anything. I wanted to take the high road, but then I heard one of them snicker again, and I turned off the high road because while I may not have had any friends in this town, I wasn't going to be anyone's punching bag, either, and the high road wasn't doing it for me anymore anyway.

"Let's call Dee when we get back to your house, Stella," I heard one whisper. I wasn't sure which one, and it really didn't matter.

"I know you intended for me to hear all of that. I don't know why you guys have a problem with me. I've never done anything to any of you, and I've never done anything to Dee Dee. So why don't you stop acting like teenagers and spare me the drama."

"Excuse me?" tall, blond, Amazonian Becky asked.

"We're all here with our kids. I don't think story time at

the library is really the appropriate forum for gossip," I said, though I was pretty sure that they didn't care.

"Then you should probably stop coming," Stephanie said. I eyed Stella, who didn't seem interested in saying anything one way or the other. She bent down and fixed a bow in her little girl's hair, like if she wasn't partaking in the conversation, she wasn't as nasty as they were.

I sighed. I stood and pressed Bo tightly to my chest, covering him with my coat as I hurried out of the library, trying so hard to understand when the entire world had gone crazy.

I didn't bother to put Bo's coat on him—rather, I held him on my hip and sprinted through the flooded parking lot, figuring that at this point, an umbrella was totally useless. When we got home I'd put all of our clothes in the dryer, and put pajamas on both of us, even though it was only 11:00 A.M. Water streamed down my face as I struggled to strap him in his car seat, and Bo whined and squirmed in his seat, kicking his feet wildly and threatening to collapse into tears. I couldn't blame him. His feet may have been dry in their ziplock-bagged sacks, but his jeans were soaking wet and his hands were cold and his little bald head was slick with rain. I held his hands up to my mouth and kissed his fingers, hoping that I could warm him enough to make it home without him screaming the whole way. I tossed my bag on the floor and buckled my seat belt, and threw the car into reverse, never, ever to return to story time at the library.

I poured myself a cup of tea when I got home and sat down

on the floor next to Bo while he played with blocks. There was no reason in the world that I should have to endure the bitchy mommies at the library, and Dee Dee and Owen, and not be able to do anything to defend myself. I hated Owen more now than I did when I found out about the affair, and that was a fact. He forced me to stay in this town while also ruining any chance I had of setting up a normal life for us. Owen was so concerned about Bo, but what about me? I'm Bo's mother! Doesn't a mother's happiness directly impact the happiness of her child? I put my mug down on the counter and glanced at my laptop, and suddenly I realized that the answer to some of my problems was sitting in front of me, and if it didn't solve my problems, it would at least make me feel a hell of a lot better. I flipped open the computer and held my breath while I pulled up Facebook and entered Owen's username and password. How did I not think of this before? I wondered. It was so obvious! It was right here! Owen had been using the same passwords for everything. I could log into anything I wanted, whenever I wanted, and with that knowledge came serious power. Part of me didn't want to do it, because it would make me look immature and vindictive, but a bigger part of me did want to do it, because I didn't care about looking immature or vindictive, I just wanted him to suffer. I began to type and type and when I was done typing I examined my work and felt satisfied with the result: *Hi everyone, I just wanted to let you all know that I'm a lying, cheating asshole who had an affair right after I moved my wife and infant from Chicago to Connecticut.*

My wife caught me and my mistress in my house while my son was sleeping in his crib upstairs. Cast your votes for father of the year here!

I posted it. I didn't know if it made me feel better. It certainly didn't make me feel worse.

I had just put Bo down for his nap two hours later when my phone rang, but I didn't know the number, so I ignored it. A few seconds later it beeped, so I removed it from my bag and listened to my voicemail: *Hi, my name is Lissy, and I'm calling for Claire? You dropped your datebook in the library after story hour. I got your number out of it and just wanted to let you know that I have it. You can pick it up anytime today. I'll be working at the stationery store in town. It's called The Stationer. Thanks.*

I probably could've gone a month before I realized my datebook was missing, and at that point I'd have no idea where to even begin to look to find it. Bo was hopefully going to sleep for an hour, but when he woke up, I'd feed him a snack and make my way into town to reclaim my planner. I'd lost enough lately. I didn't need to add anything else to the list.

THE SIGN OUTSIDE the store was small, a little too small for anyone to notice, and there was no window display at all. I probably walked by it dozens of times, as it was located right next to the coffeehouse and down the block from the train station, and never even knew it was there. I pushed the door open and struggled to get the stroller over the doorjamb, causing a small bell over the door to ring, which I found charming. You don't hear a lot of bells like that anymore. If anything, sometimes you hear a beep when a door opens to let you know that the store has an alarm system, and if you try to rob it the cops will be there in less than five minutes flat to arrest you, or you get your money back guaranteed. The store was cluttered, but not in a good way. There was a bodega near where I lived in Chicago that had somehow managed to stuff an inexplicable number of things into a finite amount of space. You could literally buy kimchi, Pop-Tarts, wheat bread, and stuffed olives in the same store, at the same time, though I didn't know why you'd want to. This store reminded me of that—minus the overwhelming smell of fermented cabbage.

I battled with the stroller for a second, trying to hold the door open with my foot, while my wet hair hung in my face before someone said, "Let me help you with that," which I appreciated. A hand reached down and grabbed the front end of the stroller, guiding it into the corner of the room. When I looked up, I realized the woman helping me was the Goth girl from story hour. I wasn't expecting that. I'd just assumed it was another mom who'd found my datebook.

"Thank you so much," I said. "I'm Claire. I think you have my datebook?"

"Yes. Here you go. I found it on the floor when I was packing up my stuff." She reached under the counter and handed me my leather day planner.

"Thank you," I said. "I can't believe I didn't notice I dropped this."

"I can't believe you still use a datebook. I don't know anyone who still has one of those."

"I'm old-fashioned, I guess. It was really nice of you to track me down."

"No problem."

"I'm not sure I caught your name on my voicemail. Is it Lissy?" I asked.

"Melissa. I go by Lissy."

"It's nice to meet you, Lissy. That's Bo in the stroller."

"'Sup, little man?" she said, as she turned around and tickled his belly. He laughed.

"I know what you're thinking," Lissy said. "You look surprised that I'm the one who called you. You were expecting a mom in a sweater set, right?"

"Do I look surprised?" I asked, embarrassed that my expression was so obvious. "I'm sorry. This has been kind of a rough day for me so far. I didn't mean to come across that way."

"It's okay. I know the Goth thing throws a lot of people, especially in these parts. Most people look at me like they don't really know what to make of me when they meet me."

"I'm sure that's not true!" I said, even though I'd bet that it was.

"It's okay. It comes with the territory, right? But I like my individuality. I don't want to wear cable sweaters etched with ponies or skirts covered in pink-and-green monkeys. Never have. Anyone who has a problem with that can just leave me alone. Know what I mean?"

"I actually do, yeah," I said. I understood Lissy better than I'd understood most people I'd met in this state so far. Check that—I understood Lissy better than anyone I'd met in this state, no question, and I'd only known her for two minutes. "How'd you end up at the library?"

"I really like reading to kids. They don't judge. They're the only people who don't care what I look like. They just care that I pay attention to them, and that I do a really good *Very Hungry Caterpillar* voice."

"You *do* do a really good *Very Hungry Caterpillar* voice," I said. I was embarrassed to think about my initial judgments of this girl. From what I could tell, she was a kind, honest, straightforward person who didn't give a damn what other people thought of her. She was everything I wished I could be, except for the nose and the eyebrow ring.

"Can I ask you a question?" she asked.

"Sure."

"I saw the way those ladies were looking at you. What's going on there? Did you bang one of their husbands?" she asked.

"Hardly," I answered.

"What's their problem with you?"

"I'm not really sure. I mean, I know why they don't like me, I just can't believe it because it's so ridiculous."

"What did you do?"

"Nothing. I married a guy from here. They're his ex-girlfriend's friends. The guy cheated on me with the ex-girlfriend, and now they're together. For some reason I guess they feel that that means they have to be nasty to me to make their allegiance clear."

"That's crazy fucked up," Lissy said, giving me another reason to like her tremendously.

"Right?" I said.

"You should come back to the library on Wednesday mornings. I do readings then, too. Those girls never come on Wednesdays, so you won't have to worry about them. Maybe we can get a drink after or something."

"At eleven in the morning? I mean, I guess I could," I said. "Why not?"

"I meant a coffee drink. Not a cocktail drink. You need to get out more."

"You have no idea," I admitted.

"Here," she said. She reached over and pulled a piece of paper off a small notepad sitting on the counter, and scribbled her phone number on the back of it. "Call me if you want to meet up sometime. I know what it's like to be an outsider around here."

"I will, thanks," I said. I had no idea why this girl had chosen to be so nice to me, and I didn't care. Connecting with someone made me feel normal and happy and that was a phenomenal way to feel.

"This store is really cute."

"Thanks. I need a new name. The Stationer doesn't really do it justice, but I'm having a hard time coming up with anything better. What do you think? Do you like it?"

"You want my opinion?" I asked, surprised that she'd be interested in my thoughts when she didn't know me at all.

"Yeah. Why not? You can be honest."

"Well, if you don't mind my saying, I don't think it's the right name for this place either. It doesn't make the store sound special at all, or even that you care that much about it. That's probably not the vibe you want to put out there."

"I know. I've been wracking my brain trying to come up with something, but I haven't been able to think of anything. Do you have a better idea?"

"No," I said, sadly. "I'll think about it, though," I said. I wanted to be cautious with my suggestions, because I sensed this store was extremely important to Lissy. The last thing I wanted was for her to feel like I stepped into her world and immediately started telling her what to do with her life like I was some kind of expert. My life was in complete disarray. I hadn't worked since I'd left Chicago almost a year ago. Who was I to tell anyone about anything?

"Okay, good. I need someone else's brain on it. The name is important, you know? I hope this doesn't sound weird, but I'm glad we met. I'm sorry those women are being bitchy to you. And I'm sorry your husband banged someone else. That sucks."

"Indeed it does," I sighed.

"Maybe you'll be able to help me come up with the right name for this place. Two heads are better than one, you know?"

"I'll certainly try," I said. "I should get going. I need to get home before this rain floods the street and Bo and I need to swim there."

"Yeah, it's brutal out there. Drive safe."

"Thank you so much again for returning this. It was really nice to meet you."

"You too. I meant what I said. Call me sometime. I'm around.

It's not like the soccer moms are inviting me over for lunch every day, you know? Life is a lot different for me here than it was when I lived in Manhattan."

"I imagine the Goth world is a lot busier in the city."

"You don't even want to know," she said with a laugh.

"You're probably right," I agreed. "I will. Have a good day."

I was just about to push the door open and back the stroller out onto the sidewalk when I had a thought. "Lissy, I hope this doesn't sound weird, but do you have any plans later this afternoon?" I asked. I knew that I may have sounded desperate, and too forward, and that if I was trying to date Lissy she would run the other way because I'd look like a cling-on, but I didn't care if I sounded desperate, and I wasn't trying to date her, so really it didn't matter.

"No. I'll be here, but I'll probably close up early. Nobody is out shopping in this weather."

"Would you like to come over for coffee or a real drink this afternoon? My friend Antonia is staying with me, but it's just the two of us, and Bo, of course. There's nothing worse than being trapped inside in the rain by yourself, right? I hope that doesn't sound weird since we just met, but if you'd like to join you're more than welcome."

"Sure. Why not?" she replied.

"Great. I'll be there, so come by whenever." I picked up a pen from her counter and scribbled my address on a piece of paper. "I'm only like five minutes from here."

"Cool. I'll close up here around four. See you after that."

"Great! See you then," I said. I waved as I pushed the stroller outside and hurried toward my car in the rain for the second time today, laughing at the fact that if not for really bad weather and a shortage of underwear to toss, I may never have met Lissy. I was happy I did. I wished I'd met her sooner.

"I'M GLAD YOU came," I said when I answered the door at 4:30. I invited Lissy inside. "This is my friend Antonia. She's staying with me for a little bit. Antonia, this is Lissy."

"It's nice to meet you," Antonia said. "Can I get you anything?" I loved that Antonia was acting like the hostess so I didn't have to. It had been a long day, and I didn't know how to be a hostess anymore, because Lissy was the first new friend to step in my house since I'd moved here.

"I'm good, thanks," Lissy answered, holding up a bottle of water.

"Claire was just telling me about how you returned her datebook. That was nice of you. You work at the library and at a store in town?" Antonia asked. We pulled up chairs at the kitchen table, and Lissy took a long drink of her water. I glanced at Antonia to see if she was surprised at Lissy's Goth attire, but if she was, she didn't show it.

"Yes," Lissy said. "I do both. I'm single so I like to keep busy. What do you guys do?"

"I work for a travel company specializing in Italian food and wine tours," Antonia said.

"That doesn't suck," Lissy replied, immediately envious of Antonia, which was what always happened when someone met Antonia for the first time.

"Nope! You won't hear me complaining. If you ever want to go to Italy, let me know!"

"What about you, Claire?"

"I guess I'm the only one here without a job," I said—well, sighed.

"So what?" Antonia asked.

"You don't get it, because you have your job—one you actually like—so you don't know what it's like to wander through your days in yoga pants with no intellectual stimulation. You don't know what it's like out here for moms in the cruel, scary jungle of suburbia. You still believe that because we're all women in this big crazy world that we're all supportive of each other, but I'm going to let you in on a little secret. The women who work are thinking about how lucky they are that they get to go do something useful with their days and how they'd just go crazy if they were home all the time, and the women who are home are thinking about how they're just so fortunate to not have to spend one minute away from their kids, and everyone is lying! We are all just jealous of one another on some level. The working moms wish they could be home more and the home moms wish they could go to work sometimes but no one wants to admit that because everyone is too busy propagating the fantasy that they love their perfect little lives. So you know what that means?"

"Everyone drinks too much wine?" Lissy asked.

"No one is actually happy," I replied.

"That's an aggressive statement," Antonia informed me.

"I stand by it. I mean, I traded my career for my marriage.

Great. Fantastic. Yay for me. Except now I have neither, and all I've been hearing is how I need to rebuild my life. Which begs the question: Which one am I supposed to rebuild first? Do I try and start over in an unforgiving industry that requires hours of commitment and let someone else tuck Bo in every night? Or do I try and find another husband so that my non-career is less like a scarlet letter and more like a selfless act? Do I chase money, or a man? Are those the only options I have? Is that what it really boils down to for all of us in the end?"

"That is seriously depressing," Lissy said. "Shit."

"Exactly. No wonder the number of female alcoholics is on the rise. Who can possibly stand to think about that? The concept of being able to have it all is a myth. You have to make a choice, but we're all trying to convince ourselves that we don't."

"I don't know why you're putting so much pressure on yourself to go back to work, and for the record, you were talking about that before you even knew about Owen and Dee Dee," Antonia said, because she had annoying recall. "Your career doesn't define your worth, but for some reason you seem to think that it will somehow make you feel better about yourself. If you want to work then go for it, but if you don't, that's okay, too. There's no one way to be a woman these days, so stop thinking that you need a job to be complete."

"I feel like people look down on me because I'm home with no job and no husband," I said. I hated that I said it, but I meant it. "Is that crazy to admit?"

"No. I get that," Antonia admitted. "I feel like people judge me all the time because I'm single. I think people are saying,

'Oh, if only she didn't work so much,' or 'She's too busy with her career to focus on finding a man.'"

"They do say that," I agreed. "But that also has to do with the fact that you're gorgeous. No one understands why you aren't married. No one ever used to say that about me. I'm not really sure if I should be insulted by that. I'll have to think about it."

"I know. And that's bullshit, too. I'm single because I haven't met the right guy. Period. And when I do, I don't know what will happen to my career. If I have kids and decide to cut back a little, so what? And if I have kids and decide to work the same amount, so what? And if I decide to never have kids and work seven days a week, that's okay, too. Who are you answering to?"

"No one. I don't know anyone," I admitted with a shrug.

"Exactly. And with that comes freedom," Antonia added.

"Ahhh, freedom. So far it's overrated," I said. "I'm a smart, educated, competent woman with nothing to show for my life. How am I supposed to feel about that? I need something in my life to work. I'm firing on zero cylinders right now."

"You should go on a dating site," Lissy suggested. "If you don't like being alone, then you totally should do that."

"No, I shouldn't," I said, but Lissy's suggestion had made my mind swirl into wonderful places. "But Owen should."

"I thought he had Dee Dee," Lissy said as she watched me jump up from the table and grab my laptop from off the counter.

"Are you doing what I think you're doing?" Antonia asked.

"If you mean am I going to sign up Owen on Craigslist and put out his phone number so that lots of random girls call him day and night, then yes, I'm doing exactly what you think I'm doing."

"Fun," Lissy said. "Can I help?"

"This is genius! Why didn't I think of this before? Between the internet and social media, I can completely torture him without ever needing to be in the same room! This is amazing!" I pulled up Craigslist and posted an ad that basically said Owen was looking for a nice casual relationship with no strings attached with someone who liked champagne and nice restaurants. I posted his phone number, laughed maniacally, and closed my computer. It took all of five minutes. The best five minutes I'd spent in forever.

"That's called bullying," Antonia said, because she was rational and no fun whatsoever.

"Only if you're a teenager doing it because you're bored. If you're a grown-up doing it to your ex because he cheated on you, it's called revenge, and it's a huge, ugly bitch of a thing. Should I put him on Grindr, too?" I asked, because it seemed silly to stop at Craigslist when there were millions of sites to subscribe him to.

"No!" Antonia insisted. "Quit while you're behind, Claire."

"He's going to get hundreds of phone calls," Lissy said. She leaned back in her chair and laced her hands behind her head. "You're kind of insane. I like that about you."

"Thank you. All is fair in love and whatever comes after love, don't you think?"

"Remind me never to piss you off," Lissy said.

"Noted," I said, feeling almost giddy. Now it was time for

Owen to see what it felt like to get screwed without even knowing it. "Anyway, to answer your question, Lissy, I was a social media consultant. Since I've been here, though, I stay home with Bo. It's okay, I guess. I miss working. I miss having intelligent conversations with people and feeling like I contribute something to the world. Why did I have to give everything up just to become a wife and a mother? Why did I decide that that was enough for me? I had a career. Then I had a son, and swapped one for the other. Why are they mutually exclusive?"

"They're not. You can have both. Anyone can. But just because your marriage failed doesn't mean you made the wrong choice. You're doing something really important. There's nothing wrong with that," Lissy replied.

"No. There's not. I know that. But it all sounds great until things go upside down and now I feel like I lost the real Claire. I used to wear shoes with heels. And shirts with buttons. And a watch. I don't even know where my watch is. It might be back in Chicago for all I know. I wake up when Bo wakes up and I go to sleep when he goes to sleep and I don't need to even know the time anymore and that's kind of sad. I should have something in my life that's just for me. I should have more than just a baby. I can handle more than just a baby."

"Then start looking at your options," Antonia suggested.

"I don't think I have any! That's the point! How can I possibly begin to coach other people on how to stay relevant in modern society when I'm totally irrelevant? I have no idea what's going on in the world anymore. Things in this space move fast. Once you take a step out of it it's over."

"Then find something else," Antonia suggested, because that was such an oh-so-easy thing to accomplish.

"I'm too old to start over," I admitted, though I hated to say it. "No one is going to hire me. I've been out of the game too long now."

"You're not old. You're just not young," Lissy said, trying to be helpful and missing the mark by a mile and a half.

"Thanks," I said.

"I could use some help. I didn't realize you were looking for a job," Lissy said.

"What do you mean you can hire me? What do you want me to do? Turn the book pages at story hour? I really think that's a one-person job."

"I could use some help at my store," Lissy said.

"Really?" I asked. Lissy's store didn't seem very busy at all, so I had a hard time understanding how she could be in need of other employees.

"How did you end up owning a stationery store?" Antonia asked. "I think that sounds like so much fun."

"It's kind of a long story. My mother bought it three years ago. It was her dream."

"To own a stationer?" I asked.

"Sort of. She was a fine arts teacher. She loved to do calligraphy. She taught me, too. Check this out." Lissy reached into her bag and pulled out a notebook. She flipped through the pages, and Antonia and I inched closer to get a better look at the gorgeous letters scrolled all over every square inch of paper.

"Oh my God," I said, completely awestruck that a person was able to produce something so perfect. "You did that?"

"Yeah. It's kind of a hobby, I guess," Lissy said modestly, which was completely crazy. It was some of the most outrageously flawless handwriting I'd ever seen in my life.

"It's absolutely beautiful," Antonia agreed. Neither one of us touched the ink, too afraid that we'd accidentally smudge it, despite the fact that they were just the doodles of a bored, yet fantastically talented girl.

"Your mom taught you well. How long have you guys worked there?"

"Actually, it's just me. My mom died about a month after she bought it. It was her dream that we run the store together, you know, a mother-daughter kind of thing."

"I don't know what to say," I admitted. It was true. I didn't know Lissy well. I was surprised that we were both willing to share such personal information so quickly. "Was it sudden?"

"She had a heart attack."

"I'm so sorry. I had no idea," I added.

"Well, we just met!" Lissy joked, and Antonia smiled at Lissy's brave attempt to ease the tension in the room. "It's okay. I don't talk about it much." Lissy stared at the hardwoods, and I knew her mind was wandering into dark corners, and I didn't want her to go there. I didn't want anyone in this house to feel sad for another minute. I was tired of it.

"I don't blame you."

"She left me the store, but I haven't really done anything with it. I dropped out of college after it happened because design school didn't really seem all that important to me anymore. I wanted to just come home and live in our house and go from there. I was only planning on being home for a few months, and then I was going to go back. But, I started reading to the kids to cheer myself up, and I really liked it, and I started going over to the store and imagining all the things I could do with it, and I liked that, too. School fell off my radar. So, that's how I ended up wearing black and reading to kids in the library, and working in a stationery store that has a terrible name that I can't figure out how to fix."

"I think that's really sweet," I said. "What do you want to do with the place that you haven't been able to do?"

"Everything. We were going to renovate it, and make it something really special, but she was the one who had the vision. I don't know how to bring her concept to life. So, I've just left it alone, which hasn't been the best idea, sadly. From a business standpoint it's not doing well, and I know it could be so much more than it is if I just put my mind to it. It's hard, though. I've never been all that great with making decisions. I used to bounce everything off of her, and without her I'm just kind of lost."

"It's hard adjusting to a new life on your own when you'd always imagined someone else being with you," I said.

"Totally," Antonia agreed. "It also sounds like you need to make all of the decisions she would've made, and that's a tough spot to be in. I don't know what I would do if I were you."

"Yeah. It's totally fine the way it is now, I guess. It's a cute little store, but it's nothing special. I wonder sometimes if this is really what I want to do with my life, or if I'm just doing it out of some kind of obligation, but I really think that this is what I want to do."

"Then you should do it," Antonia said. "I can't think of a single reason in the world why you shouldn't."

"I know, but it's not that easy. I'll never sell it, but the truth is, I don't really know how to operate a business. My mother was going to be the one in charge of everything, and I was going to do the calligraphy and the merchandising. I don't know how to take over for her."

"How can I help you?" I asked. "I'll do absolutely anything you want me to do. I'm sure I can help you get the place in order. I'm really good at organizing, usually. I recognize that it probably doesn't seem that way, but I swear, I am."

"That's true," Antonia agreed. "Don't let the scatterbrain here fool you. When she had her life together she was highly organized. This whole forgetting wallets and dropping planners in the library is kind of a new thing."

"And lucky for me it happened, or I'd never have known Owen was cheating on me, and you would never have moved here to help me, and I'd never have met Lissy, and we wouldn't all be hanging out together right now. See how well that worked out for everyone?" I teased.

"Good points. Very good points," Antonia agreed.

"I'd love to have some help. Not to mention the fact that I'm a little lonely there, and I'd like the company. I can't afford to pay you. At least not right away."

"I'll totally do it pro bono," I said. "Owen is paying me alimony. I don't need the money."

"That must be nice," Antonia said.

"Did you just say that with a straight face?" I asked. "I used to earn a paycheck and now I earn alimony. It's not exactly how I dreamed my life would be."

"Sorry," she answered. "I forgot for a minute."

"I'm serious," Lissy said. "You can start whenever you want."

"I think that sounds like a great idea. How about I make lasagna for dinner?" Antonia asked. "We can talk about the specifics. I think better on a full stomach."

"The lasagna you refuse to teach me how to make? That one?" I replied.

"That's the one. And I'm still not sorry."

"What are you talking about?" Lissy asked.

"Here we go," Antonia said with an eye roll.

"When I got married, Antonia very sweetly gave me a recipe box."

"It was more than just a recipe box. It was a recipe box with my family's recipe for pork chops and vinegar peppers—which she made to impress Owen on a regular basis—and Italian wedding soup, because it was her wedding."

"A lot of good that one did me. Do you have an Italian divorce soup recipe? Because that should really be in the box now."

"Sorry. Can't help you there. Anyway, she's botching this story. I gave her the recipe for wedding soup, and I said that I'd give her a new recipe every year on her anniversary, and eventually she'd have an entire box of Ricci family recipes and a long, happily married life."

"Now it seems I just have a box of blank index cards," I said.

"Well, you weren't the only one who didn't see your divorce coming," Antonia said.

"Just when you think things can't get worse, now I lost the opportunity to have some of Antonia's secret recipes. The hits keep coming."

"I'm sorry, bella. My family lasagna recipe is sacred. I can't just hand it out to anyone."

"I've been your best friend for thirty years."

"Ask me again after another thirty," she replied quickly.

"Fine. Then I guess that's yet another reason to be happy you moved in with me. You can make me lasagna whenever I want."

"Exactly. And tonight I'm making it because we're celebrating you getting an internship at Lissy's store, and Lissy getting some help with her dream, and me getting you out of the house for part of the day so that I can get more work done. Everybody wins."

"Unpaid internship," Lissy reminded her.

"It doesn't matter!" I squealed. "It's something for me to do! Do you have any idea how good it feels to actually choose something for myself? I haven't been this excited about anything since I got a blender with a smoothie button. I don't admit that to a lot of people."

"Good idea," Lissy said.

"I hope you can stay for dinner, Lissy," Antonia said. "You're the first person to get Claire to be legitimately excited about anything in months. Besides, when was the last time someone made you dinner?"

"Other than the chef at a restaurant? I can't remember," Lissy admitted, which made me a tiny bit sad. Losing someone you love was the worst feeling in the world. I didn't want her to endure that loss alone for another minute.

"It's settled then. You're staying," I ordered.

Antonia stood up from the table and pulled canned tomatoes out of my cabinet and placed them on the counter next to the stove, making herself right at home in my kitchen, which I loved. Four hours and what seemed like sixteen different cooking vessels later, we sat down to dinner. Lissy and I had set the table with my white everyday china, clear water glasses, and a glass of red wine for each of us. I quickly sent my mom a text, letting her know that Antonia was cooking lasagna for me and a new friend, and that she should be jealous, because she really should be jealous, and also because I wanted her to know that I had my appetite back. I pulled Bo's highchair over to the table, and was surprised to find that I was actually enjoying the smell of garlic, and the rhythm of another voice in the house, and that I didn't feel like something, or someone, was absent. "Okay, let's eat!" Antonia said. She carried the huge tray of pasta from the oven, and set it down on a trivet in the middle of the table, family style.

Chapter 6

I PUSHED MY stroller into the far corner of The Stationer a week later, sneezing and coughing because I apparently was allergic to something other than Owen, and whatever it was was driving me crazy. I took a quick peek at Bo, still tucked under his gauze monkey blanket. He'd fallen asleep in the car on the way over here, as I knew he would, and if the baby gods were friendly, that meant that I probably had about two hours until he woke up and started screaming for his lunch. Satisfied that he was comfortable, I turned to examine the store. The space itself was a small, perfect square, but still charming. The floors were covered in a red-and-pink-striped carpet, more reminiscent of Santa's workshop than a Goth's store, but it was cheerful, and unique, and clean, which was nice. Gleaming white bookcases with deep shelves held boxes of preprinted cards with palm trees, or insects, or fruit etched into the paper. I made my way to the narrow spiral staircase and climbed up to the small landing that served as the business headquarters of the store. A small white desk and a cane back chair sat in front of a lone curtained window that looked out over Main Street and appeared to get nice light during the day. There was a restroom with a teal-framed mirror and a pedestal sink, and a file cabinet that I'd be too afraid to open. I headed back downstairs and walked behind the long glass counter in the middle of the room that held the register, and a bucket of pens with furry tops. The remaining three walls were lined with floor-to-ceiling shelves, all of them containing boxes of cards and blank papers that didn't seem to relate to each other at all. She had a section devoted to all things wedding, which made sense, but it was in the back of the store, buried behind countless other invitations, which did not make any sense at all. More than anything, Lissy needed help organizing. I was good at organizing. At least, I used to be.

"This place could be really special. It just needs a format that makes sense. People don't want to search for things. They need to be able to find what they're looking for easily. Right now, it's a little overwhelming. Do you even know where everything is?"

"Not really. I'm still figuring all of that out."

"You should move the wedding section up front," I offered, as I continued doing a slow, controlled lap around the store. "If someone comes in here looking for engagement announcements, you want them to also see the invitations for engagement parties, and rehearsals and showers and luncheons. They all go together, and women these days are busy. They don't have a lot of time to shop for things, and they appreciate convenience. If everything they need is right there in front of them, you have a good chance of them buying everything at once."

"One-stop shopping for all of your wedding needs," Lissy said.

"Exactly. You should put your thank-you notes right next to

the wedding stationery, because you can't buy one without the other, right?"

"You can't?"

"Well, you can, but you'd have to have pretty poor manners to do that."

"Good point."

"I hope you don't think I'm rude suggesting you move everything around. I just think it will make all the difference in the world."

"It's not rude at all, but won't that make it look like I only have wedding stuff? I carry stationery for everything, not just for weddings."

"But weddings are where you'll make your money. That's where the large orders will come from. Plus, weddings will roll into everything else—baby showers, birth announcements, moving announcements, and so forth. If someone comes here for their wedding stationery and has a nice experience, you'll have a client for life."

"That makes sense."

"Are you on social media?" I asked, even though I knew without question that she wasn't. Lissy didn't seem much like the selfie-snapping type. It was hard for some people to self-promote, and I had a feeling that Lissy was of the "people will find me on their own" type of mentality. I get it. Unfortunately, that mentality died with Facebook.

"No. I don't like it," she said.

"Do you like making money? You need to get on Instagram, and Twitter, and Snapchat pronto."

"Why? I have a web page. I'm good."

"Congratulations. If it was 1997 that would be fantastic. It's not. You need to at least get on Instagram. It was made for this type of place. You can take pictures of all of your merchandise and blast it out for the whole world to see. You have to let your potential clients know that this place is fun, and modern, and hip, and it's right in the middle of town, and they don't even know about it. Once word gets out, you'll draw shoppers from all over the area, not just from here. We will set up a schedule. You need to post something every day, five days a week, between the hours of eight and nine A.M., and between twelve and one."

"Huh?" Lissy asked. "Why? Why can't I just post when I want to post?"

"Because posting between the hours of nine and noon is the black hole of marketing. You need the moms who are going to be checking their phones while they're waiting in line to drop off their kids in the morning at school, and then again when they're waiting to pick them up, or waiting for a friend to have lunch. In between, the women who are going to shop here are running errands, hitting the gym, showering, and slamming a million other errands into a small period of time. No one is on Instagram. Your posts will get lost in a sea of other nonsense. If you want it to have impact, you need to have it out there at the top of their feeds the moment they look at them."

"Wow. You're good at this stuff, huh?"

"Yeah. I used to be." I sighed.

"But the web is why the stationery industry has taken such

a hit. Everyone orders stuff online now. I don't want to cater to the medium that is basically responsible for putting me out of business, you know?"

"I get it, but trust me, there are some things that people will still want to do in person. I bet a lot of the girls who are ordering online are doing so because they don't know you're here. They don't know they have the option of doing it any other way."

I had an idea.

"You should host a luncheon, or have a launch party, or something. Open the store and let people come in and sip mimosas, and look through all of the books you have. You don't have samples of your calligraphy out anywhere. That's crazy! You should have calligraphy samples prominently displayed in the front window, so that people stop to stare at them when they pass by, and they will stop and stare, because they're that good."

"What do you mean, a launch party? I'm already here. I'm launched," Lissy said, ignoring my compliment.

"Only technically. I think if you rename the place, redecorate it, reorganize it, and take advantage of social media to advertise all of the great changes, it will be as if it's brand-new. Close the store while we work on it, and then reopen it with a big party in the fall, right after Labor Day weekend, so that people can become familiar with the store before the holiday season kicks into full swing. Once we have a new name I'll set up social media accounts for you. You need a brand, but that should be fairly easy for you because you're your own brand already. No one would confuse you for anyone else, you know?"

"Yeah, that's true."

"While the store is closed, we can advertise all over the place that you're having a big reopening, and get people talking. You should leave little cute cards inviting people to come at the library. The women who come to story hour are your target audience. Once you get one of them, they'll all come running."

"I thought you don't like them. Those girls made you run out of there so fast you dropped your day planner, remember?"

"This isn't about me. This is about you building a customer base, and whether or not I like them, those are the women who are going to throw tree-trimming and housewarming and Kentucky Derby and Mardi Gras parties, and will come here looking for special invitations. You don't want them to have to search through the bar mitzvah invitations or the moving announcements to find them, trust me. Then you'll be off and running."

"Oh, that's all!" Lissy said with a laugh. "You make it sound like it's nothing."

"I'm not saying it won't take a good amount of work, but we can totally do it. I'd love to help you, and when we're done you'll have the store you've always wanted. Won't that make it worth the effort?"

"You really think I should throw a luncheon? I'm not really the cucumber sandwich type of girl."

"Not a full lunch, but almost like a happy hour of sorts. Have small snacks and a waitress or two passing cocktails while people browse around the store. Trust me, I don't know a lot of women in this town, but I'll bet you any amount of money that the second one of them hears how someone ordered her Christmas cards from here, they'll all want to do it. No one will want to seem lazy ordering from iPhoto when they have the option to examine the card stock before throwing it on their credit cards."

"That makes sense. It's a good idea. See, I never would've thought about that."

"Thank you! How about this? Have you ever thought about how stationery stores are basically only for happy people?" I asked. "I don't know why this thought is just occurring to me now, although maybe once you find yourself spending way too much time in the land of the unhappy, you start to pay attention to how the other half lives."

"No, and I don't think I want to know what you're talking about," Lissy answered. She picked up a large brown box from the floor and ripped off the packaging tape. I felt so badly for her. Every minute she spent in here, every decision she made, must highlight that she was doing it alone. No wonder she hadn't been able to make any of the changes she and her mother had once dreamed of together.

"Think about it. You're selling ways for people to broadcast their happiness: wedding invitations, birth announcements, bar mitzvahs, baptisms, Sweet Sixteens, quinceañeras, retirement parties, monogrammed stationery so people can write thank-yous for all of the gifts that show up at their doors wrapped in white paper and tied with satin bows. This is where people come to tell the world how wonderful they're doing. 'I'm getting married! I got engaged! I'm having a baby! We bought a new house!' And, of course, to buy their Christmas cards, where they'll splatter the one single picture of their kids not trying to kill each other that they managed to get out of, like, ten thousand. This is where it all happens. It's the epicenter of happiness. Has anyone ever come in here asking for cards alerting the world to the fact they're getting divorced? Do you have 'my husband cheated' cards? Or 'my kid moved home because he failed out of college' cards?"

"Probably not. But I think that could be a niche. Would you have sent cards announcing your husband left you?"

"Maybe if I had people to send them to."

"That's awesome."

"All I'm saying is that you've been spending all of your working hours surrounded by happy people and you haven't even noticed it. You should pay attention to that. It must be kind of nice."

"I think you need to get some stationery with your old monogram on it. You don't need to make an announcement about it, but why don't you buy something with a nice bright . . . what's your maiden name?"

"Stevens."

"A nice bright C.S. on it? Won't that feel good?"

"But what will I do with them? They'll sit in a drawer in the kitchen forever. I don't have anyone to send them to."

"I'll send you flowers to let you know how happy I am that we're going to be working together. I'll expect a thank-you note."

"No, you won't." I called her bluff.

"What about Bo? Don't people send him presents? Aren't

there people in his life who spend time with him who deserve a thank-you?"

"I'm not writing Dee Dee a thank-you note. You've got to be kidding."

"I was thinking more along the lines of his grandparents. When is his birthday?"

"He'll be one in July."

"I'm sure people will send him gifts for his first birthday. You should say thank you. You should say thank you on these," she said, holding up an ecru card with a ladybug in the upper right-hand corner and a bright red line running along the bottom. I had to admit, they were adorable. But I was having a hard time reconciling Lissy's nose ring with the ladybug stationery she was hocking. Maybe that was part of the problem. People saw Lissy and thought tattoos, not thank-you notes. Discrimination has many forms.

"If I ever need to send thank-you notes, I promise, I'll buy the ladybugs. But right now no one is sending me gifts, or fruit baskets, so I'm all good." As soon as the words left my mouth, I regretted them. What was the matter with me? Here I was telling her that I wanted to help her, but at the same time refusing to actually buy anything from her. What kind of sense did that make? If there was one thing that my breakup had taught me, it was that women needed to support each other. We needed to pick each other up when we fell on our faces. We needed to cheer each other on when we were in need of encouragement. We needed to buy the damn insect stationery even if we had no need for it whatsoever. "You know what?" I said, reaching for a box of cards, and then another, and then one with dancing turtles adorning the perimeter because I've never owned correspondence cards decorated with dancing turtles and suddenly couldn't figure out how I'd ever managed to live without them. I tucked a green-and-yellow-striped pad under my arm, and piled leopard-print thank-you notes, and a cute glass cube holding square note cards that said "While you were out" on the counter, too, even though I was fairly certain that I would need them never. It didn't matter. Lissy needed me to need them. "I'll take these."

"All of them?" Lissy asked, a little confused, a little amused, and a lot appreciative.

"Yes. All of them. I write a lot."

"I thought you said you don't know anyone and don't talk to anyone."

"I didn't say anyone ever writes me back."

Lissy broke into a girlish laugh. Surprisingly, so did I.

"Wonderful. You're sort of my first customer. How depressing is that? I've been open for two years, and no one even knows I'm here."

"We're going to change that. You have a real niche, and as far as I know, there's nothing like this anywhere around here."

"How do you know that? You hadn't left your house in more than a month until you came to story hour."

"That's true, but I've been here long enough to know what's what," I lied. It was important that Lissy have faith in me. I needed to have faith in me, too. "I'm telling you, I haven't seen anything like this. The only thing that comes close is

Papyrus and that's like the McDonald's of stationery stores—mass-produced and overexposed. They don't have dancing turtles. I can promise you that."

"Well aren't you just a snob in normal girl clothing," she teased.

"Totally. I was the biggest bitch in the world back home. I only became nice once I moved here and got dumped. You know how it is, perspective and all that." I couldn't help but smile. I didn't realize how much I'd missed the company of women until right now. Antonia was like a sister—I'd always have her—but new friendships reminded me that maybe I still had something left to offer people. Maybe I wasn't as useless as I was making myself believe.

"Do you really think you can help me?" Lissy asked, but it was more of a plea.

"Definitely. I'm looking forward to it. I need to be useful to someone on this earth other than Bo. Trust me, I can do it."

"Okay. Let's get started!"

"I'm excited!" I said. "We're going to turn this place into the most popular store in town. We're going to get people talking. I promise!"

I picked up a package of bumblebee cards, headed to the back corner of the store, and dropped it on the floor. "Let's start with these. Go through all the boxes, and anything with insects or nature items on them should be over here in this corner. Sound good?"

"I need to ring up your order first," Lissy said.

"Right! I almost forgot." Lissy rang up my note cards and

dropped them into a white plastic bag. I handed her my credit card, the one Owen paid for, and my insides burned. I had no idea how, but I was going to break free of him. I didn't want his apologies, or his excuses, or his money. I took care of myself for a long time before he came along. I could find a way to do it again.

"It's a pleasure doing business with you," Lissy said. "And promise you'll try to come to the library on Wednesday. Bo seemed to really like it. It'll be good for him."

"Wednesdays work just fine for me."

Without saying another word, Lissy and I set about changing The Stationer into a place where women who either didn't know me or didn't like me would want to buy their stationery.

Chapter 7

I WOKE UP early Monday morning to the sound of my ringing phone.

"Claire!" Owen screamed into my ear more loudly than was necessary. "What the hell did you do?"

"Nothing. I'm in bed. Why are you yelling at me?" I asked.

"I just spent the entire weekend being harassed by psychotic women who got my number off Craigslist. What the hell is the matter with you?"

"I have no idea what you're talking about, and I don't appreciate you speaking to me in this manner," I growled, sleep choking my voice.

"Take it down! Take it down right now, Claire! These people are unhinged!"

"You're unhinged. I'm sorry I can't talk right now. I have a busy day ahead of me." I hung up. I stretched my arms above my head, and wiggled my toes, and rolled across my bed, and laughed, because waking up to the sound of Owen's frantic voice made this the best morning I'd had in forever. I quickly showered and dressed, and waited for Antonia to come in and force me to get up. I heard the door creak, and then her flip-flops flip-flopping off the back of her feet. I knew she was expecting to find me lying on my side facing the wall, the green-and-beige-paisley Roman shade I'd had specially made for the master bedroom windows pulled down so that it touched the sill, which was exactly how I was when she left my room last night. But I wasn't. I was up and dressed and standing at my dresser fastening earrings to my lobes when she entered. Today was a new day.

"Oh, look at you! You look great! I thought I was going to have to drag you out of bed again," she said.

"Nope, not today. I feel much better. Owen has been getting crazy phone calls all weekend, and you'd be surprised what that does for my mood."

"Seriously?" Antonia replied, which wasn't nearly as supportive a response as I would've liked.

"Seriously. But aside from that, I woke up this morning and realized that I actually do feel a little bit better. I think moving is going to be the answer to a lot of my problems, and I can't think of any reason why Owen would care if I move, except for the fact that he's currently very pissed off at me for the Craigslist thing. But I kind of love that."

"Take it down, Claire. You made your point."

"Have I?"

"If you want to move then you need him calm and on his heels. Right now he's neither of those things."

"Fair point. Fine, I'll take down the ad, and then I'm going to ask him to have lunch on Saturday. I'm going to take control of this mess. I'm control-alt-deleting myself. A reboot, as it were."

"Fantastic! That's going to go a long way toward helping you feel like you have your life back."

"Totally. And as part of my reinvention, I need a little pampering. It has occurred to me that I never got the facial he booked for me."

"You've had bigger problems than blackheads."

"That's true. But Owen promised me a spa day, and I think I deserve one. In fact, I think I deserve it now more than ever, don't I? I earned the right to have clear pores if nothing else."

"I like where you're going with this."

"Me too. I booked an appointment online for this afternoon. Screw Owen, and screw Dee Dee, and screw the fact that they were screwing each other and that's why he wanted me out of the house. I deserve to have an afternoon to myself. I'm taking it. Today."

"Fabulous! You can never underestimate the power of beauty treatments if you're trying to lift your mood. This is not going to be a time in your life that you'll remember fondly, but you'll get through it, and you'll look back on it, and when you do, I think you'll be so proud of yourself for taking control of your life, and for treating yourself. I don't know why I didn't think of this before, actually."

"I haven't been ready to until now. But honestly, I'm so tired of feeling sorry for myself. It's been almost two months. At some point enough has to be enough and I've decided that enough is enough today, you know?"

"God, I wish I could go with you, but I need to work. And babysit, I presume."

I glanced at the clock. It was 6:30. Bo would be up any minute. "Can you? I don't want you to feel like I'm taking advantage of you. I know you're not here to babysit so I can get facials, but I'd be lying if I didn't say that I'm really looking forward to it. My appointment is at one o'clock. I'm going to take the train in so I can read a magazine or something on the ride. I'll get my facial and come right home. Maybe we can cook dinner together tonight? Would that be okay?"

"It sounds great. I'm going to work this morning to get a few things off my plate, but then I'll take Bo for a walk after lunch, and we'll see the relaxed, restored you when you get back."

"I love you," I said. I leaned over and squeezed her.

"Love you back," she said. "There's a pot of coffee downstairs."

Bo started to whine, and I stood and pulled ballet flats onto my feet, instead of the slippers that I usually wore these days. If wearing shoes made me feel this good, I could only imagine what a facial would do for my spirits.

"Good morning, buddy!" I sang as I peeked my head into Bo's room and found him sitting upright in his crib, tugging at a stuffed zebra that hung from his circus-themed mobile. He smiled as I scooped him up and hugged him close before laying him down on his changing table to give him a clean diaper, a pair of blue sweatpants, and a long-sleeve onesie covered with fire engines. "Did you sleep well?" I asked. I liked to think that he could understand what I was saying, and looked forward to the day where he'd actually answer me back. "I slept great, Mommy. Thank you for asking," I imagined him saying. I wondered what his little voice would sound like, and if he would call me "Mommy" or "Mama." I loved his little baby phase, and I didn't want to wish it away, but still, it was so hard not to think about what would come next. What would our life be like this time next year? How different would we both be?

I sat him on my lap and fed him his bottle before getting down on the floor with him so we could play with giant blocks that my mother had sent and he loved more than anything. By 11:00 he was asleep again, and I laid him back in his crib and poked my head into Antonia's room. "I'm going to head out. Are you sure this is okay?"

"It's more than okay. Go. I'll see you later. Figure out what you want to have for dinner. I'm in the mood for pasta, so stick in that genre," she said.

"You got it," I said. I left her door open a crack and skipped down the stairs. I reached into my bag, and removed a note I'd written for Antonia on one of Lissy's frog cards. I thought about how I used to write notes for Owen when he traveled, how I'd tell him that we loved him and would miss him and he didn't deserve any of it. Antonia had been with me for everything, and had never betrayed me, and I'd never written her a note even once. Until now. I propped the card up on the counter against a container of raisins, her name written across the envelope in a green Magic Marker, and headed for the door. Husbands aren't the only ones who deserve love letters. Best friends, the ones who will be with you until death do you part, deserve them even more.

I REALLY SHOULD'VE been doing this more often. I'd basically spent the last ten months in some kind of zombie trance where I completely forgot that life existed outside of my house, and as it so happened, life was still pretty freakin' awesome. I changed into a soft white robe and the most comfortable foot-massaging flip-flops I'd ever worn in my life, and settled into a chaise in the relaxation room. Truthfully, I didn't care if the esthetician who was going to do my facial ever claimed me. I'd be perfectly happy just sitting in this room listening to Enya play through the speakers and drinking cucumber water. Before I could refill my cup, a woman appeared and whispered, "Claire?"

"That's me," I said quietly.

"I'm Maya. Please, come with me." She led me down a hallway and into a small, dimly lit room with an adjustable bed that was covered with soft blankets and pillows. "I'll wait outside while you change. You can hang your robe on the back of the door. I'll knock before I come back. Do you need anything?"

"No. I think I'm great, thank you!" I said. Maya closed the door softly behind her and I lay down on the heated bed, my body under a plush comforter, music playing, candles lit, and all I could think about was how this was the best gift Owen could've possibly given me if only he hadn't given it to me so that he could sleep with his girlfriend.

Maya returned and placed a cool washcloth over my eyes,

and painted my face with a clay that was supposed to mini-
mize my pores and make me look ten years younger. I don't
know how long I lay there before I fell asleep, but I dreamed of
Chicago—the paths I used to jog on, the churros Rick Bayless
served at Topolobampo, the townhouse I lived in with its little
courtyard and its high ceilings and the best pizza place in the
world down the street. I dreamed of Chicago as I fell asleep,
and so I fell asleep happy.

I woke to Maya gently shaking my arm.

"I'm so embarrassed I dozed off," I said.

"Don't be. That's the sign of a good facial. You should be
relaxed enough to fall asleep. It's a compliment."

"Oh, good. Honestly, Maya, that was dreamy." I wrapped
my robe around me and rubbed the sleep from my eyes.

"Would you like some lemon water? Or a glass of prosecco?"
she asked as she walked me back to the locker room.

"I'd love a glass of lemon water. Thank you!"

"Feel free to use our steam facilities. They're located in the
back next to the showers. We have a steam room and a sauna."

"A steam sounds fantastic!" I said. When I lived in Chicago,
Antonia and I would often steam after spin and before lunch,
but I hadn't done it since I'd moved here. It wasn't as fun when
you were alone, plus I hadn't gotten around to joining a gym yet.

Maya escorted me to a large bamboo door next to the showers, and handed me a cold towel from a small bowl next to the
door before she opened it for me and I was immediately wel-
comed with hot steam and the scent of eucalyptus. I laid my
towel on the tile seat, sat down, and inhaled the mist. *Okay,*

Claire, I said to myself. *Things didn't work out as planned. That's okay. It doesn't mean you can't make a new plan.* I lay down and placed the cool towel across my eyes, enjoying the steam as it breathed new life into a body that had spent most of the last year in a state of new mommy exhaustion. I was tired of being numb and exhausted. I was ready to move forward, finally understanding that the end of my marriage didn't have to be the end of my story.

When I'd finished with the steam I took a long shower, slathered lotion all over my body, dressed in jeans and a soft blue cotton shirt, and blow-dried my hair for the first time in ages. Regretfully, I dropped the robe and the flip-flops into a bin before leaving the locker room. Spa day was over. It was time to go back to real life with better skin and a new appreciation for eucalyptus.

I stopped at the desk to check out, feeling so sad to leave such a wonderful place, and promised myself that I'd book Antonia and me appointments together before she moved back to Chicago to say thank you for everything she'd done for me. A tall vase of white flowers graced the desk next to the computer, the slim woman in blue nurse's scrubs barely visible behind them.

"How were your services today? Was everything satisfactory?" she asked.

"It was absolutely wonderful."

"That's what we like to hear. How would you like to pay for that today? Cash or charge?" she asked. It was a perfectly normal question to ask, but also one that sparked a brilliant thought.

"Actually, I wanted to ask you a question about that. I had

an appointment in March that I wasn't able to keep. Do you still have the credit card on file that was used to book that appointment?"

"I can check on that for you, no problem. What's the name on the appointment?"

"Claire . . . Mackenzie," I said. That hurt so very, very much.

I waited through a few seconds of frantic keyboard typing before she looked up and told me exactly what I'd hoped she would. "Yes, we do. Would you like to charge this appointment to the card?"

"I would love to use that card. And the service was really so lovely, I'd like to add a thirty-percent gratuity for Maya on that, too. Thank you so much." I smiled. I wasn't sure if I was supposed to feel guilty about doing what I was doing, but I didn't. I felt relaxed, and refreshed, and rejuvenated, but guilty? Nope. Not one bit.

"That's no problem, Mrs. Mackenzie. I'll take care of it. Is there anything else we can do for you today?"

"Nope. You've done more than enough." I signed my name, Claire Mackenzie, because legally it still was, with a black felt-tipped pen, and waved as I walked out the door. If that was the last time I ever signed my married name on anything, it would be the perfect farewell.

I ENTERED GRAND Central Terminal and once again was struck by how it was never empty. It was 3:00 in the afternoon and the terminal was still swarming with people—one part tourists with cameras, one part National Guard with Uzis, and one part extremely busy people who didn't notice either the tourists or the Uzis. I decided that I was going to get a drink while I waited for my train, because I couldn't think of anything better to top off my afternoon of relaxation than a nice big glass of wine. I popped into Michael Jordan's The Steak House, a nice little kiosk of sorts at the top of a marble staircase that didn't seem to attract too busy a crowd at 3:00 on a Monday.

"I'd like a glass of Chianti, please," I said to the bartender, a nice-looking man with hairy hands and a tightly cuffed shirt and a tie that probably had a clip. He smiled, a tight stretch of his lips under a stubbled mustache, as he poured my drink. I placed my bag on the chair next to me, and stared at the napkin holder while I took a sip. It burned my throat in the best of ways and I remembered how Owen and I used to share bottles of red in cold weather while we watched Netflix on the couch. Now it was like none of that ever happened.

"Do you mind moving your purse?" a man asked. I turned to look at him. He was bald, and had a Tom Cruise nose without the rest of Tom Cruise's face to make up for it. He carried a stack of papers under his arm that were bound with black binder clips and rubber bands, and he threw them down on the bar next to me before I had a chance to answer. I involuntarily reached back and tucked a piece of hair behind my ear, all of a sudden conscious of the fact that I hadn't highlighted it in months, and said hair was frizzy from humidity despite the industrial air-conditioning that the city of New York pumped through its landmarks.

"I'll have a Bud draft, please," he said to the bartender. He turned to me. "Long day?" I examined the shape of his head, round and smooth, his angular cheekbones, his soft lips, and the way the outline of his beard was obvious despite the fact that he was clean shaven, and realized he was handsome. Not classically handsome, but handsome.

"I'm just killing time before my train."

"Me too. I don't usually get out of work this early, but it's slow, and it's summer, so I figured, why not?" he said. The waiter returned with a cold beer, foam running down the side of a frosted glass, and placed it on a white paper napkin. I looked at my wine, too warm and too fruity for my taste, and decided his beer looked infinitely better.

"I'll have one of those, too," I said to the bartender. I pushed my drink away from me, just in case the man wondered for a second if I was going to slug both. "I haven't had a beer in a long time, but that one looks really good," I said.

"They call it the king of beers for a reason," he replied. The bartender placed the beer in front of me and I took a long sip. My eyes watered. I was suddenly brought back to the bar where Owen and I met, where Antonia and I met for beers after work on a semiregular basis. I was such a long way from being that girl in that bar, but I wondered if maybe I liked the woman I'd become even more. "I'm Fred," he said, and I immediately thought that he totally looked like a Fred.

"Claire," I responded. I took another sip of beer, saw another flash of Owen in my mind, felt another pang of nostalgia for my life in Chicago, and then got over it.

"Nice to meet you. Are you leaving work a little early today, too?"

"Not exactly. I live in Connecticut."

"Me too. Rowayton," he offered. I didn't know anything about Rowayton, or even where it was. Just that it was a stop on the train north of mine.

"Darien."

"That's a nice town. Great school system."

"That's one of the reasons we moved there," I said, falling back into the "we" talk a little too easily. But how else was I supposed to talk about my life before my separation? It was a decision made by both of us. Wasn't it still okay to use "we" in that situation? Or did I sound like someone who didn't accept that she was now just an "I"? Was I regressing and becoming the woman in Tara Redmond's office with the wedding ring on a chain around her neck?

"Oh, you're married with kids?" he asked, and I could swear he sounded marginally disappointed.

"No. I was married. I'm divorcing, but I have a son. His name is Bo. He's almost one." This was the part of the program where I expected Fred to slug his beer and head for the tracks.

"I've been there," he said. "I got divorced three years ago. No kids, though. I can't imagine how much harder it is to deal with if there are kids involved."

"Divorce isn't easy for anyone," I said. "Are you and your wife still friendly?"

"We don't speak anymore," he said quickly. "What about you?"

"We speak a good amount because of our son. It doesn't matter. He's moved on."

"Onward and downward, I'm sure."

"Thank you. That's a nice thing to say." Fred was sweet, and understanding, and sympathetic; when he asked the bartender for the check a fleck of disappointment bounced around my rib cage before disappearing somewhere inside. I should've realized that talking about our respective divorces wasn't a really good way of prolonging a conversation. He stood, and picked up his papers from the bar next to him. "Shall we?" he asked. I had no idea what he was talking about.

"Shall we what?" I asked.

"They just announced our track. Are you getting this train home?"

"I was planning on it, yes," I said, relieved that the "shall we" referred to a train car and not a hotel room. Was I being asked on a train date? Was it too soon for that?

"Great. Want to head down there?"

"Together?"

"I thought you were getting on the next train. It's going to leave in ten minutes."

"Oh, yeah. I didn't realize it was so late. I guess the time got away from me," I admitted.

"Time flies when you're having beers in a train station bar."

"It really does." I slid off my stool and picked up the tattered leather bag at my feet. I envied the other women heading to the train, all of them leaving their important jobs, carrying important papers, going home to their husbands and their kids and the pot roasts that they put in slow cookers before their morning commutes. These women had full lives, and all I had was Antonia and a son who was happy as long as there was Similac and Orajel in the house.

The train was crazy crowded and it wasn't even rush hour yet. For a minute, I worried that we wouldn't be able to find two seats together, which would make for a really awkward good-bye in the aisle while we went in opposite directions. We walked through an entire car before finally spotting two seats tucked away in the corner, right next to the bathroom. How romantic.

Our legs touched when we sat, not in a creepy "I like you, and I want to be flirty" kind of way, but in a "these seats are way too small for normal-sized people" kind of way. I tried to squish my thighs together as much as I possibly could without looking like I was trying to avoid him because I was worried he had cooties or something. Once we were seated we had to restart the conversation, and I struggled to come up with something to talk about. Asking if he came here often seemed a little dumb. I needed something better.

"What do you do for a living, Fred?" I asked.

"I'm a corporate accountant," he answered.

"Nice," I said, even though I had no idea what that meant. "What does that mean exactly?" I figured there was no harm in asking.

"I do the accounting for some of the ad agencies in the city. It's not exactly glamorous, but I enjoy it."

"It's good that you like what you do. I always found accounting to be complicated. You lose me at accounts receivable."

"So you remember Accounting 101?" he asked.

"Only because I never made it to Accounting 102."

"You didn't miss much."

"That's good to know."

"What do you do, Claire? Are you a full-time mom?"

"Funny you should ask, I'm a most-of-the-time mom. I used to be a social media consultant back in Chicago. I'm about to start helping a friend rework her business, so I have my toe back in the working world."

"Sounds interesting."

"It is," I said. I couldn't believe how empowering it was just to say that I did something, anything, for myself. I needed some kind of job in order to reclaim a part of myself that I gave away when I got married. Lissy had no idea what her internship had done for me.

"Would you like to have dinner sometime?"

"At Michael Jordan's?"

"No, maybe at a restaurant closer to home. I spend enough time in the city for work. I like to stay in the suburbs if I don't have to be here. We could go to a train station, though, if you want."

"Thanks for offering. I appreciate it, but a restaurant will be fine."

"Great. How about the first week in June?"

"As in two weeks from now?" I asked. I hadn't been asked on a date in a long time, but still felt that it was just a tiny bit weird to ask someone out for that far in advance. I didn't expect him to clear his calendar or anything, but he seriously didn't have a single night free until June? Something about that seemed odd.

"Yes. No pressure, but next week is Memorial Day and I'm heading up to the Cape for a few days and I'm pretty busy until then. I'll call you when I get back and maybe we can just grab a quick bite. What do you say?"

This was an awkward moment. I wanted to go on the date, because I hadn't been on a date in forever. But I didn't want to go on the date, because I hadn't been on a date in forever, and because I wasn't even divorced yet, and because it didn't make me feel all that special to know that he wanted to put me on ice for two weeks. Oprah would call this a defining moment in my life, one where I could choose to either move forward, and actually see what life was like with another man, or I could choose to stay alone, and wallow in what I'd lost. I knew what Oprah would tell me to do, but I didn't know if I was ready. I also knew that I needed to decide, right now, because I was getting off at the next stop.

"I'm only recently separated. I'd like to have dinner, but it might be a little soon," I said, because if he was going to put me off until June, I wasn't going to just chomp at the opportunity.

"Okay, I understand," he said. "If you're not ready, that's fine. I have a quick question, though: How do you know you're not ready if you don't try?"

"Educated guess?" I said, even though there was nothing educated about it.

"I think you're ready. And anyway, I'm giving you two weeks to prepare. Don't say you can't do it."

"When you put it that way," I said. "Okay. I'd like that." I thought I would like that, because somehow Fred had just made me feel like I'd be making a mistake by not going out with him, and I wasn't at all sure how he did that.

"What time works for you?"

"Bo goes to bed around seven. Any time after that would be fine."

"Great. Why don't you give me your phone number. We can confirm the details later."

"Okay." He handed me his iPhone and I added my name to his contacts. It felt so amazingly weird. Was this how people dated now? Did they meet guys in bars and program numbers into cell phones? What if he did this all the time? What if a different woman programmed her name in his phone every week? Then I was just one of many sad, sad women he picked up in a bar and promised to call but never would. I immediately regretted my decision. I should've just told him I wasn't ready. I really didn't think that I was, but I couldn't stand the thought of disappointing Oprah. "If you change your mind and don't want to go, don't worry about it," I said, hedging myself so that the rejection, if it came, would sting a little less. I was never good at dating. The hiatus hadn't helped me any.

"Okay," he answered. "Thanks."

"Wait, what?" I said. The train slowed as it approached my station.

"I hope you have a good night. It was nice meeting you, Claire."

"You too."

"I'll see you soon. I'll be in touch."

"Great. That sounds . . . great." *That's awesome, Claire. Flex that impressive vocabulary.* "Shoot me a text."

"I don't text," Fred said flatly, like it was no big deal, when really it was a very big deal, because that was my predominant form of communication.

"What do you mean?"

"I'm not a teenage girl. I don't like it. No one even uses real words anymore. Everything is abbreviated and it makes no sense. 'LOL.' What does that even mean?"

"Laugh out loud," I said. I was starting to reconsider this date. What kind of guy didn't text? He might as well have admitted to not brushing his teeth. I would find that less weird.

"Well, it's not for me. I'd rather just call you."

"Okay," I said. "I guess that's fine."

"Bye," he said. I waved quickly as I slung my bag over my shoulder and headed for the door, making sure to watch the gap between the train car and the platform as the automated conductor instructed. I thought about calling my parents in the car on the way home and telling them that I had a date, but I didn't because I was pretty sure they'd never believe me, and I didn't want them to become skeptical of everything I'd been telling them since Owen and I separated. This morning I woke up and decided to stop wallowing and move on with my life. Because of that, I now had my first post-Owen date with an accountant named Fred who lived in Rowayton and who was going to call me—not text—sometime in the near future.

So, that happened.

❧ Chapter 8

EARLY SATURDAY AFTERNOON I met Owen at an oyster bar, which was where you met your almost ex-husband in the suburbs if you lived in the kind of suburb that had an oyster bar in town. The restaurant was going for that brasserie kind of look, small wooden tables with even smaller wooden chairs, brass sconces, bloodred walls, and lots of craft beers on tap because that was apparently the new trendy drink to have with oysters if you wanted to have oysters and beer for lunch. The air smelled of hops, and salt, and grease from the French fries they served with their croque-monsieurs. We'd only been here once since we moved in, not long after we arrived, and I had picked at a green salad, and stared at the lights in the lampposts that lined Main Street, and tried to drink in the fact that I was a Connecticut housewife. It didn't fit comfortably then. It fit not at all now.

I arrived first, because I decided at the last minute to bring Bo with me, and I wanted to pick the table in the corner so that I didn't have to worry about someone knocking into him with hot coffee or tea. It was inconceivable that I needed to psych myself up to meet Owen in order to have this conversation.

Things used to be easy and comfortable. Now they were difficult, and awkward. He arrived ten minutes late, dressed in his weekend jeans, his white button-down, and his brown loafers, all effortlessly preppy and casual. He looked exactly like someone who would walk down this street and think, *Hey, I haven't had any oysters in a while, maybe I'll pop in for a dozen before I go play paddle ball at the country club.* I looked down at my own mom jeans, the painfully tight Spanx underneath holding in sagging post-baby skin, all wrinkled and crinkled like used tissue paper when you remove it from a gift bag, and a pale pink sweater that had the remnant of a sticky banana handprint on the hem. I looked like I was forced out of the house on laundry day before the dryer was finished, which was frustrating, because I really tried to look nice. This was just the best I could do.

He nodded in my direction, then stopped to say hello to someone at a neighboring table. I didn't recognize the man, or the woman he was eating oysters with, but it didn't matter. When Owen was finished playing mayor of the Main Street Oyster Bar, he approached the table, and, thank God, didn't attempt to give me some kind of awkward kiss on the cheek to prove we were still friendly. He simply pulled out the tiny wooden stool across from me, put his blue-and-white-striped kitchen towel serving as a napkin in his lap, and reached for Bo's hand. "I'm sorry about that. He's a ghost from my past."

"There's a lot of them floating around," I said. He didn't realize what he'd said until it was too late. He let it go. So did I. Except, really, I kind of didn't, and probably never would.

"How are you?" he asked.

"Fine," I replied. "We're doing great." I wanted to tell him that I had a date soon, but I didn't, because that seemed wildly immature and also because if Fred canceled on me I'd have to die of embarrassment.

"Good. I'm glad to hear that," he answered. I thought I saw him relax, and realized that maybe my telling him that I'd like to talk to him about something important had him wondering if I was sick and was going to tell him I only had six months to live.

"Me too."

"How's my little man this morning?" he asked. He ran his forefinger around Bo's double chin and he squirmed and squealed in his seat. "I'm happy you brought him. I miss seeing him every day. It seems like every time I'm with him he's doing something new."

"He changes every day. He's trying to pull himself up to stand now."

"Is he really? I haven't seen that. Next time he does it can you send me a video? I don't want to miss it."

"I'll try," I said. His voice sounded so sad and I wanted to feel badly for him for everything he was missing but I couldn't because he wouldn't be missing it if he hadn't had an affair.

"Thanks. Can you please tell me why I'm finding beans all over the place? I went to put my windbreaker on last week and they fell out all over the floor. What's that about?"

"I have no idea what you're talking about."

"Seriously, Claire? That's what you're going to say?"

"Maybe you pissed someone else off and she decided to

scatter beans throughout your belongings as a reminder of your asshole-ness for years to come. Why do you think it's me?"

"Fine, Claire. Bad enough you ruined my entire wardrobe. If assaulting me with dried beans makes you feel better, have at it. But no more internet dating sites, Claire. I mean it. That wasn't funny."

"It depends on who you ask," I said. I was starting to get angry, which wasn't part of the plan. I was supposed to be calm and collected and rational, which was wonderful in theory but a lot more difficult in practice.

"Okay, whatever. Let's just move on. Do you want to have some oysters?" he asked.

"Sure," I replied, because nothing says divorce due to infidelity like an aphrodisiac in the middle of the afternoon.

When the waitress appeared Owen ordered a dozen oysters and a beer. As soon as she'd returned with his beer, he took a long slug and then checked his watch nervously, as if he had somewhere better to be.

"I'm glad we're doing this," he said. "I wanted to tell you that I found an apartment."

This was news. "Really? Where?" I asked, still trying to decide if this was something that should make me feel better, or not. If he had his own place, that meant he wouldn't be spending all of his time at Dee Dee's. But if he had his own place, then things became even more final than they already were, and something inside me clenched tightly. This man was supposed to be my entire world, and now I only saw him when he came to take Bo to Marcy's every Wednesday night and every other weekend because that was the schedule we agreed to when we agreed on how to divide Bo like a Caribbean time-share.

"It's over near the train station. It's a two-bedroom. It's in a nice building, it's clean, and quiet, and I think you'll like it."

"I don't want your girlfriend around my baby. Do you understand that? My lawyer told me that I have rights where she's concerned, and if you violate them I'll challenge our custody agreement. Don't push me on it, Owen."

"I know what we agreed to. You don't have to worry about that. I want to spend time with him alone."

"Good."

"Do you want to come see the apartment? You're welcome to come over anytime," he offered.

"Why would I want to come see your new bachelor pad?" I asked. I hadn't thought much about where I wanted to move, only because I didn't know the town all that well, and didn't know what area I wanted to live in, but I now knew I had to scratch anything near the train station off my list. Once again, Owen had managed to limit my options.

"Because I thought you might like to know where Bo is when I have him."

That was a good point. I didn't know why I hadn't thought of that myself.

"Oh," I said. "Yes. I guess I would like to see that. Have you been putting him to sleep in the portable crib you took with you?"

"Yeah, but I went to Buy Buy Baby, and had them look up

your registry, and I bought the exact same stuff he has in his room at the house. I thought maybe it would make the change easier for him. It'll be delivered to the new place."

I hated to admit it, but that was actually sweet. That was the Owen I married—the thoughtful, caring, loving man who somehow forgot he was all of those things and so he became someone else that I couldn't possibly stay married to. *My* Owen was still in there somewhere. I wish he'd been strong enough to conquer the monster that made him think that Dee Dee was the answer to a problem he never had.

"Okay. At some point after you move in and get settled I'll drop him off instead of you picking him up. I'll see it then."

"Great. That sounds great."

Yes. It's really great, I thought. *It's absolutely fabulous.* I tried to keep my face absent of emotion. It had been weeks of searching for answers that wouldn't come, of wiping away tears that wouldn't stop coming, and praying for strength that came and went depending on the day. I was exhausted, and that made it easier to appear calm and collected when I hadn't seen calm or collected since I saw Dee Dee in her underwear.

"Also, I have a really strange question for you. I can't believe I'm even asking you this, but did you recently go to Bliss in Manhattan and charge it to my credit card?"

"Yes," I said unapologetically because I wasn't sorry for it even a little.

"I was hoping that was the answer."

"You were?" I asked.

"Yeah, otherwise someone stole my credit card."

"I don't know if you remember, but something came up the afternoon that I was supposed to go, and I never made it to my original appointment. I decided I still deserved to go, so I did. It was amazing."

"You're right. I'm glad you went. You deserve more than that."

"It's too late for that now, isn't it?"

"Yeah. I guess it is." Owen pulled Bo out of his highchair and sat him on his knee, bouncing him up and down and causing him to clap and coo and I had to look away because if I didn't I knew I would cry. We should be doing this every weekend. We should be a normal family having brunch and that should be it. We shouldn't be discussing apartment rentals and Amex charges.

"What did you want to talk about?" he asked, his dark, round eyes and his feathery lashes so familiar and comforting I couldn't help but stare. I took a deep breath and summoned the courage I used to have in abundance, and now most days struggled to find no matter how hard I looked.

"After careful consideration, I think I'd like to sell the house," I said calmly. I knew that in order for me to get what I wanted, I needed to stay in control of my emotions. Owen didn't like when I flew off the handle, which could definitely happen. I wanted him to give me the okay. I wanted this conversation to be civil, and adult, and mature, and quick.

"Why would you want to sell the house?" he asked, totally incredulous, which surprised me. I wouldn't think the concept of wanting out of our marital home would warrant the kind of shock that registered on his face. If nothing else, I wanted him to understand the emotional fallout I was going through. If nothing else, I wanted him to lie and pretend he did—even if he didn't.

Because the goal was to stay calm and reasonable, I didn't want to tell him that part of the reason I wanted to move was because it occurred to me that Dee Dee probably used our bathroom and now I could only pee if I stood up. "It's too much house for just me and Bo. It's lonely, and I think I'd be more comfortable in something smaller. I'd like to sell the house and move somewhere that doesn't remind me of you. I want a clean start."

"I don't think that's the best idea," Owen said. His response left me completely confused. I'd gone over this a billion times in my mind. I made a reasonable argument. Owen was a reasonable person. This was a reasonable request. Why wasn't I getting what I wanted?

"Why not? I'm not planning on leaving town. Sorry, I guess I should've clarified that. Going forward, let's just assume that I have no intention of breaking any federal laws. I just want to sell the house and move somewhere else in town."

"I know you're not planning on leaving town. We've been through that already. But even still, I don't think moving anywhere is the best idea right now."

"Let me just give you a quick rundown of events, because I'm not entirely sure how I ended up in this situation and I think maybe you're a little confused as to how we got here in the first place. Man marries wife. Man cheats on wife. Man refuses to let wife leave state. Man refuses to let wife leave house.

Do I not have any rights at all? When does the wife get to make a decision all by herself?"

"You forgot 'Man ends up with beans in all of his personal belongings.'"

"Why do you care where I live? You don't want to live with me, so why can't I go where I want?" I asked, still trying oh so very hard to stay calm, but the effort was starting to show. I was speaking through gritted teeth. I could feel my cheeks burning a shade of red that probably matched the paint on the walls, and my nails were now digging into the flesh of my palms. Still, I tried.

"Bo is happy there. We bought the house because it was a good family house. He's dealing with enough change in his life, and I don't think it's in his best interest to move him."

"Owen, he's ten months old. I'll move his crib, and his toys, and two days after we get there he won't remember the house we're in now at all. Bo will be happy where I'm happy," I argued. I thought it was a pretty good argument.

"I've read a couple of books about the psychology of children of divorce, and they all say that consistency is key. The house is a constant. I don't want him to move."

"You were a constant in his life, too, you know. You didn't seem to care too much about that when you left us." Small cracks were starting to form in my calm veneer.

"I know. And for the millionth time, I'm sorry," he said.

"And for the millionth time I'll repeat, I don't care," I reminded him. "So that's where you got the idea to replicate his bedroom? From a book about the kids of divorce?"

"Yes. You should read it. It's really interesting, and I think it will help us parent him through this."

"Thanks for the book recommendation, Oprah. Except, I'm not here to be in a book club with you."

"Aside from that, we bought at the top of the market. The housing market has slowed and I don't want to sell the house at a loss. I'm sorry, Claire, but it's not like you're living in squalor. You're in a beautiful home in a beautiful town and for now I think you should stay there."

"This is unreal. I mean, you are really, really unreal," I said, not caring how many times I used the word "real" or that I sounded like a fifteen-year-old arguing with her parents over letting her boyfriend watch movies in her room. "It's bad enough you're keeping me in Connecticut, but now you won't even let me live somewhere that I can make my own? Do you have any idea what it feels like for me to come home to that house every day? It's torturous. It doesn't feel like home, it feels like the scene of a crime! That home is where you killed our marriage. It's a murder scene."

"I understand that, and I'm sorry. But I'm not going to throw money away because you're uncomfortable."

"We bought at the top of the market because our real estate agent sucked!" I screamed. The calm party was over. We were now moving on to the fully crazy after-party. More than a few people looked up from their European beers and their West Coast oysters and stared.

"Claire, calm yourself or I'm leaving. Bo is here, for God's sake. Do you want him to know his mother made a scene in front of the whole town?"

"You're right. That's what will be embarrassing for him. It would be horrible for Bo to learn that his mother lost her temper in a restaurant. Let's hope he never learns about what his father did in our house."

"That house is an asset. It's in my name. I'm letting you live there because I know this has been hard on you, and I thought it would be best for you to not have to worry about your living situation, and for Bo to have some continuity in his life. You can paint me as the asshole all you want, but in this case, I'm trying to help you. I'm sorry that you caught Dee Dee there, but that's not a reason to lose hundreds of thousands of dollars. If the market turns around and we can make some money on the place, we'll talk about it again, and you can move anywhere in town you want. Until then, you're staying put, Bo is staying put, and that's all there is to it. Poor little Claire, forced to live in a gorgeous colonial that, might I remind you, you once loved. You sat across the table from me after we saw it and you told me that you loved it and that you wanted it. You'll love it again. This is just a reaction to everything that's happened. Trust me, one day, you'll be happy you stayed."

"Trust you?"

The waitress placed a huge glass bowl of ice in front of us, with twelve oysters nestled in the snow, small silver cups of cocktail sauce, mignonette, and lemons resting in the center. If you didn't know better, we looked like a nice couple having brunch on a Sunday. Unfortunately, we knew better. So did the waitress, and more than half the people in the restaurant.

"Why isn't my name on the deed? We should be co-owners of the property. Why did you leave my name off it?" I asked. I pulled Bo off Owen's lap, placed him in his highchair, and sprinkled Cheerios on the table in front of him, which would hopefully keep him quiet for the remainder of our conversation slash argument.

"Don't be ridiculous. You're not on the deed because you've never wanted anything to do with the finances! You didn't even come to the closing, Claire. If you were on the deed, you would've been required to show up and sign papers and you wanted no part of that! You were pregnant and hormonal and stressed out and you wanted me to take care of it, and guess what? I took care of it. I'm sorry it ended up working out this way and now you can't force me to sell the house, but like I said, stop acting like I have you sequestered in a basement somewhere. I'm trying to set you up so that you can live a wonderful life. You're just too focused on me, and what I'm doing, to notice it. Start worrying about what's best for you and for Bo and I think you'll realize that moving is a very bad idea."

"I'm not going to ask your permission for everything I want to do for the rest of my life!" I screamed. "I didn't sign my name on this oyster, does that mean it's not mine?" I picked up a bumpy black shell, the loosened mollusk sliding around inside of it, and without thinking, threw it on Owen's lap.

"Really, Claire? A food fight?" Owen asked. He picked up the shell from the floor and plucked the slimy oyster from his lap, a wet smudge clearly visible on his pants. "I don't know why I even bothered coming here. I thought maybe we could have a civil, adult conversation. We're going to have a lot of them over the years. We share a son, remember? I'm not going away."

"I hope I signed a piece of paper somewhere saying that I own him," I said, smugly, trying to prove how stupid it was to rely on paper to prove ownership of every single thing in life. I lived in the house. It was mine. At least in part. Isn't ownership like nine-tenths of the law or something? Who said that? I made a mental note to call Tara and challenge his assertion. It smelled like horseshit.

"You did. It's called a birth certificate."

Well, he had me there.

"Why is it so hard for you to try and do something to help me? I didn't do anything to you, and I feel like you just keep beating me up again, and again, and again." The tears came, same as they did most nights during the last two months when I lay in my bed in the dark. At some point, the faucet needed to turn off; the amount of tears available in one lifetime had to be finite, and I was afraid I was going to use mine up.

"Please don't cry," Owen said. "I'm not trying to hurt you. I'm trying to keep you from making a decision you'll regret."

"That's not your job anymore."

"It is where Bo is concerned."

"I'm going to talk to my lawyer."

"Waste your time if you want. I promise you, you need me to sign off on any sale of the house and I'm not looking to sell it right now. Let's see what happens in a year or two and go from there."

"A year or two? Do you have any idea what will happen to us in the next year or two? It will destroy me, Owen. Do you care about that?"

"You're stronger than you give yourself credit for. You'll be fine," he said.

There was no point in fighting with him. I'd call Tara and ask her, but I had no doubt she'd tell me that everything he said was true. "I loved you so much," I whispered. I blotted my napkin along my lower lash line, trying to keep the mascara from spreading across my skin and leaving streaks on my face. "I left my home, my family, my friends, my job, everything, because I loved you more than I would've thought possible. I look at you now and what hurts more than anything is that I can't understand how I had you so wrong. We have a son, so I can't say I wish I never met you. But if I do one thing in this world, one single thing from here on out to be proud of, it will be to make sure that he grows up to become nothing like you."

I wanted to make some kind of dramatic exit, one where I slammed a door, or flipped a table, or spewed obscenities until the bartender had to stop pouring his fancy draft beers into frosted mugs, and escort the jilted, middle-aged mess out of the restaurant, but I didn't. I stood quietly, placed my napkin on the table, pulled Bo out of his highchair, and ambled slowly toward the exit. Part of me very easily could've made a scene, but I wouldn't allow myself to do it. Bo snuggled into the crook of my neck and I ran my hand over the back of his head, kissing his temple as we exited the restaurant. I might have been a jilted, middle-aged mess, but I was still Bo's mother—and that was not how his mother left an oyster bar.

Chapter 9

LEARNING THAT I couldn't sell the house threw me back into the depression I thought I'd worked my way out of over a month ago. I felt like I didn't exist. There was Bo's mom, and there was Owen's soon-to-be ex, but there was no Claire. It was an absolutely horrendous feeling that I wouldn't wish on anyone, and one that I didn't know how to fix.

"I can't believe he won't let me move," I said to Antonia when she came into my room and sat on the edge of my bed later that afternoon. "I was counting on it, Antonia. When I decided not to let this divorce swallow me it was largely because I thought I'd be able to start fresh on my own. How am I supposed to let the murder of my marriage go if I have to live in the crime scene?"

"I get that staying in this house isn't what you wanted, but you really did love the house when you bought it. You'll be able to feel good here again."

"I seriously doubt that. I can't believe what happened today. I was optimistic. I really believed that I'd found a small way to take back some control of my own life, and he took it from me again. I threw an oyster at him."

"So what?" Antonia said, which I appreciated.

"I made a scene. I shouldn't have done that."

"Send him an email then and tell him you're sorry. Ask him to reconsider."

"Do you think he will?"

"I have no idea. But it's worth a shot. Apologize. At the very least it will let him know he's dealing with a more rational Claire."

"Okay," I sighed, even though the thought of apologizing to Owen made me nauseous. I reached for my iPhone and opened my email. I was about to type him a very brief and very insincere apology, when my breath caught in my chest. There, right at the top of my email, was a message from Facebook, reminding me of where I was this week last year. And where I was, was my baby shower, with Owen lovingly rubbing my stomach, and my friends and family celebrating the exciting changes that were happening in my life, and it was a special kind of horror when your own pictures were thrown in your face by an algorithm that doesn't know jack shit about your current state of mind. The last thing I needed today, the absolute last thing, was to have to relive that special time in my life, when I stupidly believed that I had a perfect husband and a perfect life and was making all the right decisions.

"Oh my God," I said. I handed Antonia my phone. "Look at this."

Antonia glanced at my phone and immediately turned it facedown on the floor. "Pretend you didn't see that."

"Seriously? This is happening now? Owen used my trust

against me. Dee Dee used my house against me. And now Facebook is using my own memories against me. These are weapons of mass emotional destruction! Can't I even control which memories I choose to keep and which ones I choose to forget? Or do I not even have a right to that anymore either? Is it really necessary for my email to pop up and say, 'Hey, Claire! Remember a year ago this week when you were really, really happy? Just in case you forgot, take a look! Sorry everything sucks now!'"

"This is absurdly bad timing."

"You think? I was just handed a cinder block in the form of photos while trying not to drown in a moat made of my own tears, Antonia. Is there a good time for that to happen?"

"Admittedly, probably not."

"I need to make some changes," I said. An eerie calm descended over my body. I didn't know what was happening, but I was fairly sure it wasn't good. "I will not be the victim for one more minute. I will not live like this."

"Good. Do whatever you need to do to stay positive and focused. Burn incense, light candles, chant, meditate, I don't know what. There are a lot of things you can do to change the association you have with this house," she said, trying so hard to find the bright side of a situation that didn't have one. "We'll figure it out. Maybe you could redecorate?"

I'd stopped listening, because what she said made so much sense I couldn't believe I hadn't thought of it myself. She was right. All I had to do was make this house my own. It was brilliant. Seriously, fucking, brilliant. If I couldn't move out of this house then I was going to have to do some serious redecorating. Anything that reminded me of Owen and our time together had to go. Also, anything that now reminded me of Owen and Dee Dee having sex had to go, too. I wondered how hard it would be to rip the bathtub out of the wall. Then I realized that was ridiculous. There was no way I could rip the Jacuzzi out of the wall—I'd have to just smash it to bits instead.

"I need a hammer," I said, as I hopped up and ran into the hall closet where I kept the ironing board (hadn't used it in months), the clean sheets for my bed (hadn't used them lately), and Owen's tool kit (never used it, period).

"I have no idea what you're doing," Antonia said, as she trailed a reasonable distance behind me in case I made any sudden movements that would somehow injure her. "But you don't need a hammer. I promise, you don't."

"You're right. I probably need a sledgehammer, but I know for a fact we don't have one of those. I'll have to see what I can do with the hammer. I have rage. I think that'll help." I found the small toolbox on the shelf next to the sheets, and popped the lid. I haphazardly grabbed tools I didn't need and threw them on the floor in the hallway outside the bathroom: Allen wrench, regular pliers, needle-nose pliers, Phillips head screwdriver, the other kind of screwdriver, bags of bolts, and screws, and nails, and finally, on the bottom, the hammer. Jackpot.

"You need a sledgehammer to do what, exactly?" Antonia asked. She stepped into Bo's room and sat him in his crib, turning on his mobile so that the circus animals began to dance in front of him. "Claire, you need to calm down," she ordered, which might have mattered if she was speaking to a sane person and not someone teetering on the edge of lunacy. Calming down wasn't an option. I tried calm at lunch. It didn't work. Now I wanted to see what crazy could do for me instead.

"To smash the bathtub to bits." Antonia's inane questions were really starting to bug me. What did she care what I was doing? It wasn't her Jacuzzi. I climbed up off the floor and left the other tools where they were. It was a safe bet they'd come in handy later, so I might as well leave them where I'd have easy access. I stormed back toward the bedroom, the hammer smooth and heavy in my hand.

"What?" she asked, even though I knew she heard me. "Stop it, Claire. Put the hammer down. You are not smashing anything. Can you please just sit down and take a few deep breaths?" she pleaded.

"Why?" I asked. "Why should I take a few deep breaths? I'm happy that yoga works for you, but I don't think vinyasa is what I need right now, okay? I don't want to be calm, and I don't want to find my fucking center, and I don't want to take deep breaths, or do headstands, or imagine myself in a happy place. I want to smash shit. That's what I want to do. Are you with me?" I held the hammer over my head. Antonia seemed scared. Wimp.

Antonia grabbed the hammer firmly in her hand. "Let it go, Claire."

"Let what go? Owen, or the hammer? You'll have to be more specific."

"Both. For right now, let's start with the hammer. The bathtub stays. Go smash a vase if you want to break something."

"Fine," I agreed. "But smashing one of my vases isn't going to do anything. I don't think Dee Dee decided to do any spontaneous floral arranging while she was here to screw my husband, you know? The vases still feel like mine."

"Okay. I think maybe we should just sit down and talk—"

"Forget the vase," I interrupted, not sure why Antonia kept trying to break my concentration. "Forget the tub. I'll deal with the things in the house that aren't bolted into the floor. There are plenty of them."

"That sounds like a much better idea," Antonia admitted. "What are you talking about, exactly?"

I didn't answer her. We had done enough talking. It was time to let my actions speak for themselves.

First I'd start with the pictures. I needed to get rid of the pictures. A quick room by room accounting informed me that we had only one picture of the two of us in the house, which, now that I thought about it, was kind of strange. Most people had pictures of themselves with their husbands all over the place. I knew a girl back home in Chicago who actually made a collage of the stages of her relationship, and plastered it all over the back of her closet door. Why did I only have one picture— the shot I asked the photographer to take of us while we stood apart from the crowd at the wedding. My eyes burned as I thought about my wedding day, and how I couldn't have imagined it devolving into this. I glanced down at the photo, the memory so vivid and painful and hard.

"You're beautiful," Owen had said as he came up beside me and slid his arm around my satin-cinched waist.

"You know, I always imagined that it got old hearing that you're the most beautiful bride ever, but it doesn't. I don't care how many people tell me that today. I will never, ever be tired of it."

"Good. Because I'll never be tired of saying it."

"Hold on a second," I said. I surveyed the room and found the photographer taking a picture of the cake and waved him over.

"Can you take this picture, please?" I asked. "I want this exact shot, at this exact moment."

"No problem!" he answered as he began to click away.

That memory used to make me feel all warm and fuzzy and now it made me feel all cold and icky, so I removed the frame from its place on the bookshelf in the den, nestled between a stack of books that Owen liked to pretend he was going to read someday and candlesticks that lacked candles. I raised it above my head, and slammed it into the floor with every ounce of anger and rage that was coursing through my body. I exhaled. I felt slightly better, at least for a second, until I looked down and realized that it hadn't even cracked. Apparently inexpensive picture frames were harder to break than my marriage. Go figure.

It didn't matter. I had other pictures I needed to destroy—pictures that I was planning on actually gluing in an album that I could tuck under my bed, and show my grandkids one day when they wouldn't believe that Nana and Pop Pop had been young and beautiful once upon a time, before they started throwing oysters in restaurants and banging Realtors in kitchens.

They were under my bed.

I sprinted up the stairs two at a time, slipping on the landing and falling down on one knee. When I got to my room, I dropped to the floor and crawled toward the bed, because for some reason army crawling seemed faster than actually walking. My heart was racing and my blood was pumping loudly through my body—I could hear the *swoosh, swoosh, swoosh* of it running through my ventricles, and into my veins, and it was invigorating. I found the rectangular bin from the Container Store that held all my pictures, and pulled it toward me. It was heavy—heavier than I remember it being, but so were the memories now, so maybe that was appropriate. I tugged on the plastic clips securing the lid, and heard them click as they released. There they were. Evidence that my whole relationship wasn't some weird fantasy I conjured up because I was afraid of being alone: pictures of us happy in Chicago; pictures of us in Manhattan the weekend we got engaged; pictures from our trip to wine country in the Pacific Northwest; pictures of us on the beach in Miami. All of them bullshit. For some reason, all I could hear in my head was one of those bad used car commercials where the salesman tried to convince everyone they just had to come see the cars with the tagline "everything must go!" He was right. Everything. Must. Go.

The bin was heavy, but not too heavy for me to lift. At least, that was what I thought until I dropped it trying to carry it down the stairs, and pictures floated through the slats in between the spindles, raining down on the wooden floor below. That was fine. They were closer to the door now and that was where they were going anyway. I dragged the container down to the main floor and threw the pictures back in it, then headed for the front door.

"What are you doing?" Antonia asked as I hurried past her with the container.

"I found pictures," I said. I left out the "duh" that seemed necessary at the end of that sentence, because I didn't want to be unnecessarily rude.

"I see that. Where are you going with them?" she asked as she placed the baby on his play mat.

"The driveway. Grab the other side," I instructed, as I lifted one end up off the floor.

"Um, okay. Can I ask why?" Her tone of voice was the same one I used when I tried to get Bo to stop eating puzzle pieces. *Bo, honey, I don't think we want to chew on that now, do we? No, we don't!*

"Yard sale. We're having a yard sale," I said. My quivering voice was a little too high, a little too squeaky, my words a little too rushed, to pass myself off as normal.

"In the driveway?"

"Yes, because I don't want people walking around the yard. That's creepy—but if they walk by the front of the house and see something they like, they can take it. If I can't move out of the house, I'm moving the contents of this house out to the sidewalk. Then, I'll just clean the place within an inch of its life and I'll be able to live here. Right? Why did it take me so long to think of this?"

Antonia hadn't moved but that didn't bother me. Forget the

pictures. I'd deal with them later. I'd decided to focus my energy on the garage. Owen had boxes in there that as far as I knew, he hadn't moved out. I wasn't entirely sure what was in them, but I was pretty sure it was just a lot of sentimental stuff from his past that he didn't need, but also didn't want to throw away—you know, like Dee Dee. I decided, in his absence, that it was time to toss them. I glanced into the kitchen as I headed for the basement stairs, caught a quick glimpse of Bo sitting on his play mat trying to pick up a giant stuffed zebra, and smiled. He'd like his school. I knew he would. He could take that zebra with him if he wanted, and place him safely inside one of the cubbies, and when the day was over I would stand outside and wait for him to find me in line with all of the other mothers, and we would come home and have applesauce with cinnamon, and by then everything would be okay. By then, we would be okay in this house because there'd be nothing left that reminded me of Owen and Dee Dee. There was a small button somewhere on the wall next to the door in the basement that would open the garage door, but I was having a hard time finding it because I never went into the garage. There wasn't any need to—until today.

Finally, I located the button and pressed, the rusty chain raising the door slowly and painfully, every squeak, and scrape, and clank a reminder that we were told to replace the garage door, but never did. Dee Dee was supposed to get us the name of some places in the area that we could call for estimates. At least, that was what I thought we were talking about when we all had the conversation about replacing the prehistoric chain that threatened to snap and turn my garage door into a guillotine at any given moment. Maybe when Owen asked, "Do you know who can fix my garage door?" he really meant, "Do you want to get freaky in the kitchen when my wife's out?" It was possible. This was Connecticut, the so-called Nutmeg State, where people came to buy spices for pies and have their marriages wrecked by their real estate agents. Anything was possible.

Once the door opened the sunlight helped me locate the boxes, and I reached up and dragged them down off the shelves, hearing things clang, and bang, and break, and it felt like sky-diving and speedboating and skinny-dipping and I couldn't believe I didn't think of doing this until today. Before I dealt with the boxes, I decided I needed to clean up the trail of random pictures that lay behind me leading all the way back up the stairs to the kitchen. I grabbed the broom hanging on the hook on the wall and began to sweep anything I could reach into the garage. I formed a neat, tidy pile and brushed them all into the plastic dust pan. I carried it down to the bottom of the driveway and dropped the pictures on a patch of grass next to the blacktop. It wasn't a particularly windy day, so I didn't think they were going to get blown away, but I didn't want to risk it. I walked across the street and decided the woman who lived there wouldn't mind if I borrowed one of the large rocks lining her lawn. I brushed off a few ants clinging to the underside, and placed it on top of the pile.

I hurried back up the driveway, and into the garage, and found a lamp that Owen used to have in his apartment when we dated. It stood behind the ugly leather chair he loved more than anything that was still inside the house. It wasn't anything fancy, just a basic black iron lamp with a woven rattan shade that could've been in a million apartments nationwide, but the mere sight of it made my skin crawl. I grabbed the lamp and wrapped the cord around the base, walked halfway down the driveway, and threw it like a javelin toward the curb. It didn't make it, and I probably should've taken the lightbulb out of it before I launched it onto the concrete, so that glass didn't shatter all over my driveway, but I wasn't all that concerned with the details of its removal. I just knew I had to get it out of the house.

"Claire, you need to stop. You've lost it. You need to pull it together," Antonia said at some point during my Owen exorcism when she appeared in the driveway with my son on her hip. "You don't need to do this. We can get rid of his stuff. I get it. But there's a better way to do it."

"Nah, I like this way," I answered. I raced back up into the garage, accidentally tripped over a crack in the floor, and knocked myself into the wall. No biggie. I pushed the large blue recycling bin out of the way to expose more boxes, and began to frantically pull at them one by one until I found the one I was looking for. I opened it and was knocked backward by Owen's smell, carefully preserved for the better part of a year by masking tape and a cardboard box. I dug around inside of it until I found the sweater I was looking for, and held it up to my nose, and even though I didn't want to, because I knew nothing good would come from it, I closed my eyes and inhaled. It was the sweater he was wearing when we met, an auburn, cashmere sweater with a half-zip collar and ribbing at the cuffs. Just the sight of it immediately brought me back to that bar—the smell of the yeast from the beer and the grease from the deep fryer and the cold whipping off Clark Street every time the door opened, causing my face to flush just in case the sight of Owen wasn't enough.

My moment of nostalgia quickly passed, and now I wanted to light it on fire. The box of clothes wasn't heavy, which was a welcome change, and I dragged it easily off the shelf and carried it down to the bottom of the driveway, dropping it right next to the container of pictures, the makeshift paperweight, the broken lamp, and the shards of broken lightbulb. It was really starting to look like a legit yard sale. I was proud.

I heard a car door close, and then Lissy's voice. "Hey, guys, I'm happy you're here. I was on my way home and figured I'd swing by, I hope that's okay." Lissy walked up the driveway carrying a magazine of some kind in her hand. "I wanted you to take a look at the table and chairs I found. I thought maybe they'd make a nice seating area for people to sit and look through the books."

"Great, Lissy!" I said over my shoulder. "Just leave it on the grass. I'll take a look at it in a little bit, I'm kind of in the middle of something."

"Yeah, a nervous breakdown," Antonia said.

"What are you doing? Why is there a broken lamp at the bottom of your driveway?"

"Owen won't let her sell the house and so she's decided to get rid of all of his stuff," Antonia said, which seemed unnecessary because I thought my actions were pretty obvious.

"So she's gone crazy? Does she do this kind of stuff often?"

"No. This is a first."

"Mind if I watch?" Lissy asked.

"You're going to have to because there's no stopping her. I tried."

I decided on my next trip I'd tackle Owen's old wooden kitchen table with its three mismatched chairs, but the table was heavier than it looked. "You know what? I don't think I need to move this," I said.

"Good, I think that's the right idea. Why don't you sit down," Antonia suggested.

"Firewood. We don't have any firewood! I think this stuff will burn great, don't you think? Let's just chop it up. Where's the hammer? Can you chop wood with a hammer?" I asked. "No, of course you can't," I said, answering my own question and suddenly wishing I had a pet woodchuck. "Maybe I have an axe. Funny that I never needed one until now."

"We don't need firewood. It's May."

"I still really think we do. I'll stack it neatly next to the hearth. It's basically recycling."

"Leave the table alone, please," Antonia begged. "It's not a good idea."

"I have an axe," Lissy offered. "Not in my car, though."

"Then it's not really helpful, sadly," I said. "Maybe bring it over next time in case I need it in the future, though."

"No problem," Lissy said. I appreciated her being willing

to lend me her axe. Maybe next we could trade sweaters or something.

"There will be no axes. Aren't you supposed to be helping?" Antonia asked Lissy.

"Sorry. You're right," Lissy agreed.

No axe, no problem. I figured I'd just deal with his foosball table instead. I certainly didn't need that. In fact, I didn't know why any man over the age of twenty-three even had a foosball table, but there it was, pushed up against the wall right below the box that held my Christmas ornaments. I liked that box. That box held the tinsel-covered swags and the red-ribboned wreaths and the new ornaments I bought last year for our first Christmas together in the new house. There was a plate buried in that box that I bought for when Bo was older, a large cookie platter with the words "Cookies for Santa" painted across the top in forest green paint. I liked that plate a lot, and I'd dreamed of Bo being old enough to help me make cookies on Christmas Eve. I'd dreamed of red and green sprinkles, and of powdered sugar and nonpareils, and of aluminum cutters shaped like angel wings and snowmen. They were all in that box. That box had to do with Bo, not Owen. If a single box survived my yard sale, that would be it.

But the fucking foosball table was toast. Then I'd worry about the old kitchen set.

"Help me move this, guys," I said, my mania now at stratospheric levels. I threw all my weight against one side of the game table, and tried to force it out of the garage. "Go put Bo down, and let's get this out of here. It's not that heavy, but it's a two-person job," I ordered. I was breathless, and sweating, and the blood was still pumping loudly through my veins, *swoosh, swoosh, swoosh,* and I felt like I finally had control of this situation. As soon as the table was out of the garage I was fairly sure I'd have my life back. Then all I had to do was figure out how to get the leather chair out of the house, and rip the marble slabs off the kitchen counters, and I'd be all set. Easy peasy. Antonia hadn't moved. That was fine, because I'd changed my mind anyway. I could move it by myself.

The squad car pulled up with its red and blue lights twirling, but without the siren, so I didn't notice it at first. The officer climbed out and came toward me up the driveway, the walkie-talkie he had with him squawking, and beeping, and interrupting my concentration as I tried to drag the table down the Belgian bricks to its final resting place on the sidewalk.

"Ma'am, what are you doing?" the officer asked. I looked up at his puffy cheeks, beady, dark eyes buried deep in the flesh of his face that reminded me of the black-buttoned eyes on the Teddy Ruxpin I was obsessed with when I was little. He was so heavy his belly hung over his belt and concealed his crotch, and the various pieces of police equipment he had hanging from his belt weren't helping his situation any. Cops in the Nutmeg State would do themselves a favor to lay off the apple pies if they wanted to intimidate anyone, though I'd admit that this town wasn't exactly a hotbed of activity for the criminal underground unless they were looking to knock over stores carrying whale-patterned tie and cummerbund sets, or pig snouts.

"Hi, Officer. Yard sale," I answered, as I continued to try

and push the foosball table down the driveway, which wasn't as easy as I thought it would be. The officer stepped in front of me and put his hands on the end of the table. "Oh, thank you so much. We can just move it to the curb. Thanks for the help. You're a godsend."

"I'm not helping you, ma'am. I'm here because your neighbors complained. You need to stop dragging your personal items out to the curb."

"They're not my personal items. They belong to my husband, well, he's my soon-to-be ex-husband, technically. That doesn't really matter. I'm not allowed to move home to Chicago, and I'm not even allowed to move out of this house, and that's fine, but I really don't need his foosball table, you know? I mean, if he's going to force me to live here, then he's not going to use it as a storage locker. So, I'll just leave it down here at the curb and I'm sure in a few days some kids will catch wind of it, and it'll be gone. No harm, no foul. Everyone's happy. Now, do you want to lift that side for me, please?"

"Ma'am, you can't do this," he reiterated.

"There's that word again, can't. When the hell is someone going to come here and tell me what I *can* do, and not what I *can't* do?"

"Please put the table down. The neighbors don't want the block looking like a junkyard."

"The neighbors?" I squealed, for the first time remembering that they existed. "Why do the neighbors care if I want to give away Owen's old sweaters? I don't care about the neighbors! I don't care about these stupid sweaters! I don't care about this house, or this street, or this state, or anything right now, except getting these boxes out of here. And you know what? The neighbors are lucky that I can't lift the bathtub, or they'd have bigger things to complain about than a couple of boxes and a fucking foosball table!" I screamed. Then, without thinking, I flipped the table over onto its side, snapping one of the legs in half.

"Officer, please forgive her. She's in the middle of a nervous breakdown. I have it under control. She's just had a string of really bad luck and this is kind of the culmination of a lot of very unfortunate events. I'll take care of it," Antonia promised.

"We didn't give her the axe, if that matters," Lissy said.

"This isn't the first time I've seen a wife throw her husband's things out of the house," he answered. "I get it. But please, get her under control. If I have to come back here, we're going to have to have a different conversation. Understand?"

"Yes, sir," Antonia said, always so respectful of authority figures, even those who weighed seven hundred pounds, and yet wouldn't help me move a foosball table. Jerk.

"I'm under control!" I insisted, just in case my flushed face, frantic movements, and pupils the size of dinner plates didn't make that clear. "I just don't understand why I'm not allowed to throw this stuff out? Why do I need his permission to throw out our pictures? I'm in them. Doesn't that mean I own them just as much as he does?" I asked, so exasperated, and frustrated, and crazy that I thought about lunging at Officer Fat Ass and beating him with his own walkie-talkie. "Are you trying to tell me that I needed a notarized release in order to get rid of stuff from my garage without breaking the law?"

"I'm sorry for whatever happened to you. I really am. I'll do my best to get your neighbors to lay off you for a little while, but you're going to need to move this stuff off the curb sooner rather than later, okay? Take it to the dump, or, better yet, call the Salvation Army," he suggested, and I realized that those beady little button eyes were filled with love, and understanding, and I hoped that he went home at night and had someone to spoon in bed because he was the most compassionate person I'd ever met in my life.

"Oh," I sighed, the *swoosh, swoosh, swoosh* in my ears starting to slow to a gurgle. "Why didn't you say so?"

Chapter 10

MY NAME IS Claire Stevens. I'm a thirty-six-year-old divorcée and mother of one and I'm about to go on my first date in years with a man named Fred. "So what?" I said to myself as I examined my face, and I mean *really* examined my face, in the bathroom mirror. There she was—the quirky best friend— the one who wore sensible underwear and couldn't seem to master the art of applying eyeliner, reporting for duty in the mirror just like I knew she would. I was hoping maybe she'd call in sick and send someone sultry to fill in for her, but for some reason she was never sick. Her freckly, perky, cute-in-a- nonthreatening-way face stared right back at me. I had to restrain myself from head-butting the mirror and knocking her unconscious. I didn't want to see her tonight. Just once, I'd like to see someone else.

I went to Sephora and bought fake eyelashes for this occa- sion. I had no idea why I thought having fake eyelashes would somehow make this date any less scary, or that fake eyelashes were somehow going to help me rid myself and the mirror of my girl-next-door image, but I thought that maybe they could. They couldn't. What they could do was make my eyelids look like they'd grown fringe that could very easily be attached to the side of a cowboy boot rather than to my face. I thought I might have overdone it.

Dinner. Dinner's not a big deal. I eat dinner every night, except for the first few weeks after my life blew up. There was a while there where I couldn't manage to swallow spit, never mind a cheeseburger, and when I did eat, I did it in bed with my duvet pulled up over my chest like I was afraid the frozen pizza I managed to cook wanted to assault me or something. But that was March, and this was June, and I'd moved into the phase where I tried to put my life back together, and that meant that I'd now eat meals in public places with accountants named Fred—public places with tablecloths, and menus, and dim lighting that might help my eyelashes look less Itsy Bitsy Spider and more Marilyn Monroe. I stared at them in the mirror again, and decided that I looked like an idiot. *Pointless,* I sighed as I admitted defeat. I splashed water on my eyes in order to dissolve the glue strip holding the fringe to my skin, and watched as the spider leg lashes fell into the porcelain sink and stuck to the side of the basin right next to a crusty glob of Crest. *Down came the rain and washed the spider out,* I sang quietly, suddenly feeling very sad. There may have been a time in my life where I could've reinvented myself as a vixen if I wanted to, but that time was long gone. Now I was a nursery-rhyme-singing single mother, and there were not enough artificial embellishments to attach to any part of my body to make that fact any less true.

I shoved my feet into pumps and checked my black dress

one last time in the full-length mirror affixed to the back of my bathroom door. I was happy with the way I looked. My dress was appropriate, but still fitted, and it didn't scream frigid or slutty, the two things I was trying to avoid, and so I deemed it a success. I grabbed my enormous black bag from the foot of my bed and decided to just lug the entire thing with me tonight because I had no idea where I'd stashed my evening clutch. Respectable single mother slash divorcées didn't carry lip gloss and condoms with them in tiny little decorative bags covered in sequins or snakeskin when they left the house. Instead, I took a twenty-pound duffel bag with me everywhere I went. It held diapers, teething rings, packets of formula, a nail file, manicure scissors, wet wipes, a phone charger, no less than three pairs of sunglasses, a bottle of aspirin, and a bag of Cheerios, and that was just the list of things I could name off the top of my head. I was exhausted from worrying about my dress, and my shoes, and my eyelashes, and I simply didn't have the energy to start fretting over the size of my bag, too. It was easier to take the whole thing with me than it would be to find my wallet in it anyway.

Fred the accountant was not Owen the WASP and that was a good thing. I didn't know too much about him other than that, and that was helpful on a first date because it meant we'd have lots to talk about. I didn't know what sports he liked. I didn't know where he grew up, or what kind of music he liked to sing in the shower before work. I didn't know his favorite meal, or if he was a neat freak, or a slob, or if he had OCD or something. I didn't even know his favorite color, but I needed to make sure it wasn't purple. I decided maybe that would be my first question. I'd ask him his favorite color while we were in the car on the way to the restaurant, and if he said purple, I'd just jump out of it while he was still driving. All I knew for sure was that he didn't like to text, and that might be kind of a big problem, but I wasn't ready to worry about any other potential problems, so I decided to let it go.

I closed my eyes tightly and promised myself that when I opened them I wouldn't be thinking about Owen or my divorce anymore. I deserved to have a nice time, to laugh, and to have upbeat conversation about innocuous topics. I flipped on the TV and stopped thinking about a slut named Dee Dee, and started thinking about an accountant named Fred. I started thinking about how nice it will be when he arrives, and takes me to dinner, and tells me I look pretty, and that he likes my eyelashes just the way they are. He was a few minutes late, but I wasn't worried about it. I was busy watching HGTV and listening to a decorator assure a woman that she could change her whole life just by updating her living room curtains. It was riveting reality television.

"You look really nice," Antonia said. She breezed toward me with a cup of hot chocolate in her hand, and her notebook stuffed under her armpit. "You're going to have a great time. Just relax."

"She's totally right," Lissy said. "You need to wear lipstick, though."

"But I don't wear lipstick."

"You don't usually wear fake eyelashes either and you bought those. What's wrong with a nice red lipstick? It says 'kiss me.' That's what you want a guy to think on a date."

"I don't want a guy to think that on the first date. I don't want to look like I'm trying too hard."

"I wear red lipstick every day and I'm not trying at all," Lissy reminded me.

"Yes, but I'm not you. You've got a whole vibe working. My vibe is stay-at-home mom."

"Okay, fine. Don't wear it, but I'm telling you, you'd look great with it."

"I'm so nervous I want to throw up. Maybe I should cancel. It hasn't been long enough. I mean, is it slutty for me to do this? Shouldn't I wait a little longer? Aren't I supposed to still be in marriage mourning?"

"Don't make this a bigger deal than it is," Antonia suggested.

"You're right. I know you're right. It just feels like a really big deal."

"That's normal. But, it's not," Lissy said. "It's dinner. It's the opposite of a big deal."

"You're right. I know you're right. I need to do this. I need to grab hold of the small moments in my life that I can control. I need to change what I can change. Owen might be able to dictate where I live, but he can't tell me who to date, and he can't tell me where to have dinner, and those are two things that I'm deciding for myself and that feels good. I still have some say in what happens to me. I'm going to focus on those things for a while."

"Small things can make a big difference," Antonia said.

"Agreed," added Lissy. "I feel that way about my fifth ear piercing. It was totally life changing."

"Okay then," I said. "What's the plan for tonight?"

"We're babysitting and having a glass or three of wine," Antonia said. "How come I moved here to help take care of you, and now you're going out on a date and I'm stuck in the house on a Saturday night babysitting your kid for free?"

"Because I'm a master manipulator," I said. I'd never be able to repay Antonia for what she'd done for me, but I'd spend my whole life trying.

"Seriously! Joke's on me, I guess. At least Lissy is going to hang out with me for a little. Maybe we can rent a movie or something."

"How are you with horror films?" Lissy asked.

"I'm more rom-com than horror," Antonia admitted.

"I was afraid you'd say that. Okay, fine. Romance it is," Lissy agreed.

"I love you. I don't know where I'd be without you. I really don't," I said as I hugged Antonia.

"Under your comforter, probably."

"Definitely."

"I'm happy you're doing so much better."

"I had a lot of help."

"Nah. Plenty of people have help. You chose to get up and move forward. I think that's admirable. I'm proud of you."

"You're the poster child for divorcées. You should start a blog. A lot of women would love hearing about your journey," Lissy suggested.

"Sure. I'll start a blog about dating even though I'm not even divorced yet and have a baby at home. I'll call it Regrets Only because that basically sums up my life in Connecticut. I'm sure that'll go over real well with the other moms on the playground."

"Why aren't you meeting him there?" Lissy asked.

I checked the time on my phone. "Because Fred thinks it's 1952 and not 2016. Apparently he's very old-fashioned. And late. Am I being stood up?"

"No. He's just late," Antonia answered. "Maybe he stopped to buy you a corsage? A nice pink carnation on an elastic band."

"Don't joke. I'm trying to not let the fact that he doesn't text and wants to pick me up freak me out. Throwing the possibility of corsages at me might nudge me over the edge."

"He has nice manners," Lissy said. "Why is that a bad thing?"

"It's just odd. That's all I'm saying. I don't want to be with someone who thinks that I need to be escorted around. I'm a modern woman. I might not be able to pay my own mortgage or live where I want to live at the moment, but I can drive my own car. I don't like some other guy swooping in and trying to take away what little independence I have left."

"He's driving you to a restaurant. I really don't think he's trying to take away your independence," Antonia said with a sigh.

"It's a slippery slope. I've got my eye on him. That's all I'm saying."

"Stop finding problems where there aren't any. He's polite. You can work on getting him to text. Don't obsess over stupid things," Antonia pleaded. "If I did that I'd never date anyone. Believe me."

The doorbell rang. He was fifteen minutes late. On the line of being rude, but not over it.

"Who's obsessing? I'm just pointing out that even my mother knows how to text. That's all."

"Don't stay out too late," Antonia teased as she walked up the stairs, her bare feet sticking to the swollen, humid wood.

"Here," Lissy said as she tucked her small lipstick in my hand. "Just in case you change your mind. Good luck." She ran upstairs after Antonia and closed the door to her room.

"Thanks, you guys," I said nervously.

I hopped out of the chair, ran my hand through my hair, and inhaled deeply. *It's just dinner,* I reminded myself. *Relax.*

"Hi," I said when I opened the door and found Fred standing squarely under my porch light. He wore a navy blazer and a pair of khaki pants for our date, and I liked it. He looked like he'd put some effort into his appearance and it had been a while since anyone made me feel like I was worth any effort at all. It was a nice feeling.

"You look very nice," he said as he leaned over and gingerly kissed my cheek. I felt my body stiffen, but hoped he didn't notice. The last thing I needed was to scare Fred away before we even got to the restaurant.

"Thank you, so do you," I answered.

"I hope you like Italian. I made a reservation at this place about ten minutes from here. It's one of my favorites."

"I love Italian," I said, feeling myself marginally relax. I didn't want to go to dinner in town, where I'd have to worry about running into anyone who knew me in my previous life, when I was one half of Owen and Claire.

"Great. Let's go," he said. He stepped aside and escorted me down the two cracked porch stairs onto the path that led to the driveway. I was happy my black dress had sleeves. It was a bit cool outside, and I didn't want to be in a situation where he had to offer me his jacket or something because I appeared cold. I wasn't ready for gestures of intimacy like that. I was fine to have dinner with Fred, but I didn't want to wear his clothes.

"I like the color of your car," I said, eyeing the shiny gray Jeep in the driveway. "It's like graphite. It reminds me of number two pencils."

"Is that a good thing?" Fred asked. He smiled, a flash of orthodontically perfected teeth. They looked good on him.

"Yeah. It's sleek."

"Thanks. I was debating between this and a dark blue, but gray's my favorite color. This one seemed more like me."

Gray. Fantastic. Score one for Fred. I climbed into the front seat, and buckled my seat belt, knowing at the very least that I wouldn't have to throw myself into oncoming traffic before we got to dinner.

The restaurant was busy with married couples most likely enjoying a date night out away from their kids. Hearty laughter peppered clanging silverware on bone white plates, and opera music played softly in the background. The waiters wore white shirts with red ties, the bartender dropped chunky ice cubes into glasses on the glossy bar. The room smelled of garlic and shellfish, and if I closed my eyes I could swear I was back in Chicago at Carlo's, my favorite restaurant growing up, where I'd religiously order a huge plate of ravioli and drink Shirley Temples, and I finally, finally felt myself relax.

The maître d' escorted us to a table in the center of the room, and Fred didn't seem to mind. That was one of Owen's biggest pet peeves: he always requested tables in the corner, where he wouldn't be bothered by foot traffic and waiters carrying heavy trays laden with drinks and used dishes. He was very particular about where he was seated, and it used to drive me bananas. It was a relief to see Fred take his seat and not fight with the waiter over why we had to sit at this table and not at a different one. A delicate bud vase cradled a small white rose between two flickering votive candles. It was cozy without being overtly romantic, upscale without being fussy, crowded without being noisy. It was essentially perfect, and I was so amazingly relieved that Owen and I never came here together. I had zero negative associations with this place. There was just me, and Fred, and a large glass of red wine in my future, and that made this the best Saturday night I'd had in a very long time.

"I'm so happy we did this," Fred said. He placed his napkin in his lap and reached for the wine list. "Would you like wine?"

"I am, too," I said, and I meant it. "It's nice to be out on a Saturday. I'd be lying if I said I did this all the time. Red would be great."

The waiter appeared and took our drink order. I sipped my water and scanned the room, soaking up the dark burgundy walls and the platters of veal chops and pastas as they floated by, and I chided myself for building this up in my mind so much that I actually thought I needed to wear fake eyelashes before I was pretty enough to leave the house. I was wearing a dress—that was more than enough. I glanced at my phone and saw that it was 8:15. Bo had been asleep for over an hour, but I quickly considered calling Antonia to make sure that everything was okay. I decided against it. I didn't want to be anyone's mom tonight. I wanted to just be someone's date.

"Cheers," Fred said as he clinked my glass and I took a nice, long sip of a peppery wine that was warming and calming and hugged me the whole way down.

"Cheers," I answered, taking another sip before setting it back down on the tablecloth next to the breadbasket. "So tell me about your job," I said. Antonia told me that asking about work was how she usually started her first-date conversations, because it transferred the burden of talking onto the guy, and gave him the opportunity to talk about himself for a while so I could work out my nerves.

"I'm an accountant. Unfortunately it's not that great of a conversation piece, but I enjoy it. I grew up in New Hampshire and I have two brothers. One of them is a ski instructor and one of them is in construction, which is kind of the family business. My father owned a construction company for many years. He's retired now, so my brother runs it. They have much more interesting stories to tell when someone asks about their day."

"Construction and a ski instructor, huh? And you're an accountant?"

"I'm the geek," he admitted.

"That must be very difficult for you," I teased.

"I've spent a lot of money on therapy, but I'm doing much better with it now. Thank you for asking," he joked. The banter came easily.

"So your two brothers sound all rugged and athletic. I imagine you must have some of that in you, too. Do you ski? I'm terrible at it, but I like it a lot."

"Yeah. I grew up skiing and I totally love it. I try to go a few times every year with my family."

"Sounds like your family is all into being outdoorsy?"

"I guess so. When we were kids our parents would take us into the woods and we would go camping and kayaking in the summer. We cut down our Christmas tree every year, too. And I can build a pretty mean fire. I can't hunt deer, though."

"Check, please!" I joked, surprised at how easily it was to flirt with him.

"Happens every time I tell someone that. I really need to start holding back on the really scandalous information until the second date. Is there anything I can say to make up for that?"

"Hmmm," I said. "Maybe. How's your s'mores game?" I asked. "If you're going to have a house in the woods and a fireplace and a giant Christmas tree I hope there are s'mores involved. Otherwise the whole perfect family thing is ruined and I'm definitely leaving," I teased.

"Are you kidding? People know me for my s'mores. I actually have a following on Instagram because of them."

Fred was funny and smart and interesting and easy to talk

to and I liked that about him. I liked that he was close to his family. I liked that he didn't try to glamorize a job that was totally great, but not fascinating in the slightest. I liked that he wasn't trying too hard to pretend to be someone he wasn't, even though I did kind of wish that the someone he was knew what "LOL" meant. Still, Fred didn't seem to be the type of guy to like artificial anything. I breathed a sigh of relief that I left the false eyelashes at home.

"That sounds like so much fun. I'm an only child and I have great memories growing up, but we never cut down our own Christmas tree."

"It's one of those things you do that you just assume everyone does. You don't realize what a special memory that is to have until you're older."

"It's funny, I think about stuff like that now that I have Bo. What will he remember, what will he enjoy, how will he look back on things when he's a grown man, and how I can shape those memories for him now. I guess kids make you see the world differently. They also make you realize how much you took for granted growing up."

"What's the saying? 'Youth is wasted on the young'?"

"Exactly. Whoever said that is totally right. Do you get to go back to New Hampshire a lot? It's not that far a drive, right?"

"I go a lot in the winter. I have a little house in the woods up there, actually. I'm really busy in the spring, obviously, but in the fall and winter I try to get up there as much as I can. It's always good to hang out with my brothers. We have a good time together. My older brother, Bruce, has two kids. I wish I got to see them more. My younger brother is the ski instructor and I don't think he's looking to get married anytime soon."

"No sense in rushing, right?" I asked. Maybe I should've taken my own advice. I was in my mid-thirties when I got married, but we didn't date very long at all. If anyone ever asked me for my advice at this point, that's probably what I would say. Date for more than six months. Honeymoon periods were called honeymoon periods for a reason.

"Yeah. I'm hardly the expert on that so I usually just keep my mouth shut when the topic comes up."

"That's probably smart!" I said.

I realized that I was hungry. I hadn't been out to eat at a nice Italian restaurant in what seemed like forever, and I suddenly felt like I hadn't seen food in years. I wanted to be polite, but I was staring at the basket of bread like it was a basket of cash. I reached over and grabbed a roll, feeling the warm, crusty dough collapse under the pressure from my grip, and had to resist the urge to shove the entire thing in my mouth at once. I tore off a reasonably sized piece, and was thrilled to discover how good it tasted. Up until now, most things still tasted like cardboard—dry and coarse and impossible to swallow—but now the butter tasted sweet, and salty, and soft as flannel. I had an urge to lick my lips, but I resisted because I didn't want Fred to think I was making the moves on him before we finished our salads.

A waiter carrying a huge platter of something sizzling whizzed by the table, oil popping and crackling on a deep silver tray, and I couldn't help but track him as he delivered it to a round table tucked in the corner by the windows. I could smell rosemary, and citrus, and garlic, and I needed to find out what it was so that I could order it for myself. I hoped it wasn't something for two. I wasn't ready to wear Fred's clothes, and I wasn't ready to share Fred's food yet, either, and if Oprah had a problem with that, then that was just too bad.

My heart stopped. I wasn't entirely sure what was happening. One minute I was listening to Fred tell me about his family and his ski house and his s'mores-making skills, and the next I couldn't focus. I was suddenly having an out-of-body experience. My eyes froze on Dee Dee and Owen cuddling in a corner booth, one that he no doubt specifically requested, with a bottle of wine perched in a perspiring bucket. I hadn't seen them together since I saw them in my kitchen. Dee Dee wore a low-cut blouse, of course she did, and from my seat halfway across the room I could see the purple lace peeking out the top of her black silk shirt, and it all became too much for me to take. My stomach rumbled, and the buttered roll I just shoved down threatened to reappear. There he was. My shaggy-haired Owen, enjoying Saturday night with his steady girlfriend while I was on my first date with Fred. Dee Dee reached over and brushed the lock of hair out of Owen's eyes, gently tucking it behind his ear, just like I used to do. I gagged.

"Are you okay?" Fred asked, as I sputtered and held the white napkin to my mouth in an effort to keep from drooling red wine all over my chin. I couldn't answer him because I couldn't focus on anything except that lock of hair that Dee Dee just lovingly pushed out of Owen's face.

I hate that hair, I thought. *I hate that hair so much I can't even*

*look at it anymore. I used to love it, and now I feel like it mocks
me, and I can't stand it one more second.*

"Excuse me for one minute," I said to Fred as I dropped the
napkin and pushed back my chair from the table. I left quickly
because I didn't want him to ask me where I was going and I
didn't offer an explanation. I grabbed my purse from under my
chair, and tossed it over my shoulder as I walked toward them.
The familiar *swoosh, swoosh, swoosh* returned to my ears as my
blood rushed to my head. I could hear people talking around
me, polite dinner conversations and inside jokes, but it was all
muffled and garbled as if I were underwater.

My legs felt heavy, but I continued to lumber toward them
because there was something that I had to know. I needed my
question answered, or I'd never be able to really move on from
this. I'd never be able to look around my house and not see
Dee Dee, and I'd never be able to take a bath in the Jacuzzi,
and I'd never be able to enjoy hot rolls, and peppery wine, and
gentle conversations with accountants named Fred who liked
the color gray and can cut down their own Christmas tree. It
didn't take long for me to reach their table, but it took me a
very long time to reach the point in the healing process where I
was ready to confront those who wronged me. It took way too
long, and I refused to let it take another minute.

"Do you only have one set of underwear?" I asked Dee Dee,
which understandably caught her off guard. "You were wearing purple underwear the last time I saw you, too. It's sad that I
know that, but since I do, maybe you could go ahead and clear
that up for me."

"Oh my God, Claire," Owen said when he looked up and found me standing at his table. I'd never been so happy to not be wearing fake eyelashes. I could only imagine what he'd say to me if I were. "What are you doing here?"

"Having dinner. I do that, you know."

"Where's Bo?"

"I left him with the valet. Where the hell do you think he is?"

"Calm down, Claire. Don't do this," he pleaded. I didn't care. I just walked away from the first date I'd had in years. I was doing this. It was already being done.

"Don't avoid my question. I really would like to know. Do you?" I asked, ignoring the sweat that was running down my cleavage, and the roll that was still trying to escape from my stomach, and forcing myself to remain calm and steadfast in my search for honest answers. "Do you only own the one pair? Or is that purple number you're wearing your favorite, or something?" I asked, nodding toward the purple lace. "Or do you have an entire arsenal of purple underwear?" I wasn't sure why I needed to know. I thought maybe it would make me feel better if she only had one pair of underwear and that was why she was wearing the purple again, but I doubt that was the case because women like her always had more than one lacy matching set. No one had an affair with a married man without stocking up on the good stuff—hell, there was probably an entire section in the department stores here for mistresses who want to entice married men and ruin the lives of the unsuspecting wives buying body shapers to fix the damage done by childbirth on the other side of the store.

Owen ran his hand through his hair. I'd had it with that hair. I reached into my bag and grabbed the scissors that were tucked away in the pocket next to the nail file and my house keys. I heard some small voice of reason inside that sounded an awful lot like Antonia asking *What are you doing?* But I told the voice to shut up because Owen and Dee Dee were ruining my date and it wasn't fair. He'd taken too much from me. He took away my home in Chicago. He took away my marriage. He took away my security. He took away my confidence, and my pride, and my future, and my son's chance to grow up with a united household, and I wasn't letting him take one more thing from me.

I decided it was time I took something from him.

I decided to go with his hair.

I lunged over the wine bucket with my manicure scissors, and with one smooth motion, lopped off part of his bangs.

"Are you crazy?" he yelled as he recoiled toward Dee Dee, and grabbed the front of his hair. "What the hell are you doing?" I watched wispy strands flutter and fall like pieces of hay into his soup. It looked like minestrone.

"You just assaulted him!" Dee Dee screamed. A waiter suddenly appeared and grabbed my elbow. "He could press charges, you psychotic bitch!"

"Oh, why don't you just shut up before I hack off your stupid beach waves?" I said, not sure why I chose tonight to lose my mind when I'd tried so hard up until now to make sure things went smoothly. Of all the restaurants around here, why did we have to end up at the same one on the same night? Better question: Why hadn't Owen ever taken me here? Why was he all comfortable in his little booth with Dee Dee, and yet I'd never even heard of this place? Was this where they went to be together while we were still married? Was this where they were on nights when I thought he was traveling or working late? I needed to get out of the restaurant before I threw up all over their table. If Owen thought I made a scene in the oyster bar, he hadn't seen anything yet.

"It is not okay to play 'leggo my Eggo' with my husband," I said, as another waiter grabbed the scissors from my hand and placed them in his pocket. "You should know that."

"Ma'am, I need you to leave. Right now," the waiter said, as he and his buddy flanked me and nudged me toward the door. I felt like I was being bounced by the cast from *Jersey Boys*.

"Yeah, I'm going," I sighed, realizing that poor Fred was still sitting at our lovely little table with the white rose and the votive candles, watching his date attack her ex-husband, and also, because he was old-fashioned and wanted to pick me up, that he was my ride home.

❧ Chapter 11

THE DOORBELL RANG on Wednesday at 5:30, just as it should have, and I glanced over at Bo sitting quietly on the floor in his elephant footie pajamas, playing with a giant blue block, and wondered if I would ever have to tell him the story about how I attacked his father with manicure scissors in a restaurant. Would Owen tell him? If Bo approached him one day when he was a teenager and told him about some crazy girl who taped pictures of herself all over his locker or something, would Owen say, "That's nothing. Did I ever tell you about the time your mom cut my hair off at dinner?" I couldn't believe how fast I'd spiraled that this was now something I had to worry about. Antonia hopped off the couch to get the door, which was wonderful, because I was too tired to move.

"Nice hair," Antonia said as she opened the door and tried desperately to stifle laughter.

"Come in," I said from my seat at the bottom of the stairs. Antonia stepped to the side and Owen stepped into the foyer. He immediately scooped Bo up off the floor and stretched his arms above his head, turning my little boy into a chubby little airplane, making him laugh, and coo, and squeal, because he loved his dad. Owen's shirt rode up above the waist of his pants, exposing a thin strip of toned muscle and taut skin, and part of me wanted to go rub my hands across it the way I used to, because those feelings didn't just go away no matter how much you wanted them to.

"Do you have anything to say to me?" Owen asked. "I'm done being the punching bag, Claire. I've dealt with the beans, and the holes in my clothes, and the Craigslist ad, and even the Facebook post, but you went too far Saturday night. That was so out of character for you I'm beginning to worry that you're not stable! It stops now. All of it," he ordered. It didn't bother me much, because he didn't mean much to me anymore, so I shrugged.

"I'm sorry I cut your hair. I wish I had waited until after dinner. The soufflés looked delicious."

"Fine. Don't apologize."

"She could do a whole lot worse to you than that and wouldn't owe you an apology, Owen," Antonia said.

"Were you on a date?" he asked, which made me smile. He'd noticed Fred. I felt vindicated knowing that Owen was aware that other people were interested in me, even if he wasn't.

"None of your business," I answered, and I loved being able to say that, too, especially because it was true.

"No, I guess it's not. For what it's worth, I don't love the idea of you seeing other people either, but I want you to be happy."

"Thanks for the endorsement." I pulled Bo's diaper bag off the hook near the basement stairs, and picked his overnight bag up off the floor. I hated giving him to Owen. I hated that he had two rooms, and two homes, and two parents who couldn't make his family work as one. I kissed his soft cheek as I said good-bye.

"I'll bring him back in the morning," Owen said.

"Okay. Don't forget to plug in the night-light I got for his room. If he wakes up in the middle of the night, and it's pitch-black, he'll be scared."

"I will."

"Promise me."

"I promise, Claire. I'll plug it in. He'll be fine," Owen reassured me. "When are you going to come and see my apartment? I think you'll feel better about my taking him if you see where I live. Maybe part of the reason you've gone completely nuts is because there's still a lot of unknowns. Let's try and clear some of them up so that I don't have to worry about you ending up in an asylum somewhere. Please come."

"Yeah, that must be it. It's all those pesky unknowns that are plaguing me."

"I want you to know that I'm taking care of him. You'll have a little peace once you see his room and everything," he said. I hated to admit that he had a point, but he had a point.

"You're right. One of these weeks I'll drop him off at your place."

"Okay, good." Bo was nuzzling Owen's neck, and I felt the urge to cry, not because I was handing him over for the night, but because I had attacked the one other person in this world Bo loved as much as me, and hurting Owen was kind of like hurting Bo, too, and that was completely unacceptable to me.

The old familiar guilt wrapped itself around me, only this time I was sure that I deserved it.

"Owen," I whispered, because I could barely bring myself to say the words I needed to say out loud. "I'm sorry. What you did was awful, but I shouldn't have attacked you. I'm sorry I did that."

Owen sighed. "No. But maybe that can be the end of a long list of things neither of us should've done this year. And what about the Craigslist ad? My phone rang off the hook for a week. Do you have any idea how many wackos are on Craigslist?"

"No, I'm not sorry for that. Just to be clear. Just the scissors."

"That's a start. I'll see you tomorrow."

Owen carried Bo out to his car and I watched through the window as he secured him in his car seat, and climbed into the front seat. The headlights burned brightly, and I waved to Bo as Owen backed the car out of the driveway, even though I knew he couldn't see me. I felt like I should do it anyway.

I turned to face Antonia. "I guess that could've gone worse."

"Uh, yeah. I have to say, I'm hugely impressed by that display of maturity. I was expecting a complete disaster."

"Maybe we're making progress," I joked. "Or at least maybe I am. I don't know what's happening anymore." The tears came unexpectedly. Owen and Bo were together, and I was all alone and I couldn't imagine a time where this wouldn't feel like torture.

"What do you want to do now?" Antonia asked, which should've been a pretty easy question to answer, but nothing was easy for me anymore. Part of me wanted to go into Bo's room and sleep on the floor, and part of me wanted to go into my room and sleep on the floor, and part of me wanted to go into my room and sleep in my bed, even though the mattress was starting to mold to my body and not in a good way.

"I honestly have no idea."

"Let's go walk into town and get something to eat," Antonia said.

"I don't think so, Antonia. Can't we just order in?" I asked, because no part of me wanted to walk into town and get something to eat.

"Come on. If I'm going to live here for a while I need to get my bearings," she said, but I knew she was thinking that the fresh air would make me feel better, which was what people usually told you when they didn't know what else to say.

"I've been here since August, and I still don't have mine. You get used to it."

"We're going."

"Can't we go tomorrow?"

"No. You need to eat," she said. "No one died. You're going to get over this."

"And eating is going to help with that?"

"It's not going to hurt. Haven't you ever heard of comfort food?"

"I'm not hungry," I answered.

"I don't care if you're hungry. You're going to eat," Antonia said. "FYI, any Italian will tell you that food can cure most of life's problems, and if it can't, well, you should still enjoy your dinner while you figure out what to do next."

LIGHTS ON MAIN Street burned brightly and Antonia and I walked arm in arm through town.

"You really are doing great," Antonia reassured me, which I appreciated. I didn't know how to measure how well I was doing. I didn't know what qualified as a normal amount of crazy, and what was too much crazy, and what was just crazy enough. "You just went on a date. It takes some women years to get to that point. That should make you feel amazing. It's not easy to find nice guys to go out with, believe me, I know."

"He was a really nice guy and I scared him away. How many chances am I going to get to meet new people?"

"You don't know that you scared him away."

"I went berserk in the restaurant, Antonia. If I didn't scare him away there's something seriously wrong with him."

"So then call him and explain yourself, not that that will be easy, or think of it as a practice date. That's okay. You got the first one over with, and that's important, even if it didn't exactly go well."

"You know what really sucks about this whole thing?"

"There's only one thing?" she asked.

"I liked being married," I admitted, which for some reason made me feel pathetic. I shouldn't need a relationship to define me, and I didn't realize that mine had, but the truth was I liked being Owen's wife. I liked being Claire Mackenzie.

"You'll like being single again, too. You weren't married for that long. It's not like you spent thirty years with some guy and then got ditched for a twenty-two-year-old with a convertible."

"A divorce is a divorce. I don't think mine is somehow better than that of someone who's been married longer."

"That's not what I'm saying. It's just that you still know how to be you. You just need a little time, and then you'll remember who she is. You're going to be just fine. I think you're still in shock more than anything else."

"You'd be surprised how fast you can get used to not being alone," I said.

I was probably reimagining my own history a little where that was concerned. I may have been married, but I was still alone a good amount of the time. Owen's schedule was brutal, and when he'd finally come home he was often so tired he just wanted to take a hot shower and get into bed. I couldn't blame him. Airports were exhausting, but it would've been nice if he'd bothered to acknowledge that I'd been alone the whole week with the baby, too, and had no one else to talk to. I missed adult conversation, and the time we spent together, and the feeling like we were a team united in something. Toward the end, though, I'd felt a little bit like we had assumed our roles in the relationship, and those roles rarely intersected. He would take care of the money, and I would take care of the baby—lather, rinse, repeat.

When Owen came home from his last business trip, I think it was from Portland, I made him a special dinner, because I knew things were tense. I wanted to make him pulled pork sandwiches with homemade vinegared slaw for dinner because he loved them, and I thought it would be a nice way to welcome him home. I'd purchased a Heritage pork shoulder from the butcher in town and seared it in a huge roasting pan that took two burners to heat and spattered oil all over the stovetop. When it was browned, I placed it in the slow cooker and added beef stock, and bay leaves, and peppercorns, and chili peppers, and tomatoes, and let it braise for eight whole hours. I sliced cabbage and carrots and herbs on a mandolin even though I was terrified of slicing my hand open on the blade, and spent what felt like hours chopping, pickling, and stirring. I even made his favorite potato salad, the one with the mayonnaise and the tarragon and the hard-boiled eggs that I hated. I bought soft rolls at Whole Foods and after almost nine hours of cooking, I had my perfect welcome-home meal ready. When Owen arrived, he dropped his bag on the floor, and commented that the house smelled good, which it did, because it was impossible for a house to smell any other way if there had been a pork shoulder cooking for so long. I handed him a dark amber beer, and rubbed his shoulders and told him to sit down so that I could serve him the best pulled pork sandwiches ever made, but he said he had Taco Bell at the airport and wasn't hungry. Instead, he drank the beer, and sat on the couch watching *Vertigo* on the Turner Classic Movies channel. He didn't even taste it, or say thank you, or pretend to be hungry even though he wasn't, because that was what you did when someone you loved spent all day making dinner for you. I was hurt, but he didn't get that, because we had stopped understanding each other the way we once did. The pork went in the refrigerator, and the potatoes went in the trash, and I went to bed because I was no longer hungry either, and drained from making the effort. Still, I didn't know the next step was divorce. No one ever told me that if you stopped effectively communicating with your husband his high school girlfriend would swoop down from the Coldwell Banker office and steal him away from you.

I paused in front of the window of Farmhouse Kitchen. That was it. That was the name of the restaurant that Dee Dee told Owen that he just *had* to try because it was simply the best food in the entire world and we should totally take her word for it. The lights were dim save for a small lantern on each table, because apparently in order to be supremely trendy, you had to turn off all the lights and pretend you were dining in the pre–Ben Franklin era. Wine bottles sat on coasters on the table, encouraging people to help themselves. The diners ran the gamut of the expected: bored housewives pretending to be enthralled with their husbands' tales of war from their day at the office, first date hopefuls trying to figure out how many glasses of wine had to grace their coaster before they'd be comfortable, and insecure singles trying to prove that they weren't insecure in their single-ness by having dinner at the local nose-to-tail hotspot alone. "Let's eat here," I said to Antonia. "I've heard good things."

DESPITE DEE DEE'S claim that this place was impossible to get into, and that she could help because, of course, she knew someone, we only had to wait ten minutes for a table, so we waited at the bar. I had just ordered a glass of wine when I looked over and spotted one of the moms I'd seen at the library before, and I thought I'd seen her once in the drugstore, too, in the aisle that sold children's Motrin and Snoopy Band-Aids. We made eye contact, and I smiled, because that was what you did when you saw someone you recognized in a bar, but she looked away, and I wasn't at all sure why she did that. "I think I know her," I said to Antonia.

"Who is she?" Antonia asked.

"I have no idea," I said. "But I've seen her around. She has a little girl, I think. She has a purple stroller. I've never seen another one like it, so she's hard to forget."

"Why don't you say hello?"

"Why would I do that?" I asked.

"Because that's how you're going to make friends here and stop thinking that the whole world hates you. Come on. Be a grown-up. Go talk to her."

"You make it sound like I'm trying to pick her up."

"You are. As a friend. Go."

"Fine," I said. I had no idea why, other than to say that I felt like I wanted to get better control of my situation instead of sitting around complaining that I had none. I'd just told Owen I was sorry. Now I was going to talk to the stranger with the purple stroller in a bar. Today was a day of many firsts. I took a sip of wine and stepped toward her. "Hi," I said, giving the friendly little wave I imagined I'd give to an actual mom friend if I ever made one. "I'm Claire. I've seen you around town a few times, and once at the library. I think our kids are about the same age. I just wanted to introduce myself."

"Oh," she said with a smirk that was not an appropriate response to my friendly little mom wave. "I think you have me confused with someone else," she said.

"Really? Don't you have a purple stroller?" I asked. I'd assumed anyone who pushed a purple Bugaboo around town was cheerful and friendly and oozed rainbow sprinkles and unicorns. Perhaps I was mistaken.

"I don't think so," she said. She was lying. She was lying to me about the color of her stroller. Why would she do that?

"Oh. Okay, well, then I guess the next time I see you at CVS I won't point out that you actually do have a purple stroller, and that you are who I think you are, and we can pretend that we never had this conversation, for reasons that I don't understand in the slightest, and I don't think I want to," I said. I was bitchy, but I didn't care. I was tired of the mean women in this town kicking me around. So what if my husband left me? So what if I didn't monogram everything in my house or dress my son like Prince George? That didn't mean I didn't have anything in common with the other women here. We were all middle-aged women trapped in suburbia. We should be supportive of each other. Why was no one else seeing that except me?

"Good idea," she answered, because she was done pretending to be polite, too.

"Okay. FYI, if you want to go unnoticed, get a black stroller like everyone else. That purple thing is ridiculous. Anyways, it was nice not meeting you."

I returned to Antonia and before I could say a word the hostess approached and led us through the small room, which was crowded enough, but there were more than a few two-tops available and even one booth, so it seemed like Dee Dee was making herself out to be more important than she actually was. Shocking.

The waiter placed two rustic menus in front of us, though calling it a menu seemed like a bit of a stretch. It was more like a list of five or six things, printed on recycled paper that was supposed to look hip. He filled our water glasses from a carafe, placed a lone roll on each of our bread plates, and disappeared while Antonia and I examined the menu. I quickly snapped a photo of our table and sent it to my mother. I had no idea if she was buying any of this, but for some reason, sending pictures of myself outside of the house felt like sufficient proof that I was moving on.

"What's her name?" Antonia asked as she adjusted her bag on the back of her chair.

"Whose name?" I asked.

"The woman you knew from town?"

"I have no idea. That woman pretended she didn't recognize me. I know she did. She totally knows who I am. She just doesn't want to say hello to me because every horrible girl from high school that you wished you'd never see again once high school was over apparently lives in this town. They probably have monthly meetings and a secret password."

"Why would she pretend to not know you?" Antonia asked, thinking that I was being paranoid, which was totally not true. If you thought the whole world hated you, and they actually did, that made you self-aware, not paranoid.

"Because she's a mean mommy. That's why. She's probably friends with Dee Dee, and therefore is prohibited from speaking to me, and instead of ignoring that mandate and acting like a normal person, she's obeying it and acting like a teenager. This is what I am dealing with, Antonia. I can't even get strangers to be nice to me. It's like *Lord of the Flies* in this town."

"Maybe you have her confused with someone else," Antonia suggested, which was adorable.

"Her stroller is purple. Like My Little Pony purple. Trust me, no one has her confused with anyone else."

"That's how you recognize people these days?"

"Yes. And now is really not the time for more judgment."

"If she pretended she didn't recognize you when she really did, then she's not worth knowing anyway."

"That's how I feel about every woman here! That's why I'll never make any real friends. I'm a pariah. I'm tainted in scandal, and gossip, and at odds with the homecoming queen. No one wants to align themselves with me. I'm a made-for-TV movie, Antonia."

"That's not true."

"Yes, it is," I said. "Owen said we could reevaluate in a year or two. Maybe I only have to tough this out for a year and then we will be in a better place and he'll let me move one town over or something. I don't know. I don't want to talk about it anymore. It's too depressing."

"Okay. What do you want to talk about?"

"Dee Dee told Owen about this place the day I met her. She said he'd love it, you know, because she knows him and what he likes. I guess that goes for restaurants and for underwear, too."

"What? Then why are we here?" Antonia asked. "Claire, you need to stop fixating on her."

"You know what really gets me? When we met I remember thinking that I wanted her to like me. I remember thinking that I wanted to make sure that she knew I wasn't threatened by her, that I was fine with her being there, that she didn't need to treat me like I was radioactive. I thought maybe if I was friendly enough, she'd help me acclimate to the town. But then the waffle thing happened and it became pretty clear that she wasn't interested in helping me acclimate. She was interested in ruining my life, and that makes it kind of hard to forget her. Plus, she was our Realtor. How stupid am I to allow Owen's ex-girlfriend to be our Realtor? I mean, would you have ever done that?"

"No," Antonia admitted. "But I don't trust anyone."

"She helped us buy our house, Antonia. She helped me pick out the home in which she'd eat the waffles and drink the champagne and have the affair that broke up my marriage that ruined my life that killed the cat that ate the mouse that lived in the house that stupid Claire bought. Mother Goose should rewrite her nursery rhymes for me."

"Who cares if you remember meeting her or you don't? None of it is important."

"If we had stayed in Chicago this would never have happened. I think about that all the time. If he hadn't moved here, Dee Dee wouldn't have come back into his life and he wouldn't have cheated on me with her and none of this would be happening. We'd still be married and I'd still be happy and you and I would still be going to spin together instead of sitting in this restaurant talking about purple strollers and slutty Realtors."

"I hate to say this, Claire, but eventually he probably would've met someone else in Chicago. If he was going to cheat he was going to cheat."

"I don't know. He said they had history. Maybe there's something to that. Maybe he would never have cheated with anyone else except her."

"Can we change the topic?" Antonia asked. "Thinking like this is counterproductive. He cheated. He's scum. He's gone."

"You're right," I said. Before we could change the topic, my phone buzzed and I immediately grabbed it. Whenever Owen had Bo, I kept my phone in front of me, in case he needed me in an emergency. I checked the caller ID. It was Lissy.

Are you interested in having a drink later?

I quickly wrote her back: *At dinner right now. Welcome to come over around 9:00 if you're free.*

She replied: *See you then.*

I turned my attention back to Antonia. "I'm sorry about that. Lissy wanted to know if I was around. I told her to come by the house around nine o'clock for a drink. I hope that's okay."

"Of course it's okay. I like her. She's an interesting person. I don't know anyone like her."

"I think she might be part bat," I teased.

"She might be, but I don't mind it. She doesn't care about Dee Dee. She wants to be friends with you, and she's not a mean mommy. So see, not everyone in this town is evil. You just need to seek out the good ones."

"Agreed," I said. I liked that Antonia and Lissy had gotten along so seamlessly. I felt like I had a posse. A misfit posse, but a posse nonetheless.

"What are you going to get?" Antonia asked. "Dinner is on me. If you don't eat, I'm going to be insulted. The pasta looks good. I think I might get that."

I didn't need to read the menu, as I knew what I was having before I stepped foot in this place. I waved politely to the waiter.

"I'll have the bucatini, please," Antonia said. "And we'll have a bottle of the Santa Barbara Pinot Noir."

"Excellent choice, and for you?" he asked.

"I'll have the pig," I said. "I hear you have a wonderful pig, and I'd like for you to bring me its head and its tail. Hell, bring me the feet, too," I said. "I want the pig, the whole pig, and nothing but the pig." Antonia eyed me strangely, which was understandable, since in the course of our thirty-year friendship, I'd never ordered pig feet, or tail, even once. Hard to believe that was possible, I know.

I relaxed into my leather chair, and took a sip of my ice water, which didn't have any ice in it, because places like this charged extra for it. "I'm sorry, ma'am, but it's for two," he said.

"What's for two?" I asked.

"The pig."

"You have a mandatory two-person minimum to eat the pig? Are you kidding?" I asked. "What about the hooves? Can I just have the feet?" I didn't really want the pig feet, but I didn't like being denied what I heard was an outrageous dining experience, just because I didn't have a husband to eat pig with, or because my friend wanted pasta. So shoot me.

"No. You can't have just the feet. You can only order the whole pig, and it's very labor intensive for the chef. It's also a lot of food. We don't like to be wasteful. The meal is for two people. I'm sorry."

"This is unacceptable," I said. *Swoosh, swoosh, swoosh* went my blood as my heart pumped faster once again, indicating the onset of yet another manic episode. "Food should not be reserved for people in pairs. How can you even say that to me? We are in the midst of the most politically correct era in our entire history, and frankly, I find that policy offensive. It discriminates against single people who are willing to pay just as much as married people for an entire pig if they choose to do so. Maybe I can eat the whole pig all by myself, did you ever think of that?"

"I'm sure you can," he said. I didn't like that, either.

"What's that supposed to mean? Did you just make a fat joke?" I asked, which was absurd, because if anything I was too thin at the moment, and I knew it.

"No. Wait, what's happening?" he asked, his eyes pleading for Antonia to help.

"I won't have pasta, okay?" Antonia said, placing her hand gently on my arm. "Let's get the pig for two. No problem. I'm in."

"What about the nose? Can I just eat the snout? How many

people are supposed to share that?" I asked. "Pig schnoz, yum. Can you pair a nice red with it?" I asked.

"I'm sorry," Antonia said to the waiter, who had stopped writing on his tiny little pad, and instead was holding his pen above it, waiting for Antonia to take control. "We will have the pig. Thank you." He nodded, and shrugged, and walked back to the kitchen, and I figured as long as I gave him a nice big tip, I wouldn't have to actually say I was sorry.

"You could have just asked me if I would share it," Antonia said. "I didn't need to have pasta."

"I don't think any item on any menu should be for two people. It's hurtful. I've never noticed this until now, but maybe I'll make this my crusade. I'll take to Twitter and Yelp and OpenTable.com and get restaurants nationwide to allow singletons to order whatever the fuck they want. I'll start a hashtag: #eatme. Do you think it'll go viral?"

Antonia giggled. "The sad thing is, it probably will. You're right, though. If you want to eat the pig, you should be able to eat the pig—married, single, gay, straight, whatever."

"That's what I'm talking about. This is why I need you. You get me."

"It better be good," Antonia said. "I wanted the bucatini."

"I mean, the funny thing is, I don't even really want it."

"Oh my God," Antonia said, resting her head in her hands. "I'm going to kill you."

We laughed. The waiter brought wine. We drank it, and then we laughed again, and it felt really, really good.

Chapter 12

FRED THE ACCOUNTANT was apparently a masochist who got off on pain, humiliation, and suffering, and liked to seek out people who could make his life miserable. He had a penchant for leather chaps, and safe words, and filled a padded room in his basement with various types of perverted sex toys, and really weird porn. This was the only reason that I could think of to explain the fact that Fred called me a week after our date. His still waters must run freakishly deep.

I played the message out loud for Lissy and Antonia to hear while we sat at my kitchen table: *Well, I've never had a first date go quite like that before. If you've come back down to earth give me a call.*

"What the hell is wrong with this guy?" I asked as Bo bounced in his jumper and banged on the piano keys that played the "Can-Can." Antonia sat at the kitchen table working on her laptop, and Lissy sat on the floor near Bo so she could hand him his teething ring, which he dropped every thirty to forty seconds, but she didn't seem to mind.

"I have no idea. You assaulted Owen in front of a roomful of people. I wouldn't call you again," Antonia said. She made it sound like I punched him, or kneed him in his groin, and honestly, I thought she was making it sound more dramatic than it was.

"I'd hardly say it was assault," I said, even though it actually might have been.

"You lunged at him with scissors, Claire. You cut him," Lissy added. "Even I think that's a little crazy, and I once slashed my ex's tires."

"I didn't cut him. I gave him a haircut. Let's not make it sound like I attacked him with a meat cleaver."

"The law doesn't make that distinction," Antonia so nicely reminded me.

"Don't get me started with my problems with the laws in this country, okay? They're all bullshit."

Lissy giggled. "I still can't believe you cut his hair. I mean, it's hysterical."

"It felt good. I'm not going to lie, it felt really, really good, but I shouldn't have done it. What I can't for the life of me understand is why Fred wants to go out with me again. There's no reason on earth why he should ever want to see me again."

"Maybe he likes that you're spunky?" Antonia asked.

"Maybe he's deranged?" Lissy offered. "I've met a lot of guys who look totally cool on the outside, but are all into the Goth thing. You can never tell."

"What am I supposed to do?" I whined, which was silly since this was actually a nice problem to have. I wasn't sure why I was acting like something horrible had happened to me because Fred called. Most girls sat by their phones and came up with a million reasons why a guy didn't call when he said he would: he was hit by a bus, he was in a coma, he was really busy with work. Fred had the luxury of using fear of being assaulted with nail scissors as a perfectly reasonable excuse to pretend he never met me, but he called me again anyway. A lot of people would hear this story and think that I was the luckiest girl in the world—minus the Owen stuff. Still, at least for a little while, they'd envy my voicemail.

"What do you mean?" Lissy asked. "He called you. You call him back. That's how it typically works."

"Nothing about this situation is typical. He has no reason to ever call me again, but he called me again. Which begs the next question: If he was going to call me, why did he wait a week? What, he's a game player? I'm too old for this. If you want to call someone, call. Don't make me wait a week. Why would he do that? Isn't that rude?"

"Wait," Lissy said. "First you said you thought he was weird because he called, and now you're saying you think he's rude for waiting so long to call?"

"Yeah," I said. "Exactly." Lissy looked a bit dumbfounded, which I didn't understand. They were both perfectly legitimate concerns.

"I'm not going to sit here and listen to you talk about which reason you should go with to think that he's the crazy one, when you were the one who went nuts on your date. Either call him, or don't," Antonia said.

"Fair," I replied. I decided to just suck it up and call him. It was time I acted like a grown-up. I hit the call back button on my iPhone and he answered on the second ring. Apparently, Fred felt that he was a grown-up, too, and therefore didn't feel the need to let the phone ring a minimum of three times before answering, even though he did wait a week before placing the call in the first place. Okay, cool. We were both going to be adults about this whole thing. Good to know we were on the same page.

"I'm glad you called," Fred said.

"I honestly can't think of a single reason why," I replied. There was no reason to sugarcoat what happened. I needed to own the crazy. The only way to convince people that you weren't actually crazy was to acknowledge when crazy episodes occurred. I heard that on *Dr. Phil* one day while I was folding laundry. "I'm not sure what to say. I'm so sorry about what happened. There was no excuse for my behavior," I said, even though I still fully believed, in my heart of hearts, that there totally was, but I still shouldn't have done it. "I thought I was ready to go out with someone new, but as it turns out, maybe I'm not."

"You were a little terrifying at dinner."

"I was a lot terrifying at dinner. I know that."

"I'm not the kind of guy who just disappears after a date and doesn't let someone know where I stand with her. Even after one date, you still deserve a phone call."

"Thanks," I said, and realized that this was even worse than I'd originally thought because Fred actually seemed like a nice guy, and I'd just ruined any chance of seeing him again.

"I've never seen anything like that before in my life. But the truth is, up until then I was having a nice night. I thought we were hitting it off. Then you went crazy, and now I don't know what to think."

"I was having fun, too. I really was. Fred, I'm so sorry for making a scene, and for embarrassing you, and for terrifying you at dinner. Believe me when I tell you that I'm not proud of what I did at all. I swear, I'm not usually like that. That was the first time that I've actually seen Owen and Dee Dee in public together. I snapped. There's no explanation for me to give other than to say that I just snapped."

"I take it Owen is your ex-husband and Dee Dee is his down-trade?"

"Yup."

"That must've been pretty awful for you."

"Worse than I expected."

"I get it. Can I ask you a question?"

"There's no restraining order, at least not that I'm aware of."

"No, not that. Do you regret it?"

"Cutting his hair?"

"All of it. Telling her what you thought. Cutting his hair. Finally having the opportunity to get some of what you've been thinking for however many months off your chest. Did it make you feel any better? I'd like to know."

I hesitated, and thought again about the events from a week ago: the ice bucket, the purple bra, the way they sat so close to each other even though there was plenty of room in the horseshoe-shaped booth. I thought about the look on his face when he talked to her, and how it wasn't a look that I'd ever seen before, and I thought about the look on her face when she talked to him, and how it was the same look she had the day I met her, the same day she and Owen reconnected. I thought about the way she touched his hair and leaned in to him as if he'd always really belonged to her, and that our relationship, our marriage was really just the intermission in their adorable, enduring love story. I thought about all of it. Then, I answered honestly.

"It felt amazing," I admitted. "I shouldn't have done it, but I'd do it again. If that makes any sense," I said, realizing that it probably didn't.

"That's what I thought." He laughed. "I've never met anyone like you, Claire. That's for sure. And I don't know if that's a reason for me to hang up this phone and never call you again, or a reason to try and go out one more time."

"You'd be willing to go out again?" I asked. This was unreal. Was it possible that Fred wasn't a porn-loving, safe-word-using freak? Could he just be a really nice guy who'd been through enough of his own drama to know not to judge others when they became wrapped up in their own? Could it really be that simple? I was willing to consider it, but I still wouldn't ever step foot in his basement.

"I'm confused. I've never felt like this before. I don't want to get involved with someone who can be dangerous, or crazy, or both. But I really did enjoy the time we spent together, and I'm not convinced yet that you really are dangerous or crazy. Part of me thinks what you did was hysterical. To be honest, I'm not sure what to do."

"I don't blame you. I can't even believe you called me. I never would've thought you'd want to see me again. All I can tell you is that that night was the culmination of a lot of things, and that I know it's time to let it go. It won't happen again. I'm new to this divorce thing and I'm clearly still trying to figure out how to handle it all."

"It's hard to be on the losing end of a marriage. You're entitled to blow off a little steam, but that was taking it to another level. Like I said, I've never seen anything like it, and I'd thought I'd seen a lot."

"And you never will again. You're a really good guy for being so understanding. I don't think a lot of men would be that way."

"I might be out of my mind, but I think I might actually like to see you again, if you think you're up for it. If you're not, that's fine, but please tell me so that I don't need to worry about something like that ever happening again."

"I'd like that, too," I said. I meant it. "I'm up for it. I promise."

"I'm busy with work for the next few nights, but how would you feel about doing lunch or something next weekend? Would that work?"

"I think that would work. Bo is supposed to be with his dad on Saturday so I won't have to worry about running into Owen. It sounds perfect."

"Great. We'll go somewhere far away. Maybe we can drive to Maryland or something. Do you have any exes there?"

"None."

"Good to know. If no other place in the entire state of Connecticut is safe, we can go to Maryland."

"Sounds like a plan."

"One sign of crazy, though, and I'm done. I'm going to over-look your episode because everyone is entitled to a bad night. One bad night. Not two."

"I hear you. And I agree," I said, but it kind of bugged me. I didn't like being made to feel like I had to be on my best be-havior in order to be worthy of his company. I knew that my behavior was crazy, but he didn't have to keep telling me that. Even lunatics have feelings. "Thanks again for calling, Fred," I said. Just like Fred, I decided to ignore the transgression and let him insult me while simultaneously asking me out again. Once. And only once.

"Thanks for calling me back. I'll talk to you soon, Claire. Have a good one."

I quickly hung up, and placed my phone on the table next to my mug. I was too old to be playing games—that much was true. But, that didn't mean that I had to let him hang up first. "He wants to see me again," I said to an understandably sur-prised Antonia and Lissy. "Maybe I shouldn't go. I should just chalk that date up to a learning experience and move on. What kind of future could I possibly have with someone who knows that I'm capable of assault?"

"You need to go," Lissy said. "Any man who's going to witness a complete meltdown and come back for more is one that you need to get to know better. Actually, he sounds like someone I'd like to get to know better, too. Plus, if you guys get married, I can sell you all of your stationery. We have lots of New York

City–themed stationery that could subtly reference you guys getting together in a bar in Grand Central Terminal—in the middle of the afternoon—on a Monday. Talk about a niche."

"Very funny."

"I'll give you a discount."

"That's no way to get yourself out of the red."

"This should be simple," Antonia said. "Why are you making this a big deal? Just go out with him again and leave the scissors at home. Do you want to see him again?"

I thought about this for a minute. It wasn't an easy question to answer. If I went out with him again I was going to owe him further explanation. It was so embarrassing that it might actually have been better to just pretend that I never got the voicemail. Except, then I didn't get to go on a date with Fred, and Owen was going on lots of dates with Dee Dee, and why shouldn't I level the playing field? It was a totally bizarre motivation for wanting to go on a date with someone, but it was the only thing I cared about. If Owen was dating, then so was I.

"Okay. I'll go," I said. "But he needs to stop calling me crazy. I know in this particular phone call I couldn't defend myself, but if he thinks he's going to be able to insult me like that on a regular basis, this will never work."

"I think under the circumstances it was okay," Lissy said. "If he didn't call you crazy I'd think he was the weird one."

"Claire, have some self-awareness. You've been a little off your rocker," Antonia said.

"I admit I did some things I shouldn't have. I shouldn't have posted that note on his Facebook page. People who we haven't seen in years and never would've known anything had happened started poking around for details. It was a terrible idea. I regret that one big-time."

"And the Craigslist ad?"

"That was funny. But I probably regret that, too. I'm done cyberstalking him," I said. I might have meant it. "From now on I'm only going to use the internet for good, not for evil."

"That's progress. Keep that in mind when you see Fred again."

"I don't get a weird vibe from him," I admitted. "I really don't."

"So go!" Antonia encouraged. "I think this guy sounds like a really good dude. Do you have any idea how easy it would've been for him to run? I'm your best friend, and part of me is a little scared of you now. I like this guy. I want to meet him."

"Why don't you come to lunch with us? So far being completely unconventional is working for me. Maybe I should bring both of you with us."

"I don't do lunch. It's prissy and the lighting is terrible. No candles. Big windows. Cheery waitresses and breadbaskets with mini-muffins. No thanks," Lissy said. "Call me when they dim the lights and break out the hard liquor."

"Are you part vampire or something?" Antonia asked.

"I wish," Lissy answered. I took the wine Antonia poured for me out to the front porch, and sat down on the top step, staring at the glowing lights in the windows of the houses down the block. I imagined that most of the kitchens were bustling with activity, kids doing homework, men coming home from their evening commutes, kicking off their dress shoes, and pecking their wives on the head before they sat down for dinner. There were probably pot roasts, and chickens, and casseroles in the ovens and bulletin boards hanging on the walls next to the refrigerators that listed chores each child was supposed to complete that week in order to claim an allowance. These families had won the lottery—the American dream on a nice quiet street in Connecticut, with a good school district, and playgrounds that were clean, and safe, and free of drug dealers and prostitutes, and porches with swings. Why those houses contained happy families and mine was sad, and empty, I had no idea. I didn't know why they got to live the life I was supposed to have, and I got pushed out onto the curb. I glanced up at the sky, the stars bright, and plentiful, and winking at me like they were in on a secret.

Antonia sat down beside me with her stemless wineglass and tugged at the back of her shirt as it stuck to her neck. The midsummer heat was settling it. It was already the middle of June. Despite the fact that the days often felt endless, I couldn't believe how fast time was going by. "What's wrong?"

My shoulders slumped forward. "Every time I try and do something to help myself I feel like I get knocked down all over again."

"What do you mean?"

"I go to the library, and I run into Dee Dee's friends. I try to move so I can get a fresh start here, and Owen says no. I go on a date, and I run into Owen and Dee Dee. I keep pulling myself up and I keep getting knocked over and I'm so tired, Antonia. I'm so tired of trying. I just need something to go my way. I need to know something is going to work out for me and I swear to God there are some days when I honestly feel like I'm never going to be happy again. Do you have any idea what that feels like?" Of course she didn't. She was beautiful, and employed, and didn't need Spanx to leave the house and those are three of the main ingredients to happiness as far as I'm concerned, so she had no idea what I was going through.

"Fred just called and asked you out again. That went your way," Antonia whispered.

"Did it? What am I even doing with him? Am I ready to be dating?"

"Who's ever ready? It's going to get easier. Just remind yourself that it will never get worse than it is right now."

"I don't think that makes me feel better."

"It should. No place to go but up."

"I guess."

"Come on." She offered her hand and gently pulled me up from the step, brushing invisible dirt off my leg. Before I closed the front door behind me, I tilted my head toward the stars, just so they knew I was aware of their winking, and that I didn't like it one bit.

❧ Chapter 13

I WAS ABOUT to enter Lissy's store the following Saturday morning when my phone beeped. I stopped and pulled it out of the pocket of my tote, and involuntarily smiled when I saw that it was Fred.

So this is me, texting. It feels weird. Did we decide if we need to go to Maryland or not? What time works for you?

I sent him a quick note back: *I'm very proud of you. I was going to help a friend of mine at her store this morning. Want to meet me at The Stationer on Main Street around 1?*

I couldn't imagine how people communicated before text messaging, which was kind of a silly thing for me to say since I fully remembered life before text messaging, and cell phones, and call waiting for that matter, but I still couldn't fathom trying to maintain any kind of romantic relationship without the ability to screen, delay, and craft perfectly worded responses to such deeply personal and intense questions as "What time works for you?" It was a small thing, but I couldn't help but be flattered by Fred's gesture in not calling. I wasn't sure what that said about me.

Sounds good. See you at 1. I'm bringing a metal detector. Consider yourself warned.

I sent him back a smiley face emoji.

Please don't ever do that again.

I laughed. That was much easier than I thought it would be.

The bell chimed when I entered the store around 11:00, but there was no sign of Lissy. She'd cleared off the shelves, all of the merchandise now stored in large brown boxes she bought from the UPS Store. I stepped over one box, losing my footing briefly and stumbling into one of the empty racks. I removed a plastic bag of Clorox wipes from my bag, convinced that once we had swabbed all the shelves clean, the smell of must, calligraphy ink, and yellowed paper would dissipate.

"Hey," she said when she came down the stairs. "I heard the bell. You're early."

"Just a little. I have two fun things for you."

"Really? Let's hear them," she said.

"I spent all of last night trying to find a good canopy for the store once it's no longer called The Stationer. Without a name, it's kind of hard to pick something, so I decided that maybe something simple was best. After careful consideration, what do you think of this one?" I asked, as I handed Lissy my phone to check out the one I'd picked.

"Plain white? You think that's the best we can do?"

"That's the best we can do since we don't know what we're naming the place yet. This way we have an idea of what we want, and we know where we want to order it from, and how much it will cost us. When we name the store we can spice it up with the color of the lettering. I think this is our safest bet. We need to make some decisions or we won't ever get this place put back together in time."

"I like it. It's classy. We really need to come up with a name, though, and soon. It's hard doing all of this work when I don't even know what we're calling this place."

"I know. It will come to us. Don't worry, I think about it all the time. It's only a matter of time before inspiration hits," I said, even though I hadn't been hit by inspiration once in the last ten to twelve years as far as I could remember.

"Okay. What's the second thing?"

"Secondly, guess who is going to meet me here this afternoon?"

"Fred is coming?" Lissy asked. "He's picking you up for your date here? I'm going to meet him?"

"How'd you know it was Fred?" I was marginally disappointed. I was actually hoping she wouldn't guess. At least not on the first try.

"You don't have any other friends. I already know Antonia."

"That's true." I nodded, and thought briefly about whether or not there was anyone else in town I could at least call an acquaintance if not a friend. There wasn't.

"I'm so happy I'm going to meet this dude. Do I look okay?" she asked.

"You look great, but he's not coming here to hit on you."

"Good point. First impressions are important, though. You look great," she said. "Those pants are awesome."

"Thank you!" I felt good and it was nice to know that I looked good, because I was looking forward to this date.

"Now, let's get this place cleaned up."

I went behind the register and began to neatly stack files, before taking them upstairs to Lissy's black hole of an office. The first thing I needed to do was get rid of the paperwork and scan everything electronically. Multicolored folders were strewn haphazardly on the bookshelf next to piles of papers that didn't seem to be in any order whatsoever, and as far as I could tell, there was no functional way to keep track of pending orders or receipts. She didn't have samples of her amazing calligraphy—a huge mistake—so I was going to suggest that she create samples of her different styles that we could scan and send out on an electronic newsletter. Once I was done organizing this office space, I had to figure out what we were going to put in the electronic newsletter, how often we were going to send it, and how we were going to get the email addresses of every woman in town. Considering the amount of spam I got from vendors all over the place, it shouldn't be too hard to purchase a mailing list from one of the other store owners, but people could be weird about things, so I didn't want to count on it. Lately, I went to bed thinking about stationery (or Fred), woke up thinking about stationery (or Fred), and dreamed about fonts, ink colors, and envelope liners (or Fred) during the day. It was actually a pretty great way to go to sleep and wake up—it meant I wasn't thinking about Owen or Dee Dee, and that I had more important things on my mind. I continued to clean, and organize, and file, and stack, because it made me feel good, and because I wanted to stay busy until my date, and because Lissy wanted to make sure that the place looked good for Fred.

Go figure.

"I THINK HE'S here," Lissy squealed as she backed away from the empty store window, finally seeming like the twentysomething girl she was instead of the staid Goth woman she pretended to be. She'd been trying to fake-clean the space with a broom for the last twenty minutes, waiting for Fred to arrive. She leaned the broom against the window just as he opened the door and stepped inside.

"Hey," he said. He leaned over and quickly kissed my cheek, which immediately caused me to blush. "It's good to see you again. I'm so happy this worked out. You look very nice."

"Thanks, thanks for meeting me here. This is my friend Lissy," I said. Lissy took a step closer to me and clasped her hands demurely in front of her, like she was meeting someone's parents and not someone's second date.

"Hi, Lissy, I'm Fred. It's nice to meet you." Fred didn't seem like he was trying too hard. He didn't seem like he was trying at all, which must be nice.

"So you're the guy she picked up in the train station?" Lissy asked. "I've heard a lot about you."

"That's me. Unless she's picked up more than one guy in a train station," Fred answered.

"Hard to say with her. She's so secretive about everything."

"Very funny," I said. "I'll have you know that you're the only person I've ever met in a train station. I met all of the other guys at either the grocery store or the ATM vestibule at the Citibank in town. You were an anomaly."

"Lucky me," Fred said with a smile as he looked around the store. I wasn't sure if he was saying that sincerely or sarcastically, and it was an important distinction because one was really nice and one was really obnoxious and I wasn't interested in an obnoxious accountant named Fred even if the alternative was spending the rest of my life alone.

"You said it," Lissy agreed. I liked that she was looking out for me. I felt like she was the only person in town who really cared about what happened to me, which was weird because I hadn't known her all that long.

"I'm sorry I haven't thought of a name for the store yet. I've been trying, but it's not that easy! You need something fun, and hip, and punchy that also reflects you. It's hard to come up with something that wraps everything up perfectly. You need people to like you, and like the store, and want to shop here, and it needs to be short enough to fit on the new awning. I want it to be perfect."

"I don't care if people like me. I've never cared about what people thought about me. The haters can all kiss my ass as far as I'm concerned."

"Wait. Why can't you use that?" Fred asked.

"With all due respect, Fred, Kiss My Ass might actually be worse than The Stationer. I don't think that's really going to get people through the door," I said.

"Yeah, I know that. Thanks for that staggeringly helpful advice!" Fred answered, teasing me for thinking he'd be that stupid, which I actually kind of liked and immediately put me at ease. Unless, of course, he was being condescending, in which case it would immediately put me on edge. I wasn't sure which one he was aiming for, so I found myself in emotional limbo. I forgot how much I hated dating. "The kiss part. I'm assuming that's your thing, right? Red lipstick?" he asked.

"Why do you say that?" Lissy answered suspiciously. I had a feeling that Lissy was someone who had had her fair share of bullying over the years, and her first reaction to criticism was to assume she was being mocked.

"You're wearing bloodred lipstick. You don't seem like you're shy about your lips."

"No, I guess not," Lissy answered.

"You shouldn't be. You look great," Fred added, and it didn't seem creepy, just a genuine compliment. I saw Lissy relax.

"Thank you. I always wear it. I don't even recognize myself without it."

"I feel that way about Gwen Stefani. I don't recognize her without her red lipstick either," I said.

"You should combine your lips with something that's relevant to sending correspondence," Fred suggested.

"Like what?" we both asked.

"What about Sealed with a Kiss?" Fred said with a shrug.

"Oh my God," Lissy said. "How did I not think of that?"

"It's perfect," I admitted. I had no idea why the two of us weren't able to come up with it, but it took Fred six minutes after meeting Lissy to nail the name of her new store. What was even more strange was that I was kind of proud that he came up with it, and wanted to elbow Lissy in the side like a schoolgirl and say, "See how great my boyfriend is?" Except he wasn't my boyfriend, or even my friend, and if he called me crazy even once today he'd be my nothing whatsoever. Sigh.

"I could use a lip print as my logo, as if I had kissed the paper myself!"

"That's kind of creepy, isn't it?" I asked.

"Yeah, just a little. That's why it's kind of awesome," Lissy said.

"You're not actually going to kiss the paper, though, right?" It seemed like a silly question, but I was sure that when Lissy said she wanted the solar system represented in her earlobe, people thought she was joking, too.

"Can I make a suggestion?" Fred asked before Lissy could answer. I had to make sure to remember to circle back to it.

"Sure," Lissy said. "After that suggestion I'm happy to hear anything you have to say."

"I think you need a face-lift."

"What did you just say to me?" Lissy asked. I watched as Fred heard his own words in his head and shock registered on his face. This would be interesting.

"No! Not you! The store! Sorry, I wasn't clear. The store needs a face-lift. Your actual face is just fine."

"Just fine?" Lissy asked. "Gee, thanks."

"More than fine. It's beautiful," he stammered.

"Are you hitting on my friend right in front of me? Who does that?" I asked.

"Oh my God," he moaned.

"Relax, Fred," Lissy said as she broke into a smile. "I know what you meant."

"So did I," I agreed. "It was just too easy."

Fred laughed. "I'm sorry, I didn't mean it that way. I meant the store could use a little improving."

"We've determined that already, but the budget is a little thin," Lissy said.

"I could help you," he offered, casually, like it was no big deal. It was a big deal. It was a very big deal.

"What do you mean?" I asked.

"You don't need much. The place is small. I think if you ripped up this carpeting it would make a big difference. The stripes are kind of aggressive for a small space. I think it's making it look smaller than it is."

"I wanted to have the floors painted, actually," Lissy informed him. She walked over behind the counter and ran her hands along the glass case. "I think they'd look really great if they were painted a bright color. That's what my mom and I always talked about doing, but I don't have the budget for that right now."

"If you want, I can do it for you. I could ask a buddy to help me rip up the carpeting and I could bring over my drum sander, no problem."

"You have a drum sander?" I asked, about to pitch forward onto the striped carpeted floor. He might as well have just revealed he spoke Portuguese or used to live in a rain forest. I had no idea what a drum sander was, or why he was offering to use it on Lissy's floors when he barely knew me and didn't know her at all, but it sounded like something we would definitely need. In fact, I didn't know how we'd survived this long without one. "Sure," he replied, like that was a stupid question.

"You say that like everyone has that kind of stuff. They don't. I didn't know that you were a Bob Vila kind of guy."

"I told you my father and my brother are in construction. Just because I don't work with them doesn't mean I don't know a thing or two. My father taught me how to do a lot of things. I wouldn't attempt to rewire this place, but sanding, painting, that stuff is easy. I'm happy to help you."

"You'd do that?" I asked, completely incredulous that Fred was offering to help just because he felt like being a nice guy. Were a lot of guys like this? Is that what it was like to be in a normal healthy grown-up relationship? So many questions, and so little time to answer them because my brain was still swimming in the knowledge that Fred was going to help with her renovation because he had a drum sander and because he might actually like me at least a little bit even if he still worried that I might be nuts. This was all so hard to believe.

"I can definitely help. When are you planning on reopening?"

"The weekend after Labor Day and it's almost July. Do we still have time?"

"You have plenty of time, but you should start figuring out what you want the place to look like. I'm happy to help you out. I actually like doing that kind of stuff."

"Wow," I said. "You might be the nicest guy alive, Fred."

"I don't know what to say. You can have free stationery for life," Lissy offered.

"You guys are easy to please," he said.

"I know we just met, and I don't mean to be greedy, but do you think you'd be able to install a new awning for us above the door, too?" I asked.

"If I say no, are you going to assault me with a letter opener?" Fred asked.

"Maybe," I answered. Still confused. Still very, very confused.

"Then I should probably say yes. Where is it?" Fred asked.

"We don't have it yet, because the store didn't have a name until five minutes ago. I can order it right now and it will be here in three to four weeks!" I grabbed my phone and pulled up the commercial canopy website that I'd bookmarked for Lissy. In five minutes, Fred had turned all of our lights green, and I felt like we were finally able to move the big pieces into place. I filled out the online form, entered my credit card, and submitted my order. Just like that, a commercial canopy would soon be coming our way, and it was all because I'd decided to get a facial on Owen's credit card and then picked up a guy in Grand Central Terminal.

"It's official," I said. "We have a name, and an awning, and a general contractor who's willing to work for free. Now all I have to do is sign S.W.A.K. up on all the social media platforms and start hashtagging this place into oblivion, and we'll be in business! Well, first we need to reopen the business, and then we'll be in business."

"Is this really happening? We really are going to have a new awning and new floors, for the newly named store, just like that? Those were the big problems that have been hanging over my head, and I didn't have any idea how to fix them. Did you really just come in here and solve all of the remaining problems?"

"Looks that way," Fred agreed. "I must be one hell of a guy."

"You said it," Lissy agreed. "If you weren't having lunch with Claire, I'd ask you to lunch myself and you're not even my type. No offense," Lissy said. She gave Fred a quick hug. "Thank you, thank you, thank you." She sighed. "You have no idea how much this means to me."

"You're welcome. Now, speaking of lunch, Claire, are you ready to go?"

"I am, except I don't know where to go. I'd rather not go to the oyster bar, if that's okay."

"I don't like oysters anyway. Fine by me," Fred said. He just kept getting better and better. Next he'd tell me that he hates purple lingerie and real estate agents and then I'd have no choice but to propose.

"The pizza place around the corner is really good," Lissy suggested. "Why don't you go there? They have tables in the back."

"And plastic utensils," I added. "So you can be sure of your safety."

"Nah, I'm not worried. I'm betting that you've gotten out most of your aggression for the time being."

"If not for life," I said.

"I'm good for pizza if you are," Fred said.

"Pizza sounds perfect."

Fred opened the door for me and we walked around the corner to grab pizza for lunch—a most unlikely pair that somehow seemed to fit just right.

"SO, SHOULD WE address the elephant in the room now, or do you want to wait until after a slice of pepperoni?" I asked as I carried my two slices of pizza on a red plastic tray over to a small booth in the corner next to the refrigerator case that held nineteen different kinds of soda and a few bottles of water. Fred slid into the booth across from me and sprinkled red pepper flakes on top of his slice. "I still can't believe I didn't scare you away."

"Like I said, I think everyone handles the stress of divorce differently, and that night obviously didn't go well for you."

"No, it didn't. But I don't want to have to relive it for the rest of my life. I'd like to not talk about it again after today if that's okay," I said, then caught myself. "Assuming that we ever talk again after today. Which we may not. I get that, too."

Fred smiled. "I was having a nice time up until that point and I have to admire your passion and your spunk. You're not a wallflower. That's not a bad thing. You just need to rein it in a little . . . or a lot."

"Yeah, here's the thing about me. There are two kinds of crazy girls in the world."

"I'm pretty sure there are more than two kinds," he interrupted.

"No, hear me out. There's the good crazy kind and the bad crazy kind. I'm the good crazy kind."

"What does that mean exactly?"

"I understand your skepticism. Allow me to explain," I said.

"Okay."

"The good crazy kind is the kind that will make you laugh, and keep things interesting, and pretend you insulted her and her friend when you accidentally tell her she needs a face-lift. The bad crazy kind will slash your tires and hack your Facebook."

"And you're the good crazy kind."

"Right," I said. It didn't seem necessary to admit that I'd also hacked Owen's Facebook, because I'd already admitted that that wasn't a good idea and didn't plan on doing it ever again. No one has to admit all of their mistakes on the second date . . . or ever.

"Okay, but I would argue that the bad crazy kind think they're the good crazy kind because they don't have the self-awareness necessary to know that they're nuts. So all crazies think they're good crazy, and no one thinks they're bad crazy, so how am I supposed to be comforted by your explanation?"

"Excellent question. You'll just have to go with your gut."

"And my gut is both intrigued and terrified. So you see, I'm at a crossroads."

"I get that, and I don't want you to think that I'm a loose cannon. But, I also don't want to harp on it because to be honest, I think we've spent enough time talking about divorce since we met, and I much prefer the conversation we were having about s'mores instead. Just know that I'm embarrassed and that it's not something that's happened before. I'm sorry I did that to you. I feel terrible, and that's all I can really say."

"I think there were more than a few women in that restaurant who would've stood up and applauded you for having the guts to do that to your ex. I'm sure most women fantasize about doing something like that."

"That's sad, isn't it?"

"Definitely, but it's still true."

"So you're willing to accept the possibility that I'm not a total psycho?"

"I think so. As of now. But I reserve the right to change my mind if you start to show signs of crossing over to the dark side."

"I can live with that."

"Then should we pick up where we left off?"

"Ski houses and s'mores?"

"Where all good stories begin."

"What do you like to do on your weekends? I know you own a drum sander, and I know that you can do some basic construction work and some more-than-basic mathematics, but what do you do when you're not doing either of those things?"

"I run a lot. I've run the New York City Marathon twice and I like to play tennis, and water ski, and rock climb. I like to be outside. I think I spend so much time at my desk during the day that if I'm given the opportunity to be outdoors I usually like to take it."

"You rock climb? Like up mountains? That scares me to death. How do you do that?"

"It's not scary! It's totally invigorating. You really get to appreciate the beauty of nature when you're above it looking down. The vantage point is like nothing you've ever seen. You should really think about trying it sometime."

"I don't think climbing mountains is in my future, but then again, I didn't think most of what's now in my future was in my future until a few months ago. So, who knows?"

"You might surprise yourself someday," Fred offered.

"Maybe. But until then, I'm all for doing things outside, but on the ground. Had I known this about you I would've suggested we take our pizza to the park and have a picnic instead."

"I'm a big fan of pizza picnics," Fred admitted. "With beers. There's nothing wrong with my soda, but can we both agree that pizza really should be consumed with a beer?" he asked as he picked up his paper cup and took a sip of his Coke through a straw.

"Agreed. Though I'd say beer or wine. If it's cold outside is there anything better than deep-dish Chicago pizza and a big glass of red? I'll save you the trouble of answering, the answer is no. There's not."

"I don't like deep-dish pizza. I need to put that out there off the bat because I know for someone from Chicago that can be a deal breaker. Pizza shouldn't be eaten with a knife and fork."

"I can't have this debate anymore. We can just agree to disagree that Chicago pizza and New York pizza both have a place in this world, and I like to enjoy New York pizza when the better kind isn't available."

Fred laughed. He dabbed his chin with a napkin and

laughed at my joke and there was nothing better than having your date laugh at your joke when until then you'd been worried he thought you belonged in a straitjacket. "Okay. We agree to disagree."

"Good. So that's settled."

"Do you think we should agree to go on another date? I think this one went much better than the first one. Maybe we should stick to more casual venues for a while. That restaurant is very good, but it's formal and maybe it was just too stressful, all things considered. From this point on I think we should keep things fun and stress-free. What do you think of that?"

"I think that sounds like an awesome idea. Do you think we can do it?"

"I like our odds," Fred said. We finished our pizza and threw our paper plates in the garbage can by the front door.

"Shall we start with a walk?" I asked, because that seemed to fit our newly established criteria. "It's a beautiful day today. How would you feel about walking over to the park at the other end of town?"

"Sure," Fred said. "I'd like to hear more about your life in Chicago. Do you miss it?"

"Oh, Fred," I said as we stepped outside into the afternoon sunshine and ambled toward the other end of town. "That question becomes harder to answer by the minute."

Chapter 14

"HOW COME YOU never told me about this place?" Antonia asked as I pulled my Volvo into a parking spot toward the end of The Organic Farmer's crowded lot. Antonia opened the back door and unclipped Bo from his car seat. I'd ordered him a new outfit from Polo online, little khaki shorts and a short-sleeve golf shirt with navy blue stripes and an orange pony on the pocket. He looked like a little leprechaun, all chubby and rosy and adorable, and I had to keep myself from squeezing him to death every time I picked him up.

"Because the organic milk here costs about eight dollars and I find the whole place pretentious and annoying. I don't care if the cows only listened to Chopin while they were being milked. It doesn't justify the price tag."

"Then try not to run out of milk again," Antonia offered.

"Touché." I removed a cart from the rack out front and Antonia grabbed a basket, and I handed Bo a teething biscuit from my purse as I placed him in the seat, because I didn't want him to have an episode in the store and force me to buy him a ten-dollar teething cookie just to keep him quiet.

"So are you guys dating? If I ask you if you're dating someone, would you say yes?" Antonia asked, which made me feel like a teenager in a good way.

"I don't know! How many dates do you have to go on before you can consider yourself dating someone?"

"I have no idea. Probably more than two."

"Then ask me again after date three. Maybe I'll have an answer."

"Okay. I'm glad you had a nice lunch," Antonia said. "Now, if we are going to have a proper Fourth of July barbecue we'll need hamburgers."

"We'll also need a barbecue, and I don't think you can get one of those here," I added.

"You don't have a barbecue?"

"No. I don't grill."

"Well, then we will have Fourth of July pasta salad."

"Right. Because nothing says American independence like fusilli."

"Then you should've bought a barbecue!" Antonia chimed.

"Fair. Hey, can I ask you something?" I asked as we pushed a cart down the produce aisle that was filled with produce I'd never heard of before. Bo dropped his cookie on the floor, and it broke in half, causing him to whimper and whine until I pulled a second one from my purse and handed it to him.

"Okay," Antonia answered. She picked up a giant bunch of basil and dropped it in a plastic bag.

"You're a total foodie, right?"

"All Italians are foodies."

"When I was little, my mother would sit me in her shopping

cart, and we would go grocery shopping, right? No big deal, just a little slice of Americana in the Midwest. Good times."

"Right," she said.

"We would buy your basics: apples, pears, maybe peaches or cherries in summer, and sweet potatoes in winter, and that was about it. Now, I look around the produce aisle and have no idea what half of the stuff is, or why we're supposed to be eating it. What happened to the apples, and the pears, and the lettuce? When did kumquats, and fiddlehead ferns, and kabocha squash replace them? What the hell is a kabocha squash? I pay attention to what I eat, but isn't this whole craze becoming just a little overdone? I mean, can you even buy apples here?"

"I'm sure you can, but they won't be local since it's not apple season. They probably bring them in from Washington."

"Are kumquats local? Because I can buy them."

"I have absolutely no idea, but I'm going to guess no," she said. She picked up a mango, smelled it, and returned it to the pile. "This mango probably wasn't grown in Connecticut either."

"That's the point. Furthermore, let me ask you this: Why is it cool all of a sudden to eat vegetables that aren't the color they're supposed to be?" When you didn't leave the house for a while, when you didn't have human contact, when you stepped back from the monotony of day-to-day living, you started to notice very strange things.

"What are you talking about?" she asked.

"Look at this," I said. I picked up a pack of albino asparagus, thin, and pale, and sad-looking. "White asparagus. What's wrong with the green asparagus? Isn't it supposed to be green? Aren't we all supposed to be eating more things that are green? So why is this white now?" I gestured to an entire section of cauliflower in various colors: yellow, and purple, and green. "That cauliflower is supposed to be white, but white is the only color not represented here. Most of this cauliflower is green. Which makes no sense. The carrots are purple, the eggplants are white, but in the world I grew up in, eggplants should be purple and carrots should be orange. Which begs the next question: What color are the oranges these days?"

"Orange," Antonia answered.

"Well, thank God there are still some things in life on which I can rely," I said. I dropped two oranges in my cart, just because they were still orange, and I wanted to be supportive of their authenticity.

"Have you been watching *Seinfeld* reruns in bed at night?"

"I'm just saying I think it's silly people are falling all over themselves to pay these prices for vegetables just because they're not their normal color. It's a trend in stupidity. You heard it here first."

"Noted. Kale is still green, if that makes you feel better."

"Don't even get me started on kale. Kale is just a snobby woman's spinach."

"Okay, then. While you continue to wage a little private war with the produce section, I'm going to go check out the sushi bar. I'll pick us up some lunch."

"Sounds good," I said. Antonia grabbed her green plastic basket off the floor, and turned the corner toward the sushi bar, while I headed due north toward the organic, whole grain, flax seed–infused bread, and the juice bar, because the bottled water was right behind it.

I froze as I passed the papayas because Dee Dee and Stephanie were standing right in front of me, and I was afraid to move. They'd just come from a yoga class (obviously), and I knew that because they were all wearing Lululemon yoga pants and tank tops (obviously), and they were waiting on line at the juice bar for freshly pressed green juice (obviously that, too).

I saw another of Dee Dee's friends, drinking her juice and pushing her cart through the bulk nut section while talking into a headset on her phone. I didn't think she saw me, so I was able to turn my cart in a none-too-graceful three-point turn, and head down the brown rice, quinoa, and gluten-free pasta aisle, but before I got to the end, Stella passed me heading toward the free-range rotisserie chickens. Shit. This was not good, because now they were flanking me and essentially boxing me in where I stood.

I assumed Antonia was still somewhere in the section of the store dedicated to the South Pacific, and I had no idea which way to go to try and find her, while also not running into one of Dee Dee's minions. Stephanie, last I saw her, was heading toward the chia seeds, flax seeds, and hemp seeds, which were directly in front of me. I thought it was better to just stay still and play defense, and wait for one of them to make the first move toward the nut milks so that I could make a run for the exit. I didn't want to see Dee Dee. I didn't have anything to say to her, and I didn't want her to remind me that I acted like a crazy person the last time she saw me, and I thought it was just better if we kept in our corners and avoided all future interactions entirely. Three minutes passed and I was still immobile in the aisle. How long could one person possibly shop for chia seeds? Were there really that many different kinds? I was trapped. Any minute one of them was going to turn her cart down this aisle, and I was going to be cornered. It was like Ms. Pac-Man with shopping carts, and Dee Dee and her friends were the little ghosts that wanted to chase me, and catch me, and devour me in the aisle that contained brown rice syrup and agave.

I quickly crossed the main aisle and headed back toward the produce section near a display of heirloom tomatoes. I quickly realized that the tomatoes didn't provide the air cover I required, and so I moved over to the next display, a giant wall of organic avocados from Mexico. There was nowhere to go. Odds were slim that I could make it to the registers or the parking lot without running into one of them, and I couldn't hide by the avocados forever because it was only a matter of time before one of them came over here looking for the purple carrots, which were located right behind me. I glanced at Bo in his preppy little outfit, absorbing all the colors and shapes and sounds of the grocery store. I bent over to kiss his head, and in that split-second, he lunged over the side of the cart and grabbed an avocado from the middle of the pile, causing the produce Jenga stack to come crumbling down around us. "Oh, no, Bo! No, don't touch those!" I called as I grabbed his hand, but it was too late. No less than ten bumpy black ovals went rolling in opposite directions. I dropped to my knees and reached for the three that were about to cross into the center aisle when I heard a voice behind me.

"Claire?" Dee Dee asked. "What are you doing down there?"

I looked up and saw Dee Dee and Stella standing behind me. "Nothing," I said casually, as if people crawled around on the floor here every day. "Bo knocked over a few avocados. I'm just picking them up."

"I'm glad I ran into you," she said quietly, which was funny as I was thinking the exact opposite of that.

"I can't say the same."

"I know what you think about me." She was being aggressive, too aggressive for my taste, and it caught me off guard. I was prepared for a horribly awkward encounter, I was not at all prepared for a confrontation. Stella glanced at me sympathetically, but she didn't so much as say "hello." She just stood there awkwardly, holding on to her cart, which contained a rotisserie chicken, a bottle of coconut water, and, I imagined, her spine.

"I doubt that. Otherwise you wouldn't be talking to me right now."

"I'm going over to the frozen section," Stella said as she turned and hurried away. I wished they'd all just stay in the frozen section. I was never going over there, because I tried to avoid waffles now at all costs, and I would've been able to make it to the parking lot without any of them seeing me if they'd just steer clear of the produce, but that apparently was too much to ask.

"Hi there, Bo. How are you today?" she asked sweetly, except it was the most horrific sound I'd ever heard in my life.

"Don't say his name. Don't you dare say his name," I hissed. I squeezed my eyes closed. I could handle her. I could handle them, but the sound of her saying my little boy's name made me murderous. I tensed every muscle in my body at once, willing myself to stay silent, and still, knowing that if I gave in to my impulse to smash her head into the avocados, I'd eventually come to regret it, though probably not for many, many years. My legs burned as I squeezed my calves, my thighs, my glutes, my hamstrings, and my toes, all at the same time. Stomach acid churned, and fizzed, and burned the bottom of my throat, my ears turned hot with rage, and my vision became blurry and clouded by tears.

"I'm not a bad person. I didn't just swoop in and break up your marriage for kicks," Dee Dee said.

"Except you did."

"No, I didn't," Dee Dee responded, which really was astounding, all things considered.

"Are you really doing this right now? Here?" I asked. This was exactly what I didn't want. I didn't want to bear witness to Dee Dee's confession, or listen to the ramblings of a crazy, beach-waved lunatic.

"We're in love. I've always been in love with him. He was the one who got away. When we reconnected we both realized that we were meant to be together. I'm not just some girl who sleeps with random married men. Owen and I are kindred spirits. It's not something that either of us could deny. We're star-crossed."

I didn't know what to do, or what to say, or how to react, because I was having a hard time understanding how she could be so crazy that she'd stop and try to convince me that she wasn't a bad person, and that it wasn't her fault that she broke up my marriage because the universe gave her the thumbs-up to do it. Apparently, my marriage was just a brief intermission in Owen and Dee Dee's enduring love story. This was new news.

"He didn't get away. He got married. To me. He had a child, with me. He had a life, with me. You can tell yourself whatever you want, but don't think for one minute that I don't see you for exactly what you are. But anyway, I don't care, Dee Dee. I really don't care because I'm over it. Tomorrow is Independence Day and that's exactly what I'll be celebrating—my independence. I don't care what you do or what you say anymore. In fact, I never really did," I lied, but it sounded so perfect that I couldn't resist adding it in.

"I'm sorry for what happened to you. But I thought you should know that we're in love. It's not a fling. He was always supposed to be with me. I'm sorry you had to get hurt for that to happen."

Before I could speak, Antonia appeared at my side. "Oh my God. You're Dee Dee," she said. "Why are you talking to her, Claire?"

"She was just telling me about how Owen was the one who got away and that they're meant to be together," I said. "Romeo and Juliet in Darien, Connecticut. Who knew?"

"Did you seriously just say that? To his wife?"

"This conversation is between Claire and me," Dee Dee said, which wasn't really true because I wanted no part of it to begin with.

"Well, Claire's marriage was between her and Owen, but that didn't keep you from getting involved in that, did it?"

Score one: Antonia.

"This has been hard on me, too, you know. You're not the only one who's dealing with a difficult situation," Dee Dee reminded me, because things had apparently been so very, very hard on her.

I couldn't stand to do this for one more second. "Look, Dee Dee, I don't care what you have to say to me. I don't want to hear it. If you want to know what I think of you, I'll tell you: I think you're devious, I think you're trampy, and I think you're demented if you thought that talking to me in this grocery store was going to do anything to change my mind about either of those two things."

"I'm sorry you feel that way," Dee Dee said. "It's not true. Know that."

"I don't think she's all there in the head, Claire," Antonia said, and I agreed. I was starting to contemplate the possibility of shoving her face into the sustainable lobster tank in aisle five. I felt very strongly that I would never, ever come to regret that.

"Let's go," I said. "We need to prepare for our non-barbecue."

"That's your cue to get out of our way," Antonia added. Dee Dee turned and walked in the other direction, while Bo continued to lunge at the hundreds of avocados now located just out of reach. Dee Dee held her head high as she left, but I knew that Antonia had intimidated her, at least a little bit. And that made me happy.

"Do you believe that?" I asked, as we quickly beelined for the registers. "Oh my God, I didn't want to talk to her, Antonia. I never wanted to talk to her again. That's exactly why I don't like to leave the house. See? This is what I'm talking about. All I wanted to do was buy a few groceries. Was this type of ambush really necessary?"

"I can't believe that happened. Why wouldn't she just walk away?" Antonia asked, almost as incredulous as I was. "Why didn't she hide somewhere and wait for you to leave? What kind of mistress seeks out a discussion with the ex-wife?" All of Antonia's questions were valid, but I didn't have answers for any of them.

"Let's just go home," I said. I ran for the register, throwing my items on the conveyor belt from two feet away so that the clerk could ring up my items promptly, and then I could promptly get the hell out of there. He bagged my seven items, placing them in a brown bag made of recycled paper (because, of course it was), and then told me that I owed him forty-one dollars (because, of course that, too).

I hurried through the parking lot toward my car, which was parked way too far away. Antonia chased after me carrying Bo and a bag of groceries but I kept moving. "Claire, wait," she called, but I was moving forward, and only forward, and I wasn't stopping for anyone.

I continued to move with my grocery bag in my hand and

my eyes dead ahead. "I don't know what the problem is. I don't know what's going on here at all, but I am pretty sure I've fallen through a wormhole, and we're living in a bizarre universe where my husband leaves me and I'm the one somehow in the wrong. I can't take this, Antonia. I can't. I've tried to hold it together, even though I know that there are some days that you have to drag me out of bed, and that I never do the laundry, and that I ran out of milk this morning. I'm not proud of any of that, but I am trying. I really am." I started to sob, and then immediately hated myself for crying for the millionth time, because it was the millionth time, and it was really starting to get old. "And then days like today happen, and all I want to do is go home, and give up, and admit defeat because I will never belong here and that's probably a good thing. Dee Dee just told me that she and Owen are in love and are meant to be together and I guess that's supposed to make everything better, huh? What's next? What the hell is going to go wrong next?"

I heard a noise, and then something hit the top of my foot. I looked down, and discovered that my bag had ripped. The recycled paper handle on the recycled paper bag that was weak, and cheap, broke in the parking lot, and my three-dollar Mexican avocados rolled away on a dirty American parking lot and disappeared under a German sports car. I dropped to my knees, futilely reaching for the stupid produce I just purchased that was now trying to escape me: avocados, a Granny Smith apple I wanted to puree for Bo's breakfast, and two oranges just because they were still orange, and I wanted to be supportive.

Chapter 15

"ARE YOU HOME? I rang the bell three times. Where are you?" I asked. I stood on Owen's stoop on Saturday afternoon and adjusted Bo's shorts, more than a little annoyed that Owen couldn't even be bothered to be on time when he knew I was going to drop off Bo and see his apartment. As much as I kind of wanted to see his apartment, I kind of didn't want to see his apartment at all. It might answer some questions, but it would raise a lot of new ones. I didn't really feel like adding more question marks to my life at the moment. Still, I stood there, waiting for Owen because I said I would, and one of us still believed in following through on our promises.

"I'm so sorry. I'm stuck in traffic, but I'll be there in about fifteen minutes. I left the door open. Did you try it?"

"No, Owen. I didn't try to let myself into your house. I thought that would be breaking and entering."

"Please go inside. I don't want you guys standing in the rain. I'll be there as soon as I can. Make yourself some tea. I have some in the cabinet."

"Okay," I said. I hung up, and pushed open the door, pausing to stroke Bo's head and watch to see if he registered any familiarity with this place whatsoever. "So this is where you and Dad hang out, huh?" I asked, tickling him under his chin and causing him to squeal. I moved slowly as I walked around the living room, as if I was afraid someone was going to jump out of the closet and scare me. Owen's apartment wasn't what I was expecting. It was neat, and organized, and the couch was corduroy, not leather, and there was milk in the fridge and cereal in the cabinet and I knew I shouldn't have been snooping, but I convinced myself that I was only doing what any responsible mother would do when allowing her infant to stay in a new place. The walls were bare, but there was a picture of Bo, framed, sitting on the coffee table next to the remote control and a copy of *Sports Illustrated*. The floor was covered with a beige area rug and Bo's play mat was tucked under the window, just waiting for his arrival. I walked down the hall and stopped in Bo's bedroom, which was, just as Owen promised, a complete replica of his room at home, except for the glider that Antonia had given me, and the elephant night-light I recently ordered from a catalog that Owen doesn't know exists. I liked that Owen had taken the time to make this room comfortable for Bo. I hated the thought of him going to sleep without seeing my face and it did help knowing that he'd be comfortable in his room, even if I wasn't the one tucking him in his crib.

I paused for a few seconds before I could bring myself to stick my head in the bedroom. It felt strange seeing where Owen slept without me. It looked like a typical bachelor's bedroom: a bed with white sheets, a duvet with no cover, a pillow with no case. I wondered how he felt crawling into it at night, knowing that he'd never climb into our bed with me again. I wondered if it hurt him to think about it at all, or if Dee Dee's giraffe legs erased the nostalgia before it got the chance to fully take hold. There weren't any overt signs of a woman spending time here: no clothes lying around, no shoes on the floor, no jewelry on the dresser. I didn't bother snooping around the bathroom, where maybe there'd be a toothbrush, or more likely, a curling iron, because it didn't matter. I already knew Dee Dee was in his life. Seeing her artifacts in his apartment wasn't going to tell me anything I didn't know.

But his computer would.

I wouldn't have done it. I would never have checked his computer if it wasn't sitting open on his dresser, begging me to push the button to see what came up. I remembered what I said to him when I discovered the affair, when I'd asked how it happened, how they were possibly able to carry on for months without my ever noticing. *You started flirting with your ex-girlfriend on email. That's just awesome. I don't know about it because I'm not the kind of wife who feels the need to search your computer while you're in the shower.* I wasn't the type of wife to ever do that, but I was absolutely the type of soon-to-be-ex-wife to do it. No question.

I never knew Owen's email password, but I knew his habits, and he was as likely to have his Gmail account open on his desktop as I was to have kids' clothing websites up on mine. "Should we do this, little man?" I whispered, because I wanted some kind of affirmation from someone that it was okay to read Owen's email, even if the someone was a baby with no verbal communication skills. So, I answered for him. "You're right, I think we should, too."

I didn't know what I was looking for until I found it. I guess that was how it worked in these situations. I typed Dee Dee Haines into the search box and hit enter, holding my breath while I waited for the messages to populate. There they were, the entire secret relationship of Owen and Dee Dee on email, scrolling in front of me in chronological order. I wanted to stop, but I couldn't. Instead, I paged down until I got to the earliest messages, and one by one began to click and read, until I couldn't bring myself to read any more.

The week after we moved to Connecticut.

OWEN: *Thanks for the offer, but I'm going to be home tonight. Why do you want to get a drink with me? I'm just a boring married guy.*

DEE DEE: *You've never been boring. Come on, it will be like old times. Just one drink. You don't even have to tell Claire. I'll have you home before dinner.*

OWEN: *You know you're the only girl who ever broke up with me, right?*

DEE DEE: *One of my biggest regrets. I shouldn't have ever let you go.*

Then, the next day.

OWEN: *I must have lost my mind. I'm married, Dee Dee. I'm married and I love my wife and whatever happened between us was a one-time thing and it can't happen again.*

DEE DEE: *If you didn't still have feelings for me you wouldn't have come over. You're not being honest with yourself.*

OWEN: *I can't do this.*

Then, the week before I discovered the affair.

DEE DEE: *I hate you spending so much time with Bo when I've never had a chance to get to know him. He's important to you, so he's important to me. Why don't you book Claire a hotel and send her into the city so we can have some alone time?*

OWEN: *She would love that.*

DEE DEE: *What girl wouldn't? Let me know when it's booked. I'll come over and we can spend the whole day and night together. I hate only being able to see you for short periods of time. I hate having to hide from everyone.*

OWEN: *I'll think about it. I'm married, Dee. Let's not pretend like you didn't know that when you pursued me.*

DEE DEE: *I know. I'll take you any way I can get you. But it doesn't mean I have to like it. Think about it. It'll be good for us to spend some time together with the baby.*

I'd been wondering where Dee Dee got the idea that she and Owen were star-crossed lovers or something, and that that somehow made her less of the villain in this soap opera, and I'd just found it. She had a plan all along; from the second we met outside of our house, she knew she was going to go after Owen, pregnant wife or not. There was no point in reading any more. I knew everything I needed to know, and plenty that I didn't need to know, and I knew that I didn't want to know anything else. I was about to close the computer. I was going to close it and walk away, but I couldn't resist taking a picture of the email chain before I did. It didn't seem fair that Owen got to keep his secrets, and I was tired of things being unfair. I closed the laptop and hurried back out to the living room.

I was sitting on the couch when Owen entered ten minutes later. "I'm so sorry about that," he said. "Figures I'd get stuck in traffic the day you were coming over. Did you make yourself tea?"

"No. I'm okay," I said, even though I wasn't. What did the messages tell me? Did it make the situation better or worse to know that Dee Dee had orchestrated everything, and that if she had just left him alone maybe our family would still be intact? Did it matter? Should it? I didn't know. There was no benefit to my knowing how it all unfolded. There was only new pain, and more questions, and I didn't want either of those things. I should've left the computer alone.

"What do you think of the place?" Owen reached over and pulled Bo from my lap, and I had to fight every instinct I had to not hold him tighter, to not use him as a security blanket to comfort me as my hands trembled, but I didn't. Like so many things this last year, I had to let him go.

"It's nice. Bo's room is perfect. You were right to do that," I admitted.

"Thanks. That means a lot."

"You have diapers and everything? I didn't look in his changing table, but I assume you're well stocked. I put some in the bag anyway, if you need them."

"Thanks. I have some, but you can never have too many, right?"

"There's Tylenol in there, too. He hasn't been sleeping well lately."

"Those teeth are giving you a hard time, little man, huh?" Owen asked. He held Bo over his head and made airplane noises, and Bo kicked his little feet and giggled and I gritted my teeth and nearly choked on a scream.

"I ran into Dee Dee in the grocery store," I said. I wasn't sure why I wanted him to know, or what I wanted him to do, but I told him anyway.

"You didn't cut her hair, did you?" he joked. I wasn't in the mood to laugh.

"No, Owen. She did tell me that you two were in love, and that I should stop making things so difficult for you, because, you know, this has been hard on her."

Owen put his head in his hands for a second, and instinctively went to push the hair out of his eyes, until he realized it was no longer there. "She shouldn't have done that. I have no idea why she would say that to you, but I'm sorry. I'll talk to her."

"Don't talk to her," I ordered. "I don't need you to fight my battles for me. I just thought you should know that she had no problem confronting me while I was shopping with Bo. You got yourself a real keeper. You guys enjoy your night."

"I'll see you tomorrow when I bring Bo home," Owen said. "And then on Monday, I guess." Monday was it. The day we finally signed our divorce papers. It took four months for us to dissolve our marriage. It didn't make a difference at this point, we were already living separate lives, but the finality of it made something inside ache. "Thanks for coming over. I hope you like it, and that it makes you feel a little better about things."

"Yeah, Owen," I said on my way out the door. "I'm so happy I came. I feel much, much better now."

"WE WERE BEGINNING to wonder if you were still coming," Lissy said when I came busting through the door of the fabric store at 6:00 P.M. "They close at seven. We don't have all that much time so talk and look at the same time."

She handed me a large book filled with fabric swatches. I was meeting Antonia and Lissy at a store called Fancy Fabrics to look for something we could use to upholster the chairs we still hadn't bought. I joined them at a long rectangular counter in the middle of the store, covered with brightly patterned bolts of fabric and more than a few books of samples we could browse through in the hopes of finding something we liked. After leaving Owen's, I briefly thought about bailing on this appointment, but then decided that being alone wasn't all that great of an idea, and besides, how long could it possibly take to pick out fabric for chairs?

"I'm sorry, Owen was late," I said. I picked up a hot pink bolt of cotton and threw it to the side. "No way. This is way too bright."

"How did it go? How's the apartment?" Antonia asked.

"The apartment is fine. It's a bachelor pad with a fully decorated nursery. That's not the problem."

"What happened?" Antonia asked again. "What about this one?" She held up a bright orange and red paisley that was nice and cheerful, but probably too busy for multiple chairs. "You think this would be better as an accent fabric?"

"Probably," I agreed. "Lissy, what do you think?"

"I hate orange," she stated.

"Okay, well, there goes that," Antonia said as she placed the roll on the floor.

"I read his email," I admitted. "I read his email and I saw everything. All of the emails from the beginning. She seduced him, you guys. Originally, he said no, that he was married, and he resisted it but she wore him down. It's all there on Gmail—every sickening detail."

"What possessed you to read his emails?" Antonia asked. She'd completely lost interest in the fabric, which was fine, because so had Lissy. "I thought you said you were over the cyberstalking!"

"This is nothing like the cyberstalking. This is not a Facebook hack. The emails were sitting right in front of me. Well, they were right in front of me once I opened his computer and searched for them."

"Oh God," Antonia moaned.

"How was I not supposed to read them?"

"Nothing good was going to come of that!" Antonia said, which seemed silly because nothing good had come from any of this so that really wasn't surprising.

"Are you kidding?" Lissy asked. "Are you honestly telling me that you wouldn't have done the same thing? I so would've read them. He lost his right to privacy where she's concerned. I went through my ex's phone once. All sorts of freaky things were on there and after that I fully support snooping. What did you find out?"

"I found out that she seduced him. She pursued him and she flirted with him and when he tried to break out she basically wouldn't let him."

"Don't give him an excuse," Antonia ordered. "He's a big boy. He could've said no if he'd really wanted to."

"I know that. I'm not making excuses. I'm just saying that it was her from the very beginning. She knew she wanted him the moment she saw him. I was just a speed bump."

"Would it have made you feel better if you'd found out that he'd gone after her?" Antonia asked.

"Of course not. I don't think either option was better. It just hurt to see that it went on for so long. It was right there in front of me that entire time and I didn't see it until I physically saw it."

"Yeah, but you knew that already," Lissy reminded me.

"I know. I know, I know, I know. Except now I know exactly what I didn't know, you know?"

"No," they said in unison.

"You're almost divorced. In two days you will be totally done with this entire mess. Don't let this stupid realization throw you. You already knew everything you needed to know. That's why you're getting divorced. That's why he's in that bachelor pad to begin with." Antonia picked up another roll of fabric, pale pink squares embedded in bright pink squares that created a modern geometric pattern. "Thoughts?"

"That might make me have a seizure if I stare at that all day long," Lissy admitted. This fabric shopping thing might not be as quick and easy as I'd originally hoped.

"Tell us how you really feel," Antonia teased.

"You want to know how I really feel?" I asked, even though I knew she wasn't talking to me. "I feel so pissed off I can barely breathe. I mean, who does she think she is? What makes her think that she's entitled to just swoop in and destroy a family, a family with an infant! There was a baby involved and she didn't even blink, before she went after him. It would've been one thing if there had been an email on there that said, 'Hey, seeing you made me realize that I was stupid to break up with you back when we were kids, but I'm really happy for you and you seem to have a lovely family and I wish you all the best.' That would've been fine. That would've been the mature, appropriate, nonpsychotic thing to do. Instead, she manipulated him and just stole him away from me and if me and Bo ended up alone and devastated, well, who cares because she got her money's worth out of her purple underwear." I mindlessly scanned the fabrics that were tucked into deep shelves on the wall behind me, but I wasn't actually looking at any of them.

"What does purple underwear have to do with it?" Lissy asked.

"Oh my God, don't ask," Antonia said. "The girl is a total bitch, Claire. She's probably a sociopath or has a borderline personality disorder and I'm pretty sure a clinician somewhere with a *DSM-5* manual and a basic understanding of psychology could diagnose her with something, but it doesn't matter. Here's what matters: your husband was too weak to resist her, and too much of a wimp to come clean to you, and too much of an asshole to stop after the first time and all of that, *all of it,* is on him. Why would you want to be married to a man like that anyway?"

"I don't want to be married to a man like that, you're right. Which is good, because we're meeting to sign the divorce papers on Monday and now I'm not sad about it in the least. I can't wait to not be married to him anymore," I said with a conviction I hadn't felt about anything since this whole mess began. I also felt very strongly that it was time for people to know exactly why my life imploded, and more important, that exactly none of it was my fault. I removed my phone from my bag and pulled up the screen shot I took of the emails. If I had to see them, then everyone should see them. I opened my Instagram and uploaded the photo.

"What are you doing?" Antonia asked. "Claire, don't post that on Instagram!"

"Why not? If he's going to do this, then he should be able to own it. Everyone should have to know what kind of guy he is. No one should be allowed to do what he did and still keep his reputation."

"What about your reputation?" Antonia asked. "What about Bo's?"

"I don't care about my reputation. I don't even know anyone! Bo has nothing to do with it!"

"He has everything to do with it! Owen is his father. No matter what happens between you two, Owen is Bo's dad and he loves him and how do you think it would ever make him feel to read those emails? You put them out there now, you have no way of ever knowing if they'll come back and you won't be able to protect Bo from it forever. He doesn't need his parents' dirty laundry aired in public. Don't do this. You've made so much progress and you're moving on and all this will do is let him know that you still aren't over it. It makes you look silly more than anything. You're better than that, Claire. This is bad crazy. Fred will run if he finds out about this."

I knew she was right. I hated that she was right. I closed my eyes and counted backward from five and when I opened them I reluctantly deleted the photo. "You're right. I don't want anyone to see these. Thanks."

"You'll be happy you didn't post that. I know you will," Antonia said.

"I already am," I admitted, which made me feel like maybe I was actually making more progress than I thought. My eye caught something tucked away on the lower shelf.

"See, then it was good you read his emails. Let her have him. He's weak, and she's crazy, and they deserve each other."

"You're so right, and do you know what you deserve, Lissy?" I asked.

"A drink?"

"Yes. We all deserve a drink, but I was thinking more along the lines of this!" I bent over and pulled out a massive roll of polka-dotted fabric, bright white cotton with red and pink polka dots that were small enough to look neat but big enough to catch your attention. They were classic and fun and modern and whimsical all at the same time, which I wouldn't have even thought possible until now.

"Oh my God, I love. I love, love, love it!" Lissy said. She reached over and grabbed the bolt from my hand. "Don't you think this will look amazing?" she asked again as she unrolled it and laid it out on the table in front of us.

"It's really adorable," Antonia said. "I think it's perfect."

"Are we crazy to buy this when we don't even know what kind of chairs we are going to be upholstering? Why is it so difficult to find seating? It really shouldn't be this difficult."

"Maybe. We don't know how much we need to buy," I said. I quickly hurried over to the woman flipping through the day's receipts at the front counter by the register. "Excuse me, we want to buy this polka-dot fabric, but we don't know how much we need. Do you have this in stock or do we need to order it? How does it work?"

"That fabric is actually discontinued and I only have what's left in stock. I can't order it for you. I think we only have three bolts left so depending on what you need to cover it may or may not be enough."

"We are going to upholster chair cushions in it. But we don't know what kind of chair yet. We really love it, though."

"Why don't I put it on hold for you for a few days. If you decide that you want it, come back before the end of next week and I'll have it for you. Just until the end of next week, though. I can't hold it longer than that, I'm sorry."

"We appreciate it. Thanks so much," I said. "Okay, so that's great! We have a week to find chairs that won't need more than three rolls of fabric to cover and we will be all set."

"I'm so excited!" Lissy said. "Do you think we'll be able to find something?"

"I'm sure we will," I said, and I absolutely knew that we would, because inspiration actually hit and I suddenly had a very good idea. "I'll devote all of my free time to finding a table and chairs for you. But first, we need to go get a drink, and then, I need to get divorced."

"That sounds like a great idea to me," Antonia said. "Besides, it's six forty-five. The store is closing soon anyway. Where do you want to go?"

"Anywhere is fine with me," Lissy said. "Thank you guys so much for helping me with this. It's hard to do this kind of stuff if you don't have a second opinion, you know?"

"Totally," Antonia agreed.

"I'm so happy we found it. It's perfect, and it's going to look fabulous, and it's another thing we can check off the list."

"So where do you want to go?"

"Maybe the oyster bar," I suggested. "I think that might be the perfect place to close out this chapter of my life."

The saleswoman removed the roll of fabric from the table and tucked it into a closet at the back of the store, while Lissy, Antonia, and I went into town for a cocktail, to toast the end of Claire Mackenzie.

Chapter 16

IT WAS HAPPENING. I only signed the divorce papers two hours ago, but it was already happening. I needed a drink. I didn't care that it was Monday, or the middle of the afternoon, or what kind of drink it was, but I needed one. I suddenly understood those women with their blue cheese olives and their animal-print shirts. They didn't care what anyone else thought of them, because they signed a piece of paper that essentially erased a huge part of their lives, and that gave you a new perspective on things. They were drinking because they felt like it, and that was the only explanation they needed to give to anyone. Those divorcées were my people, and I was wrong to judge them.

The conference room where I gave up my "Mrs." and picked up a "Ms." wasn't anything special. I thought there'd be a long rectangular table, that Owen and I would face each other, that we'd slide stapled documents back and forth between before signing them in triplicate. The room was small, but neat. It was sparse, and dark, and a little bit dusty, and the gray shades that covered the windows were sad, and depressing, but then so was the occasion. The air-conditioning unit underneath the

window buzzed, and hummed, and caused the pages of the
magazine on the windowsill, I think it was *Golf Digest,* to flutter and threaten to flip. I'd been staring at it since I took my
seat, next to my lawyer, and across from Owen. Tara offered us
water, which I declined, because I forgot how to swallow when
I sat down at this table. Owen seemed uncomfortable, which
I couldn't understand. He was the reason we were here. He
should at least own it with some confidence. I couldn't bring
myself to look at him, because even though it'd been over for
four months, it wasn't really over until today. Four months was
all it took for us to pretend like nothing between us ever happened at all. Now we were just two people who shared a baby,
and who would probably be used as the archetype for how to
have an amicable divorce for all of Tara's other clients, even
though there was nothing friendly about it. We just agreed
not to fight about money because Owen was willing to give it
to me, and we agreed not to fight about Bo, because I believed
that Owen should be involved in his life, and so what else was
there to fight about, really? Once we signed these papers we'd
be nothing more than two people who traded money and custody of a baby on a regular basis. That was it. That was all we'd
ever be from here on out. Business partners and baby traders.
Not exactly 'til death do we part.

"So, I guess that's it," Owen said when it was all over, and
our blessed union was dissolved and we walked out of the office and onto the sidewalk. My eyes and nose itched thanks to
the abundance of colorful flowers that lined the street outside
my lawyer's office. I ran the back of my hand over the tip of

my nose and sniffed, trying to force the sneeze to disappear, and busied myself by staring at the paper flags still taped to the windows of the deli next door even though the Fourth of July was a week ago. My marriage ended on July 11, 2016. Would that be a date that I'd put on my tombstone? A part of me just died. Anything that happened after today was some kind of afterlife—life after Owen. Life after happily ever after. Awesome.

"I guess so," I agreed. "Except I'll still see you multiple times a week, so let's not make this some big Hollywood moment, okay?"

"Okay," Owen said. I didn't know if his eyes looked a little sullen, or if his face seemed a little pained, or if I imagined it all because I wanted him to look a little sullen and a little pained, and not happy that he was now legally free to be with his girl-friend. "I'll see you on Thursday for Bo's birthday," he added.

"Yes. I'll see you Thursday."

"Then don't forget I'm out of town next week, so you'll have Bo. I'll call you when I get back."

"Okay, then. It was a pleasure being married to you," I said. "You know, until it wasn't."

"You too," he said, and I swore I thought I saw him smile, just a hint of that crooked tooth, as if this was an inside joke the two of us would share twenty years from now when we were all just one big, modern, happy family. Maybe one day we'd all be able to laugh at the fact that our marriage ended in a heap of purple underwear and frozen waffles, but not today. And not tomor-row. And probably not for about a million days after that—give or take. "Thanks for all of the pork chops," he said.

"Wow," I replied. "You're welcome." And because I couldn't possibly think of what else there was to say, I left.

I CALLED ANTONIA on my way to the store to let her know that everything was over and that I'd grab dinner on my way home, but first I was going to make a stop at the fabric store and pick up the fabric the saleswoman had placed on hold for us without telling Lissy that I was doing it. I wanted this to be a surprise in a good way, but there was a chance that it would be a surprise in a bad way, and I'd had enough surprises in a bad way for a lifetime and really didn't want to be involved in any more.

"Are you so happy it's over? Today is a great day," Antonia said.

"Definitely. I'm happy to officially be back on the singles circuit with you."

"I'm happy to have you," Antonia said. "Are you heading over to buy the polka dots now?"

"Yes. You think this is a good idea, right? I'm not taking too many liberties by doing this without telling her?"

"No, I really don't think so. I think it's sweet and she'll be very happy."

"Okay, great. I'm going to run over there and then stop by the store and then I'll be home. I'm going to buy a nice bottle of wine for us to have with dinner tonight."

"Champagne. Get champagne because we're celebrating."

"Good point!"

"Congrats again on being divorced!" Antonia sang through my Bluetooth. "See you in a bit."

I clicked off my phone and headed toward Fancy Fabrics so that I could take my mind off my divorce for a little while and work on surprising my friend with some new chairs for her stationery store.

"SO, IT'S OVER?" Lissy asked when I pushed through the door and went directly upstairs to her office. I climbed the spiral staircase in the corner to the loft upstairs, which was piled high with boxes, books, papers, and random knickknacks that Lissy had collected for reasons I couldn't understand. There were no fewer than three bobbleheads on the shelves of the bookcase, multiple paperweights in various shapes and sizes: large three-dimensional hearts, a black onyx square, a diminutive crystal horse. I wasn't sure if Lissy was an actual hoarder, but she was probably getting dangerously close. She needed to streamline, to get rid of the junk she'd been collecting over the years, to let go of the past, and focus on all of the good things that were ahead of her.

Those who cannot do, teach.

"It's over. Just like that, it's over. It's a weird feeling."

"You should go get drunk somewhere. You shouldn't be here."

"I don't want to get drunk. Getting drunk gives me bad hangovers and I've felt crappy enough for the last few months. Instead of looking at this like the end of something, I'm choosing to look at it as the beginning of something, primarily my life as a strong, independent woman who has a job, and a nice guy to spend time with, and a son who might be the greatest kid on earth. I don't have cause for complaint."

"Wow. That's the most positive post-divorce attitude I've ever heard. Again, I really think you should start a blog."

"No thanks. No blogs for me. You need to get on Facebook, though."

"Funny you should mention that. I joined. And the first thing I did was look up Dee Dee."

"Oh my God, you didn't."

"I did. I needed to see this chick. She's not even pretty. I mean, what's with the hair? Someone should tell her she's not Gisele."

"Oh God, I know. It's totally ridiculous, isn't it? Anyway, you don't need to stalk her on Facebook for me. I like to think I'm more mature than that."

"You cut Owen's hair because he was having dinner with her."

"I like to think I'm more mature now than I was then. See?"

"Okay. Good news, though, she's apparently getting ready to go on a cruise to Alaska. There were all these stupid pictures of the scenery and stuff like she was trying to show off her vacation. Who does that?"

"Wait, what? Alaska?" I asked. "Alaska?" Without even realizing it, I slinked down on the floor, and was suddenly sitting underneath Lissy's red desk, hugging a stapler that I couldn't remember picking up. I doubted Dee Dee would be bragging about her trip if she knew that she was being offered a hand-me-down vacation. Owen and I had talked about that trip. We had talked about going. All she was doing was filling in for me on a vacation that Owen wanted to go on no matter who was with him. It didn't make her special. I held the stapler close to my chest, my heart thumping, and the loud *swoosh*ing noise returning to my ears, and my throat still burning. Why was Dee Dee packing for an Alaskan cruise while I was forced to hug a stapler like a teddy bear on the floor of a stationery store? What kind of world was this? I thought I was doing better. I thought I was past the part of the healing process that required me to be on the floor, or horizontal in bed. The fact that I apparently wasn't was extremely disappointing.

For some reason, I didn't feel the need to pull myself up. I liked it under the desk. It was cozier than I expected. Lissy kneeled down next to me, and spoke gently, like I was a scared puppy she was trying to coax out from a doghouse with a sausage.

"Are you okay?" she asked.

"I have absolutely no idea. But I'm sitting under your desk, so it's not looking good."

"I'm really sorry, Claire. Why don't you come out from under there?"

"She's going to Alaska," I muttered.

"That's fantastic. Do you have any idea how many women want their ex-husband's new girlfriend to go to Alaska?"

"She's not going alone. She's going with Owen. It's our vacation. We talked about going when Bo was a little older, because I didn't want to leave him so soon. I'm celebrating my divorce with moo shu chicken and a bottle of champagne, and he's celebrating by going on an Alaskan cruise with his girlfriend, and she's bragging about it on Facebook. Right. That sounds about right."

"Who cares? She sucks. Alaska sucks. Facebook sucks, too."

"Bo's birthday is Thursday. What if he brings her? What if he brings her to my house? She can have Owen, I don't care. She can have Owen and she can have my vacation and she can have the life that I was supposed to have, but she can't have Bo. He's mine."

"She knows that. Owen knows that. She has no intention of trying to take him away from you," Lissy said, trying to console someone who was totally inconsolable.

"She talked to him in the grocery store. I think she wants him, too," I sobbed.

"No, Claire. No. She doesn't. Oh my God, I'm so stupid for saying anything. It's just a dumb trip. It doesn't mean anything."

"I want to lie down," I said. I leaned back on my elbows and flattened myself out on the floor. I laced my fingers together and covered my eyes, willing the stupid sunlight to fade to black.

"You can stay here on the floor all day if you want," Lissy offered. She ran her hand through my hair, an intimate gesture I appreciated. This wasn't a moment you wanted just anyone to witness. In a short period of time, Lissy and I had become very close friends.

"Thanks. I think I'd rather go home," I said. I needed to see Bo. I needed to wrap him up, and kiss him, and hug him, and plant a tracking device on him so that I never had to worry about Dee Dee trying to take him away from me. It may have been irrational, but it didn't feel that way. She already stole my vacation and my husband. Why wouldn't she try and take my son away from me, too? What if nothing was off-limits? If she managed to get her hands on him, then every time Owen had Bo I'd have to stalk him to make sure that Dee Dee hadn't left my sleeping infant in a stroller next to her Mercedes while she went inside to tame her flyaways with a toothbrush and a can of hairspray. That was the type of woman Owen wanted to go to Alaska with? The type who abandoned babies in driveways?

"Don't let her get to you."

"Too late for that. She has my husband. I'm pretty sure I've been gotten."

"She doesn't want to take Bo and even if she did, she couldn't. Don't let your mind go into those dark places. They'll only drive you crazy."

"It's too late for that, too."

"Go home. I'll call you later."

"Okay."

"I can swing by on my way home if you want."

"I'll be fine. Thank you. I'm going to see Owen on Thursday for Bo's birthday. What do I say to him?"

"Nothing. He's not doing anything wrong and the only way to admit you know about it is to admit that I looked at Dee Dee's Facebook page and we both look crazy. Say nothing. Forget about it. You're divorced. Let him go wherever he wants. Call Fred and talk to him instead."

"Okay. You know, I was worried that seeing him for the first time after we were officially divorced would be a little awkward. Now I think it's going to be torturous."

"It's going to get easier. You're already doing pretty great. I don't think you're giving yourself enough credit."

"Thanks." I didn't think that was right. I was giving myself a lot of credit. I almost high-fived myself in the mirror this morning because I shaved my legs in the shower, and blew out my hair and swiped black mascara on my lashes so that I would look put together when I dissolved my marriage. I was very, very proud of that. I was giving myself all kinds of credit. I just didn't advertise it.

Ten minutes later, I pulled the car into the driveway and turned off the ignition, but I didn't open the door. I looked into the rearview mirror, caught sight of my eyes, the mascara now smudged underneath, not quite as sad and hollow as they'd looked in March, but still not bright, or clear, or shiny. It had been four months. When was the pain going to leave for good? When could I wake up in the morning and not fear that my day would end with me lying on the floor under a desk?

I threw my purse on my shoulder and headed up the porch steps. It was almost 2:00, and Bo would be waking up from his nap. I trudged slowly up the stairs, mindlessly putting one foot in front of the other, and tried not to feel like every step forward was followed by three enormous steps back.

Chapter 17

SCREW ALASKA. SCREW Alaska and screw Owen, and screw the penguins, and the icebergs, and the igloos, and the moose, and everything else that was in Alaska because I didn't really want to go there in the first place. I was far too busy having an amazing Wednesday in Connecticut—which anyone will tell you is far superior to any day of the week in Alaska—to worry about the stupid cruise anyway. Wednesday was now my new favorite day of the week, because Wednesday was the day of the week that Claire Stevens took control of everything, and actually had a routine, and a purpose, and most important, her shit together. I didn't think about regrets, or divorce, or waffles, I just focused on myself, and all that was good in my life. I woke up earlier than I needed to, so that I could shower and dress in something other than the worn-out black yoga pants and frayed T-shirts that had become my uniform since I stopped having anywhere to go. I threw on a pair of jeans and the navy blue tunic that my mother sent me for no reason other than to silently suggest from another time zone that because I was single now I needed to stop wearing ratty T-shirts every day and should wear that instead. I really did feel like the strong, independent, stylish woman I was meant to be. On Monday I got divorced and found out my ex-husband was taking his mistress on our vacation, and tomorrow my ex-husband would be coming over to celebrate our one-year-old's birthday, and I refused to spend today lying in bed thinking about it because if I did I'd go mad. I was going to grab this Wednesday with both hands and force it to be nice to me if it killed me.

I made Bo French toast for breakfast, and cut it up for him on a plastic plate that looked like the American flag, because I had some left over from the non-barbecue we had on the Fourth of July and I always liked the excuse to be festive. I picked him up and twirled him around the kitchen on my hip while I sang him Tom Petty songs I used to listen to when I was pregnant. My little slow-dancing partner smiled and giggled and when I dipped him upside down he actually squealed so loudly my heart felt like it was going to explode. I rocked and bounced and twirled him over to his highchair and then carefully sat him in his seat and fastened his white plastic tray to his chair. While he ate, I made my coffee, topped it off with two scoops of sugar and a splash of milk, and read the paper online. Antonia padded into the kitchen. "I'm going to work down here today. I usually stay upstairs in my room and work there while you're at the library, but I think today I'm going to saddle up here at the kitchen counter. I'd like to enjoy the quiet house and the chance to be downstairs without having to listen to the theme song from *Curious George* in the background."

"Sounds like a great idea," I said. "I know this place is crazy most of the day. I don't know how you've managed to get any work done in this house."

"It's not so bad."

"You must be very, very good at what you do."

"You know it," she said.

"Enjoy the quiet. There's coffee!" I said over my shoulder before I disappeared with Bo downstairs into the basement.

I buckled Bo in his stroller and pushed him down the driveway and into the street. The library was only a ten-minute walk, just past the high school and the rec center, but before the grocery store and the train station. When we arrived, I pushed the stroller by the toddlers playing on the lawn out front, and the nannies and other young mothers sitting on benches lining the rust-colored brick walkway, keeping watch over their children while drinking six-dollar lattes and typing on their cell phones. I pushed the stroller up the ramp, and parked it with the others against the far wall next to the water fountain, but out of the way of the automatic door used for the handicap entrance.

I was pretty sure that Bo liked the library, but it was hard to say since he couldn't actually tell me one way or the other. He paid attention when Lissy sang, and never cried, or fidgeted, the way he did when he wanted me to pick him up and carry him around. He clapped and babbled and stared and seemed to enjoy being around other kids, which made me happy. I liked to think he recognized Lissy, and maybe that made him more comfortable, but it probably didn't matter. If you put puppets, and music, and books with pop-out dogs in front of a baby, odds were he'd pay attention. I loved that we had this place to visit, just the two of us, where we fit in with everyone because no one knew us, and I didn't have to worry about mean mommies causing me to lose my day planner in the hallway.

Lissy was a bit of a legend at the library, at least among some of the other mothers who were well versed in kid-friendly activities around town. I heard that there had been other readers at story time, but that no one had ever been anywhere near as good as she was. I had a feeling if Lissy tried to quit there'd be a revolt, where angry stay-at-home moms would show up at her house with torches and riot gear, and refuse to leave until she agreed to come back. She played the guitar, and displayed a felt board with flowers, and trains, and the letters of the alphabet, and she let the kids place them on the board while she sang nursery rhymes. She was at home with these kids, probably because they didn't judge her, or wonder if there was something wrong with her because she decided to pierce her left ear twelve times. They only cared that she neighed like a horse, and mooed like a cow, and barked like a dog when the song she sang required her to neigh, or moo, or bark. Kids were great like that.

Since Bo was comfortable at story hour, so was I. Sometimes, we'd sit on the floor up front and not on the chairs in the back. He rocked with the music and laughed and sometimes bounced his knees like he wanted to start dancing, and it made me feel good because these were the moments where I felt like maybe Owen and I hadn't screwed him up. Maybe, because he'd never remember his parents living in the same house, his family wouldn't seem weird to him. Maybe all of my fears had been unwarranted, and a loved kid was a loved kid and that was all that really mattered. The rest of it was just geography.

Lissy broke into my favorite song, "Down by the Bay," which I wished I'd known as a child. I would have liked to make up rhymes about seeing a horse on a golf course, or a hog in a bog, or a pig in a wig. Another woman I recognized, the mother of a little girl who wore purple sneakers and carried a stuffed duck with an orange beak, made eye contact with me and we smiled as if to say "hello." We spoke briefly last week when she left her purse on the floor next to her chair, and Bo decided to rifle through it and remove her wallet. I returned it to her with sincere apologies and more than a little embarrassment that she assured me was unnecessary. She had four children, she told me. Over the years, she'd had to return more wallets, car keys, and makeup bags than she could remember. The Wednesday moms were so much nicer than the Friday moms. No one here looked at me sideways, or talked about me when they thought I couldn't hear them, or worse, knew I could hear them and didn't care enough to whisper. Nobody here knew that I was Claire of the Claire, Owen, and Dee Dee love triangle from hell. I was just the woman with the kid who stole wallets out of purses when their owners weren't looking, and that was such a better person to be.

Lissy was having a really good performance, one of her best ones yet. She was exuberant, and inventive, and her ability to throw her voice and make the cow puppet sitting on the top of her head actually look like it was talking was nothing short of spectacular. She handed out little plastic fruit rattles for the kids—bananas, and oranges, and apples, and pears that were stuffed with little beads or marbles that the kids could shake while she sang "Copacabana," but most just ate them, and she didn't seem to mind. I sat on my chair and watched my son and my friend, and decided that this was a nice moment that I'd think about for a long time on nights where I felt sorry for myself and told myself that I was the worst mother in the world. I wasn't. I wasn't the best, but I wasn't the worst, and if I was admitting that, then that meant I'd made some legitimate progress. I smiled a little wider because I'd take any progress I could get.

My phone buzzed in my bag, and for once, I actually located it in the pocket designated for cell phones, and not swimming on the bottom under loose makeup, loose raisins, loose change, and three pens that had been there for over a year. I read Fred's text. He didn't admit it, but I knew he was starting to see the advantages of text messaging over calling and that you can still be traditional while embracing modern technology.

It's quiet today, so I'm thinking of sneaking out early. Are you around?

I was, but I wasn't. After story time at the library, I let Bo play out on the lawn with the other kids, though they didn't really play with each other so much as they randomly bumped into each other and stole each other's sippy cups. Then I went home and fed him lunch, put him down for a nap, and did one of my Tracy Anderson workout DVDs on the floor in my den. I was planning on getting aggressive today, and actually using a set of ankle weights to do my leg lifts and curls, but Tracy was strong, and I suspected it wasn't as easy as she made it look in her demo, so I probably wouldn't bother. Tomorrow was Bo's birthday, so I was going to start blowing up some of the balloons I bought at Party City and clean the house so that when Owen and his mom arrived they could stare in awe at my glistening countertops. But I didn't want to tell Fred that I wasn't available, because I really wanted to see him, so I figured I'd make time and blow up the balloons while I watched the late news. I didn't want him to think that I was playing games or trying to be coy. I was a thirty-six-year-old divorcée with a baby. There was nothing coy about me and I liked that about me now.

I texted him back: *I'm free from about 1–3 while Bo naps assuming Antonia is around. Would love to do something.*

Fred: *Great. Wear comfortable clothes and sneakers. I'll pick you up at 1.*

Just in case Fred couldn't be any more promising, he encouraged me to wear gym clothes and sneakers on our date. That sounded like a perfect idea to me. I didn't give a damn about Alaska. I never liked the cold anyway.

"I CAN'T DO this. This is maybe one of the worst ideas ever," I said as I let a man strap a harness between my legs and fasten a helmet to my head. "I'm telling you this is not going to end well."

"You'll be fine! It'll be fun, trust me. Where's your sense of adventure?"

"Once you have a child you realize that adventure is not your friend most of the time."

"This is perfectly safe and it'll be a lot of fun. Come on, I'll race you!"

I stared up at the rock wall I was meant to climb, and tried not to look as scared as I was. It wasn't that I had a problem with heights or anything, it was just that I didn't think climbing up a wall using nothing but three-inch-wide fake rocks to support me seemed like the best idea on a Wednesday afternoon. I didn't want to look like a wimp, and I didn't want to disappoint Fred, but I also really didn't want to climb the wall, and so it seemed I had a problem.

"Okay, I'll climb. Hell, I'll even race you, but what do I get if I win?" I asked.

"What do you want?"

"A pony. I asked Santa for one when I was eight and I'm still waiting on it."

"Deal. And if I win, I want to come over for dinner and get a cooking class from Antonia on how to make a proper Bolognese. Mine always comes out oily and I don't know what I'm doing wrong."

I jammed my foot onto the first fake rock and used my upper body strength to pull myself up. Then I began to climb the wall like Spider-Man, if Spider-Man had worn a harness, a helmet, and a pair of black yoga pants that were pilling across the ass. "How do I know you're not using me to get to my beautiful Italian roommate?"

"You've figured me out. Damn. I was so hoping that wouldn't

happen until we at least got to the top of the wall," Fred said, as he skillfully moved to his left and climbed another three feet above me.

"Yeah, I knew you were too good to be true," I said, hoping that the altitude up here ten feet off the ground hadn't just made me lose my inhibitions and say something presumptuous I'd regret once I was back on solid ground. Things with Fred were wonderful. He was kind and smart and easygoing and he had no problem dragging his date to a rock wall and expecting her to climb and that was something I never knew I wanted until now. I never climbed anything with Owen. When I climbed to the top I looked around and smiled because Fred had been right, the view from up here really was so different than it was on the ground, and this view was of a sweaty indoor gym. I had no problem believing that the exhilaration of doing this outdoors was like nothing else, but I still had no intention of ever finding out for myself.

"I don't want to rub it in, but I won," Fred said.

"Two out of three. I really, really want my pony."

Fred loosened the slack on his cable and lowered himself slowly to the ground. "Okay. Two out of three. I'm willing to risk it if you are."

"Funny," I said as I followed him back down. "I was thinking the same thing."

Chapter 18

"HAPPY BIRTHDAY, BOO Boo Bear," Marcy sang as her overly perfumed, pantsuited body breezed into the house to celebrate Bo turning one. The air trailing behind her became instantly heavy and sticky with the scent of orchids and gladiolas. I'd always hated her perfume, because it reminded me of a funeral parlor, which frankly was where I'd hoped she'd be the next time we met. This was just not my year.

Even now, even after Owen and I divorced, and I didn't have to pretend to be happy to spend every other Christmas with her, Marcy was difficult to be around. I tried for a long time to develop some kind of relationship with her where we would talk, or text, but she never once reached out to me. She loved her son, and her grandson, but she would've preferred that a stork had dropped Bo on Owen's doorstep than have to suffer through the horror of having me as a daughter-in-law. Owen's sister, Chloe, moved to California after college, realized that her East Coast mother was bat-shit crazy, and never came home. I always liked Chloe, though I never got to know her very well. I liked to think we would've been friends if I'd had more time with the family, if Owen hadn't decided to trade me in for a different woman, like a car whose lease had come due after you'd put a few thousand miles on it and dented the fender.

If Marcy felt awkward at this being our first meeting since Owen and I divorced, she didn't show it. She removed her white purse straps from her bony shoulder and handed her purse to me in one smooth motion as she continued past me into the kitchen, treating me more like a coat-check girl than her former daughter-in-law. I opened the closet next to the basement stairs, hoping that Marcy didn't notice the vacuum cleaner hose fall on me before I was able to stuff her purse next to my winter coats, the tablecloths for the dining room table that I would probably never use, and various cleaning supplies. I'd done my best to clean the house for the party, refusing to let Antonia lift a finger, because I wanted everyone to see that I had it all under control—everyone being Marcy, Antonia, Lissy, Owen, and Bo. I also wanted to send a video of the cake and the decorations and the clean house to my mother, who was apparently buying my brainwashing, and while it was kind of scary to realize how easily you can fake your life through pictures, it was kind of awesome to realize that you can totally fake your life through pictures.

I tried my hardest to make sure that Bo felt special on his birthday. I tied blue balloons to the lamppost outside because I wanted the neighbors to know that once upon a time I was a nice, normal person who had friends, and family, and would've been able to invite actual guests to a birthday party. I bought Bo some Lego Duplos, a few new puzzles, a stuffed Elmo hand puppet, and a toy elephant that blew plastic balls out of his trunk if you pressed a button on his foot. I wrapped them in paper covered with monkeys and bananas, and tied them with bright yellow bows. Antonia made him pancakes for breakfast, and we piled them high and drenched them with syrup and lit a sparkly candle on top of the stack. We took pictures while he stared at the candle, and then again when he attacked his pancakes, even though he only ate one and threw the rest on the floor. We sang "Happy Birthday" to him, and hugged him, and kissed him, and reminded him that he was the best little boy to ever crawl on this earth. That's what you do when your only son turns one. Now that it was time for the makeshift family party I felt confident that it would be like every other little boy's birthday party, complete with pizza, balloons, a Carvel ice cream cake, royal blue paper cups and plates that I'd gotten to match the balloons, and parents who would rather not be in the same room with each other.

"Hi, Claire," Owen said. He smiled when he said it, but he didn't try and give me a kiss on the cheek or the awkward ass-out hug. He just smiled like we were mature adults who were capable of sharing a child and some pizza without the world crashing down around us, or without my breaking out a pair of scissors. That would've been all fine and good, if I didn't know about Alaska, and the whales, and the Eskimos, and the girlfriend. Knowing all of that changed this whole night for me. How much was I supposed to take? I promised myself I wouldn't say anything about it tonight. No matter what happened, under no circumstances was I going to ruin Bo's birthday by fighting with Owen. He walked past me and placed the pizza he brought over on the table next to Bo's highchair. Then he leaned down and gave him a big kiss on his cheek, and Bo reached up and grabbed his face in both of his little hands.

"Happy birthday, Bo. One year old today," he said.

"What a difference a year makes," I said.

Owen ignored me. "How are you?"

"Fine. How are you?" I asked, though I was pretty sure I knew the answer. He was finally getting that Alaskan vacation he'd been dreaming of and the fun-loving woman to accompany him on it. It seemed like a ridiculous question to ask. I'd bet he was feeling pretty good these days.

"I'm okay. The place looks great. You went all-out, huh?"

"I guess," I replied. I was happy he noticed. I glanced over at Marcy, who was crouched down in front of Bo, and had to resist the urge to kick her over.

"What's new?" he asked.

"Nothing much. I heard you're going to see the whales. That's nice. I'm glad you're able to do that." I wanted to keep my mouth shut, I really did, but I couldn't.

I hated when I broke promises to myself.

"How did you know that?" he asked, more than a little surprised.

"Your girlfriend is an immature idiot with a big mouth, that's how."

"I told you I was going away next week," Owen said.

"I thought you meant on a business trip, and you know it."

"What's the difference? Why does it matter? I told you I

won't be here, and I won't be here. I don't even know why we're talking about this," Owen argued, annoyed that he felt the need to defend himself, which I couldn't care less about because he definitely needed to defend himself even though in my humble opinion this was completely indefensible.

"It matters, Owen! What if we needed you? What if something happened to Bo and we needed you and you're on a boat in the middle of the ocean? Did you even think of that? Can you try and think about someone other than yourself for one freakin' minute? Is it possible? Or have you actually become the most selfish person on the planet?"

"If, God forbid, Bo needed me, I'd get here. You know that."

"Really? You'd leave your girlfriend in Alaska for us? Thank you. That's touching."

"This isn't the time or the place to air your dirty laundry, Claire," Marcy said, which was the first time she'd addressed me since she got here, and I much preferred she keep her mouth shut.

"It's my house, Marcy. If this isn't the place to air dirty laundry, then please tell me where that place might be."

"You have guests," she said.

"You're the only guest, and you can show yourself out at any time."

"Claire," Antonia said as she scooped up Bo from his highchair. He smiled at her and she snuggled him close to her chest. "I'm going to take Bo upstairs. There's no reason for him to be here."

"You mean other than the fact that it's his birthday?" Owen

asked. "Don't take him anywhere. Give him to me," Owen ordered, reaching out his hands to take Bo off Antonia's hip. Bo looked confused, but he adjusted quickly, and eyed Marcy curiously, probably because he wasn't sure if he recognized her, and also because he'd never seen a person without eyebrows before.

"Okay, well, there's no reason for me to be here. I'm going upstairs. Wait for me to eat the pizza," Antonia said as she hurried upstairs to no doubt close her door, turn on the TV, and start making plans to return to Chicago.

"What do you care if I'm going to Alaska? You didn't really want to go when I asked you!" Owen said.

"Bo is an infant!" I yelled, defending myself. "I told you I wanted to go. We agreed when Bo was a little older we'd go. What, you just subbed me out and subbed Dee Dee in? Was I just an interchangeable part in your life?"

"Of course not!" Owen yelled, as if the suggestion offended him. "But just because we got divorced doesn't mean I'm never going to go away again, Claire. I want to travel still, and I want to do things, and yes, Dee Dee is going to come with me. I don't know why this bothers you so much. You weren't even the least bit excited about the trip when I mentioned it to you. All you wanted to do was stay home and nest and do laundry."

"It's called motherhood. And please, no one wants to do laundry! It just comes with the territory. You didn't mind having clean boxers to take on all those business trips. Who did you think was washing them? Fairies?"

"It's called giving up," Owen said.

I gasped, and my quivering, delicate, fragile heart, the one that I'd carefully been piecing back together since March, broke all over again. He said it—the worst thing in the world anyone could ever have said to me. I gave up everything for him, and redefined myself in order to support him, and he just used my devotion as a weapon against me. "That is not fair. I didn't give up. I just decided to pursue other things, namely being your wife. Remember that? You moved me here."

"And once you were here you never wanted to leave!" Owen yelled.

"Are you honestly telling me that you cheated on me because I didn't want to jump up to go save the fucking whales?" I screamed.

"Watch the whales, not save them. Watch the whales! It's called a vacation!"

"How can you not see how messed up this is? Just when I think you can't disappoint me more than you already have, you take your trampy girlfriend to Alaska, and prove yet again that you are the biggest asshole on earth!"

"Claire, Mackenzies don't act like this," Marcy interjected. "Dee Dee isn't a tramp, and I really don't like that language. She's a perfectly lovely girl who I've known all her life. Owen and she made a beautiful couple when they dated, and her mother and I always hoped they'd reunite someday . . ."

Oh. No. She. Didn't, I thought. Then, I spoke. "That's why you never liked me? Because you're friends with Dee Dee's mom and you guys wanted to arrange their marriage? Are you serious? *That's* it?"

"I always felt that Dee Dee and Owen should be together, yes. There was always a chance of reconciliation until he met you . . ."

"Mom!" Owen yelled. "That's not true and don't say that to her!" I appreciated his attempt to defend me, but it was too late. I didn't need it. I was perfectly fine defending myself. I'd been doing it since March.

"Get out, you miserable old bat!" I screamed. "Get out!"

That was how I chose to do it.

My phone rang, and it was my mother calling to wish Bo a happy birthday, and I had worked too hard to put her mind at ease to ruin it all now because of stupid Dee Dee and her stupid Facebook and stupid Marcy and her stupid everything. I grabbed my cell off the counter and immediately changed my tone. "Hi, Mom!" I sang, so cheerful I barely recognized my own voice. "We are having the best time at Bo's little party. I really wish you were here."

"I do, too," my mom said. "Are Owen and Marcy there?"

"Oh yeah, they're both here. Owen brought in pizza and we have a little cake and we're just going to have a nice casual dinner and open some presents. I'll send you pictures of the house. It looks adorable. I even tied balloons to the lamppost."

"Oh, it sounds lovely. I'll call back tomorrow and we can talk more then. I don't want to take you away from the party. I'm happy you're all having a nice time. I was a little worried with this being the first time you saw Owen since the actual divorce."

"Oh, you didn't need to worry about that. Owen and I are

in a good place now. Marcy says hi! We love you. I'll talk to you tomorrow." I hung up the phone, and realized that Owen and Marcy were both looking at me like I was insane, which I probably was, and it didn't bother me one bit.

I turned my attention back to Marcy, and to reality, and let the fake cheerful attitude disappear as quickly as it came. "Why are you still here?" I asked. "I said get out!"

Marcy froze, her mouth stretched into a stern, thin line, the lipstick feathering off her lips onto her dry, flaky skin. But she didn't move, which confused me, because I thought my instructions were pretty clear, and I had repeated them twice now.

"You don't get to come into this house and say that to me," I informed her. "Not ever. You don't get to defend her, you don't get to tell me how you're happy they're back together, you don't get to say anything to me except, 'I'm sorry that my son betrayed you,' which for the record, I'm still waiting for you to say. And you have the nerve to come here, and tell me what Mackenzies do? Are you kidding? Let me remind you, Marcy, that I'm *not* a Mackenzie. I'm a Stevens! So let me tell you what Mackenzies don't do. They don't honor their marriages, and they're not honest with the people in their life they're supposed to love the most. That's what Mackenzies *don't* do. Actually, I'd like to add one more thing to this list. They don't celebrate Bo's fucking birthday with him, either. Get out!" I screamed, for a moment stunned that I actually dropped an F bomb on a septuagenarian, even one who deserved that and oh so much more.

"I don't owe you an apology! I haven't done anything,"

Marcy gasped, as if the mere concept of telling someone you're sorry for their troubles was completely unheard of. I shouldn't have been surprised. Marcy firmly believed that Owen could do no wrong, probably because if she admitted that, she'd maybe have to admit that she wasn't the best mother on earth. Marcy was never going to let anyone tell her that she was anything less than perfect—certainly not me. It was completely infuriating, and even more unhealthy, and I decided right then and there that Bo didn't need to ever be exposed to her brand of crazy ever again. He was going to have to deal with enough crazy from me. Bringing her into the mix was an unnecessary stressor for everyone.

"Exactly. You didn't do anything. You've never done anything, and that's exactly why Owen is the way he is, and why you are no longer welcome in this house." I stormed over to the closet and threw open the door, forgetting for a second that the vacuum cleaner was jammed against it, and it fell with a thud when I grabbed Marcy's purse. I shoved it in her hands. "From now on, if you want to see Bo, you go through Owen. I don't ever want to see you again. Now, get out of this house!"

"Owen, are you going to let her talk to me like that?" Marcy asked.

"Why don't you just calm down, Claire. We don't have to do this now. We can talk about this later," Owen offered. "I get that you're upset. We can talk about it," he said, as if talking about his cruise was going to make me feel better about it. Maybe he could post pictures on Instagram, or Snapchat, so that I could be downright elated.

"Why do we have to do this later? You're here now. Why can't we just do it now?"

"Because it's your son's birthday party, for starters," Marcy reminded me. "Why don't you think about what's best for him?"

"Marcy, so help me God if you don't get out of this house I'm going to physically remove you," I threatened. I took a step toward her and clenched my fists at my sides. I didn't own this house. But I lived in this house, and that meant I could decide who was welcome here and who wasn't. Marcy wasn't welcome here when Owen and I were married either, but I couldn't do anything about it then. Now, I could. So at least I had that going for me.

"Stop," Owen said. "Please, relax. Don't do this on Bo's birthday. You'll regret it."

"You want to talk to me about regret? Are you serious right now?" I squealed. "Don't worry about my regrets. The more the merrier. I'm going to have a blog. It's all working material!"

"You're impossible to talk to when you're like this. I don't know why I even bother trying." Owen sighed, because you know, it was frustrating dealing with your ex-wife after you blindsided her with an affair.

"You're right, so let's just stop talking. You can show yourselves out," I said.

"Fine," Owen said. He placed Bo in his jumper and turned to Marcy. "Let's go, Mom."

"You own this house. You don't have to leave on your son's birthday if you don't want to, Owen."

"Try me, Marcy. Just try me." I stormed out of the kitchen,

stepped over the vacuum cleaner, and held the front door open. "Marcy, it's been lovely knowing you, but I honestly hope that you and I never lay eyes on each other again."

"You know what, Claire? That's it. I'm so damn sick of this!" Owen snapped.

"What are you going to do, Owen? Divorce me? Oops! Been there, done that already!"

"I'm not even going to try anymore!" he yelled. "If you want to be bitter, and angry, and miserable for the rest of your life, you go right ahead. We don't have to be civil. We don't have to be anything. I've been far more tolerant of your antics than I should've been, and any leg you once had to stand on is gone. I tried, but it's clear you're incapable of having any kind of normal interaction with me. You got what you wanted. We're leaving. Let's go, Mom."

Owen reached out and escorted Marcy by her elbow out the front door. Neither one of them looked at me as they walked to their cars parked in the street. I slammed the door behind them and then kicked it for good measure. I wished I'd been wearing something other than a flip-flop. My foot throbbed.

"It's all clear," I called upstairs to Antonia after I'd closed the door behind them. I headed straight back to the kitchen where I'd left my wineglass. I glanced around at Owen's beer, still unopened on the counter, and the ice cream cake, starting to melt and leak out the sides of the box, and could still smell the stench of Marcy's perfume in the air. The balloons were still tied to Bo's highchair. The pizza was still sitting in the box.

Everything was exactly as it should be, except nothing was the way it should've been.

The doorbell rang, and for a second I feared it was Marcy, because if I had to lay eyes on her again I was fairly sure I was going to drop-kick her off the porch. The door opened a crack and Lissy called in a singsong, "Happy birthday, Bo! I'm sorry I'm late. What did I miss?"

"Oh, nothing," I said. "I just threw Bo's father and grandmother out of the house. No biggie."

"I always miss the good stuff," Lissy said as she closed the door behind her.

I reached over and removed Bo's presents from under the table. I handed him one and watched as he banged on the box, and ran his hand over the paper, and laughed. I tried to think about how today was my little boy's first birthday, and how even though it had been the worst year of my life, it had also been the best. I tried not to think about the fact that I'd just threatened his grandmother with physical violence, or that I just ruined my beautiful, innocent, cherubic son's birthday party. Years from now, when I looked back on today, I had no doubt that I'd be embarrassed, and ashamed of my behavior. The only thing that kept me from being the absolute worst mom in the world was knowing that Bo was thankfully too young to remember it. It was also hugely unfortunate that I would never forget.

IT TOOK TWO weeks for me to finally stop seething over the fact that Owen and Marcy had ruined the memories of my little boy's first birthday, and two weeks for me to stop hating myself for it, too. The emotional roller coaster I'd been on since March was old, and I didn't know how much longer I could take the swings. One day I was happy, then I was sad; I felt optimistic, then I felt depressed. I felt calm, then I felt rage. I couldn't predict it and I couldn't control it and it wasn't healthy. I had to find a way to settle my nerves and my anger and my life before it ruined everything that I had left.

"Let's go for a walk," Fred said on a steamy early August morning. He arrived at my house with bagels, scallion cream cheese, and large coffees for both of us, which I gladly accepted. I didn't know if you could call what we were doing going steady—we were probably too old for that—but I was pretty sure that we were going steady. We'd spent a lot of time together since we met and I'd grown to really love his company. We saw movies, and shared meals, and went for walks, and had real conversations with each other about anything you could imagine. I wasn't sure what the turning point was for me—when Fred stopped just being a guy I was seeing and became someone I cared about—but there was one. It had seemed impossible to think that there would ever be a time when I had another man in my life, but I did, and he was sensitive and kind. He would never refuse to eat homemade pulled pork sandwiches because he'd already gone to Taco Bell. He just wasn't the type.

Owen and I had barely spoken since the party. We traded text messages to discuss the logistics of picking Bo up or dropping him off, and that was it. Something about it wasn't sitting right with me, but I wasn't sure why, because it shouldn't have mattered. Fine, my timing was less than perfect, but so what? I still didn't think I was wrong to say what I said. I may have been wrong to throw him out of the house. I wasn't sure what I thought about that one yet. I was still working on it.

It was painfully humid outside, the air thick with the smell of cut grass and flowers and mulch from the landscaping trucks that made their rounds through the neighborhood starting at about 8:00 A.M. No one here mowed their own lawns, which was odd to me. Back in Illinois, there was a riding lawn mower in every garage right next to the rake, the leaf blower, and the huge aluminum shovel used for clearing massive snowdrifts off of walkways in winter. The only person you paid to mow your lawn was your kid, and the going rate was around five dollars, barely enough to get a slice of pizza and a soda from the pizzeria in town. Things here were done differently, and I'd bet that if I threw open every garage door on the block, I wouldn't find a single lawn mower. It was funny what I'd come to miss about home.

"Okay," I said, as I slathered cream cheese across a halved sesame bagel and took a bite. The dough was soft, and warm, and comforting and I was so happy to have my appetite back it was hard to remember the time where food made me nauseous and eating was a chore, even though that time was only five months ago. "Let me just get Bo's shoes." Antonia had gone spinning, continuing the Sunday morning routine she'd had back in Chicago, and I thought it would be nice for Bo and I to go for a walk before the sun became too hot to bear and we spent the rest of the afternoon hunkered down inside in the air-conditioning. Antonia had been eyeing a purse in a store window in town, and I wanted to cruise by the store on our walk and buy it for her, because she was right when she said that little things could make a big difference, and I wanted this little thing to convey a big thank-you for being an amazing friend. I shuffled into the hallway and removed the small blue sneakers from the basket on the floor and strapped them on Bo's pudgy feet, then headed down to the basement to clip him in his stroller. Bo was getting ready to walk. He pulled himself up on the side of his stroller and tried to appreciate his new vantage point on the world. My little baby was now a little boy. A new phase of our life was about to begin.

"Have you talked to Owen at all?" Fred asked as we walked.

"Just the usual, why?" I wondered.

"Just curious if you guys talked about anything since your last argument."

"No. There's not much to talk about. I'm not saying that I shouldn't have handled things differently, but honestly, Marcy should've kept her mouth shut, and Owen should've kept his pants zipped, so there was plenty of blame to go around."

"It doesn't sound like you feel all that bad about it," Fred pointed out.

"I'm just so tired of finding out important information about Owen's life by accident. He's my son's father. If he's going to Alaska, I should know. What if there was an emergency? Am I wrong to think that?"

"No. You're not wrong. You should work on your delivery,

though. Throwing Bo's grandmother out of the house might have been a little extreme," Fred said. One of the reasons I liked Fred was because he always stayed calm and steady. Calm and steady were two things that eluded me recently, and I liked having that kind of influence in my life. I wasn't entirely sure why Fred was interested in me, unless calm and steady people were drawn to those who seem to summon chaos as easily as people hail cabs.

"You don't know her," I reminded him. "I've wanted to throw Marcy out of the house every time she stepped foot in it."

"True." He paused, but I knew he had more to say and was searching for the words. Fred was good like that, and I should try to do that more often, instead of just spewing whatever came to mind out into the universe without stopping to think about anything. "It does show, though, that you're still volatile. I'd be lying if I said it didn't make me a little nervous, Claire. It doesn't matter what happened to you. At some point you need to get your emotions under control. What am I supposed to think when you tell me that you threw your son's grandmother out of the house? It's not exactly . . . what's the word I'm looking for?"

"I honestly have no idea," I said. I shouldn't have told him anything. I thought we were past the part of the program where I had to prove my sanity to him. I thought he'd understand my feelings where all of this was concerned, but now I worried that we were right back into the "you're bad crazy" mindset and I was done defending myself against that. You could be emotional without being nuts, and if he didn't get that then he didn't understand women in the slightest. He either liked me and wanted to be with me, or he didn't, but if he did then he was going to have to like all of me and that included the part that wanted to punt Marcy to the curb.

"Attractive. It's not attractive," he said, casually, as if that wasn't one of the worst things you could ever say to a woman in any situation, period.

"Wow. Well, that's an interesting piece of information. Thanks for that," I said.

"There's something I want to talk to you about," Fred said, which might be the second worst thing you could ever say to a woman, period.

"Okay," I said, waiting to be knocked down again, waiting for him to reach inside my chest cavity, grab my newly restored heart with both hands, and squeeze the bejeezus out of it.

"I wasn't completely honest with you when I told you about my divorce," Fred said. He blotted the grooves in his forehead with a handkerchief, sweat dripping down the back of his neck and causing his shirt to stick to his back. He kicked a small rock, and it skipped off the curb and disappeared under bushes lining the sidewalk. I wished I could've disappeared with it.

"Oh my God. You're still married. Are you kidding? You know what I've been going through, and you're still married?" I stopped walking and stepped on the brake pedal by the back wheel of Bo's stroller. My legs shook beneath me, and my body went numb, my fingers and toes tingling from hypoxia. "This isn't happening. I don't want to be Dee Dee. I don't date married men!" I felt the blood rush to my head again. I don't care what Fred thought of me. I wasn't going to let another man make a fool out of me. Not again. "I should've known. I should've known there was something seriously wrong with you the second you agreed to go out with me again. Why would you do that? Why would anyone want to see me again after what I did to Owen? My friends asked me that, and I asked myself that, and I chalked it up to you just being a good guy who understood a little bit how hard this situation is for me. But that wasn't it at all. You were just using me like Owen did. You have a wife at home and you just figured it didn't really matter if I was crazy, because I was never going to be anything except the other woman. So why did you make me defend myself? Why did you make me prove to you over and over again that I wasn't a raging lunatic? Why would you do this to me? Is every man on earth seriously demented? Do I need to join a convent? Is that where my life is heading? Are you—"

"Stop," he said, calmly. "Put a sock in it and stop with the incessant questions and let me finish before you say something you'll really regret."

"See, lucky for me regret is not really something I care about. I'll just add it to my Regrets Only blog. I think it could go viral. At this point I have so much source material I could probably get a book deal or a miniseries on Netflix!" I screeched, which caused birds to fly out of the trees on the other side of the street.

"Claire!" he yelled. "I'm not married. I didn't lie to you when I told you that I was divorced. I am. I was." He corrected himself, which was confusing. He is divorced? He was divorced? How was this possibly a confusing concept?

"Fred, I swear to God, I can't take any more disappointment. I need to believe that there are still good people in this world. I need to believe that not everyone is out to get me. Otherwise, I'm going back to bed for the next year. Spit it out."

"I don't really like to talk about it, which is why I didn't tell you in the beginning, but now I feel like it's time for you to know. I've been waiting for the right time."

"Time for me to know what? What, exactly, didn't you tell me?" I glanced down the street at the normal, happy people enjoying the beautiful summer morning: an elderly couple shuffling in the crosswalk, holding hands and cups of coffee from the bakery three blocks away; a gaggle of preteens, maybe eleven or twelve years old, in tiny shorts and tank tops carrying field hockey sticks and bottles of orange Gatorade; a young father with his son on his shoulders, promising him that the next time they reach a tree he'll stop so the little boy could grab the branches. A few minutes ago I felt as normal as they were, just a nice couple pushing a baby stroller down a tree-lined street in suburbia. Now, I felt like an outsider, who was once again forced to examine life in this town from the cheap seats.

"She died. Two years ago," he said, answering my question. "I didn't tell you that she died."

"Your wife died? You're a widower?" I asked. This changed everything. I thought we shared the divorce card. I thought we understood each other, because we had both been in the trenches, and had worked our way out of them. I thought that was part of our bond. If he was a widower, then I didn't understand him at all.

"No," Fred said. "I'm sorry. I'm not explaining this well. I've never had to talk about it before, and I guess I'm not very good at it."

"No. You're not," I said. "I guess you're not perfect either."

"I'm divorced. We got divorced first, but she died two years ago. I'm sorry I haven't told you until now, but I wasn't sure what to say."

I was about to tell him that I didn't need him or his stupid drum sander, but I paused before I actually uttered a word. "I don't know what to say either," I finally admitted. This was a first for me. Was I supposed to offer my condolences? Was I supposed to say that it was a good thing he divorced her before she passed away? Was I supposed to ask what happened? What was the right thing to say when your new boyfriend told you that his ex-wife was dead? "What happened?" I asked.

"She had an aneurysm. It was instantaneous. She was over at a friend's house. I wasn't there, obviously. I didn't find out until the following day," he admitted. I tried to think about how I would feel if Owen was suddenly gone, and my body immediately reacted as if I'd eaten something spicy. My eyes watered, and my throat and stomach burned and itched and threatened to close up.

"I'm sorry," I sputtered. "How long had you been divorced?"

"Over a year. Still, it was an awful thing to go through."

"I can't imagine. Just because people leave your life doesn't mean you want them to really leave your life."

"It's strange. More than anything I kept thinking about how my life would be if we'd stayed married. What if things had been great between us and we were living out our happily ever after, and that happened? Then I'm a widower, and not just a guy who's divorced and who had already gotten used to living life without her. The universe had already decided that we were never going to have a life together. There was always a clock counting down above us until our time ran out, but we didn't know it."

"It's crazy to think about it like that," I said, which was true, but I still was getting really tired of people treating the universe as an active participant in their life. The universe didn't kill Fred's ex-wife, and it didn't bring Owen and Dee Dee together. An aneurysm and a U-Haul did those things. That was it.

"I know. My whole life could've been different. Instead, I was just the ex-husband at the funeral, the guy people looked at sideways wondering why I'd bothered to show."

"I'm sure nobody thought that," I said, even though I'd bet there were more than a few people who did.

"It's not something I like to talk about, and it's certainly not an easy thing to work into conversation, but I wanted you to know. I didn't want you to think that there was an ex-wife out there waiting to pop out of the bushes and sabotage what we have."

"How do you know I was thinking that?" I asked.

"Just a guess."

"I'm so sorry, Fred. I feel horrible for you for having to go through that. I feel horrible for her, that she was so young and had her whole life to look forward to. I feel horrible for your family."

"What I hate the most is knowing that our divorce caused so much stress for her the last few years of her life. She wasted so much time fighting with me over stupid little things: who was going to get the flat-screen TV in the basement, and who got to keep the house. At the time it all seemed important. Then she was gone, and I realized that none of it mattered. It was too late then to tell her I was sorry, or to try and make things easier on her—on both of us. It shouldn't take something like death to give you some perspective on your life but it did."

"Why are you telling me this now?"

"I don't want to watch you make my mistakes. I know Owen hurt you and you hate him and you have every right to. I guess my advice to you is to not get mired in anger. Find a way to see the bigger picture. I wish someone had told me that, so I wanted to tell you."

"So when I asked if you still spoke to your wife you lied to me," I said. I didn't know why I chose to focus on that. Probably because it seemed easier than trying to admit that he was right and that I needed to forgive Owen. And probably Marcy, but definitely Owen.

"No. I told you that I hadn't spoken to her in a few years. That's true."

"Technicality."

"I didn't even know you. I didn't want to divulge something so personal. I can't apologize for that. I won't. If you don't get that, I don't know what to tell you."

I had to admit he was right. "I don't blame you. Thank you for telling me. Do you want to talk about her?"

"No," he said, firmly. "Don't forget we were divorced when she died. We didn't have the best relationship, but I like to remember the good stuff. I think I'll just keep that for myself if that's okay."

"It is."

"You should focus on the good times. Nothing is going to change what happened between you, but you can either remember the parts of your relationship that made you happy, or you can remember the parts that made you miserable. It's entirely up to you. Things can change in an instant."

"They already have," I said as we approached the park. We sat down on a bench near the pond, Bo's stroller tucked next to me under the shade of a giant tree, and I reluctantly allowed my mind to scroll through my ever-growing list of regrets.

Chapter 19

LABOR DAY WAS fast approaching, and once upon a time that would have bothered me a lot, but now I was actually excited about fall and everything that lay in front of me because life was finally back in my house. The bad memories of Owen were starting to fade and were being replaced with new ones I created for myself with the people I loved. Now I just needed Fred to rip down the insect wallpaper in the powder room and this house would totally feel like home.

Bo was starting to say words: "Mama," which I loved, and "Da Da," which I didn't love, and if he woke up one day and said "Dee Dee" I'd have no choice but to hurl myself out of a second-floor window, so I tried not to think about that possibility too much. Living with a baby made it impossible to ignore the passage of time. Every day there was a new word, or a new skill, or a new tooth, and it was all happening so fast I could barely believe it. He walked holding on to things, but he was getting ready to let go and go it alone. Every morning I woke up and wondered if today would be the day that he decided he was brave enough to move without the help of a table or chair or leg to support him. I knew one of these days he'd do it, and it would be the first steps he took away from me, and out into the world on his own. It was a wonderful time for him, but a scary time for me, because I wasn't ready to let him go—not even a little bit. I decided that Antonia could never, ever leave the house. She was going to have to be in this with me for the long haul.

Lissy officially closed the store a week ago, and Fred had been sanding the floors all weekend. We only had a few weeks left until our opening, and he said it would take him about two days to finish, and that was two days ago, and I was starting to get nervous. I wanted to go down there and check on his progress, but he made me promise that I'd stay away from the store until he was finished, because sanding floors was apparently noisy, and dusty, and you had to wear a mask over your mouth, and protective goggles over your eyes to keep the wood dust from burning your retinas, and I didn't have either of those things. When he was finished sanding the floors we were going to paint them, and that meant we needed to buy paint.

Lissy, Antonia, and I met in the parking lot outside of Home Depot, and that was a place that I never would've imagined Lissy, Antonia, and I would meet on a Sunday morning. I had no idea that Home Depot was so enormous. We stood in the middle of the warehouse, right in front of the automatic doors, waiting for someone with a nametag and a clue to come give us directions, or a map, or some breadcrumbs we could drop on the floor in case we got lost and couldn't find our way out. I wasn't planning on being here long, but now I realized that it was going to take us twenty minutes just to find the paint section, and that we probably should've just gone to the local hardware store, and grabbed some of those cards with different shades of paint on them that Benjamin Moore lets you take home for free. We were in way over our heads.

"Do you think we could paint them red?" Lissy asked after a very nice man escorted us what felt like three miles from the entrance to the paint section of the store.

"I think red might make the space look small," I suggested. "Maybe a pink would be better? Besides, your logo is red, and some of the accent trim in the store is red, and you will obviously have red lips, and we don't need to hit people over the head with it. Pink is a nod to your color, but a little more subtle."

"I agree," said Antonia. "Let's look at the pinks."

You'd be surprised how many shades of pink there are, but after thirty minutes of searching, we found some promising contenders: Easter Bunny, Bermuda Breeze, and Rhododendron being the early front-runners.

"I don't like Rhododendron," Lissy said, dismissing it immediately. "We had one at the bottom of our driveway when I was little and bees swarmed all over it. Half the time I was afraid to leave my house."

"Okay. No Rhododendron," I agreed. "We can find another one that doesn't remind you of an agoraphobic time in your life," I teased.

"Thanks," Lissy said, missing my sarcasm entirely. "I don't want there to be any negative associations with this place."

"Believe me, I get that," I told her, and I did.

"I like Easter Bunny," Antonia said.

"Me too," I agreed.

"I like it, too," Lissy added. "I just don't know if we should buy it right now."

"Why not?" I asked. We were in Home Depot. Why were we there if not to buy paint?

"Maybe we should just take a sample, and once we're allowed back in the store, assuming that Fred hasn't sanded the floors down to matchsticks and there's still a floor to stand on, we can see what the paint looks like in natural light," Lissy said.

"Never underestimate the importance of good lighting," I said, remembering Tara Redmond's office and wondering what happened to the thread-puller.

"I think we're overthinking this," Antonia said. "Let's just pick a color. We can stand here for ten hours and decide, or stand in the store for ten hours and decide, but it's not going to make this decision any easier. Let's just do it now and move on. What do you think?"

"I think that sounds scary," Lissy admitted. I wasn't so sure. There was something to be said about just ripping off the Band-Aid. I took out my phone and snapped a picture of the paint samples.

"I just sent a picture of them to Fred. Let's see what he thinks."

"Sure," Lissy said. "Because a heterosexual man is obviously the right person to ask if you're looking for a second opinion on a pink paint color called Easter Bunny."

"He's good at this stuff. It doesn't matter if the paint is pink! He'll know."

"Awwww, isn't it so cute to see our little Claire in love again?" Antonia asked.

"I never saw her in love the first time," Lissy said. "Was it this sickeningly cheerful?"

"Worse," Antonia added. "Someday I'll tell you about it."

"Oh, stop. I just think that he knows a thing or two about DIY and we know less than a thing or two about DIY so we'd be silly not to ask him. A professional decorator might advise that we stay very far away from the color, but we can't afford a decorator, so we are going to have to rely on our own instincts, and Fred. It's unfortunate that none of us have ever done anything like this before, but sometimes, you just have to wing it. This is one of those times." I felt like the team captain—like it was my job to push this team over the finish line.

I knew Lissy was nervous because she had turned her store, and in some ways, the memory of her mother, over to my boyfriend and his very large sanding machine, and she wasn't really all that familiar with either of them. It would've been easy for me to tell her that she had absolutely nothing to worry about, that Fred was a pro and that when he was finished she'd have the most beautiful store in town and it wouldn't have cost her a dime. I wanted to tell her all of this, but I had absolutely no idea if it was true. Fred certainly seemed knowledgeable about the art of drum sanding, but he was an accountant, not Ty Pennington. I was terrified that if something went horribly wrong, Lissy would never forgive me, and then Fred would be responsible for ruining the only friendship I'd managed to nurture since I'd moved here. There was a lot riding on this for everyone, and it wasn't like the floor was a small thing that we could afford to screw up.

"Okay," Lissy agreed. "Just let me sleep on it. I'll come back and buy the paint tomorrow, I promise. I just want to think it over for a few hours before we commit. Okay?"

"Okay," Antonia and I said simultaneously. It was a simple request, but we had to make a decision by tomorrow, or we were going to risk not finishing everything on time. We said good-bye to Lissy in the parking lot, and I watched as she stared at the two paint cards while she walked to her car. I was happy that Antonia and I had decided to surprise her with our little DIY project. I just hoped she loved it as much as I wanted her to.

"You ready to go back inside and do that all over again?" I asked as we watched Lissy's car disappear into the road.

"Let's do it!" Antonia cheered. We locked our arms together, and quickly scurried back into the store.

ANTONIA AND I returned to the house and laid out the entire Sunday *New York Times* across a large patch of grass in the backyard. I opened the bag from Home Depot and removed the sandpaper, paint cans, and two paintbrushes. We were ready. I was sure of it. I was pretty sure I was sure of it.

"Are you sure you know how to do this?" Antonia asked.

"No! I have never done this before, but it's spray paint, not open heart surgery. I imagine you just point and shoot."

"That doesn't mean it's easy. Maybe we should wait for Fred, or someone else, to come and help us."

"Fred is helping enough. Speaking of, how long does it take to sand floors anyway? Shouldn't he be done by now?"

"Are we sure he knows what he's doing?" Antonia asked.

"I'd really rather not answer that question right now."

"I just hope we don't ruin the whole set and end up still needing to buy something. We don't have a lot of time left before she needs to reopen."

"Don't be so negative! Besides, how hard could it be? What's the worst thing that happens? We wreck a perfectly good kitchen set and the grass in my backyard? So what? I don't care about either of them."

"Okay. You're right. Let's go get it," Antonia said, looking hysterical in denim overalls, a baseball hat, and a pair of sneakers, because that was apparently what you wore if you wanted to spray-paint your best friend's ex-husband's kitchen set in the backyard.

"I'm so happy I didn't let you smash this to bits," Antonia said as we descended the stairs to the basement.

"One girl's trash is another girl's treasure."

"Isn't that why Dee Dee is dating Owen?" Antonia joked. For a second my breath caught in my throat, the air fighting through knots, and lumps, and muscles in the midst of spasms, trying to escape. Then, all of the tension eased, and I surprised myself by managing to smile. "I'm sorry. Is it too soon?" she asked.

"No," I answered, liking so very much that it was true. "It's been almost six months. It's definitely not too soon," I said.

"Anyway, I'm happy she'll be able to use it. I think it'll be perfect."

The rickety garage door still worked, though it was only a matter of time before the chain broke in half and the door slammed into the pavement and splintered into a million pieces. The table and chairs were exactly where they were the last time I'd gone looking for them, when I wanted to chop them up and light them on fire in the driveway. I hadn't been in the garage since, mostly because I promised Antonia that I wouldn't go near it again until I needed to get the Christmas decorations, but also because there was nothing in there that I needed.

Until today.

We carried the table and chairs one by one into the backyard and set them down on top of the newspaper. Antonia strapped on her goggles. "Here we go," she said. She began to paint the chairs while I stood next to her and sprayed the table with glossy white paint. Neither one of us was good at this type of thing and it showed, because I wasn't even done with my first can of paint and my clothing, hands, and lawn were arguably more evenly painted than the table sitting three feet in front of me. I needed this paint job to work, because I refused to go back to Home Depot and tell the man who got stuck helping us that we messed it up and needed to start over.

We were just about finished when Antonia finally brought up the conversation I'd been hoping to avoid at all costs. "We need to talk about when I'm going to leave," Antonia said. She ran a small paintbrush around the bottom of a chair leg, making sure that every last bit of wood was covered, even though every last bit of wood was covered ten minutes ago.

"No, I don't think we need to talk about that at all, actually," I said. I knew this conversation was coming, I just kept hoping that the longer she stayed, the more at home she would feel, and maybe she'd want to stay forever. Was that too much to ask?

"You don't need me anymore. You've got your groove back. My leaving is the last thing that needs to happen before you can close this chapter in your life for good."

"I don't want you to go. I love having you here. What will I do in this house by myself? Who will make us lasagna?"

"I'm not saying I'm leaving tomorrow, but at some point, I'm going to have to go home. I just don't want to blindside you with it when it happens. It's on my radar, okay?"

"Okay," I lied, because it was so definitely not okay. "Can we talk about something else?"

"You got it. What do you think?" Antonia asked as we stood back and admired our work, and also the fact that my lawn was sprayed white in patches like we were trying to create a football field in the backyard.

"I think they look freakin' awesome. It looks like a whole different set!"

"Do you think we'll have a hard time with the upholstery?"

"Probably. I only say that because so far this is going way too smoothly, and eventually something has to go wrong."

"I'm so happy we were able to go back and buy the fabric

without her knowing. I love it! Should we take the seats and recover them now?"

"Do you mind if I take a quick shower first?" I asked, looking down at my hands and my arms, wondering how long it would take this spray paint to dry and set on my skin so that I had to scrape it off with a trowel. "I'm a mess."

"Go for it," Antonia said. Her own hands and arms were still clean. I had no idea how she managed to do that.

I took a hot shower, leaving my paint-covered clothes in a little mound on my bathroom floor next to the pile of sheets and towels that I hadn't gotten around to washing just yet, which you could do if you didn't share your bathroom with anyone else. That was one good thing about being single—no one asked you if you washed his undershirts, or replaced the hand towels in the bathroom, or bought more toilet paper because the powder room on the first floor was out. Now, if I didn't want to replace the toilet paper for weeks, I didn't, and it was no one's problem but my own—which reminded me that I needed to buy more toilet paper because I was one roll away from running out.

I'd put on a few pounds, which was how I knew that I was finally happy. My mother would describe women in town who were starting to look a little plumper than usual that way, and I never understood it. I was sure if she was here right now, she'd say, "Oh, honey, you look beautiful. I haven't seen you this happy in a long time," and she'd be right. I turned and looked at my butt in the mirror, and while I certainly wouldn't be appearing under the "bootylicious" definition in the dictionary anytime soon, there was a little roundness there, keeping my jeans from hanging off me the way they usually did. My face was a little less pale, and a little less angular, and my eyes were a little less dull and a little less empty. I still had a few more pounds to gain in order to be back to my old self, but a few more weeks with Fred would take care of that soon enough.

I pulled on a pair of jeans, and a brown sweater, and brushed my hair into a low ponytail before I headed back downstairs. I heard a courtesy knock on the front door as I hit the landing, and Fred came lumbering in smelling like a wood chipper and covered in dust. I held my breath, waiting for him to tell me that his drum sander went crazy and now we could see through the floor of the store into the basement, but instead he gave me two thumbs up and a smile. I hoped one day I'd be able to stop expecting the worst. The world wasn't out to get me. Everything was just fine. My life was mine again, and this time it was going to stay that way.

"They look great. I'm really happy with how they came out," he said. "And I have a surprise for you girls."

"What?"

"I painted them. Well, two of my buddies came over and helped me, but they're done. Lissy is going to love it."

"What do you mean you painted them?" I asked. We hadn't definitely picked out a paint color yet. I also couldn't understand how he possibly could've managed to do that in the time it took us to buy five cans of spray paint and coat a table and chairs in the backyard. We must really suck at this.

"I went to Home Depot and bought the paint color you sent me."

"I sent you three different colors. Please don't tell me you picked Rhododendron."

"You said you thought you'd decided on Easter Bunny."

"We did. Sort of. We weren't definite on that!" I said.

"Trust me, you wanted to go with Easter Bunny."

"This is a strange conversation."

"I wanted to surprise you, and do it today. I know how it's been stressing you out to have everything on hold until the floors were finished, and I didn't want to be the one responsible for slowing down this train. As of tomorrow, you guys can start moving everything back downstairs."

"You're serious? Lissy is going to freak out! Assuming she likes the paint. If she doesn't she's going to freak out in a bad way."

"I'm serious. Look, I'm not your target audience, but I think they look great. You're going to be really happy with it."

"Did you take any pictures?" I asked, gesturing toward his phone. "Please tell me you can show me what it looks like."

"I had a feeling you'd ask me that," he said.

I wrapped my hands around his neck and kissed him, not minding that he smelled sweaty and dirty, and woodsy, and those aren't three things that I ever thought I'd find attractive in a man—but I did. We went upstairs, leaving Antonia outside with the newspapers and the empty paint cans, and the wet furniture, and I dragged Fred into the shower with me, even though I'd just gotten out of one, and my hair was already partially dry, because that was what you did with your boyfriend after he spent his entire weekend sanding and painting your friend's floor.

Chapter 20

THE REST OF August flew by in a whirlwind of planning and cleaning and social media postings and before I knew it the month was almost over and our grand opening was just around the corner. The Friday of Labor Day weekend was a beautiful day, the kind of early fall day where people want to open their windows, and turn off the air conditioners, and start looking for their sweaters instead of their flip-flops. The grand opening of Lissy's revamped store was only a week away, and there was so much to do between now and then. I'd been promoting the store on local social media, but I needed to stop by the office of the town paper, and see how much it would cost to run an ad. I wanted to swing by the high school and see if one of the secretaries in the attendance office would mind if I left stacks of party invitations on her desk so the senior girls who cut class the first week of school would see them when they reported for detention. I needed to double-check with the caterer that we'd be using red trays for the passed hors d'oeuvres, per Lissy's orders, and I wanted to stop in town and get a small gift for Fred to say thank you for everything he did for us. I knew the last week before the opening would be crazy busy, and I couldn't remember the last time I had so much to do. But first, I had to do something else.

I dug through the bottom of my closet, and finally found my black ankle boots, the ones that I'd sworn I'd never wear again when I'd been terrified about accidentally falling down, killing myself, and leaving Bo alone. My black pants were fitted, and showed off the curve of my butt without looking trashy. My cotton sweater was a beautiful mossy green that J.Crew introduced for fall, and while I was sure half the town would be wearing it for the next few months I didn't care. I didn't own anything this color. It was new. I felt pretty. And, it didn't remind me of Owen at all. I ran a comb through my hair and brushed it straight back into a ponytail. I added two thin bangles to my wrist, and a swipe of cream blush to my cheeks. Then, I took one more look at myself in the mirror, and nodded at my reflection. *Hi, Claire,* I thought. *It's good to see you again.*

"Are you ready to go?" Lissy called from downstairs. "I need to be there a little early."

"I'm ready," I replied. I turned off the bathroom light and left the master bedroom to head downstairs. I wasn't going to let those women bully me into staying home on Friday mornings for the rest of my life. I wasn't going to let them dictate my movements, my mood, or my attitude. Bo liked the library. I didn't care that it was a Friday, or that I had a million things to do, or that they were likely to be there. We were going to go to story time, and we were going to sit in the middle of the room, right up front where everyone could see us. I was over them. Nobody puts Claire in a corner.

I smiled at the elderly lady manning the front desk. Her name was Barbara, and she'd been working at the library for the last fifty years. She'd seen young children grow up, marry, and return with their own kids and even grandkids. She stashed a glass jar of lollipops at her feet that those in the know could ask for on their way out the door. She'd told me that she used to keep them on her desk, and let the kids help themselves, but that was before food allergies and an all-consuming hatred of artificial preservatives and refined sugar forced her to hide them under her desk like some people hide porn. She was a wonderful woman who'd donated her time for her entire adult life to the children's section of this library. I hoped I could be like her someday.

Lissy took her seat on the dais and removed her favorite cow puppet from the bag. Personally, I liked the puppet shows the best, because they really showed off the span of Lissy's talents. She was more than just a good storyteller—she was part ventriloquist, part stand-up comic, part babysitter, and part fairy godmother to these kids and that made her one of the most special people I'd ever met in my life, and without her I'd probably still be back home trying to take a sledgehammer to my own bathtub.

Purple stroller lady was there, but I didn't even look in her direction, because I was over the fact that she didn't want to be my friend, or even tell me her name. Becky and Stephanie showed up, just like I hoped they would, but Stella apparently decided to skip this week. It didn't matter. Showing two of them that I didn't care what they thought of me was just as good as showing all of them. I hadn't seen the playground mommies with the thermoses since that day at the park. I hoped they didn't go to rehab, but I didn't wish to be friends with them anymore either, because I had a nice little life brewing here, and hanging out with the day-drinking girls no longer seemed so appealing, though I reserved the right to change my mind on that. I took a seat on the floor, right in the middle of the room, and pulled Bo on my lap. They slid into chairs in the last row, like it was a high school math class and the cool kids needed to sit in the back of the room, and talked loudly as if no one else was there. I finally saw them for what they were, and I almost felt bad for them, because twenty years ago they had Mommy's looks, and Daddy's car, and everyone's attention, and they weren't ready to let it go. I felt bad for them because now they were middle-aged, and Mommy's looks weren't quite what they used to be, and the car was a minivan, and they still got people's attention, but not for the same reasons. I might have been closer to forty than twenty, but if there was one thing I could embrace about aging, it was that I didn't give a shit about girls like that anymore. I couldn't believe I ever did.

They didn't notice me, probably because it never occurred to them that I'd go back after they told me I shouldn't, and their conversation stopped me in my tracks.

"Do you believe he broke up with her?" Becky asked. Her little boy was wearing an argyle sweater vest and knee socks, and he crawled up to Lissy and tried to grab the puppet off her hand. I kept my eyes glued on Bo, but my ears were very much tuned in to their conversation. I couldn't believe what I was hearing. They broke up? Actually, it was even better than that. Becky didn't say that they'd broken up. She'd said that *he* broke up with *her.*

Was this really happening?

"I never liked him. I'm sorry, I don't care what anyone says, he was never a good guy. Never," Stephanie added, which was hysterical, because if I wasn't mistaken, just a few short months ago, she was the one claiming to know that Owen and Dee Dee were always meant to be together.

"She was about to start shopping for wedding dresses. I mean, who leaves his wife for someone he doesn't want to marry? Is he deranged? Was this all just fun and games for him?"

Nothing fun about it, I thought. Maybe that was Dee Dee's problem this whole time—maybe she never understood the seriousness of the situation. Maybe she just saw it as some great, romantic love story she could brag about to her friends, and never bothered to look at it for what it really was: a very bad ending to a very good marriage; a very difficult beginning to a very complicated living situation; and a very different life for a very little boy. She didn't care about any of it, because she was too worried thinking about herself. I was very happy to discover that karma had very badly kicked her in her selfish ass.

Bo got up and wobbled up to the front of the room, and stood at Lissy's feet. She smiled as she pulled him up onto her lap, and he gave her an enormous toothy grin. My little boy was walking now. Pretty soon he'd need a haircut. When did that happen? When did he morph from a chubby baby into a little boy? Lissy rang her bell indicating that class was over, and people filed out, heading to the park, or the grocery store, or home for morning naps, but I hung back and waited for Lissy to pack her bag.

"He'll never do better than her," Becky said, as they lingered in the back of the room so they could finish their gossip session. And it was just too good of an opportunity to pass up.

"Excuse me," I said. "About that. Yes, he will. In fact, he already has."

"THEY BROKE UP! Do you believe this?" I asked Lissy the second I came barreling through the door, almost ripping the bell off its string. I'd dropped Bo at home with Antonia and returned to S.W.A.K. for a few hours to help with the finishing touches at the store. I felt like I was flying. It may have been immature to take pleasure in the misfortune of others, but I was taking an absurd amount of pleasure from this unfortunate turn of events. In fact, I couldn't remember a time when anything had pleased me more. Whatever. I wasn't even going to pretend to feel bad about it. I wasn't planning on applying for sainthood anyway.

"Of course I believe it," Lissy said. She finished placing a few stacks of cards on the top shelf of the display case, and climbed down the ladder. "You didn't think they were going to get married, did you?"

"I don't know! I don't know what I thought. I guess I figured if he was going to leave me for her then they'd at least be together for a while, but it hasn't even been a year! Wait a second, is that supposed to make me feel better or worse?"

"It doesn't matter. All that matters is that she's gone. She's gone because he told her to scram, and you just totally stuck it to her friends. You're having one hell of an afternoon."

"I know!" I said. I paused for a second and looked around the room. "This place is stunning," I gushed, so overwhelmed with how beautiful it looked I temporarily forgot about everything else, including the awning that Fred was going to install while I was at the library.

I turned and raced out onto the sidewalk to examine the crisp white canopy covering the façade above the door. It was simple, it was elegant, it was clean, and it showed off the script lettering beautifully. Lissy and I had agreed that the words "Sealed with a" would be in black ink, and the word "Kiss" would be in red, and it looked so amazing I had to resist the urge to scale the wall and lie on top of it so that I could kiss it myself. There was no missing this place now. Everyone would know that Sealed with a Kiss was in business, and also that it was awesome. Mission accomplished.

"I'm having a hard time believing that it's the same place. How did this even happen?"

I didn't like to brag, and Lord knows, I hadn't had much to brag about lately, but we'd done a really wonderful job making the tired store look bright and shiny and ready for a real grand opening. Fred had been right when he said that painting the floors in Easter Bunny was the way to go. We'd gotten it exactly right. The original glass counter and display cases and carousels kept the space looking open and airy, and, in my opinion, toned down the pink, white, and red color scheme enough so that you didn't feel like you were buying your letterhead in a candy shop.

"We never got chairs. I looked everywhere but everything was either too big or too expensive. Do you think that's going to hurt us if we don't have them by the party?"

"I'm so happy you mentioned that. I have a surprise for you," I said. I dragged Lissy out back by the parking lot, and there was Fred, just as he promised, delivering our gift.

The small wooden table and mismatched chairs I'd wanted to hack into matchsticks looked like they were custom-made for S.W.A.K., the table and chair seats painted white, and their legs painted Lissy's signature red. The red, pink, and white polka-dot fabric we found was perfect, and thanks to a lot of time in front of HGTV and more than a few tutorials on You-Tube, Antonia and I had been able to reupholster the chair cushions with little more than a staple gun, a glue gun, and some minor burns on our hands. I knew they'd look perfect tucked into the nook in the corner in between the register and the stairwell. "Do you like them?" I asked. I walked over and ran my hand over the tabletop. It was hard to believe it was the same furniture, or that it had ever been anywhere but here.

"They're amazing! Where did you get these? I've been looking all over the place for seating and haven't been able to find anything like it. This is exactly what I would've picked if I'd seen it!"

"I had the table and chairs, but Antonia and I refurbished them. Do you really like them?" I asked, so happy that Lissy seemed to love our gift.

"Are you serious? You guys did this? For me?"

"Yes. We wanted to do something to surprise you. Antonia did two, and I did two. Mine are obviously better," I joked.

"I love them. I really, really love them. I don't know what to say," Lissy admitted.

"I know the feeling."

"I don't mean to ruin the moment, but shall we bring these inside? I need to get going soon, and I don't want to leave you guys to do all the heavy lifting by yourselves," Fred said, ever the gentleman.

"You got it," we said. We carried the table and chairs into the store, positioned them in the corner, and admired our work.

"I couldn't possibly have imagined this looking any better than it does. It's a dream come true," Lissy said.

"On that note, I'll take off. Claire, I'll see you later." Fred blew me a kiss as he reached for the door.

"Thanks so much for being my moving man. And my awning man. And just my man," I said with a wink.

"And general contractor," Lissy said. She walked over to Fred and gave him a firm kiss on the cheek, leaving her lip imprint on his skin.

"All in a day's work. Except now I need to go home and do my actual job. Bye, ladies," he said.

"I'm going to send you a hundred emojis to say thank you for this," I called after him as he headed toward the parking lot. "Hearts and smiley faces and thumbs-up and dancing ladies and red lips and stars and that's just off the top of my head!"

"Don't even joke, Claire! That kind of nonsense is exactly why text messaging will be the demise of all basic communication skills. Don't make me revoke your text privileges!"

I smiled. I'd been doing that a lot lately. "Okay," I said as I picked up a rag from a pile on the floor. "One last scrub before I go?"

"Agreed!"

I buffed, and scrubbed, and polished until every surface was gleaming and every single fingerprint was erased from the glass. I inspected the displays, and was convinced we'd covered all the bases. There was something for everyone: note cards with ladybugs, sophisticated monograms, birth announcements with trains, rocking horses, and bumblebees for boys, and stripes, flowers, and kittens for girls. There were save-the-date cards with sketches of the New York City skyline, and classic cards trimmed in grosgrain ribbon that could be used for anything. The shining star of the case, Lissy's beautiful calligraphied envelopes, were displayed on a large Mariposa silver tray I'd gotten as a wedding gift and never had a chance to use. It was perfect to showcase Lissy's amazing talent, her handwriting, scrolls, and flourishes so perfect it was hard to believe it wasn't manufactured by a letterpress. People were going to be knocked out of their leather moccasins when they saw those beautiful envelopes. I knew without a doubt that if nothing else, that calligraphy would get her a ton of business. And, if we were lucky, eventually some publicity on one of the big wedding websites. That was phase two of my plan for this place. First we needed to get through the grand opening. We had another full week to go, but we were ready.

It was just after 4:30. "I need to get going," I said to Lissy, who was polishing the glass counter with Windex for the fiftieth time. "I'm going to post a picture before I get my car. Then I need to drop Bo off at Owen's. I don't know how I'm going to see him and not ask him what happened. It's going to kill me."

"Don't ask him. Let him tell you himself. Otherwise, it'll look like you still care."

"Good point. Fine, I'll keep my mouth shut. I'll check in with you later."

"Okay. This place really does look good, doesn't it?" Lissy asked. My heart ached for her.

"Your mom would be so proud of this place. You've done her justice while making it your own. As a mom, I can tell you that you can't ask anything else of your kids. You did a really terrific job."

"Yeah," she said. "I think she really would've liked it. I think she'd be proud of me. That's probably a ridiculous thing for a grown woman to worry about, huh?"

"She already is, Lissy," I said, knowing that it was true. "You're kind, and honest, and thoughtful, and generous, and if those aren't the things all mothers wish their children would be, then they're not wishing for any of the right things."

"Thanks," she said, getting slightly choked up, which for Lissy was an epic display of emotion probably on par with my meltdown in the Italian restaurant. It was nice to see.

"Bo's lucky to have you. I don't know if anyone has ever told you that. You should know."

I walked over to her and hugged her tightly. "That's the nicest thing anyone has ever said to me."

"Then I repeat, you really need to get out more," she joked. "Now get out of here and don't forget to wear red lipstick at the party on Saturday."

"I have to wear the lipstick? That's your thing. I'm more of a mauve girl."

"Of course you have to wear the lipstick!" she squealed in horror like I had just asked her if I had to wear pants to her big opening. "It's my brand. There's a lip print on the awning. There's a lip print on the business cards. I wear red lipstick, and when you're here, you wear red lipstick, too. We're a team, and you're the one who told me we need a brand. That's our brand."

"Okay. I'll go and buy a red lipstick before next Saturday, I promise. Can I be a pinky red? I feel like one of the Robert Palmer girls playing guitar in the 'Simply Irresistible' video when I wear red lipstick."

"No. Bloodred. Vampire red."

"Hollywood siren red."

"Whatever you're comfortable calling it. You know what I'm talking about. Don't wuss out."

"Okay. That's the least I can do for you. Bye."

I stepped out onto the sidewalk, the air noticeably crisper than it was even a week ago. It wouldn't be long before people would be wearing quilted vests and soft cotton scarves around their necks, blankets would be draped over the legs of toddlers in strollers, and Pumpkin Spice Lattes would be the morning coffee of choice. Maybe Owen was right. Maybe there was something to the whole fall in New England thing after all. The leaves hadn't started to change yet, summer just officially ended after all, but I had no doubt that when they did, the town would transform into something really special. I thought I'd actually enjoy it. It had been five months since things ended with Owen, and I was now finally at a place where I knew we'd be okay. I had Bo and Antonia and Lissy and Fred and that was all I needed for my life to be full. I wished I'd known things would turn out like this from the very beginning.

I turned my back to the road and stepped toward the curb, so that I could take a picture of the new awning. The crisp white stood out against the dark brick, and the red lettering was both attention grabbing and appropriate. I held up my iPhone and captured the entire façade with a few branches from the tree on the sidewalk leaning into the side of the frame. I examined it, and decided that it didn't even need a filter. It was perfect just the way it was. I couldn't wait to post this on Instagram, Facebook, and Twitter. I also wanted to scan it on flyers, and hand them out outside the organic grocery store and in the parking lot at the high school before the Labor Day parade on Monday. There was still so much to be done.

"That looks amazing," a woman walking by said as she stopped and gazed at the new façade. "What a great name! Sealed with a Kiss! How smart is that? I love it!"

"Isn't that just the best name for a stationery store?" I asked, loving the compliment so much I almost jumped up and down right there on the sidewalk.

"It really is totally adorable. Has this store always been here?"

"It has, but it's recently gotten a full makeover inside and out. We're having a grand reopening next weekend. You should come by. The holidays are going to be here before you know it, and she's going to have some of her cards available for preordering at a discount," I said, thrilled that someone had already noticed the new storefront. I wanted to reach out and hug this little blond woman for validating everything we'd done, for proving that it hadn't all just been a huge waste of time. "Here's a business card. The store hours are on there, as is the email address. Lissy, the owner, does really beautiful calligraphy, too."

"I had no idea. It's hard to believe that it's almost time to start dealing with holiday cards, but I'll definitely come by. See you next weekend," she said. She tucked the card into a pocket in her purse, and continued down the street. I took a deep breath, felt the cool air burn the air sacs in my lungs, and as I exhaled I decided that maybe Connecticut wasn't so bad.

There, I said it.

I wasn't going to beat myself up for the way I handled the last five months of my life, but I wasn't going to tackle the rest of the year the same way. I controlled my mood, and I controlled my happiness, and I had a lot to be happy about, so I was going to focus on all of the things that were good in my life, instead of the things that weren't. Fine, things didn't turn out anywhere near the way I'd hoped they would, but that was okay. Maybe the way I wanted them to turn out wasn't right for me anyway. Going forward, I was only going to worry about living in the now. I was going to be a positive example for my son, a good friend to the people who were good friends to me, and live my life with my new mantra: no regrets.

I uploaded the picture and began to scroll through my emojis looking for the bright red heart before I posted it to Instagram. As it turned out, I shouldn't have been worried about the selfie-stick-wielding millennial plowing me over. The millennial, however, should've been really worried about the middle-aged idiot trying to cross the street while posting a picture of a stationery store to every social media outlet in the free world. I didn't see her coming, and that was probably a good thing.

Chapter 21

THE ACCIDENT WAS a blur. I didn't remember too much of it, just that I was crossing the street while simultaneously trying to post something on Lissy's Instagram to help promote the new store opening, and ended up bouncing off the hood of someone's car and landing on my back in the middle of the road.

There were lights. Bright, pulsing, blinding lights. There was pain. Stabbing, throbbing, shooting pain. There was yelling, and screaming, and shrieking. Someone kept telling me not to move, and that I was going to be okay because she was a nurse and I guess that meant that she wasn't going to let me die on the pavement in front of a stationery store. Lissy appeared out of nowhere, and dropped down on her knees next to me.

"Oh my God. Claire? Claire, can you hear me?" she asked. "Please say something. Talk to me."

"I don't think my Instagram picture posted. You might have to redo it," I whispered, once again babbling things that were completely inappropriate given the situation.

"That's okay. We'll worry about Instagram later."

"Okay," I said.

Lights continued to flash on and off in front of my eyes. I squinted. Squinting hurt. Every time I squeezed my eyes shut I felt like someone in my brain was trying to punch my eyeballs out of their sockets from inside my skull. It was as rhythmic as a bass drum, over and over and over.

"An ambulance is on the way. I'll come with you, okay? You don't need to worry about anything. You're totally going to be fine, but you need to stay calm," Lissy ordered, which was strange since she was the one panicking and I hadn't moved at all.

"Mm-hmm," I agreed. "I'm totally fine. I don't need an ambulance. Just help me up. I need to go get Bo," I said. I tried to move. I couldn't.

Somewhere off in the distance a woman was crying. "I didn't see her!" she wailed. "She just walked out in front of me!" *What's her problem?* I wondered. *I'm the one who just got hit by the car.* Some people could be so dramatic.

"Why can't I get up?" I asked.

"You're in shock," the nurse said. She held her finger up in front of my eyes and moved it back and forth like the metronome my childhood piano teacher kept perched on the top of her Steinway.

"Oh," I said.

"Can you tell me what hurts?"

"Everything," I answered, which probably wasn't very helpful to her, but when I said everything hurt, I meant it. The asphalt was hot, and something sharp was digging into the skin on my arms—small razor blades inflicting a million little cuts.

The back of my head felt wet. I was fairly sure it was blood seeping out of my skull. This was my worst fear. I was going to die. I was going to die because of Instagram. Thank God I had my death folder on my computer. I needed to make sure Antonia knew about it before it was too late, because I never actually got around to showing it to her.

"Can you feel this?" the nurse asked. She touched the bottom of my foot with something, I have no idea what.

"Yes. I can feel it."

"That's great. That's really wonderful," she said.

"Can someone do something about the flashing light?" I asked. "It's so bright."

"Oh my God, she's seeing lights? No, Claire!" Lissy shouted. "Stay away from the light! Somebody do something!"

"Stop it! You're upsetting her!" the nurse ordered. "She probably has a concussion."

"You're right," Lissy said, calming. "You're right. That's fine. We can fix that."

"Claire, I'm fairly certain you have a concussion, and probably some broken bones. We're going to get you to the hospital," Nurse Find-the-Bright-Side-of-Everything said.

"Lissy, I need you to call Antonia. Tell her to call Owen. I was supposed to bring Bo to his house tonight. He's going to have to come pick him up."

"Okay. No problem. I can do that."

"Also, tell Antonia that I have a death folder on my computer and to not forget that Bo really likes his sweet potatoes mashed with coconut milk."

"Okay, sweetie. I'll tell her," Lissy said, and even in my post-accident state of shock, I knew she was going to chalk that comment up to my head injury and not take it seriously. That was not acceptable as I'd never been more serious about anything in my life, and this very well may have been my dying wish.

"Tell her. Tell her it's saved on my desktop," I said. I was starting to get fuzzy. I thought about my tombstone once again. Claire Mackenzie died on July 11, and Claire Stevens died on September 2. I wasn't sure how that would read. I hoped the guy doing the inscription would have some ideas on how to handle it.

"Oh, seriously? You have a death folder? About potatoes?"

"Someday, you'll understand," I muttered. With that statement, my transformation toward becoming my mother was complete. I felt like maybe it was the perfect time for me to leave.

THIS HAD NOT been a good year. Antonia told me that someday I'd look back on this time in my life and realize that it wasn't as bad as I thought it was, but I was pretty sure that even with the benefit of time, wisdom, and perspective I would not ever think that 2016 was one of my better years. I laid on the adjustable bed in the emergency room, my clothes cut off and probably thrown in a Hefty bag somewhere, never to be seen again, which sucked, because I liked the outfit I had on a lot. Instead, I now wore a standard white and blue hospital gown that I didn't like very much at all, and an itchy white plaster cast on my leg that I downright detested. Lissy sat in a small plastic chair against one of the curtained walls of my cubicle, trying very hard not to show her fear. "It's not your fault," I said, quietly. My lips were dry and my tongue felt fat in my mouth, like it didn't really fit in there.

"If you weren't posting on stupid Instagram for my stupid store, you wouldn't be here."

"Maybe I would've walked faster and the car in front of the Toyota was a Hummer that would've steamrolled over me. Did you ever think of that?"

"Oh my God, don't even say that."

"It was an accident. I'm a big girl. I know I'm supposed to look both ways before crossing the street."

"It was really scary, Claire. Thank God you're going to be alright."

I looked down at the cast on my left leg. This was certainly not something I was planning on dealing with, but all things considered, it could've been a lot worse. "Did you call Antonia?" I asked. It occurred to me that this accident might end up being a blessing in disguise. Antonia would never leave me now. If nothing else, I just assured myself another two months with her. The accident might have been worth it just for that. "Where is she?"

"She's with Bo," Owen answered as he entered the room.

"What are you doing here?" I asked.

"Antonia called and told me what happened. Instead of picking up Bo I asked if she could keep him. I wanted to come down here and see you. Are you okay? You're lucky you weren't killed, Claire."

"I know. Thanks for coming. I appreciate it, I really do. But, you should've stayed with Bo," I said. It wasn't his responsibility to take care of me anymore. I could take care of me just fine—though today admittedly didn't do a whole lot to support that point.

"Claire, no matter what happens, you're still Bo's mom. You're the most important person in the world to him, and that means you'll always be one of the most important people in the world to me. Did you honestly think I was going to hear that a car ran you over and sit at home? Do you think I'm that evil?"

"I do," Lissy said, which I appreciated. I pushed the call button for the nurse.

"What are you doing?" Owen asked, ignoring Lissy's comment.

"If you're going to be here, I'm going to need some more painkillers," I said, only half kidding.

"It's going to get worse before it gets better," Lissy said, looking guilty and staring at the sterile beige floor for an inordinate amount of time.

"Why?" Owen and I both asked simultaneously.

"I didn't think Owen was going to be here. I called Fred, too."

"Who's Fred?" Owen asked.

"You did?" I asked.

"Her boyfriend. And yes, I did," Lissy answered.

"You have a boyfriend?" Owen asked. "Who? Wait, don't tell me the guy from the restaurant?"

"Yes, the guy from the restaurant. His name is Fred, and we've been seeing each other for a few months. There wasn't a reason to tell you."

"You didn't scare him away when you attacked me with a pair of scissors?"

"Believe it or not, no."

Talking about Fred made me think about the conversation we had about the fight at Bo's birthday party. I'd been waiting for the right time to do it, but it never came, except oddly enough now I thought it had. "Listen, Owen, I want to talk to you," I said. "I realize that this is kind of a strange time."

Owen leaned in a little closer to my bed. "Okay. You scared me today," he admitted. "You scared me to death."

"I wanted to apologize for some of the things I've done since our split. For example, I'm sorry for the hair incident. Really, I am."

"Thank you," Owen said.

"And I'm sorry for throwing your mom out of the house on Bo's birthday. I'm not proud of my behavior that night."

"Thanks, again. The truth is, Claire, I can't say I blame you. What I did to you was horrible. Things got really messed up for you, really fast. I don't know how I'd have reacted if that had happened to me."

"Yeah, they did."

"I'm sorry for everything I did, too. I really am," Owen said. I believed him.

"We shouldn't have to go through the rest of our lives mad at each other. We can't do anything about the past, but I'd like Bo to grow up with two parents who respect each other if nothing else. That's not too grand a dream, is it?"

"No, it's not. You're right. I'd like that, too."

"Good. Do you think we can do it?"

"I think we can. We're a good team when we're being a team."

"Yeah, we are."

"How come you've gone all Dalai Lama on me?"

"A wise man told me to focus on the positive, and to practice forgiveness."

The curtain rustled, and a doctor entered in his light blue scrubs, his Crocs, and his starched white coat, just so that no one confused him for a nurse. I couldn't blame him. If I went through what he went through to become an emergency room physician, I'd wear my coat, too. Hell, I'd probably sleep in it.

"Claire Stevens?" he asked. He was kind of cute. Not traditionally cute, like a soap star playing a doctor on TV, but realistically cute, like a doctor playing a doctor in real life, and who therefore didn't sleep a lot. He had fair skin, brown eyes, and a full head of brown hair interrupted by white streaks that reminded me of the coffee cake my mom used to get at the bakery on Sunday mornings. His voice was deep and commanding without being intimidating—more Morgan Freeman than Darth Vader—and he was a doctor. As long as he wasn't a fugitive, or married, he was perfect. Actually, as long as he wasn't married he was perfect. I could get over the fugitive thing. Who hasn't made some mistakes in life? My list was certainly long.

"That's me," I said. "Forgive me for not getting up."

"You're very lucky," he said.

"So I've heard."

"I'm sorry, am I interrupting?" Fred interrupted, popping his head into the gap in the curtain. "I came as soon as I could."

"Hey there," I said, trying to sound flirty so that Owen would be annoyed, and Fred would be flattered. I realized that I'd never been in bed with three men in the room before. If I'd ever imagined it (and I hadn't), it would've looked a little different. I wouldn't have asked to be in a ball gown or anything, but I probably could've gone without the steri strips, the hospital gown, the broken bones, the bruises, lacerations, and concussion. The painkillers I would keep. "Come on in. The party's just getting started."

The doctor looked at Owen. "Are you her husband?" he asked.

"We're divorced," Owen said.

"I can come back later," Fred offered.

"Absolutely not," Lissy ordered. "You should stay. Claire wants you here."

"I do," I added, the drugs making me slightly worried that I may have just gotten remarried, and I hadn't even shaved my legs.

"Okay," the doctor continued. "You have a broken tibia, some superficial cuts and bruises, and a mild concussion. Honestly, you're a very lucky woman. I can't believe you only have one broken bone. It could've been much worse."

"I think I've fulfilled my bad luck quota for the year. It's about time that something worked out in my favor."

"You're going to be in a cast for the next eight weeks, but after that, you should be as good as new. The bruises and the scrapes will heal. You'll be pretty sore for a while, but we can give you something for the pain."

"Whatever you've given me here is amazing. I'll take more of these."

The doctor laughed. "I hear that a lot."

"Can I ask you a question?" I asked.

"Sure."

"Are you single?" I waited for the reaction from the peanut gallery.

"What?" Fred, Owen, Lissy, and Doctor Morgan Freeman asked.

"I think she's had enough painkillers," Lissy said, trying to assuage what could be a very awkward situation for the perfectly lovely Fred, who raced down here to have to sit in a cubicle made of curtains with his drugged-up girlfriend and her ex-husband.

"No, I definitely haven't had enough painkillers, but that's beside the point. I mean it. I don't mean to be rude, but I'm actually wondering if you're single."

"I was in a relationship until recently, but I'm single now, yes," the doctor answered.

"This is good to know," I sighed. I closed my eyes. This could work. I really believed that this could work. If these last five months had taught me anything it was that there really might be a plan for everyone.

"It is?" he asked. "Why's that?"

"I have a friend named Antonia," I said.

"Ohhhhhh," Lissy, Owen, and Fred sighed.

"Is she coming here, too?" the doctor asked. "You're running out of room."

"No, she would be here but she's babysitting my son right now."

"She really is a wonderful girl. Very pretty," Fred added. I knew Fred was a great guy. He had proven that more than once. He stuck around after the dinner debacle. He loved spending time with Bo. He encouraged me to be friends with my ex, and he sanded Lissy's floors, and he delivered her furniture, and he came here to see me in the hospital, and he believed me when I told him that I was good crazy, and he didn't have to do any of those things. Now, just in case it wasn't clear, he was trying to help me find Antonia a boyfriend without her knowledge. If that doesn't say "keeper," then nothing did.

"And she's age appropriate," Lissy added. "Assuming you don't only date twenty-three-year-olds."

"I really think we should get back to talking about your injuries, Claire. But thanks for trying to play matchmaker," he said.

"You probably get it a lot, huh?" I asked.

"Two to three times a week, and every single time I call home to talk to my mother."

"Where's home?" I asked.

"Chicago."

"Get out of here! That's where she lives!" This was fate. Now, I was sure of it. God cracked me with a Toyota so that Antonia could finally meet the perfect man. It all made sense.

"She's babysitting your son in Chicago?"

"No. Well, she technically lives there, but she moved here for a bit to help me out after Prince Charming over here banged the Fairy Godmother of Real Estate. It's a long story."

"I think maybe it's time I go," Owen said.

"No, don't go. I'm sorry. Old habits die hard, I guess. I meant what I said before, okay? We're going to be friends. Besides, Dr. McCoffeecake doesn't care about our past. Neither does Fred."

"My name is Blake." Blake laughed. For some sick reason, I thought he was actually enjoying this little crazy carnival, which made me even more sure that he and Antonia would hit it off big-time.

"Blake what?" I asked.

"Carpenter."

"Dr. Carpenter Blake," I repeated. "That's interesting. I like it."

"No. It's Blake Carpenter. Blake is my first name."

"Ohhh, I see. You want to be on a first-name basis then," I said. I was starting to get tired, groggy, and apparently, confused.

"Can we please get back to your broken leg and head issues and worry about Dr. Blake Carpenter's personal life later?" Lissy asked.

"Fine. That's so boring, though," I said. I yawned, and poor Fred was still standing in the corner, probably wishing that he'd stayed very, very far away from here.

"The nurse will be in with some discharge papers, and a prescription. You're going to be fine. Just rest. You need to lie down for the next few days, and keep your leg elevated. Make sure you take the pills with food. You said you have someone staying with you?"

"Her name is Antonia. She's thirty-seven, a Sagittarius, and gorgeous. She makes a fantastic lasagna, and I really think you guys should meet."

"That's true. It really is delicious," Lissy agreed.

"She sounds great," Dr. Blake Cake said. "I assume someone here is going to drive you home?"

Everyone looked at each other. Lissy nodded in Fred's direction. "I'll take her home," he said.

"Great." The doctor left.

I smiled. I had a man to take care of me. A good man. A man named Fred with Tom Cruise's nose and a handsome face and a heart even more beautiful than all of that. The doctor was right. I was lucky. And, Percocets were amazing.

"I'd like that," I said. "Also, this is Owen. Owen, this is Fred. I don't think you guys have formally met."

Owen stood and shook Fred's hand. "Nice to meet you, man. I wish it was under better circumstances."

"Me too. Good to meet you."

"I'll follow you back to the house and pick up Bo. You get settled and figure out how well you can move around with the crutches. He can stay with me as long as you need. I'll take time off work if I have to. Don't worry about it."

"Thanks. That'd be great, actually," I agreed. "I don't want him to see me until I can clean myself up a little bit."

I wasn't someone who felt like it was necessary to be friends with an ex. I mean, what was the difference? But in this moment, I realized that Fred was right. There would be a lifetime of accidents, injuries, and celebrations, and it would be so much better for everyone if we could all just get over it. I was going to work on that. Right before I got run over by a car, I was thinking that maybe Connecticut wasn't such a bad place to live. I didn't want to let a little thing like a near death experience kill my Zen state. I worked so hard to get there to begin with.

"I'll meet you at the house. Lissy, thank you for everything. You're a good friend," Fred said.

"Thanks. I'll come over tonight. I'll bring dinner or something."

"Are you going to cook it?" I asked.

"I was going to pick it up from Citarella."

"Sounds great. Actually, swing by Sephora and pick up a red lipstick for me, too. I don't think I'm going to have time to get there before the party next weekend, and a promise is a promise," I said.

"Oh my God, who cares about the party? You don't need to come. It's fine. I'll handle it all."

"Lissy, I know that I'm cracked out right now, and that I was just hit by a car, and that makes anything that comes out of my mouth questionable at best, but let me be clear: I am coming next Saturday. I don't care if Fred and Owen have to put me on a chair and carry me into the store like we're doing the hora, but I will be there. I wouldn't miss it for anything."

Lissy kissed the top of my forehead. Then, she left, leaving me with Owen and Fred and a potentially awkward situation that actually wasn't awkward at all because Owen and I had declared a truce, and also because I was high.

"Owen," I said, noticing that there wasn't any anger in my voice when I said his name. "I heard about Dee Dee. I feel like I should say I'm sorry it didn't work out. But I'm kind of not."

"I know you're not. I'm not either," Owen agreed.

"I want you to be happy. Just not with her. Maybe someday I'll feel differently, but for now, I'm happy she's gone."

"Thanks," he said. "I'm happy she's gone, too. She hasn't changed much since high school. Originally, I thought that was what I needed in my life. It got old fast. Turns out I need a grown-up."

"Go figure," I said.

"I'm sorry I hurt you. I really am. I totally forgot about everyone who meant anything to me. I don't know what I was thinking, and I'll never forgive myself for what I did to our family. Not ever."

"I know. I want you to know that I'm happy. It took me a while to get here, but I am finally happy. Fred here is a great guy. I think you two will like each other when I decide that it's okay for you to spend any kind of time together. We aren't there yet. Even on drugs I know that I don't want that right now."

"Good," Owen said. "You're crazy, but you deserve to be happy," he teased.

"Thanks. I'm good crazy, though. Not bad crazy. I just want to make sure that's clear."

"Okay," he said, a little confused, which was fine. He didn't need to understand me anymore. I wasn't even sure that he ever did. "Listen, don't worry about Bo. When you're ready to see him let me know, and I'll bring him over."

"Make him French toast tomorrow for breakfast, okay? He loves it. You need to get the real maple syrup for when he's at your house. You use that imitation crap. He knows the difference."

"You're turning him into a food snob?" Owen asked.

"Antonia has had a lot to do with it, but yes, we are. In a few years I'm going to introduce him to the wonders of eating snout to tail."

Owen laughed, getting my joke just like I knew he would. We were going to be just fine. It helped that he was a good father, and that he was sorry for what he'd done, and ironically, that he didn't let me move back to Chicago. If he had, I would've never met Fred, and I liked that I had Fred in my life. I also liked that Dee Dee and her manufactured beach waves were gone. That made it easier to forgive him, too.

"I'll go," Owen said, kissing me on the forehead the same way Lissy had, like if anyone touched me I might crumble and break like a cookie gone stale. "It was nice to meet you, Fred. Take care of her. If I can do anything, just call."

"You too, Owen," Fred said. "I'll keep you posted."

Owen waved and Fred turned to me, alone in my corner of the emergency room for the first time since he'd arrived. "I can't believe this happened," he said. "You could've been killed."

"Nah. It takes more than a little car accident to kill this girl. I'm indestructible. Didn't I tell you that?"

"You didn't, but I probably should've guessed."

"I guess it's a good thing we got in that rock climbing date, huh? I don't think I'll be doing anything too active anytime soon."

"Good thing the weather is about to get colder. You know what that means?"

"Red wine and movies on the couch?" I asked.

"Bingo," Fred said.

"Then my broken leg timing is perfect because I can't think of anything I'd rather do more."

"Except eat pizza with a knife and a fork," Fred teased.

"Right. Except that."

"Are you ready to go home?" he asked.

"Yes. All I want is to get out of here. Will you make me a cup of tea when we get there?"

"You got it. Do you want me to get you a wheelchair? Or are you okay to use the crutches the nurse left for you?"

"I can crutch. I'm good. Wheelchairs are for sick people, and ironically, this is the best I've felt in months. If you help me, I can do it. Let's go."

Fred leaned over and kissed my lips, not my forehead—the way any boyfriend would kiss his girlfriend when he came to see her in the hospital after she'd been hit by a car while Instagramming in a crosswalk.

❧ Chapter 22

FRED WENT TO Sephora. That was how I knew we were seriously serious. What kind of man stepped foot inside the beauty mecca that was Sephora and purchased no fewer than seven different red lipsticks, and some concealer for bruises, for someone he didn't like a whole lot? No one did—unless he was a cross-dresser, but I'd moved past the phase of our relationship where I feared he had some freaky demons, and instead had resolved myself to the fact that he was just a straight-up nice guy. Imagine that.

"Until today, I would've thought that red was red. Now I know better. And I wish I didn't. It's too complicated," he said. "That place is insane. You can get lost in there!"

"Yup. Beauty isn't effortless. Don't let anyone convince you otherwise."

"There's an entire section devoted to fake eyelashes. I didn't know that was a thing."

"That's the least of it. There are fake eyebrows now, too," I added. I thought about telling Fred that I'd almost worn fake eyelashes on our first date—that I was trying to look sexy, and hip, and thought that that would somehow help. It was crazy to think that I was recently that stupid.

"Why in God's name would a woman believe she needs fake eyebrows to be beautiful? Who notices eyebrows? You could shave yours off entirely, and I don't even think I would notice."

"Yes, but you also don't mind my Spanx. You're an anomaly. Not everyone is as wonderful as you are," I said. It wasn't forced. The compliment slid off my tongue the same way the oyster slid out of its shell and onto Owen's lap four months ago. It required very little effort.

"Nah, I just know what's important." He leaned down and kissed the top of my head. "How do you feel?" he asked. "You know, Lissy would understand if you weren't up for it. To be honest, I think you're pushing it a little. You should probably stay home and rest."

"Under no circumstances am I staying home today," I said, as I examined red lipstick number four, an orangey-red called Firecracker, by the window next to the armchair. "This one is too orange," I said. "This isn't easy. A lot of women are totally obsessed with makeup, and could probably pick out a color without even trying it on, but I can't. It was never my thing," I said.

"That's because you don't need it."

"Sweet talker."

"Aren't you just full of compliments today?" he asked. "Thanks."

"No, that's the name of this lipstick," I said. "I think this is the one." I swiped the color on the inside of my wrist, and it seemed perfect—not too orange, not too blue, not too pink. I ran the matte stick across my mouth and held up my blush compact to examine my face in the mirror. I was right, I looked like I belonged in a Robert Palmer video, which meant that Lissy would totally approve.

I was worried when I woke up this morning that it might rain, but the stormy skies had given way to gorgeous sunshine and sparse clouds, which was exactly what we wanted. It was cloudy enough to keep young mothers out of the park, but nice enough to bring women out shopping. If you were going to order weather to go with a store opening on a Saturday, this would be it.

"You look hot!" Antonia said as she bounded down the stairs in jeans and an eggplant-colored sweater. "You should wear red more often!"

"Do you think it goes well with my cast?" I asked, holding up my white plastered leg. My head still hurt, and I had to spend a large part of my day in bed, which was not where I wanted to spend my days anymore. Ironic.

"Oh, definitely," Antonia said.

"You look nice, too," I said as I surveyed her. She was wearing flats, which was totally appropriate, except I wanted her to change her shoes. "Why don't you wear those suede boots you have?"

"With the heels? They're uncomfortable as hell. What's wrong with my flats?"

"Nothing. Absolutely nothing," I answered, which was true.

"I really like the boots, though. Come on, put them on. I can't wear anything on my left foot. Let me live vicariously through you."

"You're weird, you know that?" Antonia asked.

"Yes. I do," I answered.

"Okay. I'll change my shoes. I'll be right back," she said as she turned and made her way back upstairs.

"Are you sure this is a good idea?" Fred asked.

"Of course it is. Why wouldn't it be?"

"I'm just asking. I don't know how I would feel if someone did this to me."

"Trust me, it's going to be fine," I said, with more confidence than I actually felt. I had no idea if it was going to be fine. I just really hoped it would be.

"Are you ready to go?" Fred asked as he walked over and handed me my crutches.

"I am." I clasped Fred's hands and let him pull me up onto one foot, then gingerly placed my crutches under my armpits and began my slow, steady limp toward the front door.

THE WEATHER WAS at once both a blessing and a curse. That, and the fact that there was really nothing to do in this town on weekends except shop and eat oysters, explained why the store was so crowded for the grand opening that people could barely move. I huddled in the corner holding my crutches in front of me as a barricade lest someone accidentally bump into me, and smiled through my pain. We worked hard for this opening. I didn't want my little injury to ruin it, so I tried to go unnoticed, which wasn't exactly easy since I was wearing bright red lipstick and a giant plaster cast.

Fred had been sitting next to me for a good part of the afternoon, but it quickly became obvious that we didn't hire enough waitresses to serve the champagne. "I'll be back," he said as he grabbed a tray and began to pass around drinks to the groups of Burberry-clad women roaming the store. I watched him chat, and flirt, and politely offer cocktails, and found it impossible to believe that had I not gone into Manhattan on that exact day, we'd have never met. I was starting to wonder how I ever lived here without him, and then realized that in a lot of ways, I hadn't.

Lissy looked fabulous, her long hair clipped behind her ears and with a short black dress that highlighted her slender legs. A beautiful gold locket dangled on a wisp of chain around her neck that I'd bet belonged to her mother, because I knew it was important for her to feel like her mother was with her today. Every few minutes, she grabbed the pendant and slid it up and down the chain like a zip-line and I wanted to run over to her and reassure her that she looked beautiful, and that everything was going great, and that her mother would be so proud. It was sweet to see her so nervous. She may have decided to hide herself behind her makeup and her piercings, but inside, she was just as soft as the rest of us—my Goth Princess friend with a heart of gold.

Antonia sat down next to me and handed me a glass of champagne. "Did you take any of your painkillers today?" she asked. "I don't think you should drink this if you have."

"I didn't. I wanted to be able to toast our hard work. I didn't want to be loopy for the big opening."

"You guys have done a great job. I've overheard a lot of people talking and it sounds like you're getting rave reviews. I think she's going to have a lot of new customers after today."

"I hope so. She deserves it."

"Claire, I have to say, I think you should really look into working again."

"Huh? I just got hit by a car, Antonia. Can't I get a break for a little? No pun intended."

"You're so good at this kind of thing."

"Organizing stationery stores?"

"Marketing. Branding. Business development. There's so much you can do. You should think about getting into something at least part-time. You have so much talent. I know you think it's too late, but it's not. You can reinvent yourself in your career, too."

"Thank you. I've been thinking about a few things. I have some ideas but whatever I decide to do, I want to make sure that I can spend a good amount of time with Bo. I've been so worried about what women at the playground, or Dee Dee, or the purple stroller lady, or the mean mommies thought about me and God it feels good to say that I don't care about any of them anymore," I said. "I know who I am. I don't care what anyone else thinks. I'm happy. That's all I care about." Maybe there'd be a career for me going forward, or maybe not. It didn't matter, because I wasn't defined by a business card or lack thereof. I wasn't going to spend another minute dwelling on what I'd given up or what was taken away. It was so much better to focus on what I had and what I'd gained.

"Then I'm happy, too." Antonia looked down at the chairs we were sitting on and knocked her fist on the top of the table. "We do good work."

"It looks pretty good here, don't you think? This is where it belonged."

"You've come a long way since you were running around your house looking for a sledgehammer, you know."

"I had a great support system."

"Yes. And I have to say, I'm very proud of you, bella. You went through hell, and you got hit by a car, but you're here and you're happy and you pushed through it all and I don't know that I would've handled it as well as you have. I really don't."

"I hope we never find out."

"I've decided that if ever there was a person who deserves this, it's you." She reached into her bag and removed a small card. It was the lasagna recipe, written in Antonia's beautiful, perfect script.

"Oh my God. Are you sure you want to do this? Once it's out there, you can't take it back."

"As long as you swear on our friendship that this recipe will remain a cherished secret, then I firmly believe that the Ricci family recipe belongs with you. Use it wisely. Use it for Fred. He's a good man."

I placed the card over my heart and reached over to hug my oldest friend, my closest confidante, and the one true love of my life. People always said they married their best friend, and

I didn't understand why that should be a goal. It would never be for me. A husband or a boyfriend was one thing, and a best friend was another thing entirely. No matter what my relationship status, that title would always be reserved for Antonia, and I'd never allow her to share it with anyone. "I don't know how I'll ever thank you," I said. "Without you, I'd still be lost, and alone, and scared, and pouring beans in Owen's belongings, and I can't think of a worse way to be."

"You'll come up with something," she joked.

I looked up and caught sight of a very cute man with hair that reminded me of cinnamon streusel coffee cake. Even without his white coat, he was handsome, which was good. I was a little worried when I called him that the narcotics had altered my perception, but I needn't have been worried. Handsome, check. Doctor, check. Single, check. All systems go. "I already have," I said as I raised my crutch slightly to catch his attention. He was wearing a button-down and brown cotton pants, and I couldn't believe he'd actually agreed to come.

"You didn't," Antonia said.

"I did. I had to do something to get you to stay in Connecticut for a little longer. I don't want you to leave. Bo and I need you here. You belong with us."

"And you thought a man would make me stay?"

"I was hoping it would delay you. Maybe indefinitely. Italians believe in love above all else, don't they? Except maybe pasta? Maybe it's pasta, and then love, but either way love is right up there."

"I'd be offended, but he's actually really cute. Who is he?"

"The emergency room doctor who took care of me."

"You're joking."

"Nope. And I already checked to make sure he's single. My work here is done. Now, it's up to you."

"And you're a matchmaker now, too?"

"For one night only. Then I'm going into permanent retirement."

He easily breezed through the crowd, because every woman in the place stepped back in order to get a better look at him. He grinned just enough to expose the dimple in his cheek, his white teeth, and as expected, his fledgling interest in Antonia.

"I'm so happy you could make it," I said. I shook his hand and tried not to notice that he was looking at Antonia intently, and not turning away. I was no matchmaker, but sometimes you just have a sense about things. "This is my friend, Antonia. Antonia, this is Dr. Carpenter."

"Blake," he said. He shook her hand, she smiled, and I realized that I was already the third wheel, and that I should be hobbling off. I crutched over to Lissy, who was standing near the front door.

"It's going great," I said as I glanced around the room at the throngs of women fondling everything in sight.

"Antonia's fake date, or the store opening?" Lissy teased.

"Both, don't you think?"

Before she could answer, the bell above the door rang, and Stella entered, her vest still zipped up to her neck, her sunglasses perched on the top of her head. I knew it was possible that Dee Dee's friends would stop in, in fact, it was probably a good thing. They may have been obnoxious, but they were also popular and social, and the reality was that they'd be good clients for Lissy. Still, I was hoping I'd be able to avoid them, or at least not have to stand next to one of them. So much for that.

"Welcome to Sealed with a Kiss. If I can help you with anything, please let me know," Lissy said politely.

"Thank you. Wait, you look familiar," she said, not at all trying to be rude and yet simultaneously being so insulting it was almost comical.

"She's the reader at story hour," I said.

"Oh my God! I didn't recognize you without any of your jewelry and with your hair off your face."

"I took the earrings out for today," Lissy said.

"You look very nice," she said. I think with sincerity.

"Thank you."

"The store is really adorable. We could use something like this around here. I order most of my stuff online because it's easy, but I'm never happy with the quality. I think there's a bit of a backlash going on now with the internet. People like knowing exactly what they're buying, and who they're buying it from, you know?"

"We do," I answered. "In fact, we're counting on it."

"I'm Stella," she said, finally offering her hand and introducing herself. It was totally stupid that we were having this conversation to begin with. She didn't like me, I didn't like her because she didn't like me, and that was okay. We should just stay in our opposite corners, literally, and pretend we didn't see each other. That was the civilized thing to do.

"Lissy," Lissy said. "And this is—"

"Claire," she interrupted.

"We've met," I said. "I'm going to go sit down."

"Wait," Stella said. "Before you go, I just wanted to tell you that I'm embarrassed by how we treated you," she blurted.

"Excuse me?" I said. Lissy turned and walked away, leaving me alone with Stella and an awkward tension in the air.

"We weren't very nice to you. We didn't even know you, and we didn't make any effort to try and get to know you. I'm not going to speak for anyone else, but for what it's worth, I'm sorry."

I didn't care at all anymore about them not being nice to me. Don't get me wrong, the apology was nice and everything, but it really didn't matter. I didn't need their friendship and I didn't want their acceptance and I didn't care if they looked at me as the girl who lost her husband to Dee Dee before Dee Dee lost him to absolutely no one. I was past all of that. I was happy in my life. I knew I really didn't care anymore, because of how easy it was to forgive her.

"You weren't mean. The others were, but you never actually did anything. You were just quiet."

She quickly brushed a curl out of her face. "We've been friends since we were kids. I'll always be friends with them, but I don't agree with a lot of what they do and say. I should've spoken up sooner. I guess I just don't want you to think that

I'm like them. I'm not. I don't want my daughter to think that her mother is a bully, or that it's okay to treat people that way. It's only a matter of time before they start picking up on things. Having a kid makes you take a hard look at yourself, I guess."

"Yeah. It definitely does. I appreciate the apology. Thank you," I said.

"I stopped going to story time with them. I decided to take a step back."

"Take it from me, don't let anyone keep you from bringing your daughter to story time. Lissy is too good at what she does."

"She really is. What happened to your leg?" she asked. I wasn't sure if she actually cared, or if she was making conversation, but I guess it didn't really matter much. My injuries were nothing if not a good conversation piece.

"I got hit by a car."

"Seriously? Oh my God."

"Yup. Owen wasn't driving it in case you were wondering."

"I was going to ask if Dee Dee was," she joked, making me wonder for a second if maybe we could somehow become very unlikely friends. "You've had quite a year, huh?"

"Yeah," I answered as I waved for Fred to help lead me to Lissy at the register. "I guess I have."

"Well, it was good to see you. Maybe I'll see you at the park or something one day. Your son is adorable. My daughter is almost two."

"I'd like that," I said. "I go to the library on Wednesdays. It's a nice crowd. You should come."

"I will. Bye," she said. She exited the store, and I watched her leave, and found that I was happy to see that not all the mean mommies were really mean mommies. Some of them were still trying to figure out who they were, and I understood that completely. Fred stood next to me and helped to gently move people out of the way as I crutched over to the counter.

Lissy continued to ring up customer after customer buying preprinted note cards and thank-you notes and made appointments to meet with women who wanted to get their Christmas cards done early, just like I knew they would. I wanted to be part of this because I'd never been involved in anything like this. I hobbled over to the counter and helped bag the purchases after Lissy finished ringing them up. I stuffed each white paper bag with red tissue paper, affixed a round sticker with our name, address, phone number, email address, and a lip print onto the middle of the bag, and tied the handles together with red ribbons. I admired the bags and thought they looked beautiful, appropriate, and just edgy enough to be interesting. Originally, Lissy thought that maybe we should put giant lip prints in the middle of each bag, but collectively, we'd decided that it might look more like a trampy lingerie store than a stationery store, and all it would take was one person to think the bag contained furry handcuffs for the well-heeled women in town to never so much as walk past the store again. We wanted people to think modern Emily Post, not Heidi Fleiss, when they came to S.W.A.K. I handed the bag to the customer. "Have a nice day," I said.

"You too, dear. Feel better," she offered, noting my current disability. I smiled at the next customer, an impeccably dressed woman with a bright pink scarf tied around her neck and giant diamond earrings that were so big I wondered if maybe they were purchased at the jewelry kiosk in the mall. I placed three packs of note cards in her bag, which seemed appropriate. She looked like a woman who believed in sending proper notes. She probably didn't even know what email was.

"Who does the calligraphy?" she asked as she pointed at the tray in the glass case. Lissy bent down and removed the tray so she could place it on the counter in front of her. The woman gently ran her pale pink manicured finger across the letters on the envelope, checking to see if the ink smudged on her index finger. I could smell her hand lotion, a combination of jasmine and lavender that reminded me of my grandmother. When she saw that it hadn't, she picked up one of the envelopes and examined it closely. "It's absolutely stunning."

"I do, actually," Lissy said.

"You did all of these yourself?" she asked, fully impressed at Lissy's talent level just like I knew she would be.

"Yes. I learned when I was a little girl. My mother taught me."

"It's incredible. It's not easy to find people who know how to do this kind of work anymore. Everything is done by machine now. It's beautiful, sure, but it's not the same."

"I agree," I said. "I think it totally went out of the window when we started expecting drones to deliver our orders from Amazon.com."

"You're probably right," she agreed with a small giggle. I liked her. Turned out there were plenty of nice people in this town after all. Who knew?

"She can do any style you want. It makes any formal invitation infinitely more special, doesn't it?" I asked.

The woman nodded. "Do you have a card?" she asked.

Lissy reached over and handed her a business card. "I'd be happy to meet with you at your convenience to discuss doing invitations for you if you'd like."

"Are you open on Sundays?"

"Yes. From ten to four."

"Wonderful! I'll come in on Sunday. I'm having a dinner party next month for some colleagues from my husband's office, and I think you have some really beautiful things to choose from. I'm so happy you're here."

The woman walked away and Lissy turned and looked at me. "I've been here. How have these people not noticed that I've been here the whole time?"

"Because people are all on autopilot. They think they know everything so they don't pay attention. Now you've got everyone's attention. Trust me, that awning won't go unnoticed by anyone."

"Kind of like me," Lissy joked.

"Exactly like you," I agreed.

THE PARTY WAS over. Empty champagne bottles filled the coolers on the floor in the office upstairs. Crumpled red napkins were strewn all over the shelves and the counter, and crumbs from quiche covered the floor. The ladies had all come and gone, and when Lissy tallied her orders she realized she'd done more business in one afternoon than she had in the last six months. It was a huge success. Fred, Lissy, and I sat at the small table and enjoyed the quiet, but sitting in quiet made me realize that I needed to leave. I wouldn't have missed this party for anything, but the truth was every bone in my body ached and I was past the point where Motrin was going to help. I needed a painkiller, and to lie down, and to crawl under the duvet that had made me feel safe so many nights when nothing else had. The only difference now was that I wanted Fred to crawl under it with me.

"I should probably get going," I said.

"I can't believe you came," Lissy said.

"Of course I came," I answered. I leaned over and hugged her. "You're going to do so well here."

"I know. I can't help thinking about how not that long ago I was living in the East Village in New York City and didn't care about a career or working or anything. I just wanted to party and stay young forever. Now here I am, a business owner, with a beautiful store, and an awesome seating area, and a path forward in my life, and I didn't have to give up who I am to get any of it. I wouldn't have thought that this was possible."

"You're a badass. You have the whole town at your feet. Just keep working hard and being you and doing your amazing calligraphy and the business will come. I'm going to check your Instagram religiously, though. If I don't see you posting I'm going to come over here and clock you with something."

"As long as you don't cut my hair," she joked.

"Nah. I'm retired from that game. I'm just a boring suburban mom now. And that's pretty awesome."

"Mom, yes. Boring, never," Fred said.

"I don't know that it would have been possible without you, Claire," Lissy said. "If you ever want to help me with my marketing or my social media stuff, I'd love it."

"Count on it. You can't get rid of me that easily. How many women willing to work as unpaid interns are floating around this town anyway? Ten? Twenty max."

"Before you go, I have something for you," Lissy said. She reached under the counter and produced a small box tied with a giant red bow.

"You got me a present?"

"Sort of. Open it," she ordered.

I slid the bow off the box and ripped off the paper to reveal a small box of thank-you notes, the ones Lissy had shown me the first day I came to The Stationer, with the small ladybug in the upper right-hand corner, and my name, Claire Stevens, imprinted on the bottom.

"You are Claire Stevens. You should have the paper to prove it," she said. "I don't want you to ever forget who you are again."

To say that I was touched by Lissy's gesture would be an understatement. It might have been the most perfect gift anyone had ever given me. "I love them. Thank you, Lissy. Do I need to buy thank-you notes so that I can properly thank you? Is this just to make sure I spend more money here? I'm on to you," I teased.

"I think we can just call it even."

"Deal."

"I'd never have been able to do this without you guys," Lissy said.

"Yes, you could have," I reassured her. "Well, definitely without me. Probably not without Fred." I turned to Fred and continued, "Your being handy with tools, equipment, and all things renovation certainly helped."

"I'm happy I was able to be a part of it. It was a great day," Fred said. "You pulled it off, Claire. You got hit by a car in the process, but you really pulled it off."

"Yeah, I told you that sometimes being a little crazy comes in handy."

"Good crazy. You're definitely good crazy."

I was touched. That was one of the nicest things he'd ever said to me and that included the earlier comment about not needing makeup to be beautiful. It was probably better. "Thank you for saying that. It means a lot. Hey, I want to take a picture and send it to my mom. It's funny how this whole time I've been trying to convince her that I was happy. Let's see if she can tell the difference now that I actually am."

"Oh, she'll know," Lissy said. "You're like a whole different person."

"I feel like a whole different person. I think it's time that I try and go back to work. And when I say go back to work, I mean start my own business."

"I think that's a great idea!" Lissy said. "I love working for me."

"I loved working for you, too. But I think I have something to offer. I have a niche and maybe it's time I start thinking about what I want for me. I don't want Owen to pay my mortgage. I don't want to move anymore, but I want to pay for my own house. I want to pay for some things for Bo on my own. I remember when you came to my house that day I said that I could handle more than a baby. I can. I can handle a business, too. I just need a name for it."

"Here we go again," Lissy said.

"Maybe Antonia will have some ideas. Where is Antonia anyway?" I asked, looking around and realizing she'd left without saying good-bye, which was very un-Antonia-like. Unless . . .

"She told me to tell you she was going to have a beer and some oysters with the doctor," Fred said. "She snuck out."

"That's fantastic! They're on a date! I knew it!" I yelled. I held my phone up and Lissy and Fred leaned in close so I could take a selfie of the team that helped make Lissy's dream come true. I sent it to my mother with a lip print and the words "Sealed with a Kiss."

"They're only having a beer. Don't get ahead of yourself," Fred advised. "She's probably still going home to Chicago. Just prepare yourself for that. I don't want you to be hurt if she sits you down one day and tells you she's leaving."

"I know she might," I admitted, even though the thought of it made me feel ill. "But, she might not. Maybe things will work out for her here, too. Who knows?" I asked, optimism oozing out of me from the same place where doubt, fear, and negativity had recently dwelled. "If this year has taught me anything it's that life is totally unpredictable. And isn't that wonderful?"

Acknowledgments

I'M SO GRATEFUL to the entire team of people who helped make this book possible, but to two women in particular:

Thank you to my agent, Erin Malone, for working so hard with me on this book, for having such great thoughts on the early drafts, and for once again having my back. As always, you're awesome.

Thanks so much to my talented editor, Emily Krump, who somehow made this book better than I ever hoped it could be. Thank you for all of your time, all of your energy, and all of your thoughtful comments. Working with you on this was so much fun. Thanks, Em!

In addition, thank you to Jenifer Foley, Esq., for giving me your time and expertise in the field of family law. I can't tell you how much I appreciate it.

Thank you to Telicha Waldron, for taking such good care of my little squad so I can make time to write. We are all so lucky to have you.

Thank you once again to my family and to all my friends who encouraged me to keep going when I wanted to stop and who pitched in to help with anything and everything so that I could finish this book. I love you guys.

Insights,
Interviews
& More . . .

About the author

2 Meet Erin Duffy

About the book

3 Behind the Book

9 Bo's Pear and Applesauce Recipe

Read on

11 More from Erin Duffy

Meet Erin Duffy

Elena Seibert

ERIN DUFFY graduated from Georgetown University in 2000 with a BA in English and worked on Wall Street, a career that inspired her first novel, *Bond Girl*. She lives in New York with her husband and children.

She can be found on Facebook and Instagram: @erinduffybooks.

Behind the Book

I didn't sleep very much while I wrote this book. Not because I had three young children who screamed and cried and insisted I console them for one reason or another at all hours of the night, but because most of the time I'd crawl into bed and my mind would stumble and trip over all the ways in which working had caused me to fail at motherhood. The list was always long, and often redundant, but as I neared the third month of insomnia, I began to seriously worry that, barring professional intervention, I'd never sleep again. There was the fact that I'd spent most of my afternoons writing, and so I hadn't been available to greet my kids when they woke up from their naps. I hadn't read to them, or sang to them, or even played with them, really, because I was too invested in Claire's life and her family to pay attention to my own. One day, in an attempt to keep up with the mountainous pile of laundry accumulating on the floor in my bathroom, I dumped all of it into the washing machine, and then in the dryer, and accidentally shrunk my son's sweater to roughly the size of a cocktail napkin. Awesome. For weeks I'd been working during every free minute I had. I pawned my kids off on their baby-sitter, wore headphones to block out their crying, ▶

Behind the Book *(continued)*

and ultimately determined on more than one occasion that they didn't really need baths before bed because I was too tired to deal with it. Then, the icing on top of my ever-growing cupcake of failure, I fed them boxes of macaroni and cheese for dinner multiple times a week, and let them eat it in front of the TV while I wrestled with the writing of Claire's nervous breakdown. Ironic, I guess, as I was pretty close to having one of my own. I was just too busy to notice.

One afternoon as I was nearing the completion of *Regrets Only*, I drove to an empty parking lot not far from my house, stared blankly at the asphalt, and fought the urge to cry. There I was, clad in a ratty sweatshirt and mismatched socks, listening to the radio alone, legitimately believing that that was a perfectly normal thing to do. I began to wonder if this was how it was for all women who tried to balance a family and a career. Were there millions of us all over the world sitting in empty parking lots thinking about the canyon of things they didn't do? Thinking about the myriad of reasons why they failed to embody the archetype of the modern female? Thinking about the ways in which they, quite frankly, sucked? I sincerely hoped that most were better than me and that they at least managed to put on shoes before they took their minivans out for joy rides to nowhere, but I couldn't say for sure because no one ever talked about it. One thing was clear: I'd hit my breaking point, and I didn't like the feeling of being broken all that much.

I fully believed that I should be better than that—that my inability to make a balanced dinner, not ruin the laundry, and sing "Rubber Duckie" to three kids under the age of two in the bathtub for thirty minutes while simultaneously trying to write a book made me a poor excuse for a parent. And so goes the mind of the modern working mother—so intent on proving she can do everything that she's never satisfied with anything. I spent months stuck in this cycle, snuggling up with guilt every night like it was a long-lost love because I wasn't able to do everything and therefore managed to disappoint myself, my family, my agent, or my editor—or the Chernobyl scenario: all of the above. I was a wreck—which, by the way, only made me feel worse—and exhausted, because constant self-inflicted emotional abuse is actually quite tiring. And so after a silent pep talk, I decided it was time to get off this hamster wheel and abandon the absurdly high expectations that were quickly inching me toward the psych ward. Great in theory, but admittedly easier said than done.

This cycle is part of normal life for ▶

Behind the Book *(continued)*

a lot of women with children—the constant push-pull of trying to be a good mother while also taking some time—any time—to do things for yourself. I've spent a lot of time talking with girlfriends who all basically feel the same way. The stay-at-home moms fear their brains are turning to mush and wish they could exercise their talents in some way that doesn't involve Play-Doh or puppetry, and the working moms are suffocating from FOMO on crack because they're not able to spend time with their kids during the day. We blindly adopted the mantra that women can have it all—that we don't have to choose—but how is that a realistic (or healthy, or practical, or obtainable) goal? Somewhere along the way we set the bar so high for ourselves, we have to pole-vault to clear it. Before I escaped to the parking lot, I'd written ten pages—ten solid pages that I liked a whole lot—but that wasn't enough to make me feel good about myself. Instead, I thought about all the things I didn't do: the cries I didn't soothe, the music class I didn't attend, the sweaters I shrunk (yes, plural—I admit there was more than one), the homemade dinner I didn't make. And worse than all of that was the truth I was afraid to admit to anyone for a very long time: I really enjoyed the hours I spent alone with my laptop.

If I hadn't, I'd never have finished this book. When I got home, I hugged my kids, realized that they were just fine without me for a few hours, and tried to forgive myself. I accepted that becoming someone's mother didn't mean that I had to stop being me—that I wasn't required to trade one title for another. I also realized that if I chose to wear all the hats at once, I could—I just shouldn't expect to look good while doing it.

It didn't happen overnight, but slowly, I stopped hearing the ever-present voice in my head telling me that what I was doing wasn't enough. I stopped thinking that the world was going to end if my kid ate mac and cheese out of a box, or skipped a bath (or two or five). I stopped putting myself atop the list of things to sacrifice every single day, and I'm okay with that. I'd like to ensure that my two-year-old daughter learns to be okay with that, too. I don't want her to wind up sitting in a deserted parking lot one day because she's foundering under the weight of too-great expectations. I want her to know what it feels like to be satisfied, and content, and somewhat balanced in her life. I imagine that's a pretty nice way to feel.

If there's one thing I learned while writing *Regrets Only*, it's that it's okay to allow my priorities to change daily, instead of trying to make everything my number one priority 100 percent ▶

Behind the Book *(continued)*

of the time. I love Claire so much because she's able to finally get to a place where she says, "You know what? I'm good where I am. I'm done thinking about everything I'm *not* doing and am going to be happy with what I *am* doing instead." I hope I can get to that place, too. I still have a ways to go, but I've promised myself that I'm going to try. ᴄᴗ

Bo's Pear and Applesauce Recipe

Ingredients:

1 apple
1 pear
½ teaspoon cinnamon

Directions:

1. Rinse, peel, core, and dice the apple and pear.

2. Steam the apple and pear pieces in a steamer basket over simmering water for 3-4 minutes, or until tender.

3. Move the fruit to a food processor and add cinnamon. Puree until blended. ∽

More from Erin Duffy

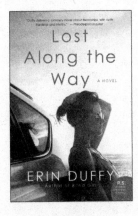

LOST ALONG THE WAY

The story of three friends who find
themselves on a laugh-out-loud
life adventure, *Lost Along the Way*
illuminates the moments that make
us, the betrayals that break us, and
the power of love that helps us forgive
even the most painful hurts.

"Duffy effortlessly explores complex
issues, especially how much pressure
women put on themselves and one
another to be perfect and have
everything together."
                              —*Library Journal*

More from Erin Duffy *(continued)*

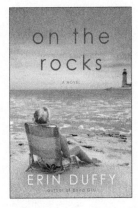

ON THE ROCKS

A witty and heart-warming novel about the perils, pitfalls, and dubious pleasures of being a young, single woman in the Facebook Age.

"Alternately humorous and touching, this novel is a fast, fun read."
—*RT Book Reviews*, four stars

BOND GIRL

A fast-paced, hilarious odyssey in four-inch heels, *Bond Girl* is *The Devil Wears Prada* meets *Wall Street* with a touch of Emily Giffin—a novel set in the financial world leading up to the (infamously) tumultuous year of 2008.

"Erin Duffy is a fresh, funny, and fabulous new voice in literature. . . . Great story. Delicious debut."

> —Adriana Trigiani, author of *Lucia, Lucia* and *Brava, Valentine*